DELORES FOSSEN

SWEET SUMMER
Sunset

HQN™

ISBN-13: 978-1-335-04106-7

Sweet Summer Sunset

Copyright © 2019 by Delores Fossen

Recycling programs for this product may not exist in your area.

Printed in U.S.A.

SWEET SUMMER
Sunset

CHAPTER ONE

EQUALITY FOR RODEO HEIFERS!

Nico Laramie silently cursed when he saw that. The protest demand was on a canary yellow sign that the protest organizer, Liddy Jean Carswell, had adorned with tiny cowbells.

What she'd written on it probably wasn't legible enough for most folks in his hometown of Coldwater, Texas, but Nico had had plenty of dealings with the octogenarian so he was well aware of the message.

A stupid message.

Some people did indeed protest mistreatment of rodeo animals. Mistreatment that Nico would never have allowed in his own business. Liddy Jean knew that, and she also knew that his track record was clean, but clearly she felt he needed to spur a radical change in the rodeo industry. She also apparently thought Nico could orchestrate the change that she'd spelled out on the back of her sign.

Allow Heifers in Bull Riding!

And there it was. Liddy Jean's main cause in a nutshell.

Nico had tried to explain to the woman that the sport was called "bull riding" not "cow riding." He'd even gone into detail about how bulls tended to be larger and more aggressive than cows and were therefore more suited to a competition like that. But Liddy Jean was sticking to her guns and had protested at least a dozen times since Nico had started using this office on Main Street three months ago.

Nico flashed the woman a smile, and it wasn't bragging for him to admit he was good at that particular facial expression. It often worked either to soothe hurt feelings or heat things up. Heck, he was downright charming. Plenty of people had told him that. Not Liddy Jean, though. Charm and smiles apparently didn't work on her. Neither did logic.

As she had on her previous protest days, Liddy Jean was wearing khaki shorts that went to her knobby knees and a plaid shirt covered with patches and decals that publicized her other *cause*.

Stop Vilifying Snakes in Movies.

Nico wasn't sure if, when or where the woman actually protested the reptile thing, too, but Coldwater likely wasn't a good target audience for her on that particular topic. There was no movie studio anywhere in the vicinity and no one with even weak connections to that industry.

"It's too hot for you to be out here, Miss Liddy Jean," Nico commented. It was already well into the nineties, and it was barely eight in the morning, but that was Texas in July weather for you.

"Equality for heifers!" she snapped in her crotchety tone, and just kept on prancing up and down the sidewalk as fast as her vein-streaked legs would carry her.

Sighing, Nico turned to unlock the door of the office building, but Liddy Jean said something else that stopped him in his tracks.

"Sorry about that woman dying," she grumbled.

Just like that, the annoyance of her protest vanished, and in its place came the grief. Grief like a thick layer of sweat covering him. It felt so real that Nico was certain it would rub off on anyone who touched him right now.

"She was like your real mom, I heard," Liddy Jean added with what sounded like genuine sympathy in her voice.

No. Brenda Calhoun had been a heck of a lot better than his actual mom. She'd been his rock, and until Brenda had died two weeks ago, she'd been the most important woman in his life.

Liddy Jean wasn't the only person in Coldwater who knew about his situation with Brenda. Everyone did. This was a small town that dished up talk as often as the bakery did their snickerdoodle specials. It didn't matter that Brenda had never lived there, that her home had been nearly an hour away in San Antonio. Brenda had visited Nico enough so folks would still know how important she'd been to him.

And that's why even a protestor who disliked him now looked at him with sad, pitying eyes.

Sadness and pity from women were new experiences for Nico—as an adult anyway. With his reputation for playing around and blink-and-you-miss-it relationships, women usually gave him different kinds of looks. Either a *come here, cowboy* or *keep your jeans zipped around me.*

He didn't like the pity, but until this grief ran its course, he couldn't see a way around it. That didn't mean he was going to try sex with those *come here, cowboy* lovers to try to console himself. No need to add guilt to his grief.

"Thanks," he told Liddy Jean after he swallowed the uncomfortable lump in his throat.

Nico got moving again, unlocked the door and, once inside, he went up the stairs to the second floor. His assistant's desk was empty—it was still early yet—so Nico started a pot of coffee. However, before he could make it across the hall to his own office, his phone dinged with a text message.

Dear Naughty Cowgirl,
I'm hooked up with one hot guy! He can't keep his hands off me. I'm talking three, four times a day, and I'm loving his hands—wink, wink—as much as I love him. So, here's my question. How do I keep the heat this high…like forever? The dirtier, the better.

Signed, Pleasured in El Paso

Nico read through the message and frowned. He was betting most guys didn't get texts like that at seven thirty on a Monday morning. Or any other time for that matter. He frowned again at the plea for help from the person who'd sent the text. His best friend,

Eden Joslin, who owned the *Naughty Cowgirl Talks Sex* blog.

Got any good suggestions for dirtier/better? Eden had tacked on to the copy of the blog letter.

He gave it about thirty seconds of thought.

Tell Pleasured in El Paso to play naked pin the tail on the donkey. Don't use pins but a feather or vibrator.

Okay, not his best effort, but maybe he could add more after he had some coffee. Eden didn't often ask him for advice with the blog, which meant she was still going through a dry spell. That was natural, he supposed, since she was in a bad dry spell in her life, too. He really did need to figure out a way to pull her out of the slump. While he was at it, he might also figure out a way for himself.

Work. That was what he needed now to forget about the grief. And thankfully, he had plenty of it. He needed to find four bulls suitable for a rodeo in Austin and then arrange for the transport of his own livestock that he'd be providing. There were invoices to check, emails to answer, calls to return.

Nico didn't do any of those things.

Instead, he shoved his hands into his jeans pockets and walked to the shelf behind his desk that was lined with framed photos. Pictures of him with his three brothers, Callen, Judd and Kace, including a recent one that had been taken at Christmas. Another one of their foster father, Buck McCall, who'd raised them after Social Services had placed him and his brothers here in Coldwater when Nico had been eleven.

Then, there was the picture of Brenda.

Nico automatically smiled when he looked at it. Man, even in a picture she could light up a room. And she was gone much too soon at the age of just forty-five.

Damn cancer.

It was a mean greedy bastard, all right. It had also claimed Brenda's husband when they'd only been in their thirties.

Along with being his fourth-grade teacher, Brenda had become his first foster mother. Well, the first one that counted anyway. Plenty of folks had thought she was too young to take him in. Barely twenty-four at the time, but there weren't a lot of fosters clamoring for a nine-year-old kid with an attitude. Brenda had not only taken him in, she'd treated him like a son.

Pushing that all aside, or rather trying to, Nico went back across the hall, filled his World's Okayest Bull Rider mug—a gift from one of his brothers—and carried his coffee back to his desk. The emails he had to answer didn't have anything to do with sex advice, cancer or protestors. It was business as usual that he found comforting in a *going through the motions* sort of way.

About a half hour later, Nico heard the clomp of boots coming up the stairs, and he looked up to see his assistant, Wally "Hog" Hannigan, step into the doorway of his office. Hog was a hulk of a man, and he was true to his name, thanks to a nose that'd been broken and poorly set so many times that it now resembled a snout. His hair didn't help. It was a mix of pale ginger and gray spiky sprigs that looked pig-pink in the wrong light. Somehow, it always seemed to be the wrong light.

There must have been something telling in Nico's expression because Hog sighed. "You okay, kid?" the man asked.

Kid. Not Nico. It didn't matter that Nico was nearly thirty-one and that he was Hog's boss. The man had called him that since they'd first met when Nico had been sixteen and learning to ride bulls. Nico figured he had a better chance of stopping Liddy Jean's protests than he did of getting Hog to call him anything else.

"I'm fine," Nico assured him, and that was mostly true. *Mostly.*

Hog nodded, but his faded green eyes let Nico know he wasn't buying it. Nor would he push it.

"You know how bad news comes in threes?" Hog asked, but he didn't wait for Nico to say anything about that. "Well, sorry, but you've got a big-assed set of three." Hog held up his index finger, counting them off. "I just got the word that you drew BYB for the Bluebonnet Charity Rodeo."

Well, hell. That definitely got Nico's mind off his blue mood. BYB was the "family-friendly" name for Bust Y'all's Balls, an ill-tempered Brahma mix that most rodeo riders hoped they didn't get in the random drawing to assign riders to bulls.

Since the Bluebonnet Rodeo was local and plenty

of his friends and family would be there, Nico had wanted a good ride, one where his eyes remained firmly in his sockets and his teeth didn't get rattled. But because Bust Y'all's Balls was also true to his name, Nico was pretty much guaranteed that wasn't going to happen. Still, this was part of the job so he'd get it done.

He was a livestock contractor first and foremost, and the owner of Laramie's Bucking Bulls. It was his job to locate bulls for rodeos, but he also felt it necessary to keep his finger on the pulse of the actual business, and he did that by trying to keep his butt on an often-ill-tempered bull for eight seconds. That meant occasionally getting his balls busted. But the kick of adrenaline and publicity he'd get from it would be worth it and would outweigh the pain.

Nico hoped.

Hog held up a second finger to let Nico know he was continuing with the three bad news things. "The crazy protestor lady is back. She was marching out front with that heifer sign again."

"Yeah. I saw her when I came in," Nico verified.

"Did you also see her swing her sign at your brother when he told her to move on and quit blocking the sidewalk? She hit him with it, and one of the cowbells cut his head."

No, Nico had missed that little drama, and now he went to the window to see his brother—Sheriff Kace Laramie—putting Liddy Jean in the backseat of his cruiser. It appeared that had riled two of Liddy Jean's friends because one of the women was fussing at Kace, and the other had taken over holding the protest sign. Something like this would set tongues wagging, and it wouldn't put Kace in much of a good mood, either.

When Nico turned back to Hog, his assistant held up a third finger. Bad news number three was coming, but Hog didn't jump to volunteer it. He hesitated, his gaze drifting to Brenda's picture before he said, "Right before the protestor lady smacked Kace, I saw Eden walking just up the street. I'm pretty sure she was bawling."

Shit on a stick. It hadn't been that long since her text for dirty advice, and Nico wondered what the heck had gone wrong in that short period of time. If she was crying, it was something big.

Since Eden had recently gone through a divorce, her tears probably had something to do with that, but he shouldn't have had to guess about what was happening with her. He shouldn't have let his own grief get in the way of helping someone who'd been his friend since sixth grade.

"Eden was going into Roy's?" Nico asked, already getting his hat so he could head out. Roy's was Roy Eccleston, Attorney at Law, where Eden worked part-time as a legal assistant.

Hog nodded and checked the time on his battered Timex watch. "You got that rodeo guy from Kerrville coming in at nine so there's time if you wanta go ahead and see Eden."

Even if visiting Eden took longer than that, then Nico would just have to be late for the meeting.

When Nico came barreling out of the building, he figured that he'd see Liddy Jean's protest buddies still loitering around, but the woman he saw was significantly younger.

Silla Sweeny.

She definitely fell into the *come here, cowboy* camp, and she flashed him a smile that could be considered foreplay. Silla was beautiful, rich and considered a mean girl. That last label was the reason she'd never been in Nico's bed. Most folks might be surprised to learn that he had standards when it came to lovers, but Silla ticked off one of the no-go boxes that he had.

The *M* boxes.

He didn't sleep with married or mean women, and that's why, even if he hadn't sworn off sex, he would have still brushed off her advances—like the one she was giving him now.

"Nico," she greeted. Her voice had some foreplay in it, too, and just in case he'd missed it, she sent him a let's-get-naked invitation with her eyes. "I was on my way to the diner for breakfast. Want to join me?"

"Can't." He tipped his head to Roy's office. "I've got some business to take care of."

And with just that short explanation, he saw the change in Silla's expression. Pity. "Oh, this is about your foster mother," Silla concluded. "I was real sorry to hear about that."

The grief was sure working overtime today. "Thanks—"

"Does the death of your foster mother have anything to do with the reason Eden was crying?" Silla interrupted. "I mean, I heard that Eden knew her and all, but I didn't know they were that close. Or was she crying over Damien again?"

Great. If Silla had seen Eden, then the crying would soon be all over town. If it wasn't already. Eden was a private person, and she wasn't going to like that.

As for what had made Eden cry, Nico figured it was definitely Damien, her ex-husband. Eden had indeed known Brenda and had liked her, but it was Damien who could bring her to tears.

After muttering an absent goodbye to Silla, Nico ran across the road. Not much of a distance and very few vehicles to dodge, considering Main Street was just two lanes and had one stoplight. The only time there was anything remotely close to a traffic jam was when the librarian's pet longhorn broke fence and moseyed its way onto the street.

Nico stepped into Roy's, his attention immediately going to Eden's desk. Empty. Ditto for Roy's office.

And then Nico heard it.

The rustling around from the bathroom that was just off the reception area. He went straight there and knocked. "Eden, it's me. Open up."

First, Nico heard her groan, followed by an, "I'm okay."

Like Hog, Nico knew that wasn't true. Unlike Hog, Nico definitely was going to push it. He opened the door, figuring she wasn't using the toilet, and she wasn't. Eden was at the mirror, and there was makeup scattered about the vanity.

"What part of 'I'm okay' didn't you understand?" she snapped.

"The *I'm* and the *okay* parts," he snapped right back.

Neither one of them had any real bite to their tone. No eye contact, either, since Eden stayed facing the mirror. In profile, she looked like her normal self. Her explosion of brown curly hair that she'd tried to tame by pulling it back into a clip. The loose cotton blue dress with her cowboy boots—practically a uniform for a woman her age in Coldwater.

Eden straightened her shoulders when she turned to face him and hiked up her chin. The facade would have been a whole lot more effective if she'd had both eyes made up. One was cosmetically fixed with mascara and some shadow stuff on her lid. The other, her right one, was red and still showing signs of those tears that both Silla and Hog had witnessed.

Nico shut the door and went to her so he could pull her into his arms. "What happened?" he asked.

At first Eden just shook her head, causing some of those stray curls to whop him in the face, but then a sob broke from her mouth.

"Damien and I have only been divorced six months, and he's already asked someone else to marry him." The words just rushed out with her breath, and they kept on rushing. "It's Mimi Bakersfield. Did you know about this?"

Oh that. "I knew they were dating, but I didn't know about the engagement."

That was the truth. Nico hadn't exactly cut Damien out of his life, but they weren't nearly as close after Damien had filed for a divorce from Eden and moved to San Antonio. Damien had told Nico about dating Mimi, but he'd also said they were keeping their relationship under wraps because they were trying to avoid dealing with the folks who still wanted him to get back together with Eden.

"Mimi didn't say anything to you about it?" Eden pressed.

Nico shook his head, but it was a valid question. Along with being the local minister's daughter, Mimi was an accountant who kept the books for his business. Nico and she spoke often. Heck, she'd even had lunch with Brenda and him a couple of times when Brenda had come to town for a visit.

"Mimi was with Damien this morning because he was bringing her to his mom's," Eden went on. "I was walking here, and they saw me while I was on Main Street. They got out of his car so Damien could tell me about the engagement. God, Nico. She's barely twenty-four. Her boobs are big enough for their own zip code, and she's got this perky little butt."

Okay. There was plenty in that for him to decipher, and Nico tried to figure out which of those things would have upset Eden the most so he could tackle it first.

"How perky were her boobs?" he asked, knowing it would get Eden to push back from him and frown.

It worked.

She dished up a frown that was hard, fast and came with a side order of narrowed eyes.

"Hey, tits and asses are a man's weakness," he added, hoping it would make her smile. Something they usually managed to do for each other. Not today, though. So, he went in another direction. "Damien's a dick."

It felt a little sleazy to dick-label a man he still considered a friend, but it was the truth. That's one of the reasons it had bothered him when Eden and Damien had gotten married a little over three years ago. Nico had been worried that it might not last.

That's because Damien was too much like him when it came to women.

Unlike Nico though, Damien didn't have any *M* boxes to rein him in even in a small way. Bedding women had been a hard habit for Damien, and it showed a lack of respect for Eden.

Of course, now that Eden and he were divorced, Damien did have every right to find someone else— and get engaged. But it'd been pretty dick-ish of him to spring a fiancée on Eden.

"Don't tell me you didn't notice Mimi's butt and boobs," Eden grumbled.

Oh, he had. Nothing short of blindness or neutering would have prevented that, but Mimi didn't exactly flaunt her assets. She dressed, well, like a preacher's daughter. Probably the way that Eden's folks would have preferred her to dress.

"Damien's a dick," Nico repeated, because he

thought that might be the root of all the other stuff that'd made her cry.

His conclusion caused Eden's eyes to fill with more tears, but he thought these were of a different variety. Not from the "kick to the gut" feeling of seeing your ex with someone else. An ex-husband you likely still loved. No, these tears seemed to be moving on to the next level and were about something other than Damien and his perky-butted sweet thing. Nico got confirmation of that a moment later.

"Lots of people saw me cry." Eden's voice cracked. "Ruby Deacon, for one. She'll tell my folks, and they'll harp on me again to see a counselor or something."

Yeah, they would. Willard and Louise Joslin were pillars of the community and owned the hardware and feed store. They loved their daughter—who was their only child—and they wouldn't want to see her unhappy. Of course, the way they would try to fix that unhappiness would likely mean some major interference in Eden's life.

"Silla Sweeny saw me crying, too," Eden added. "That means soon all the mean girls will know."

Silla had likely fired off a mean girls group text. None of them would be nasty about it to Eden's face. In most cases, meanness in Coldwater still had a "bless your heart" civility to it. But there'd be behind-the-hand whispers and poor, pitiful looks that would take on the critical tinge of, "You should've been able to hang on to your man."

"Look, I know how to fix this," Nico said. "I'll just give the gossips something else to talk about."

Eden's frown returned. "You're not going to sleep with Silla and then post about it on social media. Nico, I hate to break this to you, but your sleeping with someone won't stir a whole lot of talk. It's what people expect of you."

It was. He couldn't argue with that, but he could turn the town's expectations in any direction to help Eden. "I'm swearing off easy sex. When that news gets around, there'll be plenty of talk, and that'll take the heat off you."

Eden shook her head, sighed and looked ready to spell out why she was neither impressed nor surprised by his idea, but she stopped when she heard the voices in the reception area. Nico stopped, too, because they were familiar. Roy, for one—that wasn't much of a surprise since it was his office. But Nico was pretty sure he recognized the other one, too.

"Rayelle," he muttered. Brenda's sister, Rayelle Devereaux.

Nico turned to go see her, but Eden caught on to his arm. "Don't let them know I'm in here," she whispered.

That was a given. Nico made a locked motion over his mouth. "Your secrets are safe with me." And yes, that was plural. He hadn't told anyone about her blog or just how unhappy she was.

"Thanks." Eden still kept her voice low. She paused. "I didn't even ask if you were okay. Are you?"

"Sure." The lie just slid right off his tongue. But he wasn't.

Hearing Rayelle's voice brought on the grief again. And more than a brushstroke of discomfort. Rayelle and he weren't close, and she hadn't been around at all when Brenda had fostered Nico. In fact, he hadn't even met her until after he'd been moved from Brenda's care and placed with Buck. Eden studied him a moment as if she might call him on the lie, and then she motioned for him to leave. Nico gave her another hug and walked out, but he'd check on her as soon as he cleared up whatever was going on with Rayelle. And there was indeed something going on or the woman wouldn't have come to Coldwater.

Since it wasn't a big building, he saw Roy right away. It would have been impossible to miss the lumberjack-sized lawyer with the shock of stark white hair and an entire set of spare tires around his gut.

Rayelle was dwarfed next to him and barely came up to Roy's shoulder. Since she was Brenda's younger sister, it was always a jolt for Nico to see that somewhat-familiar face on someone else. Familiar but way different, too.

Rayelle was not someone who could light up a room.

She had the same brown hair as Brenda, but it didn't halo softly around her face like her sister's. Rayelle had hers yanked back and slicked into a tight stubby ponytail, and while Brenda had practically lived in jeans and T-shirts, Rayelle's usual was skirt sets and dresses. Plain ones.

He supposed it was the kind of outfit Rayelle thought she should wear since she was an elementary school librarian, but she dressed a lot older than most women her age. Heck, she was only thirty-seven.

Nico was a hugger, but he didn't go to Rayelle and do that. Nope. Rayelle put up invisible walls when it came to emotions, and as usual she had her arms crossed over her chest.

"I went to your office," Rayelle said when she eased back from him, "and your *assistant* told me you were here to see Eden."

Nico nodded. "I came over here to talk to her, but guess she's not in yet," he lied.

"She should be here soon," Roy said, checking his watch.

Good. The man didn't know Eden was in the bathroom. If he had, Roy wouldn't have been able to cover it. He had no poker face whatsoever.

"Your assistant's…not an ordinary-looking assistant," Rayelle added with her lips twitching in disapproval.

"Yeah, Hog and I go way back." That probably wasn't what Rayelle had been looking to hear, but no way was Nico going to diss the man. "Not as far back though as Brenda and me," he added.

Her mouth tightened again at the mention of her sister's name as if the mere sound of it had brought back something unpleasant for her. But then Rayelle had that reaction about most things. Nico had known the woman for about ten years now, ever since she'd moved back to San Antonio to be near her sister, and he'd never seen her truly smile. The best he ever got from her was a slightly upturned lip twitch.

Roy gave Nico a friendly slap on the back. "Brenda showed me pictures of you when you first went to live with her," the lawyer said. "You were such a scrawny little boy. But look at you now. All grown-up. Brenda always said the ladies just couldn't resist you."

Brenda had indeed said that, and she hadn't meant it as a compliment. Probably because she'd known that Nico hadn't done much resisting in that department, either. Brenda's interference in his life was much more subtle than what Eden got from her folks, but Brenda had made it clear that she wasn't pleased that Nico hadn't settled down yet.

"How are your brothers?" Rayelle asked. It was polite small talk, something that she no doubt thought was expected of her since she didn't know his siblings that well. Nico had been the only one of the Laramie brothers to end up with Brenda, but Brenda had kept in touch with all the Laramie "boys," and she had certainly kept Rayelle in the info loop.

"They're good," Nico answered. "One got married, another's engaged." The other had just gotten assaulted by a senior citizen protestor, but Nico didn't share that. "How's my sister?"

"Sister," Rayelle repeated. "Piper."

Rayelle sounded as if she wanted to correct him. That's because Piper Drake wasn't his biological sister, but she was in every way that counted. Well, every way that counted to Nico.

Piper was sixteen now, and Brenda had been her

foster mother for more than a decade. After Piper's parents had been killed in a car accident when she was five, there'd been no one to take her so she'd ended up in the system. Just as it had happened with Nico. Fortunately, Piper hadn't gotten a bad placement her second time in foster care but had instead ended up with Brenda. Piper had not only moved on from her painful past but had thrived.

Nico had gotten close to Piper over the years when he'd visited Brenda. And he'd worried about her after Brenda had gotten the cancer diagnosis. Heck, he was still worrying. Even though Brenda had talked Rayelle into fostering Piper, Nico still wasn't sure that was the best arrangement. Not with Rayelle's rigid outlook on life.

Nico waited for Rayelle to answer his question as to how Piper was, but she didn't. Instead, she pulled back her shoulders even straighter than they already were. "I need to talk to you a minute. Do you have time?"

"I'll make time," he assured Rayelle, but he felt the twist in his gut. Something was wrong.

Nico was about to leave with her, but the front door opened, and Eden came in. He sighed, knowing that meant Eden had climbed out the bathroom window into the alley and come around front so that Rayelle and Roy wouldn't know that Nico and she had been alone in there together.

Appearances.

Eden was darn good at that. Even though neither Roy nor Rayelle would have gossiped about it, she wouldn't have wanted it getting back to her folks that there might be something going on between Nico and her. It wasn't always easy for a man and woman to have a no-benefits friendship in Coldwater, but Eden had managed to stave off the potential gossips by taking steps like climbing out a bathroom window. Even though absolutely nothing inappropriate had gone on in there.

"Rayelle," Eden greeted. The full *appearance* was in place now. Eden had redone her makeup, and there wasn't a trace of the tears. Well, not unless you looked close enough. "It's good to see you."

The woman definitely didn't return the warm greeting. "I heard about your divorce. Brenda was upset about it."

Eden swallowed hard before she spoke. Then, nodded. "My ex and I are moving on with our lives."

Well, Damien was anyway. With Mimi Bakersfield. The jury was still out on whether or not Eden was actually doing any "moving on."

"Is everything okay?" Roy asked, sliding glances between Nico and Eden.

"Fine," Nico answered, and he figured everyone knew that wasn't quite the truth. Still, he wasn't sure yet just how un-okay things were and wouldn't know until he'd spoken with Rayelle.

"I was about to take Rayelle to my office so we could visit for a while," Nico volunteered. "I'll call you later," he added to Eden.

Eden nodded but didn't thank him for the bathroom TLC. No need. And besides, it would mess up the whole *appearances* thing.

"I brought papers," Rayelle said the moment they were outside. Her tone was all business, and she took an envelope from her purse to hand it to him. "It's a copy of Brenda's will and a letter she left for you."

Nico figured it was just plain muscle memory that kept him walking and had his hand closing over the envelope.

"Brenda left you some money," Rayelle explained, her tone as brisk as the walking pace. "About twenty thousand dollars. She said you probably wouldn't take it, that you'd donate it to someone who needed it more than you."

Nico would indeed donate it. It didn't seem right taking money from someone who had given him so much. Besides, he had plenty of his own money. Maybe he'd put it in a trust for Piper.

Rayelle let the silence crack and sizzle between them, and she didn't say anything else until they were across the street and inside Nico's office.

"I'm sure you already know this, but a few months before my sister got sick, Brenda bought a little house just a few miles from your place," Rayelle continued. She sat down across from his desk—after she brushed off the seat that hadn't had a speck of dust or anything else on it. "A log cabin, actually. It's right on the creek."

Nico nodded. He knew about it and had been keeping an eye on it for her. Brenda had bought it because she wanted a place to spend summers with Piper. That way, they'd be able to see him more often, and the visits wouldn't interfere with the girl's school schedule.

"Brenda left that cabin to you, too," Rayelle went on, "but she had, well, plans for it. Plans that include me." Her mouth seemed to tighten even more with each word, and she dusted off the chair arms.

Oh. "Brenda didn't mention that. But feel free to use the cabin anytime you want," he said, hesitating both before and afterward.

Her huff confirmed what Nico already knew. Rayelle wasn't the cabin-using type. She was as city as could be.

"I don't *want* to use it," Rayelle went on. "But Brenda insisted on it. In fact, it was the last thing she said to me before she died."

Because he no longer felt steady on his feet, Nico eased down in his desk chair. "I don't understand." But he was getting a bad feeling about this. The sort of feeling he was sure he would almost certainly have right before his bull ride with BYB.

"Brenda made me promise to bring Piper here for the summer. So that you could help the girl get over Brenda's death." Rayelle motioned toward the envelope she'd given him. "It's all in the letter."

A letter. From Brenda. Nico felt two things—the good and the bad. He wanted to read whatever Brenda had to say to him. A sort of message from beyond the grave. But it worried him, too, especially considering that Brenda had wanted Rayelle to come to Coldwater with Piper.

Rayelle stood. This time, she dusted off her suit.

"Read the letter," she insisted. "I think Brenda spells it out better than I could."

"Spells out what?" he asked.

Boy, did that tighten her mouth even more. "That Brenda had reservations about you being around Piper. Trust me, I have them, too. In fact, I have so many of them that I'm hoping..." She stopped, and Rayelle didn't spell out what had caused her to change her mind about what she'd been about to say.

"Just read the letter," she added, and she turned and walked right out of his office.

Nico managed a goodbye, but his attention was already on the letter that he took from the envelope. It wasn't a short note but rather three handwritten pages. He wouldn't have nearly enough time to go through all of it and then steel himself up again before his appointment. For now, Nico just skimmed it, looking for the part about Brenda's reservations about him.

And he found it.

Well, hell.

Nico got it then. Something he hadn't especially wanted pointed out to him, even by someone he'd loved. But there was no mistaking it.

Nico now knew that he, too, was a dick.

CHAPTER TWO

Dear Naughty Cowgirl,
Help! I'm getting married to the greatest guy in Texas. Seriously, the greatest! We've been together for over a year now and we've acted out all our fantasies. LOL, yes all. I'm talking three or four times a day. Now, I'm looking for something extra special for our honeymoon night. Something he'll never forget. Any naughty suggestions?

Lovey Dovey in Abilene

EDEN'S FINGERS WERE poised over her laptop keyboard as she read through the post again. Normally, it was a snap to answer one like this. After all, it was her specialty. Well, the answering was anyway, but that was what counted for the *Naughty Cowgirl Talks Sex* blog. No one—including the advertisers on her site—would come to her house and demand to do a spot check to see if she practiced what she preached.

Good thing, too.

She'd personally only tried a handful of the naughty suggestions that she'd come up with in the past five years, and the prospects weren't high that she would be trying them in the near future. Hadn't been since Damien had divorced her.

Eden didn't tear up at the thought of her ex's name. No. She was past that. Past the humiliation of the totally unexpected divorce, and now she'd moved on to some particularly pissy anger.

Nico was right. Damien was a dick, and she was just going to have to get past the pain and misery he'd caused her. She thought the anger might help with that. The right amount of anger could smother the flames of heartache—which was a line that she'd used once in her blog.

Eden gulped down a decent-sized swig of Diet Coke and eyed her gray tabby, Miss Kitty, who was eyeing her. He was sprawled on his back on the floor, his belly bulging out on both sides of him, and as usual he had that look of disdain.

She was certain of it.

Miss Kitty blamed her for Damien leaving, and because of it, he'd been giving her the cold shoulder treatment along with acting out.

Of course, maybe the cat also had a bad attitude because of his name.

His previous owner, one of Eden's elderly neighbors, had thought Miss Kitty was female when she'd gotten the feline as a kitten. After the neighbor's death when Eden had taken the cat, she'd considered changing it to something more masculine. However, since everyone else continued to call him Miss Kitty, Eden had gone with the flow.

Lovey Dovey, for now, in Abilene, she wrote, once she got her fingers moving on the keyboard.

Three or four times a day is too much. You'll go blind from having that many orgasms.

Eden stopped, hit the backspace key and was about to give it another try when her phone dinged with a message. From Damien. She couldn't stop the low growl in her throat when she read his text.

Heard you were still upset. Just checking to make sure you're okay. I'm at my mom's most of the day if you want me to stop by.

Mentally, she ripped that text apart, word for word. No. She wasn't okay, and yes, she had been upset, but she'd eat the dying row of cacti on her living room windowsill before she'd admit it to Damien.

To anyone for that matter.

She'd followed all the rules with Damien. Hadn't jumped into a relationship with him. Heck, she hadn't had sex with him until after he'd told her he loved her and wanted to spend the rest of his life with her.

Apparently, his notion of "the rest of his life" was thirty-two months and eleven days.

She downed the Diet Coke as if it were a shot of alcoholic courage, slapped the can on the coffee table and tackled the blog again. This was her job, Eden reminded herself. One of them anyway. It paid the bulk of her bills, and she needed to suck it up and get it done. Plus, she did enjoy writing it.

The blog had been a sort of release valve from the pressures of living in a small town and trying to still be herself with her parents' strict restraints. A way of also spicing up her own sex life with Damien. That's why she'd started it. Small at first. Basically, just a simple webpage, and no one was more surprised than she was about the way it had taken off. She now had over twenty thousand subscribers, a reminder that she was doing something right. Even if it didn't feel so right at the moment.

Lovey Dovey, for now, in Abilene, she wrote.

Seriously, is he really the greatest guy in Texas? Or will he break your heart into a thousand little pieces when he dumps you and finds a perky-butted Mimi?

Clearly, she was going in the wrong direction again and gave the backspace on her keyboard another workout.

Her phone dinged again. Twice. The first was from her mom, and it had the name of a dating site she wanted Eden to use. Not a surprise. The last sixteen messages from her mother had been for dating sites or attempts to set her up on blind dates. As Eden had done with those other messages, she didn't respond. Anything she said right now would only encourage her mom to continue.

The second text was from—who else?—Damien. It began with the poop emoji.

Feeling like this. Afraid I hurt your feelings when I sprang Mimi on you. Can I come over and talk it out?

This one she did answer. Eden texted him back a supersized poop emoji with the single word No and forced herself to focus on her work.

Lovey Dovey in Abilene, she started.

Keep your hands and mouth on your guy as often as possible during the honeymoon. Many couples who've been together for a while jump right into sex. Don't. Make sure there are plenty of long, lingering kisses. Then, gallop up the pace Naughty Cowgirl style by touching, tasting and teasing to give him a honeymoon night to remember.

It wasn't her best effort, but sadly it wasn't her worst, either.

Ever since her breakup, it had been hard to solve other people's relationship concerns when she hadn't been able to solve her own. But her readers wanted more than what she'd written here. They wanted specific tips, positions and settings. They wanted her to map out some foreplay for them.

Lovey Dovey in Abilene, she tried again.

Naughty up your honeymoon with a new move. While your honey's on a chair or the couch, strip and sit on his lap. Lean back until your body is resting against his lap and your head is by his legs. This will give him

a spicy new view of you while you have naughty sex.
Enjoy that naughty orgasm you'll both surely have.

She hit the save button just as she heard the knock
on her door. *Damien.* He'd likely come to rid himself
of the guilt that he was feeling over upsetting her. It
was small of her, but Eden didn't want him relieved.
She wanted him to wallow in misery for falling out
of love with her and falling right onto Mimi and her
massive breasts.

Eden set her laptop on the coffee table and went to
the door to tell him that. It wasn't Damien, though.

It was Nico.

One look at him, and she knew his day hadn't been
any better than hers. Maybe even worse. She should
have expected as much after he'd left the law office
that morning with Brenda's stiff and starched sister.
Now Eden was the one who felt guilty because she
should have checked on him after finishing her shift
and coming home.

With his hands bracketed on her doorjamb, their
eyes met. His were gray, but they were like one of
those strips that you stuck into swimming pools to
determine the chemical level. The color was always
changing. Right now, that gray was too dark, more
like gloom-and-doom storm clouds. Not his usual.
Most of the time his eyes were like spring rain.

"On a scale of one to infinity, just how bad was
your day?" he asked.

"Infinity," she said. It was a scale Nico used for

lots of things like pain levels from injuries, drunkenness and moods. "You?"

"Infinity," he agreed.

Eden took hold of his arm and tugged him inside but not before she got a glimpse of her neighbor, Sherry Winslow, peering out her front window at them.

Sherry had a knack for growing the best verbena in Coldwater and believing the worst was looming on the horizon. The woman wasn't a big gossip, but she probably suspected that Eden was suicidal and that's why Nico was there.

Eden nixed her plan to get him a beer and instead went to the kitchen cabinet to pour him a good-sized shot of Irish whiskey. When she went back into the living room, Nico was already seated. Except Nico didn't actually sit. He more or less lounged in a "been there, done that" sort of way.

Nico had his legs stretched out in front of him and the back of his head resting on the sofa. He would have looked at ease to most people, but Eden knew him too well. There were those stormy eyes and the tight set of his jaw.

"Did you just get back from a ride?" she asked. Because she smelled the scent of saddle leather and pasture grass on him.

He nodded. "I needed to check on some bulls and thought a ride would help."

Obviously, it had, but he didn't volunteer what was eating away at him. Correction: he didn't volunteer exactly what had gone wrong with Rayelle's visit. Maybe it was just that the sight of the woman had brought back the grief, but Eden thought it might be something else.

She sank down beside him, waving the whiskey under his nose until he took the glass from her. He lifted his head and downed the whiskey in one gulp. As if that'd cleared his head some, Nico glanced at her, then the laptop.

"You're working," he said.

"More like failing at working," she explained.

Now that Damien had moved his veterinary practice to San Antonio, Nico was the only person in Coldwater who knew about her blog. He'd even helped her with responses a time or two. Now he sat up, his eyes skirting over the laptop screen as he read what she'd written to Lovey Dovey in Abilene.

"If the greatest guy in Texas doesn't keep a grip on her hips, she's going to slide off him and hit the floor," Nico grumbled. "Plus, unless he's fast, she'll get lightheaded in that position. Instead, tell her that sex is just an itch that needs scratching, and she should quit playing around and scratch."

Obviously, that wasn't Nico's best effort, either. Normally, he could help her work out the logistics of positions and such, but scratching and itching weren't exactly romantic words. Eden wasn't sure if Nico had said that because of his bad mood or if it truly was stellar advice. She didn't press him to try to figure it out. Not when they obviously had bigger things to discuss.

"I should have checked on you sooner," he said at the exact moment she said, "What happened? Why are you giving up sex again?"

"You first," Nico insisted.

Since Eden wanted to get to his problems, she didn't argue, something that would only waste time. Instead, she rattled off her laundry list of woes.

"Damien keeps sending me pity texts. Roy's still walking on eggshells whenever he's around me. I have blog-block and can't give a decent Naughty Cowgirl answer. My mom is trying to set me up on dates so I'll get over my broken heart. And I think Miss Kitty's neutering failed and he knocked up the neighbor's calico."

Nico stayed quiet as if going through each of those, one by one, and then his attention shifted to the cat. Yes, the very cat who hadn't moved a fraction of an inch since Nico arrived.

"He's sneakier than he looks," she insisted, "and he's mad that he can't stay with Damien all the time instead of just one week out of the month. But a week is all Damien wanted." Eden nixed the subject of the cat and gave Nico's arm a nudge. "Now, spill it. What's wrong?"

"I'm a dick," Nico said without hesitation.

She waited for more, but apparently that was it. "I'm going to need a tad more info than that if you want me to give you words of sympathy or wisdom. The best I can manage from that is a *hmmm* or a questioning grunt."

The tad more started with him cursing some, but all the profanity seemed to be aimed at himself. "I sleep with women who think of me as a notch on a bedpost. Heck, I sleep with women, period. Too many of them. It's like a blur once the mind-blowing pleasure is gone."

Okay. That helped her fill in some of the blanks. This wasn't exactly a revelation since she'd known Nico for nearly twenty years. He'd nailed nearly every one of her friends. Heck, he'd even nailed some of his *own* friends. In fact, it was possible that Eden was the only nonmarried, nonmean woman in Coldwater who hadn't been in his bed. That was because in his mind, she'd always been Damien's. In her mind, too, until Damien had walked out on her.

Eden didn't nudge Nico this time. She patted his arm instead. "You're a nice guy with a good heart."

Nico groaned and quickly shook his head. "I don't respect sex."

That filled in another blank, but that was because she remembered overhearing a lecture that Nico had gotten from his oldest brother, Kace. It'd been around the time Nico had turned sixteen, so Kace would have been about twenty-one, and he'd sounded like the authority when he'd told Nico that if he didn't treat sex with respect, then he might as well jack off in the shower.

At the time Eden had blushed at the advice. Had blushed even more because she'd just stood there listening to a private conversation. But Kace's advice had resonated with her even though she hadn't been entirely sure she'd given it the right interpretation. To her, respect meant feelings. As in feelings more than mere horniness. And that's why she hadn't gone all the way with Damien until she'd been sure that his feelings for her were love.

Of course, now she knew that was a crock. Love could be as fickle as a man's erection.

Nico dragged in another of those deep breaths, drawing her attention back to him, before he reached in his pocket and pulled out some papers. A letter, she realized.

"It's from Brenda," he said. "She left instructions for Rayelle to give it to me after she died."

Oh mercy. Obviously, this had punched Nico in the gut and he figured it would do the same to her because of the effect it was having on him. "You want me to read it, or you want to tell me the gist?" she asked.

He seemed to have a mental debate with himself and handed her the letter. "Page two, third paragraph," he instructed.

Eden skipped straight to the second page, and she zoomed in on what had put Nico in this state of mind. Brenda had written:

Piper looks up to you, Nico. You're her big brother in every way that counts. She wants to spend the summer in Coldwater so she can be with you. I think she needs that, too, so you can help her get over losing me and starting her new life with Rayelle. But, Nico, I'm worried. You know in your heart that you might not be the best influence on Piper.

Eden groaned, ready to defend Nico, but he stopped her.

"It's the truth," he insisted. "You know it's the truth," he amended.

As his friend, Eden wanted to argue with that, but she couldn't. Piper was sixteen, a vulnerable age. And while Eden seriously doubted that Nico's reputation would cause Piper to start sleeping around or having sex without respect, this might mess with the girl's head in very bad ways.

"Page three, paragraph one," Nico prompted her.

Dreading what might be there, Eden went to that page and continued to read.

So, I'm begging you to do right by Piper. For the time that Piper and Rayelle are with you, make them believe you're the man that Piper already thinks you are. The man that I've always known you could become.

Lord love a duck. Talk about a guilt trip. Part of Eden wanted to blast Brenda for putting this on him, but the other part of her got it. Man, did she get it.

"So, what are you going to do?" Eden asked, because she had no idea what else to say.

"Page three, last paragraph," he answered without even sparing her a glance.

Her attention zoomed down, all the way to the bottom of the letter, and this time when Eden thought, *Lord love a duck*, it was for a different reason. Now she did blast Brenda.

"You need to clean up your act," Brenda had insisted. And she sounded exactly like a mother.

For two months, let Piper believe that you can be content with just one woman. A good, decent woman who you already respect. You might be surprised how much happier and complete that can make you feel.

Everything inside Eden went still.

"Turn the page over," Nico instructed.

It wasn't necessary. The *already* had said it all. "Brenda wants you and me to pretend to be a couple," Eden concluded.

"Turn the page over," he repeated.

Even though Eden was certain of what she would see written there, she did as he said and flipped over the paper. It wasn't her name, though, but it was one from very recent memory.

Well, crap.

The name Brenda had written as Nico's intended mate was none other than the perky-butted Mimi Bakersfield.

CHAPTER THREE

"MIMI?" EDEN CHALLENGED.

Nico heard the surprise in her voice. That same emotion was in her expression, too, but as he expected, it quickly morphed to anger.

"Mimi?" she repeated, her tone a little harder now. "Brenda thought Mimi should be the woman of your dreams? The ideal female to prove to Piper that you're not a bad influence?"

He'd never considered himself a genius, but Nico was smart enough to know that Eden's venom wasn't solely aimed at Brenda and her poor choice of candidates for his potential partner. Eden's feelings about her ex were also playing into this.

Nico's foster mom hadn't known that Mimi had been seeing Damien and was now engaged to him. Also, Brenda almost certainly hadn't been aware that beneath Mimi's often-prim attire was the body of a woman who could ignite jealousy and hurt in Eden.

"Why the heck wouldn't Brenda think of me for something like this?" Eden went on. "I'm a good decent woman who you already respect." She stopped. "Did Brenda know about my blog?"

Nico quickly shook his head. No knowledge of

what Brenda would have considered a dirty blog. And since Eden wrote under a pseudonym, Brenda wouldn't have guessed if she'd just happened to come across *Naughty Cowgirl* when she'd been surfing the net.

"I suspect the reason Brenda didn't suggest you is because she knows we're friends," Nico explained. He further suspected that Brenda was trying to do some matchmaking. "Maybe Brenda believed if I spent two months with Mimi that I would come to my senses and stop sleeping around."

"More like you'd start sleeping around with Mimi," she grumbled. Then she stopped again. "Did you ever have sex with Mimi?"

"No." He couldn't say that fast enough.

And he thanked his lucky stars that Mimi and he had never crossed paths sexually. Eden had been way-laid with news of the engagement, and it wouldn't have helped for her to hear that her best friend had banged her ex-husband's fiancée.

On a heavy sigh, Eden slumped lower on the sofa. "What are you going to do? What will you tell Rayelle?"

Both good questions. Nico didn't have the answers. Well, not the answers that would please anyone anyway.

"I'd already decided to give up sex," he reminded her. "Of course, Rayelle isn't likely to believe I'll be able to actually do that."

"You can do it," Eden piped in. "You can," she repeated when he looked at her.

Yeah, he could. Still, ending the casual sex was only the tip of the iceberg.

"I can think of better ways to spend a summer other than under Rayelle's watchful eye," Nico went on, and he was being generous with "watchful." The woman was a prude and would scrutinize his every move. Along with all the moves of everyone else in Coldwater. "Plus, folks around here know how I am, and even if I try to clean up my act, Piper would soon hear about my *unclean* past."

Eden's sound of agreement was quick. So quick that it stung a little. But then Nico was already coming face-to-face with the fact that he hadn't led a life that would have pleased Brenda. And it sure as hell wouldn't please the persnickety Rayelle.

It clearly wasn't pleasing him, either.

The words in Brenda's letter burned into him. He'd always described his lifestyle as fun and not doing anyone any harm. But it had obviously given Brenda some uncomfortable moments about her possibly not having raised him right. She'd probably felt that way not just because of his string of sexual partners, but also since she could have seen this as his inability to commit.

"Put roots on your boots," Nico muttered. "Brenda used to tell me that's what I needed. That by chasing women I was actually running from my past."

Eden made another sound of agreement, causing Nico to turn his head toward her and scowl. "You'd rather I lie to you?" she asked.

Maybe. He was feeling a little raw and bruised

right now. But he had to shake his head. Eden was the one person he could count on to tell him the truth. That grounded him in a way that nothing else could.

"You had nothing to do with your mother running out on you," she continued a moment later. "You were just a kid, and she was messed up on drugs. That still doesn't mean it won't haunt you. She's like those little wisps of breaths in cold weather. Nothing much to it, but you can't stop it. Thankfully, the wisps are gone before you know it."

He frowned because it sounded like something she'd once said in one of her blog posts. Still, it was true. His druggie mother's leaving had forced him and his brothers into foster care. Not together at first, either. Nico had ended up with Brenda, but her place hadn't been big enough for four boys so his brothers had been placed in other homes. That had gone on for two years until they'd finally gotten moved together. That had meant Nico leaving Brenda and being placed in a hellhole where one of the caregivers had nearly killed him.

That was another of those wisps of "breath" that haunted him.

Brenda had saved him then, too, by reporting the abuse and working to get the Laramie brothers all moved to a good home with Buck McCall in Coldwater.

Even though everything had worked out in the end, a therapist would probably conclude that Nico's inability to form lasting relationships with women was because of abandonment issues. And the therapist would be right.

"So, you'll talk to Rayelle and tell her not to bring Piper here for the summer?" Eden asked.

Nico nodded. That was pretty much the plan he'd come up with since Rayelle's visit. The trick would be to convince Rayelle to ditch the deathbed promise she'd made to her only sister.

Yeah, that would be fun.

"I'll go see Rayelle," Nico explained.

Though part of him wanted to chicken out and call her instead. He wouldn't. This was something better done in person. Then he could square things with Piper along with checking on her to see how she was dealing with Brenda being gone.

There was a knock on the door, and as if he'd been hit with a cattle prod, the cat sprang off the floor, running toward the sound.

"It'll be Damien," Eden grumbled, and she clearly wasn't pleased about that. Unlike Miss Kitty, who started to howl and claw at the door. "The cat must be able to smell him or something because he always acts like that whenever Damien is nearby."

Nico stayed put, but several moments later he got confirmation that it was indeed Damien when he came in carrying the tabby. Miss Kitty was purring and bumping his head against Damien's chin, and it was obvious the cat was the only one in the house who was glad to see him.

"It's not your week to have the cat, and I didn't invite you in," Eden snapped.

"I noticed that. But I thought I should check on you." In contrast, there was no heat in Damien's voice. Just sympathy. Which was probably genuine. That wouldn't make Eden any happier about this visit.

"I'm fine," Eden snarled, proving that she was as far from fine as possible. She was spitting mad, maybe at Damien's just waltzing in. Maybe because her ex still caused her to feel, well, whatever she was feeling.

Damien shook his head, throwing in a "hello" to Nico before he turned back to Eden. "You're upset. It's all over town that you were crying this morning."

Nico wondered how Damien could know so little about Eden. That comment was like tossing gasoline on a fire, and Nico got to his feet to try to put out some flames before this turned into a full blaze.

"I'm sorry it upset you when I told you about Mimi," Damien went on before Nico could speak. Still stroking the cat, Damien strolled into the living room, glancing around as if looking for signs of any changes she'd made to the decor. "I didn't mean to blurt it out that way, but I knew you should hear it from me."

"Eden's fine about Mimi and you," Nico lied. "She was upset about Brenda's death. That's why she was crying."

Damien stopped in his tracks, his gaze volleying from Nico to Eden. "No," Damien concluded as if any deep emotion just had to be because of him.

"Yes," Nico and Eden said in unison.

Damien dismissed that with a grunt, walked to the

coffee table and glanced down at the laptop. "And now you're having trouble answering your blog. The only time that happens is when you're upset about me."

"I'm not having trouble with the blog," Eden insisted.

But that didn't stop Damien from reading over the response she'd written to Pleasured in El Paso. "You should tell her to keep the fire alive with the two-grip hand job for her man, and then explain in detail to her how it's done. That'll add some spice."

Eden gave Damien a look that could have frozen Lovey Dovey in Abilene, but that didn't stop the man. Obviously, he was accustomed to giving Eden sex advice—even when the advice was unwanted.

"If she wants to spice up the honeymoon, she can add nipple clamps and a cock ring," Damien added. "Of course, you haven't had any experience with that," he said to Eden, "but you fake a lot of the advice."

Then with that zinger fired, Damien practically did a double take when he saw the way Nico and Eden were staring at him.

But Eden was doing more than just staring.

She was seething, and Nico didn't have to guess that she was about to say something she would soon regret. Despite her anger, she still cared for Damien. She was hurt. And when she spoke to him, it would likely be the pain that was talking.

Nico didn't mind Damien getting a little verbal flak, but he knew that the only person it would end up hurting was Eden. That's why he hooked his arm around Damien's shoulders and got the man moving toward the door.

"Come on," Nico insisted. "We need to talk."

"I can handle this," Eden protested.

Nico had no doubts about that. No doubts, either, that he could handle it without having a meltdown. And he could do it in a way that would smooth all of this over and get Damien out of her face.

"Let me fix this for you," Nico whispered to her. "Please."

He figured the "please" would do it. That, and the fact that Nico rarely asked her to take a step back about anything. But the sight of her tears was still way too fresh, and he didn't want her going through that again.

Despite the cat's howl of protest, Damien plopped Miss Kitty on the sofa and headed toward the front door with Nico. Of course, Nico didn't give Damien much of a choice about that because he kept his arm around him and practically muscled him out onto the front porch. Nico braced himself for Damien to complain about the strong-arm treatment, but the man only shook his head and sighed.

"I hate seeing Eden like this," Damien said, and that took some of the angry wind out of Nico's sails. "It brings out the worst in me."

Nico hated seeing her like that, too, and it was impossible to put the blame for her broken heart solely on Damien. Yes, Damien had walked out on her, but if he'd stayed, there would have still been hurt since it was obvious Damien no longer loved her. Nico wasn't on Damien's side of this breakup, definitely didn't like the way Damien had handled things, but Nico was holding on to hope that this would be better for Eden in the end. She deserved better.

From inside the house, Miss Kitty continued to howl, and Nico could hear the feline clawing at the door. That couldn't be pleasing Eden since he was her cat. She'd had him for several years before marrying Damien.

"I don't think Eden can get past us," Damien continued, still shaking his head. "I don't think she'll ever get over me."

Well, that sounded more than a tad arrogant, but for the moment, it was true. Eden wasn't past them, and Nico wasn't sure if she would be anytime soon. He also knew Eden was listening.

Or rather trying to.

She probably had her ear right at the door, and that's why Nico did a little more strong-arming and got Damien off the porch, through Eden's postage stamp of a yard and onto the sidewalk.

"What the hell happened between you two anyway?" Nico asked. He'd already put that question to Damien in various ways since the breakup, but he hadn't been satisfied with any answer he'd gotten from the man.

Damien lifted his shoulder. "I just got bored with her. And don't tell me you don't understand that. Your attention span for a woman is like that." He snapped his fingers.

Yeah, it was, but then Nico had never been married. If he had, he would have figured out a way to deal with the boredom.

"You loved her," Nico pointed out.

Damien shrugged again. "Sure, but love can't get you past sleeping with the same woman night after night."

Nico was certain he looked at Damien as if he'd sprouted an extra nose. "Then why the hell would you get engaged or married again if you feel that way?"

"Because it'll be different with Mimi," Damien answered without hesitation. Without convincing Nico, too.

Oh, Nico was certain that Damien believed that "different" theory, but Nico knew that Damien hadn't been able to stick with one woman when he'd married Eden. And Nico doubted that Damien would stick to Mimi, either. But that wasn't his rodeo, wasn't his ball-busting bull.

"I just need Eden to be okay," Damien went on. "Then, I'll stop feeling like shit. People will finally stop looking at me as if I've stomped all over the town's good girl. You and I both know she's not that good. Not with that sex blog she writes."

The sex blog didn't make Eden good or bad in Nico's eyes. It just made her the author of a sex blog. But he figured most folks, including her parents, wouldn't feel that way.

"Eden just needs time," Nico said, remembering that his job here was to make this better for Eden. That meant making Damien understand that he shouldn't repeat his dick-like behavior. "And maybe it'd help if she didn't run into Mimi and you for a while. You know, until she can get used to the idea of you starting a new life with another woman."

"I can't stop her from running into my fiancée. Not with Mimi still living and working here. Plus, the only way Eden will get used to our marriage being over is for her to see Mimi and me together." Damien huffed again. "Eden and I have been divorced for six months. That should be plenty enough time for her to have moved on."

"You two dated from the time you were thirteen," Nico pointed out just as quickly. "That means you were together for nearly seventeen years."

Something that Nico couldn't even fathom. But in a way it endorsed his own lifestyle. After all, if Eden and Damien couldn't make it work after all that time, then maybe he was right to stick with his one-week stands.

Nico geared up to drive home his point about Eden needing more time, but he stopped when he saw the cruiser approaching them. His brother, Kace, was behind the wheel, and he eased to a stop next to them.

"Everything okay?" Kace asked.

"I was about to ask you the same thing," Nico admitted. There was a bandage just above Kace's left eye, and the Equality for Rodeo Heifers sign was on the backseat of his cruiser.

Kace ignored his comment, and he aimed a darn effective cop's stare at Damien. "Eden's neighbors called," Kace told him. "Three of them. They seemed to think there was some kind of trouble going on here."

Damien cursed and threw his hands up in the air. "See? This is what I've been talking about. All this crying and moping that Eden's doing is causing people to gossip. It's putting folks off being around her."

Nico hadn't reached that same conclusion. Yeah, Eden had been crying. Maybe doing some moping, too. But it wasn't putting people off. The calls to Kace had likely been because Nico had taken the discussion outside, which could have led the neighbors to believe that Damien had needed some cooling off. That, in turn, could have caused them to have some concern for Eden. In other words, the opposite of putting folks off.

"We're just talking," Nico told his brother.

Kace was darn good at that cop's stare. So good that it always made Nico want to confess to something just to get him to look away. It seemed to have the same effect on Damien.

"Eden's practically falling apart without me," Damien stated like it was a fact. "She won't get on with her life because she wants to punish me, to get back at me for leaving her."

Well, that was bullshit. Eden was hurting, period, and her crying spell hadn't had anything to do with getting back at Damien. Just the opposite, since Eden hadn't wanted a soul to know about it.

Apparently, Damien felt the need to just keep on confessing. "I can't be sucked into Eden's drama," he continued. "It's not my fault that no other man is interested in her."

And Nico felt it then. The breaking point. He rarely felt the rise and churn of temper this fierce, but he was sure as hell feeling it now. There'd been a couple of other times he'd wanted to punch Damien, but the *want* was turning into a fast *need*.

"Excuse me?" Nico snarled. "No other man is interested in Eden?"

Damien pulled himself out of his trance and looked at Nico as if remembering he was there. What Damien didn't do was take back his remarks and admit that he'd said them in a whiny-assed fit of self-indulgent temper. In fact, judging from Damien's suddenly steely stare—which still looked whiny-assed to Nico—he was going to dig in his heels when it came to his opinion of his ex.

An opinion that dickweed Damien had no right to have.

"No other man is interested in Eden," Damien restated like a challenge. "You don't know about her sexual problems."

No, Nico didn't know about those. Nor did he want to. Well, not immediately anyway, but this was the first he was hearing about Eden having any problems with sex. Of course, Nico challenged Damien right back. In fact, he tossed aside common sense and any other troublesome logic, and he jammed his thumb against his chest.

"I'm interested in her," Nico declared. "Very interested. And you'd better get used to it."

Damien's mouth dropped open. That was quickly followed by a "have you lost your mind?" groan from Kace. Nico ignored both of them, and he turned to go inside. Because he was well aware that he'd just tossed the gauntlet and drawn a big-ass line in the sand.

Now the question was—what was he going to do about it?

Leaving his audience—Damien, Kace and the nosy neighbors—Nico walked to the door, and when Eden opened it lightning fast, he realized she'd been part of that audience, too.

And she wasn't happy about what she'd heard.

Welcome to the club. Nico wasn't especially thrilled with any part of that conversation, either.

"You're not going to ask me about that sexual problem, are you?" she said right off.

Of all the things she must have heard, it didn't surprise him that she'd latched on to that one. But for Nico, it had been the straw that'd broken the camel's back.

"I couldn't let Damien get away with saying that no other man was interested in you," he whispered.

Yeah, that was going to stick with her for a while. Not good. Eden's self-esteem had already taken too many shots because of Damien.

Nico saw the instant change in her expression. The anger that had lit her eyes cooled some. Eden lowered her shoulders, and she caught her bottom lip between her teeth to steady it.

"What an ass," she grumbled, shooting a steely glare over Nico's shoulder.

Nico glanced back, too, and saw that Damien and Kace were now talking in hushed whispers. Damien was probably trying to justify why he'd just doled out that ass-like behavior to a woman he'd once loved.

"He is," Nico verified. "And I'd like to give him a dose of something to bring his ego down a notch."

That got her attention, and Eden's gaze quickly shifted back to him. She didn't ask him what he planned on doing, but she did study his face. Then, his mouth.

"You're going to kiss me?" she asked, her voice not thick with heat—no surprise there—but with deep concern.

Nico didn't let on that he was in the concern mode, too. That's because he was still steaming over Damien and wanting to teach his former friend a lesson. It didn't matter if this was likely the worst teaching tool in the history of teaching tools. He just went with it anyway.

Nico slid his hand around the back of her neck and leaped right into the mistake. He kissed his best friend. In the grand plan he'd semiformulated in his mind, he meant to keep it short and sweet. Mentally chaste.

That didn't happen.

The moment his lips touched her soft mouth, he felt the heat slide through him, all the way to the brainless part of him behind his zipper. The part of him that usually landed him in women's beds and other places he shouldn't be.

Strange that he would feel this heat when it was Eden's mouth. And Eden's breasts touching his chest. It was wrong. All wrong. Even when they'd been teenagers, he'd trained himself not to think of her as anything but a friend.

As Damien's girl.

She couldn't have been anything else without it tearing apart their friendship. Well, it was darn sure doing some tearing now because she shouldn't have tasted like this. Shouldn't have felt like this.

Nico moved away from her, his grip easing off the back of her neck. He manned up, meeting her eye to eye so he could determine just how much of an apology he owed her. Nico knew it would need to be a big one when Eden muttered two little words.

"Well, shit."

CHAPTER FOUR

LET ME FIX this for you. Please.

Along with several other things, those words had continued to play through Eden's head for the past two days. It was what Nico had said to her when he'd taken Damien outside for a chat. And while she hadn't expected a miracle in the fixing department, Eden also hadn't thought that talk would lead her to where it did.

To that kiss.

Over the years, she'd seen Nico kiss other women. Mercy, had she. She'd even considered how it might feel to be kissed by a man who seemed to be a champion at it. Heck, a time or two she'd even fantasized about him. She was a woman after all.

One with twenty-twenty eyesight and fully functioning nether regions.

No way could she have completely ignored all that hotness. But it had gotten easier for her to do that once she'd become Damien's lover. Then his wife. Then, she'd saved all her fantasies for him.

More or less.

For the sake of her marriage, she'd moved Nico firmly into the best-friend compartment of her life.

That meant that other than the occasional dream or lapse, she hadn't thought about his own fully functioning nether regions.

That kiss had opened new doors. Ones that Nico and just about everyone else thought should have stayed closed. She wasn't his type, people were probably saying. And she was his friend's ex-wife. That had to cross a boundary or two. But probably the biggest concern of the gossip would center on one hashed-over question.

Was she Nico's "new" woman?

Of course, Nico and she knew the answer to that. No. She wasn't. He'd kissed her for just one reason. To get back at Damien for the mean things he'd said about her. That'd been Nico's sole motivation, and like her, he probably hadn't expected to feel anything when he'd planted that lip-lock on her. Well, nothing except some "nanny nanny boo boo" aimed at Damien.

But there'd been heat.

Oh yes.

And in that handful of seconds that the kiss had lasted, Eden had gotten enough carnal knowledge about Nico to understand why he got frequent invitations to women's beds. Of course, his looks had helped with that, too. All that thick tousled black hair. The sizzling eyes.

Things she shouldn't be thinking about. No. She needed to focus on the big picture here. The kiss had fixed the Damien problem. Well, it had if she considered his storming off like a cranky toddler fixing things. She'd very much enjoyed that fit of temper. Not as much as she'd enjoyed the kiss but still…

The kiss hadn't fixed other things, though. After the gossips had hashed out that kiss, the talk would be of Nico and her as a couple. That could be a good thing, considering Nico might be looking for someone to meet Rayelle's approval. And Rayelle might indeed see Eden as stable enough so that Piper's sensibilities wouldn't be warped.

Might.

Or Rayelle could just see this as another rung on the ladder of the poor relationship decisions that Nico had made over the years. Nico might be on board with that possible assessment, too.

Despite that kiss and what he'd said to Damien, Eden knew Nico was having second and third thoughts. Not only about the possible pretense with her as his "stable" woman but also second thoughts about Piper's and Rayelle's visit to Coldwater. He loved Piper and would definitely want to make sure she was okay, but Nico wasn't just going to buy into Rayelle's theory about his needing a woman to keep Piper on whatever course in life that Rayelle had deemed the right one.

Her phone dinged with a text. From Damien, of course. Since the "blowup" with Nico, her ex had texted her multiple times a day, including when she'd been at work earlier at the law office. He'd also tried to call her, but she had let those go straight to voice mail.

The only reason she hadn't outright blocked the

number was because their divorce agreement had spelled out he needed to be able to reach her for "custody" arrangements/plans for Miss Kitty. That didn't mean though that she had to talk to him about anything else. She deleted the texts and instead had used the dinging sound as a sort of thump upside her head. A reminder for her to get back to work and stop letting her thoughts drift.

Eden went back to what she should be doing—working on the blog. She didn't need to write a new response today, but she did need to sort through previous posts for her "best of sex advice." It was something she did several times a year, and it always garnered her the highest page hits, something her advertisers most certainly noticed.

She bookmarked "Hot in the Saddle" to be included. The poster had asked for tips on having creative sex with a horse trainer. Eden had written it BTD— before the divorce—so it didn't have the snarky, disillusioned tone of some of her more recent stuff.

"Use the saddle, of course," Eden had written. "Put it on the bed or floor, get naked and hop on with your hot-to-trot trainer. Then, gallop up the pace Naughty Cowgirl style by putting the reins on him. Tug, pull and wrangle him in."

Eden had added some more suggestions that involved a creative way to use the saddle horn and horse collar. Successful suggestions apparently since the person had sent a video to prove she'd followed Eden's instructions. Of course, Eden had deleted it without watching it—too much.

She thought of that video now. Heck, she thought of sex, which wasn't that much of a surprise, considering she was reading about it. BTD, the blog posts had been a sort of foreplay for Damien and her. Not that she'd needed a whole lot of that what with her peculiar "problem." But the foreplay nudge had stopped after Damien left.

Except she felt a little tingle of it now.

She smiled, enjoying the little buzz. A buzz that vanished when the image that came into her mind was Nico. Specifically, of Nico standing up to Damien. Of Nico lounging on her sofa. Of the way his jeans fit his amazing butt.

Of Nico and his jeans when he lounged on her sofa.

Her phone dinged again, the sound causing her to make a startled gasp. Another text from Damien and also her cue to move on, so that's what Eden did.

She shook her head to clear out the last of the tinglies and went back to work, scrolling through the files of posts. The next one she bookmarked for "best of" was "Sneaky Tongues" from a woman who wanted to keep her sexual relationship a secret.

"Go for phone sex," Eden had advised. "But while talking to your guy, send him photos of yourself to let him know what his words are doing to you. Then, gallop up the pace Naughty Cowgirl style with you wearing just a Stetson and boots."

This time her phone didn't ding. It rang. And Eden automatically flicked away the annoyance of Damien trying to call her again. But that wasn't his name on the screen.

It was Piper's.

Eden didn't have annoyance to flick away but rather concern. It wasn't the first time the girl had called her. They had spoken several times when Piper had been trying to figure out what she could get Nico for Christmas or his birthday. But the timing of this particular call made Eden think the topic would be a little more serious.

"Piper," she answered, and Eden tried not to sound worried.

"Do you know what's going on with Nico and Aunt Rayelle?" the girl demanded. Piper didn't even attempt a no-worry tone.

Since Eden wasn't sure she had the latest update from Nico about this, she went with a noncommittal, "Sort of."

The huff Piper made was loud enough that people in Vermont probably heard it. "Please try to talk Aunt Rayelle into us coming to Coldwater. The woman won't listen to me. She keeps saying how Nico is inappropriate parental material."

Eden figured those last three words were verbatim from Rayelle. "And what does Nico say about that?" Again, Eden was going for noncommittal.

Another huff. "That he wants me there with him for the summer, but that it's up to Aunt Rayelle since she has custody and all. You can talk her into it. I know you can."

The girl had a lot more faith in Eden than she did. "I'm not sure Rayelle even likes me."

"She's not happy about you getting a divorce, but

she doesn't call you 'inappropriate parental material.' I think she'd listen to you if you explained that Nico is grieving and that I could help with that."

Eden had been about to go for a third noncommittal round, but that last bit stopped her. Nico was indeed grieving. And so was Piper. Heck, Rayelle was, too, but they weren't anywhere near on the same pages with that grief.

"Please talk to her," Piper pressed. That was apparently it. The end of the girl's argument. And it was a darn effective one, too.

"All right," Eden said but had to pause when Piper squealed in delight. "First though, I'll speak to Nico about it."

"Today," Piper insisted. "Talk to him today."

Since Eden had planned on doing that anyway, she assured the girl she would and ended the call so she could text Nico with a simple message:

Got time to meet up? Piper wants me to convince you to let her visit.

She wasn't sure how busy his schedule was or if he'd want to put off seeing her awhile longer, so Eden set her phone aside. She figured she'd have to wait at least a couple of minutes for him to respond. But he texted her back instantly.

Gray Mare in twenty was his response.

The Gray Mare was the only bar in town and was just up the street from her house. It was an Old West–style saloon, and it wasn't unusual for them to go there since Nico's brother's girlfriend owned the place. But Eden hoped he hadn't picked the location because he needed to drown his sorrows. If so, it wouldn't take long. Nico was a lightweight when it came to liquor. But his speedy response told her that he was anxious to talk to her.

Eden tried not to wince about that.

Nico was no doubt ready to apologize for that kiss and ask her if they could figure out a way to cram everything back into the Pandora's box they'd opened. And she supposed she should agree to it and pretend the kiss never happened.

But what if she didn't want to agree?

What if she wanted that kiss to lead to more kisses and maybe even sex? And it wasn't as if she had no carnal knowledge whatsoever of Nico. Well, she had visual carnal knowledge anyway.

Once when Damien and she had been sixteen or so and on a double date with Nico and Sandy Kellerman, Damien had driven them to a popular make-out spot by the creek. Damien and she had been in the second base stage. Lots of French-kissing and touching through the clothes. In other words, no chance of sex happening, which meant it would be the same for Nico and Sandy. Nico had almost certainly been the only nonvirgin in the car that night, and since none of them would want an audience for their de-virgining, it was going to stay that way.

During their making out, Eden had glanced in the backseat at Nico and Sandy. Lots of French-kissing going on there, too, but then she'd seen something that branded itself into her memory.

Nico had had an erection.

Hard to miss since it strained like a baseball bat against his zipper. The perfect outline of it. And then while his mouth had been occupied with Sandy's, he'd slid his hand down into the waist of his faded jeans to give himself an adjustment. Moving that bat to the side, probably so he'd be more comfortable. Oh, but it had given Eden a moment to remember.

And remember.

Even years later, she could still see his hand disappear into his jeans. Could feel the way it'd caused her pulse to skitter when she thought about what he'd touched. Most women wouldn't have felt a heated flush or gotten a skittery pulse, but for some strange reason, both had happened to Eden.

And still happened when she thought about that night.

She figured it had been memorable for all parties, too, because as she'd shifted in the seat to get an even-better look at Nico, her foot had landed against the horn. It'd been loud, too. So loud that it'd caused curses and shouts from others making out in the vehicles around them.

Despite the horn interruption, the image of Nico was still strong in her head, and it gave her another round of tingles as she stepped outside to start her short walk to the bar. Of course, the sticky humid heat hit her at once and pulled her out of her thoughts, but Eden forced her mind back to the what if.

Nico and she were adults and actually had stuff in common. Some stuff, anyway. Similar tastes in music and books. Hardly a foundation for a relationship, but that and the newfound attraction were more than enough to have an affair. Then, maybe they could do a Pandora's box restuffing and still be friends.

That was pretty much a best-case scenario since Nico didn't do long-term.

She stepped into the bar, thankful for the cool AC that immediately spilled over her. Thankful, too, for the friendly greeting.

"Hey there, Eden," the owner, Cleo Delaney, called out.

Cleo was behind the bar, serving up drafts to two ranch hands seated in front of her. She gave Eden a smile and lifted her finger in a "be with you in a sec" gesture. Eden nodded, glanced around but didn't see Nico.

"Nico's not here," Cleo said, coming out from the bar to give Eden a hug. They'd known each other for years but had only recently renewed their friendship after Cleo had moved back to Coldwater. That move had been coupled with Cleo buying the Gray Mare and getting engaged to Nico's hunky brother, Judd.

Of course, that hunkiness applied to all four of the Laramie brothers. Eden figured hearts had broken all over the state when first Callen had gotten married and then Judd had asked Cleo to be his wife. Those broken hearts were now looking to Nico and Kace to fill the sexual void. Kace wouldn't be game for something like that, and until recently Nico had been doing his best to make up for the shortage of available Laramie men.

"I heard about the kiss," Cleo said, easing Eden away from the door and next to a table so they'd be out of earshot from the guys at the bar.

"I'm sure you did. It's all over town." Eden shrugged. "The good news is that it's put a stop to some of the pitying looks I'd been getting."

Cleo stared at her with those exotic amber eyes and took Eden by the shoulders. "So, be honest. Just how *friendly* have Nico and you gotten?"

For reasons that weren't exactly clear, Eden had always been up-front with Cleo. Maybe it was the fact that Cleo had a criminal past and owned a bar. Or it could be that with Cleo what you saw was what you got. If Cleo had been writing *Naughty Cowgirl Talks Sex*, she wouldn't have felt the need to keep it under wraps. And her advice would have probably been a heck of a lot better than Eden's.

"It was just a kiss," Eden explained. "And not even a real one. Nico did that because he was riled at something Damien said about me. It was sort of a kissing pissing contest between former friends." And Eden had no doubts, none, that the *former* label was spot-on.

Cleo frowned, her chin tipping down. Obviously, she wasn't happy about the non-genuineness of that kiss. Well, neither was Eden now that she'd given it some thought.

"Sometimes though, I do think about kissing Nico," Eden admitted.

"So do half the women in town." Cleo laughed and let go of her shoulders so she could give her a playful nudge with her elbow. "I would tell you to just go for it, but I know the other things going on." She paused. "Rayelle has called all the brothers, Buck McCall and me."

Eden didn't have to guess what the topic of conversation had been. "Let me guess. Rayelle heard about Nico kissing me or, even if she didn't, she's concerned about the influence I'll have on Piper because I'm a divorced woman."

"She heard about the kiss," Cleo verified. "And no, I don't know how she learned about it. She wouldn't say. Said it would be gossiping if she mentioned her source."

That sounded like Rayelle. She preferred to back up her judgmental ways with facts. Such as a divorce. It wouldn't matter to Rayelle that 50 percent of Americans were divorced because she would still see it as a character flaw. A character flaw that Rayelle had avoided since she'd never married.

"Rayelle thinks both Nico and I will be a bad influence on Piper?" Eden concluded.

"Yep, she does. But I think Rayelle could be a bad influence on her, too."

"I'm in complete agreement with that." And it was why she was here. To talk to Nico as she'd promised Piper and see if they could work out a solution. One that probably wouldn't include kissing or hands in the pants.

"Bottom line is this for me," Eden said a moment

later. "Is Rayelle trying to find a reason not to bring Piper to Coldwater?"

Cleo shook her head. "Nope. As far as I can figure out, she wants to keep that deathbed promise she made to her sister. In fact, it would eat away at her if she didn't keep it."

Of course, it was eating away at Nico, too. He was worried that he might agree to bring Piper here only to mess up the girl's life.

The front door opened, and Eden steeled herself up for the chat with Nico, but it was Beckham Morrelli, one of the three kids Cleo was fostering. He was carrying two large boxes, one stacked on top of the other, and judging from the way his muscles were straining, they were heavy.

"I picked these up from the post office," he said to Cleo in that mutter-mumble-put-out kind of way that only a teenager could manage.

"Thanks." Cleo went up on her toes to brush a kiss on the boy's cheek. One that caused Beckham to make an "awww, Mom" grunt in response. "Just put the boxes in my office."

"He's growing like a weed," Eden commented. It had only been a few weeks since she'd seen him, and it seemed as if Beckham had added a couple more inches to his already-six-foot body.

"Oh yeah," Cleo confirmed, "he's sixteen, going on thirty, and that pretty face complicates things. Judd's lectured him about turning into another Nico."

So, Nico was now a cautionary tale. One who at that exact moment stepped into the bar. He glanced at

Cleo and her, his forehead creasing as if he'd known he was the topic of discussion. If so, he didn't address it. Nico gave his soon-to-be sister-in-law a gentle arm squeeze and a kiss on the cheek.

"Whiskey," Nico told Cleo.

Eden only sighed, ordered a glass of wine and led Nico to the booth all the way at the back of the bar. It wouldn't ensure them absolute privacy, but it was the best she could manage. Besides, if Nico had wanted a privacy guarantee, he would have gone to her place. The fact that he hadn't told her loads.

That he didn't want to risk kissing her again.

They sat across from each other in the booth, and even though Nico didn't dodge her gaze, he didn't exactly jump into an apology, rationalization or whatever else was on his mind.

"Piper called me and wants me to convince you to allow her to stay here this summer," Eden volunteered, even though that clearly wasn't a news flash. "I just heard from Cleo that Rayelle doesn't want to renege on the promise she made to Brenda. That means there probably isn't a way around Piper and Rayelle coming here for the summer."

Nothing, other than a grunt that could have meant anything. Or nothing.

"You'll just have to make Rayelle believe that we won't psychologically damage Piper," she went on. "That won't be easy, but if anyone can do it, it's you. Remember, you're the charming Laramie brother."

She'd added that last bit as a little tongue-in-cheek, but Nico didn't bite. He stayed under that dark and dismal cloud that he'd walked in with. Obviously, she just needed to go for a good air clearing, one that could flick that cloud away.

Eden slid her hand over his. "Look, I've been honest with you for twenty years, *mostly*, and I'm not going to fudge things now. I'm glad you kissed me. Glad you put Damien in his place. But I'm sure this has probably caused you some troubling moments..."

There. It was a spelled-out start for him, leaving her words hanging for him to pick up where she'd left off. All he had to do was pipe in and either confirm or deny the trouble. On a scale of one to infinity, Eden was just one eyelash short of infinity that it would be a confirmation. But he still didn't speak. His silence went on so long that Cleo had time to deliver their drinks and then slink away.

"When we were kids and I first noticed that you were a girl," he finally said, "a girl interested in my best friend, I put on blinders. Stupid ones."

Now it was Eden's turn to grow silent. This was the first she was hearing about Nico ever noticing her, much less the blinders.

"Stupid blinders?" she asked.

"I imagined you as a rodeo clown." He paused to have a sip of his drink. "Big red nose, floppy shoes. Once you got breasts, I pretended they were coconuts."

Eden continued her silence, but that's because she was stunned. "Huh?" she managed.

"Coconuts," he said with disgust. "And don't ask about what *blinders* I used for other parts of you, but

I had to come up with something that time we all went swimming and your right butt cheek slipped out of your bikini."

Color her clueless. Eden would have been less surprised if he'd just confessed to being a serial killer. Obviously, this wasn't putting Nico at ease, either, because he muttered some really bad curse words, shook his head and looked ready to throw himself under a stampede of longhorns.

"Now you have proof I'm a dick," he grumbled.

Stop! she wanted to yell. He was beating himself up for having normal teenage responses. Though the way he'd handled it was, well, unique. Coconuts, huh? Well, that did put an odd image in her head.

"I'm not blind or stupid," he went on. "I know you're attractive, but I'm also your friend, and I crossed a big line when I kissed you. Now, I'm afraid I've screwed up things with you—"

"I got hot once when I saw you put your hand in your jeans," she blurted out. In hindsight, Eden should have given him some of the backstory on that because it caused Nico to give her first a blank stare, then a confused shake of his head.

Eden leaned in and hoped she wasn't blushing as much as she thought she was. It felt as if her face was on fire. "You know how you asked me not to question your choice of blinders for my butt cheek, then please don't question what I just said."

He'd already opened his mouth, no doubt to do just that, but he closed it a moment later. Reopened it. Closed it again. Then, he went with more cursing and another hit of whiskey.

"Clearly, we're aware of the attributes of each other's gender," Eden continued. "But that's not what the kiss was about. That was about Damien—I know that. Still—"

"What sexual problem do you have?" he asked. "Or was Damien just making up shit?"

Eden hadn't thought her face could flame up any more than it already was, but she'd been wrong. Now she did some mental reopening and closing of her mouth, trying to figure out if she should snap the lid shut on her secret. Especially since she'd already blurted out his hand in the jeans thing.

"No fudging," he reminded her.

It wasn't easy to hear her own words used against her. But she'd told him the truth when she said she'd been mostly up-front with him, and she'd be up-front with him now.

She just wouldn't give him many details.

"I have problems with orgasms," she said.

He let out what seemed to be a breath of relief. "Heck, lots of women do. Sometimes, it takes a while to find the right way for things to work out."

"Uh, not that kind of problem." Though she was intrigued by how Nico *worked out* that sort of thing. She imagined hours and hours of foreplay. "It's the opposite for me. I sort of jump the gun on things. I don't last long," she added when he gave her the blank stare again.

"For real?" he finally asked, and she nodded to

confirm it. "Well, most men wouldn't see that as a problem."

"Exactly!" Eden said that a little louder than she'd planned, causing the hands at the bar and Cleo to glance in her direction. "Exactly," she repeated in a much softer voice.

The fact that Nico agreed with her made her feel vindicated and pleased. It didn't last, though. Not when she realized she'd been discussing a very intimate part of her sex life with the king of sex lives.

Nico cleared his throat and tossed back the rest of his drink. "I'm sorry."

There was the apology Eden had been expecting. The one she didn't want. "I know. We're friends, and I've only been divorced six months."

"And let's not forget what happened could possibly be a rebound because of your busted self-esteem," he added.

"Yes, let's not forget that," she mumbled in agreement.

Too bad she couldn't deny it, either, but this heat was possibly rebound-ish. After all, she'd had some lusty feelings for Nico for years. Judging from the coconuts and clown blinders, he'd had some for her, as well.

But they hadn't acted on them.

Not before Damien and she had become a couple and not in the six months after the divorce.

"So, a truce," he went on. "Some thinking time."

That sounded more mature of him than she wanted. That's because Eden was still buzzing from the sex-heat vibes that Nico threw off just by breathing.

"And what about Piper and Rayelle?" she asked.

The sigh he made was long and dripping with weariness. "They'll come here. God help me, they'll come."

Yes, they would. And at that moment Eden realized something else. This heat she was feeling for Nico wasn't going away. He had now become an itch that she was just going to have to scratch.

CHAPTER FIVE

NICO TOOK ONE look at his brother Callen and realized he wouldn't be making as quick an exit from his office as he'd hoped. Callen, who owned and also shared the building with him, rarely made trips up the stairs to Laramie's Bucking Bulls, but there was no doubt he was headed here now. And Callen was sporting a big brother/are you ready for a lecture? look.

Hell.

Nico didn't have time for this. He needed to head to the cabin and make sure it was all cleaned and ready for Rayelle and Piper. But he doubted he was going to be able to put off Callen with some of his usual joking and charm. Nope. Callen was bullheaded and focused, not a good combination when it was aimed at him. Nico knew for a fact that he was the target. And he knew why.

Rayelle and Piper, with a side dish of Eden.

"Let me guess," Nico said to him. "There was a family meeting about me, and you drew the short straw to tell me the outcome."

Callen's jaw tightened. "I think Judd and Kace cheat. And it wasn't a short straw. It was a coin toss."

Yeah, the pair cheated all right. Kace was levelheaded and, as the oldest brother, firmly on the top rung on the family ladder, but he was good at delegating—and cheating—when it came to touchy subjects. Judd, the second oldest, wasn't levelheaded, but he wouldn't have wanted to get in the middle of whatever was going on in Nico's personal life.

Nico checked the time. "Can you make the lecture short? I need to get out to the cabin."

Callen nodded but didn't say anything until he was inside Nico's office and had the door shut. "You need to quit dicking around. It won't do Piper any good, and it'll just cause Rayelle to keep calling the rest of us to 'voice' her concerns."

Voice went in air quotes, letting Nico know there'd been a whole lot of complaining during those phone conversations. Considering that Rayelle hardly knew his brothers, that was a surprise. Not really, though. Rayelle wasn't shy about sharing her opinions with others, and she knew Nico was close to his brothers. She likely figured they had plenty of influence over him.

Nico nodded. "I'm giving up sex while Piper's here."

The flat look Callen gave him let him know he was skeptical about the outcome of that. "For two months." Callen waved off any response Nico might have been about to offer. "Celibacy won't clean up your reputation. You'll need to give Rayelle some kind of a game plan for when word of your reputation gets back to Piper."

Nico nodded again. "I was going to sit down and

talk to Piper, to tell her that my life's on a different path."

There was no way Callen's look could flatten out any more. "And that's why you kissed Eden, because of a different path?"

"No, that was because Damien was being an asshole." At least that's how it'd started, but the kiss hadn't exactly stayed on Eden's front doorstep. The effects were still lingering in all the wrong places. "Don't worry. I'm not going to mess up things with Eden."

"Good." His brother said it so quickly that Nico didn't have to guess that it had been on Callen's mind. "She's been through a tough time."

Yes, thanks to the prick she married. Nico had to mentally shake his head and wonder if Damien had always been that way or if the divorce had brought out the worst in him.

"What kind of man talks about his ex-wife's sex problems?" Nico grumbled to exactly no one. He certainly hadn't intended to grumble it loud enough for Callen to hear, but that's what happened.

"Sex problems?" Of course, Callen latched right on to that.

Nico waved it off. No way would he fess up to anything Eden had told him, but it wasn't exactly something he could just shove aside. Hard to believe that it was something Damien actually found to bitch about, but then Nico had never been with a "quick draw" kind of woman. About the only downside he could see to something like that was Eden would never make it as a porn star.

Which obviously wasn't a negative at all since Eden would have never considered something like that.

In his way of seeing things, if a woman had a quick orgasm, then he would just give her another one as things moved along. Nothing wrong with a twofer, though Damien clearly hadn't seen it that way.

Callen snapped his fingers in front of Nico's face. "Sorry to bore you with this talk."

Nico wasn't exactly bored with thinking of orgasms, but he put his focus back on Callen so that he didn't have to explain his lapse in attention. "Consider your duty done here. You can go back to our brothers and report that you've lectured and that I listened to every word you had to say."

Callen was just as good at glares as he was at flat looks. And huffs. He could have blown out birthday candles on a senior citizen's cake with that snorting huff of air. "Look, just be on your best behavior. It's not a good time for family drama right now."

That caused everything inside Nico to go still. It hadn't been that long since Buck had battled cancer, and while the doctors were confident they'd gotten all of the tumor, Nico knew there was always a chance it could return.

"Buck?" Nico managed to say.

Callen shook his head. "Buck's fine." He paused again and rubbed his fingers against his temple for a second. "It's Shelby."

That didn't ease the sudden tension in Nico's gut. Shelby was Callen's wife and, like Piper, Nico also thought of her as a sister.

"Shelby's pregnant," Callen added a moment later.

The tension vanished, and Nico whooped with joy along with giving Callen a backslapping hug. Callen smiled a little but made a "yeah-yeah" sound to stop the celebration.

"Don't make a public announcement about it," Callen warned. "She wants to keep it a secret until she's past the third month, just in case there's a miscarriage."

Callen was usually a serious person so it wasn't unusual to see his stern expression or hear his firm tone, but this was different. "You're worried about her?" Nico asked.

There was a long silence. "Scared shitless, not because of the pregnancy but because I'm worried I'll suck at fatherhood. But if you tell her that, I'll drown you in a pool of bull piss while I beat you with a shovel."

Nico smiled not just in spite of the threat but because of it. It was going to be fun to see the unflappable Laramie brother get a little flapped. Besides, Callen wasn't going to suck at parenthood. Neither would Shelby.

"You'll be a good father," Nico told him. "And I'm happy for Shelby and you. Really happy," he emphasized.

Callen nodded and muttered a thanks, but Nico

made a mental note to repeat that "good father" assurance to his brother at least a dozen more times.

"Gotta go," Nico said, checking his watch again.
"I need to get to the cabin and make sure it's ready.
Rayelle and Piper will be here in a couple of hours."

Callen nodded. "Rayelle called about that, too. She
wanted to make sure the place wasn't a dump. Judd
sent Beckham over to see if anything needed to be
cleaned."

He didn't mind the boy's help. Beckham was a
good kid, but this wasn't his responsibility, and a
teenager likely had something better to do on a nice
summer day than clean a cabin.

Nico left his office, calling out to Hog that he'd
be gone for the rest of the day, and he barreled out of
the building to find the protesting Liddy Jean. She
wasn't alone today. There were two other women with
her, and all three were carrying Equality for Rodeo
Heifers signs.

Minus the cowbells.

Apparently, Kace's injury had caused Liddy Jean
to rethink the way she expressed herself on a sign.
However, it obviously hadn't stopped the protest
itself. When he had more time, he would ask the
woman how she'd managed to recruit supporters for
her strange cause, but for now that was a question
for the ages.

Nico drove his truck out of town and toward the
cabin, passing his own house and ranch along the
way. It wasn't much of a spread, only ten acres, which
was postage-stamp size by Texas standards. Even-

tually, he'd need a bigger place. Maybe even sooner than eventually since he wanted to make sure he had enough pasture for his livestock and an adequate training area for the bulls.

His business wasn't in the booming stage. Not yet. However, he'd rented the office space from Callen with the hopes that someday Hog and he would have so much business that they'd need room to grow. But neither the business nor his ranch was likely big or successful enough to impress Rayelle. Of course, that wasn't a news flash since not much impressed the woman.

The cabin sure wouldn't.

Nico took stock of the place as he pulled to a stop in front of it. *Small* was the first word that came to mind. Only about a thousand square feet and made out of rough-hewn logs that would appeal to a camper but not necessarily someone like Rayelle. But it did have two bedrooms and a fully functioning kitchen. And then there was the view.

Even the disapproving Rayelle wouldn't find fault with that view. The cabin was right on the edge of the creek lined with a small sandy bank and dotted with plenty of live oaks, mountain laurels and cedars. The limestone rocks in the bend of the creek formed a ledge, creating a small waterfall. The sound it made was something people paid for in those sleep machines.

Nico pulled to a stop behind a truck that he instantly recognized as belonging to his brother Judd. Judd was there all right, nailing a board in place on the porch. There was no need for Nico to tell him that his help wasn't necessary. He could have gotten it all done himself, but he did appreciate it.

"Did Callen bust your balls?" Judd asked when he looked up from his task. "He lost the coin toss."

"Some ball busting took place," Nico assured him. Some movement on the creek caught his eye, and he spotted Beckham's Lab, Mango, darting in and out of the water. "Did you cheat on the toss?"

Judd nodded. "Damn straight I did. I don't want to talk to you about keeping your jeans zipped. The only thing I want is for you to convince Rayelle to quit bugging me."

It was a reasonable request, especially considering that Brenda had never been Judd's foster mother. Brenda, and therefore Rayelle, were part of Nico's past. A good part with a few exceptions. Piper definitely fell into the good category, and thankfully his brothers had always been accepting of her. Judging from Judd's scowl though, his patience was wearing thin.

"I figure Rayelle will put in a token stay," Nico explained. "She'll be around just long enough to fulfill the deathbed promise she made to her sister. Piper will likely get bored, too. I mean, this isn't exactly a haven for a teenage city girl. Then, they'll return to San Antonio and things will go back to normal."

Nico frowned. *Normal* didn't sound as good as it should have. And besides, he wasn't sure going back to the way things were was even possible. He got a reminder of why that was when he heard the approaching car. Not Rayelle. But Eden.

She got out of her gray Ford Focus, dragging two bags of groceries from the backseat. She smiled when her attention landed on him, and while Nico thought it looked genuine enough, he still studied it for any signs of pretense. There didn't seem to be any.

After he gave a nod of greeting to Eden and a silent, narrow-eyed warning to Nico, Judd went back to hammering and Nico went to help Eden.

"You didn't have to do this," he told her, glancing in the bags. Not chips and such as he'd figured. There were fresh cherries, wrapped deli sandwiches and some salads.

"I didn't have to work at Roy's this morning so I drove into San Antonio to that gourmet marketplace. And, yes, I did that to get in Rayelle's good graces."

Eden had obviously also taken her clothes into consideration for the good graces. She was wearing a perky yellow dress with sandals instead of her usual cowboy boots. For reasons that Nico didn't want to explore, it made him notice her legs.

Well, hell.

Was this how his life was going to be now? He was going to see Eden and think of things that should never be on his mind when it came to her.

"Are you looking at me with clown blinders right now?" she whispered as they walked toward the cabin.

Nico considered a lie, but what would be the point? "Yeah, squeaky red nose and everything."

He hoped she wasn't imagining him with his hands in his pants, though. Which made him want to ask her about that. When had she seen that anyway? It was a burning question that he might not ever get answered because talking hands in the pants or sex with Eden was *not* the way to cool him down.

"You've been avoiding me," Eden added, and she set the grocery bags on the small kitchen counter.

"I have," he admitted, and he wanted to wince. This was the problem with crossing a line with a friend. He wasn't used to putting on mouth filters when it came to Eden. "I wanted to give us both some time."

Her eyebrow came up, and she huffed before she mumbled some frustrated profanity under her breath.

"See?" he snapped, as if that proved all the arguments going on in his head. "We're uncomfortable with each other, and it's all because of the kiss that shouldn't have happened."

She stared at him a moment, caught on to a handful of his shirt and yanked him to her. She kissed him. Hard.

Nico felt his body jolt, an almost involuntary reaction that nearly made him dive in for more. After all, good kisses should be deep and involve some tongue. It was like stripping off a layer of clothes or going to the next level. But those were places that Nico stopped himself from going. Before their tongues could get involved, he stepped back from her, and she let go of him, her grip melting off his shirt.

He felt the loss right away when her mouth was no

longer on his. The loss and the realization that Eden was a real, live, breathing woman. An attractive one with breasts, legs and everything.

Oh man.

He didn't want to realize that. He wanted his friend. And he wanted that friendship almost as much as he wanted to French-kiss her.

"Now, we can also be uncomfortable because of that kiss I just gave you," she said, as if that proved whatever point she'd been trying to make. It proved nothing. Well, nothing that should be proved anyway.

Nico stared at her. "Eden, you're playing with a thousand gallons of fire," he warned her—after he'd caught his breath.

"I know, and I'm going to be honest about that. In fact, I'm going to insist we be honest with each other so that we don't ruin our friendship."

That was very confusing, and Nico wondered if this was some kind of trick. Except Eden wasn't a trick-playing kind of person. "What the heck do you mean by that?"

Her gaze stayed level with his. "It means if you want to kiss me, you should. If you don't want to kiss me again, then don't."

He was still confused. About what she was saying anyway. Nico was reasonably sure that the wanting-to-kiss-her part was highly charged right now.

"I just don't want you to avoid me because you're struggling with this possible curveball that's been tossed into our friendship," Eden went on. "That kiss makes us even," she added with a firm nod.

No. It didn't. And Nico was certain he could have come up with a good answer to that. Something along the lines of *there shouldn't be a curveball at all*, but this seemed a case of closing the stable door after the horse was already out. The ball had been thrown, and it had smacked him upside the head along with letting the horse out.

This was one of the few times in Nico's life that he was actually glad for an interruption. He heard the sound of an approaching car engine, followed by Judd's gruff announcement. "Rayelle and Piper are here."

Judging that there wouldn't be enough time for him to say anything significant to Eden and also because he still didn't have a clue what to say, Nico just hit the pause button of, well, whatever the heck was happening, and he went out on the porch to greet his guests.

Nico couldn't help but smile when he saw Piper. She was petite, barely five-one, and built like a fairy. She sort of looked like one, too, with her golden blond hair and sky blue eyes.

Piper returned the smile, not with a very big one though, but she bounded out of the car and up the steps to throw herself into his arms. "Thank you so much for talking Aunt Rayelle into this," she whispered.

Despite the fact that there could be multiple problems with this visit, Nico brushed a kiss on her temple. "It's good to see you. You'll behave yourself while you're here?"

That should have earned him at least some stink eye, a sarcastic chuckle or an elbow nudge. It didn't. "Thank you," she repeated.

The words were right, but she seemed... Well, he wasn't sure. Something was off. Maybe she was just having a bout of grief over Brenda. He'd certainly had his own bouts over the past couple of weeks.

"You're sure you can handle being in this cabin with Rayelle?" Nico kept his voice at a whisper even though Rayelle was too far away to hear them. She had popped the trunk on her car, and Judd had walked out to help her with some luggage.

"Well, I was hoping I'd get to spend some time at your place," Piper answered.

Nico had no problem with that. The trick would be to convince Rayelle that Piper wouldn't be walking into a den of sin.

With his arm looped around Piper's shoulders, Nico led her down the steps so he could take the suitcases from Rayelle. Or rather try to do that, but Rayelle held on. "It's okay." She paused, glanced away. "I have some personal things in there."

Of course she did. Suitcases often carried personal things, and in Rayelle's case, she must mean her underwear. It wasn't as though he was going to get a clear mental picture of them just by touching the container that held such things. Still, maybe she just didn't like a man, any man, being within fondling distance of her panties. Not that he would ever have any intentions of doing that.

Piper went around them, going after her own suitcase so she could haul it into the cabin. Rayelle didn't follow her, and her attention settled on Eden when she came up behind Nico.

"I understand Brenda and I made the wrong recommendation when it came to Nico," Rayelle said.

It took Nico a moment to connect the dots on this, but Eden picked up on it right away. "Mimi Bakersfield is engaged to my ex-husband."

"Yes," Rayelle muttered. She took slow steps toward the cabin. "Well, obviously Mimi was the wrong recommendation if she's taken up with a man so soon after his divorce."

That was something at least. Rayelle wouldn't be trying to push Mimi at him, but that had to sting Eden because she was the second half of that divorced team, which probably meant Rayelle would consider her off-limits, too.

"It's going to be okay," Nico told the woman, and yes, he cheated and used some of that charm people were always telling him he had. He smiled at her and gave her hand a gentle squeeze once she'd set her suitcases in the living room.

Rayelle glanced around the place, but her attention settled back to him. "Please tell me you'll do everything to make sure this visit isn't a mistake for Piper."

"I promise." And to seal that, he pulled Rayelle into his arms for a hug. She wasn't exactly the hugging sort, but Nico thought in this case they could both use it. It felt surprisingly good, and Rayelle didn't go stiff.

But Nico did.

With the way they were standing, he had a perfect view through the big window in the kitchen that overlooked the lake. In fact, it was one of the best views in the cabin, and he had no trouble seeing Piper, who'd obviously gone out back. She had her hand braced on one of the trees, her phone pressed to her ear, her head down.

Everything in her body language was a Texas-sized red flag for Nico, and he needed to check on her. First though, he had to distract Rayelle because if what had upset Piper was something she wanted her aunt to know, it would already be out in the open.

"Rayelle, why don't you let me help you get settled into your bedroom?" Eden asked. Nico saw Eden's glance flick to the window, probably to let him know that she'd also seen Piper and was now giving Rayelle the distraction that he needed to go to the girl.

Eden didn't take no for an answer, either. She tried to pick up one of the suitcases, but as Rayelle had done to him, she stopped that and snatched them up herself. That's when Nico noticed there was a little lock on one of the bags. That seemed extreme even for Rayelle.

Putting her hand on the small of Rayelle's back, Eden got the woman walking toward the bedroom. Eden was persistent, too, and even launched into some small talk about the food she'd brought from that gourmet place.

Nico didn't waste any time. He hurried out the back door and made a beeline for Piper. She no doubt heard him coming because she issued a quick goodbye to the person on the other end of the phone line. What she didn't do was look at him, but Nico had no trouble hearing the sniffing sound she made.

Hell.

He went to her, pulling her into his arms. "What's wrong?"

She shook her head, either attempting a denial or letting him know she didn't want to talk about it. Tough. She would talk.

"Is this about Brenda?" he asked.

Piper went still and with the seconds crawling by, she finally looked up at him. "Yes," she said.

Nico groaned. He had no doubts that her grief was part of the reason for those tears she was blinking back, but there was something else. He'd held enough crying women to know that.

"Spill it," Nico insisted, and it wasn't hard for him to use his big brother tone for that demand.

There was more head shaking, even some gaze dodging, before her eyes finally locked with his again. "God, Nico. I've really screwed up." The words rushed out, along with a stream of breath.

Nico wished he'd done a better job of reining in whatever expression formed on his face. It had to be a bad one—one laced with shock and, yes, fear—because it caused Piper to gasp and back away from him.

"Sorry," she quickly added. "It's okay. I swear, it is." She dismissed it not only with the wave of her hand but a little bobble of her head. "I just broke up with my boyfriend, that's all. That's a good thing.

I'm better off without him," she added. "I'd better go in before Aunt Rayelle comes out looking for us."

Nico didn't stop Piper when she flashed him a fake smile and hurried back to the cabin. He wouldn't press things. For now.

But Nico sure as hell knew bullshit when he heard it.

CHAPTER SIX

EDEN WAS ARMED and ready for the town's Bluebonnet Rodeo where she knew she'd run into (1) well-meaning folks who would pity her or ask her about kissing Nico, (2) her parents, who'd also quiz her about that kiss, (3) Damien, (4) Mimi, (5) Nico, (6) Rayelle and (7) Piper.

She didn't mind seeing Nico or Piper, but maybe she could stave off having close encounters with the rest. Her weapon of choice was the stench coming from the deep-fried onion blossom on a stick she'd bought from one of the food booths. It smelled more burned-grease than savory, but just in case that didn't do the trick, Eden had also bought a huge cone of fungus-green cotton candy.

She wasn't sure why the All Things Sugar booth had decided to use that particular color dye, but hopefully it was enough of a repellant that it would keep at least some of her persons of concern at a distance. If that didn't work, she'd go for an off-putting slab of the bacon and pickle ice cream that the vendor was using a machete to cut.

People saw, and ate, all sorts of weird things at a small-town rodeo.

Keeping a firm grip on her cotton candy and

blooming onion, Eden walked around the fairgrounds, taking in the sights. The handful of rides and row of carnival games. The bulls and broncs waiting in the corrals. Nico would be riding one of the bulls so she knew he'd be there. Knew also that he and Callen would have had a lot to do with putting this together.

She went closer to the corrals with the bulls and frowned when she spotted the gray Brahma. It was by far the biggest and the meanest looking of the bunch, and Eden wondered if this was BYB, the one that Nico had drawn to ride. If so, Nico was going to be in a whole world of hurt in the handful of seconds that he managed to stay on the bull.

Hurt that he might not even share with her.

That stung, but there was no way around it—Nico had been avoiding her again. Eden didn't have to guess that the two kisses were part of the reason for that, but she also suspected Rayelle and Piper played into it, as well. It'd been a week since they'd arrived at the cabin, and they were no doubt keeping Nico busy.

Eden had checked on them, too, but she hadn't exactly gotten a warm and fuzzy feeling from Rayelle. Not that she'd expected one. She was tainted goods, and Rayelle was likely still hearing talk about the kiss. Talk that she would be trying to keep from Piper so that the girl wouldn't think her brother was, well, easy.

Rayelle's attitude was somewhat understandable, but Piper's mood wasn't. Considering she had insisted on coming to Coldwater, had even lobbied hard for it, Piper didn't seem to be having a good time. Just the opposite. She was sulky and down. On the day of their arrival at the cabin—the last time Eden had actually talked to Nico—Nico had mentioned that Piper was upset about a breakup with a boyfriend.

Maybe.

Eden wasn't exactly a breakup expert since she'd only dated Damien in high school, but it seemed to her that if it was just a breakup, Piper would have wanted to stay in San Antonio to try and mend things. Of course, that was assuming there was something worth mending. Perhaps there hadn't been. And perhaps the boy had mistreated Piper.

"Who are you avoiding?" someone asked, interrupting Eden's thoughts. It was Cleo. She didn't have any food products to mask her identity, and she peered around the fried onion glob at Eden.

"Many people," Eden readily fessed up. "Not you, though." She was reasonably sure that Cleo was the one woman in Coldwater who wouldn't judge her if she found out about the blog. Or if she learned that Eden had this hot fetish thing for Nico's hand in his jeans.

"Is Nico one of those people you're avoiding?" Cleo plucked off a bit of the cotton candy and popped it into her mouth.

"No, but he's made sure he hasn't run into me. I would be hurt and insulted if I didn't know he was going through a rough time."

Cleo made a sound of agreement, sniffed the onion concoction and made a face. "Of course, you're going through a rough time, too." She tipped her head to the other side of the corral, where Damien was standing with Mimi. "I didn't know Damien that well before your divorce, but was he always a jackass?"

"Probably, but when you're in love and lust, faults aren't always easy to see." But she was seeing them now. And had heard him when he'd insulted her with *No other man is interested in Eden*. That put him in the rat-bastard category forever as far as she was concerned.

"So, if you don't mind me asking, what went wrong in your marriage?" Cleo said.

Cleo probably wanted to know so she could make sure it didn't happen in her own relationship, and Eden wished she could assure her that it never would. But Eden honestly didn't know where Damien and she had gone wrong.

"We just drifted apart, I guess," she tried to explain. "We were together since middle school. Were each other's first lovers. Joined at the hip." Joined, too, with Nico since he'd always been there. Just not for the intimate parts. "Then, one day that wasn't enough for Damien. He obviously wanted a woman with a perky butt and massive boobs."

Cleo made another sound of agreement and kept her attention on Damien and Eden's replacement. "I think he might have done you a favor."

Oh yes. Eden was beginning to see that, too. Though that didn't mean Damien hadn't crushed her heart.

"Say, I know it's too late for this with Damien," Cleo went on, "but I found a blog that offers advice about heating things up. It's called *Naughty Cowgirl Talks Sex*." She chuckled.

Eden tried not to choke on her own breath. As perverse a thrill as she got from doing the blog, she had an equal fear of being outed. And the reason for that fear came walking her way. Her parents.

Willard and Louise Joslin.

They looked like a cake topper for a senior citizens' wedding. And they were indeed seniors now they were in their late sixties. They'd had Eden fairly late in life, probably about the time they'd given up on having a family.

Her dad was wearing a silver bolo tie and gray suit coat. Yes, at a rodeo. He always wore them, along with his jeans that had such heavily starched creases, he could have probably used them to chop wood.

Her mom wore her own version of her usual suit. Petal-pink pants and top. Her top and pants always matched and never strayed out of the pastel color palette. Ditto for never changing her hairstyle. It was pure white, like a pile of whipped cream squirted on her head. There was zero chance of the breeze budging even a strand because of the Aqua Net Extra Super Hold that she favored. In fact, her mom favored it so much that she carried a travel-sized container on her key chain.

Her mother started the visit with a sigh, and for something that wasn't even a word, it managed to convey a whole lot of disapproval. Maybe because her mom didn't care much for Cleo or it could be the neon green toenail polish that Eden had slapped on when she'd realized she wanted to wear sandals. Any number of things could set off her mother's disapproval button.

Thankfully, her father wasn't quite as judgmental as her mother. He tipped his cowboy hat to Cleo, and managed a friendly smile. Of course, he tipped his hat to everyone so it wasn't necessarily a special greeting, but it was better than her mother's sigh.

"It's good seeing you, Mr. and Mrs. Joslin," Cleo greeted. She glanced around. "But I need to be rounding up my kids so we can get to the arena. Wouldn't want to miss the bull riding."

Neither did Eden, and after Cleo left, she started strolling in that direction. Of course, her parents strolled right along with her.

"Damien came with that woman, I see," her mother said, and she was especially good at aiming some stink eye in Damien and Mimi's direction.

"What?" her dad practically yelled. In addition to being polite, he was practically deaf.

"The battery in his hearing aid died," her mom added. "We ordered a new one, but it hasn't arrived yet."

Well, that was going to make this conversation even more challenging than Eden had imagined it would be.

"Damien's here with his new fiancée," Eden relayed to her dad, and then lowered her voice to answer her mom. "Of course Damien came with Mimi. They're engaged." The words only stuck in her throat a little this time.

Her dad did more hat-tipping and greetings as they continued their walk to the arena, but her mom's attention was firmly fixed on Eden. "I heard about you kissing Nico." Her mother's voice was barely audible and was tight and clipped.

"What?" That was from her father.

"I kissed Nico," Eden relayed, though this time she definitely didn't shout. Not because she thought the kiss was a secret to anyone but because she didn't want to garner unnecessary attention.

"Oh," her father concluded. There was no judgment in his tone, but that was possibly because he hadn't actually heard what she'd said.

"I figure that kiss happened because you're lonely," her mother went on. She risked leaning in very close to the cotton candy so she could deliver the rest of her semiwhispered lecture. Eden wanted to warn her if her helmet hair brushed against the spun sugar, they might never get them apart. "I understand that, the loneliness. But that should only prove that you're ready for a man in your life."

Eden was under no illusions, none, that her mother didn't mean for that man to be Nico. Since she didn't want her father to yell another "what," Eden gave him an explanation he stood a chance of hearing.

"Mom's worried about me because of the divorce," she said. There, plain and to the point. Eden finished the rest of that point with her mother. "I don't want to date anyone from the Cowboys.org site you sent me. If I wanted a cowboy, there are plenty to choose from around here."

And at that exact moment, Eden caught sight of a cowboy.

Not one from the dating site, either. She spotted the real deal. Nico in the arena.

Oh mercy. He was wearing a leather vest and chaps that framed the front part of his jeans. She'd never understand how an item of clothing could look so hot. Nor could she understand why a man about to risk a ball busting didn't have something protective over that part of him.

"You should give the dating sites a try," her mother pressed. "And buy a different color of toenail polish. Was that on sale or something?"

It was the "or something." Eden had felt a rebellious streak when she'd gone into the town's small drugstore to buy the polish. She'd had five choices. Four pinks and the green. She'd decided on the green when Silla's tweenaged cousin—who was following in Silla's mean footsteps—had giggled at her and mumbled something about that not being the right color for an "older" woman. Eden had bought the polish on the spot.

"That toenail polish is a little ugly," her dad piped in. Either he'd heard that part of the conversation with her mother, or maybe he had come to his own logical conclusion.

Her mother gave another of those sighs when she glanced at Eden again. "Look, I know you're tired of me making suggestions, but it hurts to see you so sad."

Yes, and that was the reason Eden hadn't told her

mom to mind her own business. The bottom line was that her parents often were sticks-in-the-mud, deaf as fence posts and harsh critics of fashion and cosmetics. But they loved her. They wanted what they thought was best for her. And in their wants and love, they had sometimes put her in a little box that they wanted to fit nicely into their world. Well, Eden had tried their world, and it hadn't worked.

Still maneuvering the cotton candy and onion thing, Eden leaned against the arena fence to wait for Nico's ride. Her dad moved to one side of her. Her mother, the other.

"Nico." Her mother said his name on a sigh when she saw what had snagged Eden's gaze. "Please tell me you won't leap before you think this through. Nico's all wrong for you."

Eden was already scowling, but her father spoke before she could say anything.

"Nico's a fine man," her father stated. "He's got that quick-draw zipper problem, but I think a good woman could cure him of that. Ever thought about going out with him?"

Her mother threw him a look that could have frozen West Texas in August, but her father didn't see it because of the food obstacles. Her mom didn't get a chance to add words to her glare, either, because Eden saw Nico get into the bucking chute where he got on the bull.

"To start the fun, here's our first cowboy of the day," the announcer said, his voice booming over the microphone. "He's our own local boy, Nico Laramie, owner of Laramie's Bucking Bulls. Let's get behind him and make a lot of noise."

The crowd obliged by clapping and whooping. Of course, since this was Nico, there were plenty of female cheers in the mix. Eden saw more than a few of them in the bleachers. Even if she hadn't recognized them by their faces, their tube tops, skinny jeans and high heels would have given them away. She hadn't missed that Nico's taste in women ran a little to the less conservative side. Which, sadly, might explain why he'd been resisting her when she'd practically thrown herself at him.

"Our own local cowboy drew BYB for this ride," the announcer went on. "Whew, that's a rough one." But despite saying that, he chuckled as if there was an inside joke. "Come on, folks. Cheer Nico on."

Again, they did just as the chute gate opened, and BYB torpedoed out. BYB lived up to his job title of a bucking bull. He instantly kicked up his back legs, the front of his body nosing down almost to the ground. Nico managed to stay on for that. But not for the second one. BYB seemingly bucked every one of his legs, muscles and head at the same time, and he sent Nico flying.

The crowd made a collective groaning-ouch when Nico splatted on the ground.

"Hope he hadn't planned on having kids," Eden heard someone in the stands say.

"Or sex," someone else piped in.

It had indeed looked like a bad fall, and Eden wanted to rush out into the arena and help him to his feet. Nico managed that on his own, though. It took him a couple of tries, but he got up and waved to the crowd. Somehow, he smiled. Then, he hobbled toward the office that was just off the exit. Eden was about to head there, but when she turned, she saw Rayelle and Piper making their way to her. Like Eden, Piper had a whiskey-barrel-sized amount of the green cotton candy.

Even though her folks had known Brenda, they hadn't yet met Piper or Rayelle so Eden made introductions. Eden didn't miss the fact that Rayelle, too, was wearing a petal-pink outfit, but hers had a skirt rather than pants. The two women nodded at each other as if giving silent approval.

"I was going to come out to the cabin this week to welcome you," Louise said to Rayelle. "I was just waiting to make sure you were all settled in."

"That's so kind of you," Rayelle answered, and it seemed as if they were about to gear up into a polite conversation that would go on longer than Eden wanted. Of course, right now a minute was too long.

"Uh, I'll be right back. I just need to make sure Nico's okay," Eden interrupted, and before anyone could object to that, she practically ran in the direction of the arena exit.

Unfortunately, the blooming onion became a casualty when she collided with two teenage girls who were glued to their phones. The greasy, crusty breading flew much as Nico had done in the arena, and chunks of the slimy onion strips landed on the girls and everyone else who was in the general vicinity.

Eden rushed out an apology to anyone who wanted to hear it, dumped the rest of the blooming bits in the garbage and made it to the door.

And immediately spotted Nico.

He was inside the arena corridor and standing in front of the office. This time she hardly noticed the crotch-framing chaps, *hardly*, but instead she saw his bunched-up forehead and grimace.

"You're in pain," she said. "On your scale of one to infinity, just how bad is it?"

"I might need something more than infinity to answer that," he grumbled. "BYB stands for Bust Y'all's Balls, and that's exactly what the bull did. I'll never accuse him of not earning his name." He looked at her, his gaze sliding over her, and he plucked a batter blob from her hair before tossing it aside. "You don't even like onions."

"I know. My food choices were dictated by size, not taste."

"You didn't want people to see you." His comment hung in the air. It definitely wasn't silent around them. Not with the sounds of the crowd and the announcer prattling out the info about the next rider. "I'm sorry I've been avoiding you. Are you okay?"

She nodded, and because she hoped it would make him smile, Eden added. "I didn't have an encounter with BYB and even if I had, I don't have any Bs to bust."

He did smile. Not one of those panty-melting ones but slow and sweet. Intimate somehow. One that friends would share. The friendly moment lasted only a few seconds though before the concern slid back into his eyes.

"I can't lose *us*," he said. "I can't lose what we have. And before you start telling me that won't happen, it always happens."

Ah, logic. Well, Eden had a cure for that, and it was more logic. "Have you ever had sex with a friend?"

He cursed. "Hell, I'm just getting used to the idea that I've had my tongue in your mouth. It could be a while before I can work my way up to actual sex." Nico stopped, paused, and the smoldering look he gave her made her notice the chaps again. "A short while maybe," he amended.

Eden couldn't help it. She laughed, and God, it felt so good to do that. She'd always been able to laugh with Nico, and she'd missed that down to the bone over the past week. And now there was the added bonus to her feeling good—that he might actually consider taking things to the next level.

Their eyes stayed connected, with so many things passing between them, and then Nico cursed again and shook his head. "I've got some business to take care of." He glanced back at the office. "But I'll call you later."

Nico lifted his hand as if he might touch her. Then his gaze dropped to her mouth as if he might kiss her. But he didn't do either of those things. He grumbled some profanity, repeated, "I'll call you later," and disappeared into the office.

Considering he hadn't touched or kissed her, Eden was surprised at the swarm of heat that sizzled right through her. Oh, mercy. She hadn't wanted this attraction for Nico to vanish, but she didn't need it bowling her over like this, either. She didn't need to be thinking with the specific parts of her body that suddenly wanted Nico more than her next breath.

Eden had taken only a few steps out of the arena when someone carrying one of the huge wads of cotton candy moved in front of her. When the candy carrier peered around the gob, Eden saw that it was Piper. The girl was chewing on her bottom lip, and her gaze was darting around as if a puppet master had put her eyes on strings.

"I need to talk to you," Piper insisted, and she took Eden by the arm, leading her away from the crowd.

Piper didn't stop until they were on the back side of the arena. Obviously, the girl wanted some privacy, and she more or less got it. There were a couple of smokers a few yards away, but they seemed engrossed in their own conversation.

"I lied to Nico," Piper said, her voice definitely rattled. "Well, I sort of lied."

Eden snapped toward Piper so fast that she swiped her hair against the green sugar fluff. "About what?"

Piper lifted her shoulder and then took her time answering. She didn't even start with the explanation though until she'd huffed. "Nico saw me crying right after I got to the cabin, and I told him that I was upset because I'd broken up with my boyfriend, Jax. I am upset about that," Piper added in a grumble.

Piper was fidgeting now, running the fingers of her

free hand down the side of her jeans and then picking at some nonexistent lint on the front of her shirt.

"So, why were you crying?" Eden pressed.

Despite the urgency in Eden's tone, it still took Piper several snail-crawling moments to speak. "Like I said, I was upset. Jax hurt me when he broke up with me. He wouldn't return my calls or texts, and I'd had enough of begging him to talk to me. The day I got to the cabin, I left him a voice mail and told him never to get in touch with me again."

Okay, Eden was starting to see the picture here. Nico had seen Piper crying, and even though she'd told him about the breakup, the girl had probably held back, maybe fudging the truth about exactly how upset she really was. And she'd likely done that so Nico wouldn't go after Jax.

Eden tossed her cotton candy in a trash can and did the same to Piper's so she could put her arm around the girl. "I'm sorry."

Piper attempted another shrug. "I should have known not to go for Jax. He has *badass* written on him. I mean, it's actually on him. He has a tat."

Eden didn't point out that if you had to advertise it, then you were likely a badass wannabe. Still, a wannabe could break a heart just as fast as the real deal could.

When Eden pulled back from the hug, she saw Piper blinking back tears. "Want to have a girls' night out? We could binge on ice cream, watch movies and trash Jax and his tat? Heck, we can trash other things about him, too."

That didn't help put an end to the tears, and Piper certainly didn't jump on the idea. Maybe teenage girls no longer did that sort of thing to cheer themselves up. Too bad Eden couldn't recommend what had finally gotten her out of her down and out mood over her own breakup. Nico was her cure, but clearly Piper didn't see her foster brother as helpful for her own situation or the girl wouldn't have lied to him.

"What can I do to help?" Eden came out and asked because it was squeezing at her own heart to see those tears.

More snails crawled long distances before Piper said anything. Then, her words came out in a rushing flood. "I had sex with Jax, and I might be pregnant."

Eden felt as if six Mack trucks had just slammed into her. *Oh crap.* And she just kept mentally repeating that. She had no experience with this, not even on her blog, and this was going to be bad. Beyond bad. It might give Rayelle a heart attack, and Nico would…

Eden couldn't even finish that because she had no idea what Nico would do. However, she was betting there might be a butt-whipping or at least some very mean threats in Jax's near future.

"I haven't taken a test yet," Piper went on, "but Dotty is over two weeks late. That's what I call my period," she added in an uncomfortable mumble.

Eden was experiencing some extreme discomfort, too. And panic. Yes, that was the main thing. But she tried to tamp all that down so she could help Piper. It was obvious the girl was feeling mountains more panic and fear than Eden was.

CHAPTER SEVEN

NICO STOOD IN the shower and let the scalding hot water spew over him. It wasn't helping the dull ache in various parts of his body. Neither was the extra-strength ibuprofen he'd taken. Still, he stayed in the shower and hoped for a cure to the fist-sized bruise he had on his left ass cheek.

BYB had done a number on him, but it had gotten him the publicity he'd wanted, along with two seconds of the adrenaline that his body often craved. Tonight though, the only craving he had was for a beer, whatever he could find to eat in the fridge and some sleep—even if that sleep would need to happen on his stomach.

After he dried off, he pulled on just his boxers, not bothering with anything else since he'd be crashing soon. While he went to the kitchen, he checked his phone. And frowned. There were two texts from women who wanted to know if he could hook up with them tonight.

Clearly, the town gossips were falling down on the job. If they had been in top form, both women would have known he was off the market at least for the next six weeks or so because of Rayelle and Piper's visit.

Unless his mind and body did a serious one-eighty, that hiatus would continue at least until he could figure out what the hell was wrong with him.

He grabbed a beer from the fridge, opened it and had a long pull while he contemplated what was going on in his head. Of course, Piper had a lot to do with it. He didn't want her to think that if sleeping around was good for her brother, it would be good for her, too.

But Piper was only part of the reason for this hiatus. Brenda was in that mix, as well. He was still grieving for her, and that might not go away anytime soon. Heck, he wasn't sure he wanted it to go away. The grief and memories were the only things he had left of her, and he didn't mind hanging on to all the little pieces.

And then there was Eden.

Oh yeah. Definitely in the hiatus-reasoning mix now, and he honestly hadn't seen that one coming. A week ago, she hadn't been a sex interest but rather his best friend. One who was trying to get over a divorce from another friend. Now he was at odds with Damien and couldn't put up enough clown blinders to stop him from seeing that his best friend had breasts. Breasts he wouldn't mind touching. She had a mouth, too, and yes, he wanted to kiss her.

He drank more of his beer and considered if there was a large enough rock in his yard that he could use to hit himself on the head. Obviously, he needed something to knock some sense into him.

What's the worst that could happen if you go for

her? he heard a little voice in his head say. But he knew that little voice more often than not doled out BS rather than sound logic.

Nico threw open the freezer, and while he was contemplating his extremely limited selection of dinner choices, there was a knock at the door. Followed by a real voice that gave him a pure shot of adrenaline and lust.

Eden.

"It's just me," she said.

There was a whole bunch of irony in Eden's greeting. Because for only a "just," she was certainly occupying a lot of his thoughts and testosterone urgings.

"I need to get my jeans on," he called out to her.

"Uh. Are you alone? Should I come back?"

Shit. Now he heard the hurt in her voice, and even though it was a dumb idea, he went to the door, threw it open so that she could see he was alone. Of course, she could also see that he was nearly naked. Since he had no doubts that being half-dressed around Eden was a bad idea, he motioned for her to come in and then headed to his bedroom to grab some clothes.

He located a pair of jeans, dragged them over his sore butt. "Help yourself to a beer if you want one," Nico said in a loud enough voice for her to hear.

It was a rote kind of comment. Something he'd said to her too many times to count over the years. But now it seemed a lot more than just an invitation for friends to share a beer together.

Because it was.

He seriously doubted this was just a "dropping

by to say hi" visit. Nope. He'd seen that sparkle in Eden's eyes at the rodeo. Specifically, the way she'd checked out the parts of him that his chaps hadn't covered. And that meant she was likely here for sex. She wouldn't be that obvious, though. Wouldn't throw herself at him the way Silla did. However, the look she'd give him would make it clear as to what she wanted.

Or not.

Nico was still pulling on a T-shirt when he came back into the living room, but he had no trouble seeing that there wasn't a sex-look on Eden's face. Something was bothering her.

"What happened?" he immediately asked. He went to her, ready to give her a hug, an ear or whatever the heck else she needed. "Did Damien say something else stupid?"

Eden shook her head and opened her mouth, but her phone dinged before she could say anything. Because he was watching every little twitch of her face and body language, he saw her relax. He also saw the message on her phone screen.

A message from Piper.

Squee!!!!!!! Piper had texted.

Dotty came. No need for you to do that favor for me. Thanks bunches though.

The rest of the screen was filled with happy face emojis.

"Dotty?" he questioned.

Eden blinked. "Uh, her friend."

Nico had never heard Piper mention anyone by that name, but it was obvious that she was thrilled about the visit. That's good because she'd been moping about her breakup ever since she got to Coldwater.

"What favor did she want you to do?" Nico asked, and he went to the counter to retrieve his beer and to get Eden one from the fridge.

She waved it off, took the beer and had a long drink of it. The kind of drink a person would take if they were dying of thirst. Eden drank it so fast that her eyes were watering a little when she lowered the bottle.

"I wanted to make sure you were okay," she said. "I mean, after that fall from the bull."

He stared at her a moment, wondering why the heck she'd just lied to him. He didn't doubt that she was worried about his bruises and such, but if that's all there was to it, she would have just called or texted, and she wouldn't have waited the six or so hours since his ride. No. There was more to this visit than that, and Nico was pretty sure he knew what was going on.

"The blinders I'm trying to use on you aren't working." He was surprised at the relief he felt when he got out that confession.

Eden, however, seemed to feel no such relief. "God," she grumbled. A moment later, she said, "Jesus."

And Nico didn't think she was praying.

He helped her out with the ball of frustration,

doubt and heat that she was obviously dealing with. All right, it was just as much help for himself, he admitted, as he leaned in and kissed her.

Oh man. It was good. He knew that right from the start. Even though he hadn't had a lot of practice with her mouth, none was needed. Eden tasted like a hyped-up mix of Christmas, birthdays and summer. All the things he liked.

She made a sound of surprise, a little *eep* that got trapped in their mouths, but that was her only hesitation. She wrapped her arms around him and went in for the melt of her body against his. That was yet another of "all the things" he liked.

Since he was still partly sane, he knew this had high potential for being a mistake, but there was that feeling of relief again. As if a too-tight cork had finally been let out of a bottle.

Eden seemed to be experiencing some relief, too, because she really got into the kiss. No pulling back when he deepened it and went French. She just gobbled up everything he was doling out. Which, of course, led him to a big concern.

She wasn't going to stop at just some kisses or slides of her body against his—which she was doing.

Nope.

This could lead straight to the bed. Along with the consideration that his bruised butt might not be able to do justice to this moment, there was also the problem of how this would play out after some satisfying orgasms. And Nico was certain they would be very, very satisfying.

He pulled back, setting their beers on the counter before he met her gaze. Though he wasn't sure she could actually see him clearly through her lust-glazed eyes. "Second thoughts?" he asked.

"Oh, I had those days ago. I'm well past that now."

He wasn't sure if that meant she was on to third and fourth thoughts or no thoughts at all. He decided it was the last one, and she proved it with another body slide. Her breasts—yes, the very ones he'd been dreaming about touching and tasting—brushed against his chest. Nico knew he was wearing a T-shirt, but it suddenly felt as if there was nothing between her bare skin and his.

Because of that, he kicked things up a notch by sliding his hand under her top, shoving down the cups of her bra, and he got busy with the touching. Her nipple tightened when he pinched it with just enough pressure to give her a nip and pleasure at the same time.

"I'm counting on you to be very good at this," she muttered.

At least that's what he thought she said. Hard to decipher every word when they were still Frenching. But if it was good she was after, he could indeed give her that. For once, he wasn't ashamed of all the practice he'd had and could put it to good use.

Nico lowered his head, ignoring the protest Eden made when his mouth left hers. The protest didn't last because he kissed her nipple. She liked that. No doubts about it. She yanked him closer and let him feast on her.

Yep, this was going to lead to the bed.

At first Nico thought the roaring that he heard was the sound of his own heartbeat, but when Eden froze, he knew that it wasn't. Crap. They had a visitor. One on a motorcycle, judging from the sound of it.

Later, he'd maybe think the interruption was a good thing, that it would give Eden and him more time to decide if they should go through with this, but right now Nico definitely wasn't seeing the benefits of anyone coming to his doorstep.

"Excuse me a second," he grumbled, but before he could walk, he had to give himself an adjustment. He slid his hand into his jeans to do that.

"Oh my," Eden practically moaned out. "That's my fantasy."

He hadn't forgotten that she'd said something about that when they'd been at the Gray Mare. A fantasy, huh? Well, he was glad it revved her up, but for him it had been a necessity.

"Hold that thought," he told her.

Nico dropped a kiss on her still-moaning, sighing mouth, and he stormed across the room to give whoever was out there a very unfriendly greeting. Someone knocked, though, before he even threw open the door, and Nico got another hit of relief. It was some teenager he didn't know. That meant it was likely just someone who was lost. Nico would give him quick directions and send him on his way.

"Nico Laramie?" the guy immediately asked as he gave Nico the once-over. He had shaggy blond hair and hit right about six feet with a lanky build. The build was easy to see because of the muscle T-shirt he was wearing. He had a helmet tucked under his arm, and the porch lights revealed the motorcycle parked in Nico's driveway.

"Yeah, I'm Nico Laramie. Who are you?"

"Jax Russo," he said as if that would mean something to Nico. It didn't. But judging from the speed that Eden came racing to the door, it likely meant something to her.

"He's Piper's ex-boyfriend," Eden supplied and then turned to Jax. "What are you doing here?" she said at the same moment Nico had been about to ask her how she'd known that was the ex-boyfriend's name. It didn't matter, though. The only thing that mattered now was that he was the ex. And that he'd crushed Piper's heart and made her cry.

"What the hell do you want?" Nico snarled. He could do badass when called for, and this was definitely a situation where it did.

"Uh, I came to see Piper. I asked around town to find out where she was, and some folks at the diner said she might be here or at a cabin you own. I thought I'd start with you, and if she wasn't here, then you could give me the address of the cabin."

"You thought wrong," Nico quickly informed him. "Piper's very upset, and in turn, that makes me very upset, too."

Eden touched Nico's arm, rubbed gently. Probably a gesture meant to soothe him so he'd throttle back, but Jax looked like a cocky turd who needed to be taken down a notch. Of course, Nico figured that's because his big brother feelings for Piper were playing into this, but he wasn't going to let this turd crush Piper again.

"Uh, sorry about Piper and you being upset," Jax said. "Especially Piper." But he eyed Nico as if he were a rattler ready to strike. "All right. Maybe I'm sorrier about you right now."

Well, that at least meant the boy had some brains.

"If Piper had wanted you to have the address of the cabin, she would have given it to you," Nico pointed out.

Jax didn't deny that. He nodded, then gave a weary shake of his head. "I was a…jerk." It seemed as if he'd been about to use a much harsher word but had decided not to add possible gasoline to Nico's flammable temper. "And I need to tell her I'm sorry. She won't talk to me. And, man, I'm worried. Really worried."

"Uh, I can call Piper," Eden said. "I'll let her know you were here, and if she wants to phone you back, she will."

Eden would have shut the door in Jax's face if both Nico and he hadn't caught on to it. Obviously, neither one of them felt they'd hashed out whatever needed to be hashed.

"Why are you so worried about Piper now that you've dumped her?" Nico demanded, aiming his index finger at the boy.

Jax didn't seem so cocky right now. His shoulders actually dropped. "I got scared, that's all. It was just such a big-assed shock when she told me, and I didn't handle it right. I dumped her and walked away. But I'm sorry about that now. Piper's prime, not just pretty and all but smart, too, and I didn't treat her right."

Because he was several steps beyond merely being pissed off, it took Nico a couple of moments to pick through all of that and find a big red flag. "A shock when she told you?" Nico paraphrased.

If it'd been up to Eden, Nico wouldn't have gotten an answer to that because she moved to shut the door again. Nico stopped her, shot a "stop that" glare and made his glare even harder when he turned his attention back to Jax.

"What did Piper tell you that shocked you?" Nico growled. "I want to hear it word for word."

Jax swallowed hard, twice. "I'm guessing you just want to hear me admit it. I get that. It's like manning up or some other sh…crap," he amended, "that older folks want you to do. So, here it is." Another hard swallow. "Piper said she might be pregnant with my kid."

"Oh, crud," Eden mumbled

She thought she'd dodged a bullet after Piper had texted to tell Eden that she'd gotten her period. Piper had almost certainly felt that she'd dodged a thousand bullets. She wasn't pregnant, and therefore Eden hadn't had to tell Nico about it.

Except that Nico had just learned anyway.

Nico made a growling sound. There was no other way to describe it. It was something feral that had come from deep within his chest. Eden had never

seen him get violent, but then he'd never been con-
fronted with anything like this. Just in case he was
about to punch Jax in the face, she stepped between
the two of them.

"Hold on to whatever you're about to say or do,"
she warned Nico, and she shot the same warning to
Jax as she took out her phone. "Both of you will get
an explanation in just a few seconds."

They obeyed and stayed quiet, but Eden wondered
if that was because Nico's jaw muscles were too tight
for him to speak. In Jax's case, he looked frozen as if
he couldn't decide what else to do.

Eden sent a quick text to Piper:

Jax is about to call you. Answer it. It's important.

Of course, it would be terrifying once Piper
learned that Nico knew about the pregnancy scare,
but Eden was hoping she could soften that blow by
telling Nico that his sister hadn't gotten knocked up
by some guy Nico wanted to knock out. Piper would
be on her own when it came to telling Jax, but Eden
figured once they got past the shock of Nico knowing, they'd be relieved.

"Call Piper," Eden told Jax, "and then you can
leave. Nico and I have to talk."

Apparently, Nico didn't agree with her plan because he tried to block her from shutting the door in
Jax's face. Then, Nico's eyes met hers, and she realized that not all the anger he was feeling was for Jax.
Some of it was aimed at her.

"You knew about this," Nico snarled.

She nodded, sighed. Even though Jax hadn't put his call on speaker, she heard when Piper answered. Eden pried Nico's hand off the door so she could shut it and give both the teens and themselves some privacy for the conversation they were about to have. Eden was betting there'd be a whole lot more jubilation in Jax's call than in her talk with Nico.

Since there was no way to sugarcoat this, Eden started blurting. "Piper told me at the rodeo that she might be pregnant. She wanted me to tell you because she was afraid of how you'd react."

"Afraid?" Nico snarled, but it wasn't a question, and it only seemed to piss him off even more.

"She's sixteen," Eden reminded him. "She made a mistake, and even though she didn't come out and say it, I believe she wanted you to get past the initial shock and anger so you'd be more rational about it when you saw her."

His eyes narrowed. "There'll be nothing rational when it comes to this. That shithead knocked up my sister."

Nico reached for the door again, but Eden slid in front of him, which put them face-to-face, and at the moment his was a very mean face.

"No, he didn't knock her up," Eden went on, speaking very fast in case Nico decided to move her aside and go out in the yard. "It was a false alarm. Right after I got here, Piper texted that she'd gotten her period. So, no baby. No reason to pulverize Jax."

Nico stayed quiet, dangerously so, for a moment.

"Yeah, there's a reason. The shithead had to have had sex with her for her to think she might be pregnant."

Eden huffed and wondered why she hadn't expected this big brother logic. "Teenagers have sex," she reminded him. "You sure did when you were Piper's age." She aimed her index finger at him. "And don't you dare say that's different."

He didn't say it. Maybe didn't even think it, not in the insulting way it could have been had Nico believed it was okay for boys but not girls to have sex. Clearly, he didn't believe that.

"She's my sister," he snapped.

"I know, and that makes this hard to take, but it's over. They had sex, there's no baby and therefore there's no reason for Rayelle to know any of this."

That got Nico's attention, and his gaze fired back to hers. "Shit."

"I'm in total agreement," she said. "If Piper wants Rayelle to know, then she'll tell her. It won't come from us."

And she was betting it wouldn't come from Piper, either. Rayelle's prudishness would soar to epic proportions if she found out that Piper was having sex. A baby scare might send the woman off the prudish ledge and result in Piper being grounded for life. While Piper did deserve a good talking-to about safe sex and such, Rayelle could and would dole out a lot more than that.

Nico didn't jump to approve of what Eden had just laid out, but at this point she doubted he would agree to anything other than beating up Jax. Still, Nico finally nodded. Then, in a sneaky move, he hooked his arm around her waist, moving her, so that he could push the door open.

"I'm going to see Piper," Nico insisted just as Jax said, "Piper wants me to come to the cabin so we can talk."

Eden could see an immediate problem with that. "Rayelle will be there."

Jax nodded and looked marginally less uncomfortable than he had minutes earlier. "Piper's going to tell her aunt that she's going for a short walk, and then she'll meet me at the end of the road that leads to the cabin."

Eden was shaking her head before he even finished. "Rayelle will hear the motorcycle." She knew that wouldn't put the boy off going. Didn't want him to put it off either since it was obvious that the teens needed to talk. She also couldn't see a way to stop Nico from joining in on at least a portion of that chat. A portion where he could do his big brother thing for Piper and maybe scare Jax into never having sex again.

"We'll go in my truck," Nico insisted. He shot Jax a glare. "That way I know you won't be staying too long or doing something you shouldn't do, and I won't have to kill you."

Yep, Nico was going for the "scare the crap out of Jax" angle. It might work in the short term, but even Nico was no match for teenage hormones. He of all people should know that.

Since Jax looked somewhat terrified of getting

into the vehicle with Nico, Eden got in first, and she slid into the middle. Jax took shotgun, and Nico got behind the wheel. He took off as soon as they had their seat belts on.

"Should I text Piper and let her know that you'll be with me?" Jax asked, and mercy, he sounded rattled.

"No," Nico snapped. "She'll know soon enough."

Yes, Piper would because Nico was practically flying down the country road. Eden considered making some kind of small talk, but the only thing that seemed a safe topic was the weather.

"Nice night," she commented. "It's cooled down a little."

The stony silence from Nico and the nervous aura bursting off Jax let her know that even that hadn't been a good choice of conversation.

She moved closer to Nico to give him a whispered reminder not to yell or Rayelle would hear it, but the moment Eden leaned in, Nico did, too, and her mouth ended up brushing over his ear. There was some breath involved, too, since she'd geared up to speak.

"Shit," he grumbled. "Not there. Not now anyway."

Obviously, his ear was a "sensitive" spot for him, and while Eden hadn't been looking for anything like that at this moment, she would file it away for later and put it to good use.

That's because Eden had decided that sex with Nico was going to happen.

After that kissing circus in his kitchen, she couldn't see him trying to figure out a way to stop it. Nope.

Once they had this situation with Piper resolved, there'd be more kisses—including ones solely devoted to his ears—and then they'd land in bed. Eden refused to think what would happen after that.

Eden spotted Piper as soon as Nico pulled into the road that fronted the cabin. Piper was using the flashlight on her phone to illuminate the path she was pacing, and she looked about as comfortable as an embezzler facing a tax audit.

Nico stopped the truck, bailing the moment he'd put it in Park. There was an immediacy in Jax's exit, too, but because of her middle position, their "chat" had already started by the time Eden got out of the truck.

"You should have come to me with this," Nico growled to Piper. "You should have told me about him." He hiked a thumb in Jax's direction.

"I know. I'm so sorry." That's all Piper had to say, and Nico no doubt heard the swarm of emotions in the girl's voice. Thanks to his truck headlights, he could see it, too. Along with seeing the tears shimmering in her eyes.

That caused Nico to curse, groan and scrub his hand over his face. After he'd done all of that, he pulled Piper into his arms and kissed the top of her head.

"You should have told me," he repeated, but this time there was love mixed in with his anger and concern.

"I know, but I was afraid of what you would think of me. Afraid of what you might do to Jax."

Nico eased Piper back a few inches and stooped down a little so he could make eye contact with her. "I wouldn't have thought less of you. *Never.*" He paused. "Jax is a different matter." Nico shot the boy a glare from over his shoulder. "He had sex with you and then broke up with you when you thought you might be pregnant. That's an asshole thing to do."

"It was," Jax readily admitted. "And I'm sorry. But I'm here now, and I want to do what's right." He went closer to Piper as if he might continue to plead his case, but Nico kept his grip firmly around his sister.

Eden didn't think Nico was just going to encourage a conversation between the two teens so she moved in closer, as well. She started to whisper to Nico that they should give them a few minutes alone, but she remembered his sensitivity in that area.

"Nico, they need to talk," Eden said, keeping her voice calm and low.

That didn't get him to budge. Or stop him glaring at Jax. "How do I know he won't hurt her again? She cried, you asshole," he added to Jax.

Eden understood the groan that Piper made. The girl wouldn't want a heart-crushing ex to know that she'd been crying over him.

Jax didn't back away, and he did look sorry about Piper crying. "I said I was wrong," the boy repeated. "I didn't handle it right."

"No shit, Sherlock." Nico snapped. "Did you even use any protection when you had sex with her?"

Piper groaned again, and this time Eden joined her in a chorus of groans. "Nico, that's something that should be discussed in private. But if you didn't use protection, you should have," Eden softly added to the teens. "I'm sure this is something you've already clued into, but you're both too young to risk a pregnancy."

Because of the whir of Nico's truck engine, Eden didn't actually hear the footsteps as much as she sensed them, and she practically snapped in the direction of the cabin.

And there was Rayelle.

Even now, the woman was wearing one of those plain dresses she favored. Mint green this time. And she was sporting a very troubled look.

Oh God.

Obviously, Rayelle had walked up on their conversation, but it surprised her when the woman didn't turn that look on Piper but on Eden.

Rayelle pressed her hand to her chest. "Sweet merciful heaven. Eden, did I just hear you say that you're pregnant?"

CHAPTER EIGHT

PIPER HAD BEEN about to start digging a hole that she could climb into, but her aunt's question stopped her. She'd been certain that Rayelle heard what Eden said, but she hadn't.

And now all eyes were on Eden.

Piper held her breath because it was possible that either Nico or Eden was going to spill everything. But she knew that there was no chance of Jax doing that because he was standing there looking as scared spitless as Piper felt.

"Well, are you pregnant?" Rayelle demanded as she went closer to Eden. "Because if you are, it's definitely not a good idea for you to be around Piper." Even though Rayelle had dropped her voice to a near whisper for that last part, Piper was still able to hear her every word.

Eden laughed, surprising everyone around her, and she gave a dismissive wave of her hand. "We were talking about horses. One of Nico's mares will foal soon, and Piper was wondering if she'd be around to see the colt or filly."

Heck, Eden was a lot better liar than Piper would have ever thought, and Piper appreciated it all the way to the marrow of her bones. However, a lie, even a good one, wouldn't necessarily get her out of the hot seat because it was possible that Aunt Rayelle wouldn't believe it.

Piper could almost see what Rayelle was thinking. Had she really misheard? Maybe, too, she was working out a way to apologize to Eden about being so snippy with her about being knocked up.

As it turned out, her aunt didn't say she was sorry. She just shifted her attention to Jax. "What are you doing here?" Rayelle asked. "You and Piper broke up."

Jax nodded. "I just wanted to talk to her and try to work out some things."

"Then you can do that at a more reasonable hour," Rayelle scolded.

It was 7:00 p.m., which was plenty reasonable for a lot of things, including talking. No one pointed that out, though. Piper, Eden and Jax all nodded in agreement, but Piper figured no one actually agreed. She hated when her aunt got all pissy like this, but considering what she'd done by nearly getting knocked up, Piper wasn't going to judge. Especially since Rayelle had stepped up to take her after Mama Brenda had died.

"Jax was just leaving," Piper explained. "I'll call him tomorrow, and we can talk then."

That would hopefully give her time to settle her nerves. Right now, she was straddling a kind of high because of the relief of getting her period while tamping down the fear of nearly being caught.

"Just give me a second to say goodbye to Piper," Jax begged. Like Eden's laugh, that surprised Piper, too. She would have thought he would have turned tail and gotten out of there as fast as he could now that they had dodged a Rayelle bullet.

Nico wasn't getting out of there, either. He was giving Jax and her a hard stare. "We'll talk soon," Nico finally snarled in a whisper as he brushed a kiss on Piper's head.

Oh joy. That would be a fun chat. Nico wasn't usually a pain-in-the-butt kind of brother, but there was no way he was going to let her get away with a pregnancy scare without giving her a serious lecture. Piper felt another safe-sex chat coming on. Unfortunately, this time he would have a good reason for giving it.

"Good night, Rayelle," Eden said.

Eden gave Rayelle a cheery wave before she took hold of Nico's arm and got him moving back to his truck. Of course, they couldn't leave, not since Jax had ridden with them, but at least Nico was no longer standing in front of Jax and glaring at him.

"I'll be inside in just a few minutes," Piper told Rayelle. While she tried to sound adamant, Piper knew she was bargaining with the woman, and she added as much of a smile as she could muster, hoping it would help.

Again, Rayelle had the debate expression on her stern face before she ground out, "Ten minutes. Then, you and I can work out some visiting rules. I don't want Jax showing up here at all hours."

Piper nodded, ready to grovel or do whatever it

took to get the woman to leave. And her aunt finally did. Not before giving them yet another glare. Even though Rayelle's wasn't as good as Nico's, it still worked. Piper knew she was going to have to work hard to get into her aunt's good graces.

Once Rayelle was on her way back to the cabin and out of earshot, Piper set the timer on her phone for eight minutes. No way did she want to be late getting back, or Rayelle might ground her.

Piper whirled around toward Jax. "I don't know why you came here," she snapped. "You're the one who broke up with me." He opened his mouth to say something, but there was nothing she wanted to hear from him. "I'm still grieving my mom's death, was worried I could be pregnant and you broke up with me. What kind of loser does something like that?"

"The lowest of losers," Jax readily admitted. He groaned. "God, Piper. I'm so sorry. I was just scared. I mean, there's no way I'm ready to become a dad."

"And you think I'm ready to become a teenage single mom?" Somehow, she managed to keep her voice lower than a shout though she wasn't sure how. She wanted to punch Jax. Curse him.

But at the top of her list was something that disgusted her.

She wanted him to hold her. To pull her into his arms and tell her that everything was going to be all right. Apparently, she was stupid. This was the guy who'd run out on her at the lowest point in her life. And it wasn't as if he'd been a one-night hookup or anything. Nope, he'd been her first.

Her only.

It had taken her weeks to decide to sleep with him, and along with laying out her body for him, she'd laid out her heart, too. A heart he'd crushed, and here she wanted him to hold her again.

"Will you forgive me?" Jax asked.

Well, crap. Of course, he sounded sincere, but Piper could have probably resisted that. After all, he'd been plenty sincere the night he'd had sex with her. Safe sex, she mentally emphasized. They'd used a condom, had been responsible, and yet her period had still been late. In hindsight, that was likely because of the stress of losing Mama Brenda, but Piper had gotten so caught up in the fear and panic, that she had only considered the pregnancy.

"Please forgive me," Jax amended.

Damn him. More sincerity. And he looked so good. Of course, he always did. She'd had a thing for him since ninth grade when she'd first noticed his amazing blue eyes and warm smile. Most people didn't think warm, nice or kind when they saw the motorcycle and tat, but Jax was all those things.

Piper tried to wrestle down the warm buzz she was getting at being so close to him. Better yet, she tried to make sure Jax didn't notice it. But he did. She could tell because his mouth stretched into a slow smile.

"I want to kiss you," he said, his voice all hot and low. "I want to show you how much I've missed you, but I'm afraid your brother will beat me with a tire iron."

"He wouldn't, not really, but don't push it. Don't push anything right now."

Piper silently cursed the tears that started to sting her eyes. She didn't want Jax, Nico or Eden to see them. Crying was all she'd done for the past three weeks since Mama Brenda had died, and it wasn't going to help.

"Hey, hey." Jax risked touching her arm. "What is it? Talk to me."

She shook her head and purposely turned to the side so that Nico wouldn't see any hint of her watering eyes. "You've got two parents, and you don't understand."

"Then help me understand." Jax said it in a way that made her believe he was worried about her. That he cared for her. And maybe he did. But it didn't matter. Rayelle didn't approve of him, and she would never make it easy for them to be together.

Even if Piper was certain that she was in love with him.

"Help me understand," Jax repeated, and he ignored it when Nico flashed the truck lights at them. No doubt her brother's way of telling her to hurry things along.

Then the timer beeped on her phone.

"I have to go," Piper insisted. She gave Nico and Eden a quick wave. Gave Jax one last look, too, before she turned and hurried back to the cabin.

"Piper," Jax called out to her.

"I'll call you," she said, so that he wouldn't follow her.

No way did she want him to see her now that she was really losing the battle with her tears. Besides, there was no way she could make him understand. Jax had two parents, a mom and dad who loved him. And while they wouldn't have been one bit happy if he had gotten his girlfriend pregnant, they wouldn't have done something that Aunt Rayelle could do to her.

No.

That was something Jax would never understand.

NICO'S IDEA OF a Sunday lunch was a burger or pizza. Or leftover burger or pizza. It wasn't his dream lunch to sit through the roasted chicken meal with Rayelle and Piper. A meal he'd picked up from the diner since he was a lousy cook. Still, he would have put up with his own cooking to be able to spend this time with Piper.

Now he needed to figure out how to spend some of that in private so they could talk. So far, Rayelle hadn't given them a chance to do that, and this wasn't a conversation Nico wanted to have over the phone. But he had a plan to get his sister away from Rayelle's prying eyes and ears.

"Ready for that ride?" Nico asked Piper the moment she'd finished the last bite of chicken.

Rayelle looked up from her plate, her forehead already creasing with concern. "You mean as in a ride on a horse?"

Nico nodded, and Piper and he started clearing the table. Of course, he was clearing a little faster than Piper was, no doubt because she was dreading this little chat with him, but she'd agreed to it after a series of texts and knew that it had to happen. Nico hoped she knew that it wouldn't be any more comfortable for him. Talking about sex with his kid sister was even a rung higher on the discomfort ladder than having lunch with Rayelle.

"It's been ages since I've gone riding," Piper said. It was a teen's version of gushing with some emo on the side.

"But it's so hot out there," Rayelle protested, and she even checked her watch as if time would be a factor. It wouldn't be. It was only a little after noon, and when Nico had issued the lunch invitation, he'd suggested Piper and she stay all afternoon, that they could watch a movie and then go into town for ice cream.

"We'll ride by the shade trees where it's cooler," Nico explained. He'd already prepared himself for that argument.

"And I really want to ride," Piper put in. "We won't be long."

Piper didn't invite Rayelle to come along, not with the woman wearing one of her usual dresses. Besides, he doubted Rayelle had ever been on a horse. Nico didn't wait for her to object, either. Once the table was cleared, he told her they'd be back soon, and Piper and he headed out of the house and to the barn.

It wasn't a long walk, only about thirty feet, but Piper glanced over her shoulder, no doubt to make sure Rayelle was staying put. When Nico glanced back, he saw her standing in the still-open doorway, and he gave her a wave and a smile.

"She knows something's up," Nico grumbled.

"Yeah," Piper readily admitted. "She's been asking a lot of questions about Jax and me."

Nico didn't bother to tell her that he'd be asking plenty of questions, too. That's because Piper already knew that.

Piper saddled one of the mares just as Nico had taught her to do, and even though it'd been months since she'd ridden, she climbed right on. Nico did the same, and they rode out of the barn and away from the house. And yes, Rayelle was still in the doorway watching them.

"First of all, thanks for not saying anything about the pregnancy scare to Aunt Rayelle," Piper started. She looked at everything but him. "And second, Jax and I used a condom when we had sex. Believe me, you drilled that point home often enough to me."

So that eliminated one of his questions. Piper had listened.

"After my period was late," she went on, still dodging his gaze, "I started worrying that maybe the condom was defective or something. I panicked and was sure I was pregnant."

"You should have told me then and there," he insisted.

Now she looked at him and gave him something she rarely did. Some teen snark. "Yes, because talking to my brother about sex and possibly being pregnant was something I was chomping at the bit to do.

I knew you'd be pissed, and you were. Don't deny that," she quickly added.

Nope, he couldn't deny it. Some piss-ery had indeed been involved. "I was upset about the situation, not with you." He shrugged when she leveled a stare at him. "Okay, maybe I was also upset with you. I didn't want you going through something like that. Not just because of a possible pregnancy but because of how Rayelle would have reacted."

Bingo. He knew he'd hit the mark when he saw her expression soften.

"And just because the crisis is over," he continued, "that doesn't mean I don't want to tear off Jax's dick."

"I wanted to do the same thing after he broke up with me." Piper's voice was a barely audible—and embarrassed—mumble when she said that. "It scared me, Nico."

He sure heard that last part loud and clear. Hell, he felt it in the pit of his stomach. Because it scared him, too, that she'd had to deal with so much emotional stuff on her own.

"I just haven't kept close enough tabs on you," he added. "And no, I don't mean tabs so you wouldn't have sex. I knew that would happen sooner or later. I was just hoping for the later. Maybe like when you were thirty."

She smiled, but the humor didn't make it to her eyes.

They continued to ride in silence for a few minutes while Nico gathered his thoughts. "You were always such a smart student. A good kid. Never gave Brenda any problems. So, I guess I just thought you didn't need much…" And that's where he drew a blank.

Parenting? Supervision? Brotherly attention?

None of those seemed to fit.

"Don't worry. I won't need whatever it is you think I need," Piper assured him. "Eden's taking me to a doctor in San Antonio, and I'll get on the pill."

Well, Piper had obviously made some plans and decisions. With Eden. Not that Nico was surprised that Eden would have stepped up to help. Nor was he surprised that she hadn't mentioned it to him. Eden would want Piper to be the one to tell him. If she chose to.

"The pill," he repeated. "That means you're planning to have more sex." He was well aware that he sounded like a sourpuss. An old one.

"I just want to be prepared. I don't want a repeat of what almost just happened."

Nico supposed he should commend her for doing that, but after all, he was still her brother, and he didn't like the idea of some guy doing things with Piper that Nico himself did with women.

The image of Eden flashed into his head. Of course, it did. Her image had been making regular appearances in his thoughts and dreams. No blinders for that, and it was having an effect on him. So had those scalding kisses.

"People like Jax don't understand," Piper said, drawing his attention back to her. "He's never been in foster care. He doesn't know what it's like."

No. But Piper and Nico sure had that in common.

And more. Before Piper had been adopted, the girl had been in a bad situation. A home where she'd been neglected and even physically abused with whippings for even the smallest infractions. The same had happened to Nico after he'd been moved from Brenda's. Except Nico had nearly been killed when his then foster mother's boyfriend, Avis Odell, had beaten him up, leaving Nico with broken bones and a punctured lung.

"Aunt Rayelle is strict," Piper went on. "But at least she doesn't hit or scream." Her voice broke. "God, Nico, I'm afraid she's going to give me back. Afraid she'll put me back in the system."

Nico reined in, catching on to Piper's mare to do the same, and he managed to move in closer to her. "That's not going to happen."

Piper shook her head. "But it could."

Ah, hell. Now, there were tears in her eyes. That got Nico out of the saddle, and he pulled Piper off the mare and into his arms. "That's not going to happen," he repeated, brushing a kiss on her hair. "If Rayelle ever tried to do something like that, I would take you."

Piper eased back, looked up at him. "You were arrested for a bar fight and being drunk and disorderly. And while I suspect you had a good reason for that—more or less—you still have a record."

Nico did indeed have a good reason. Years ago, when he'd been celebrating a rodeo win, some jerk in the bar took it upon himself to try to mess up the "pretty cowboy's face." Nico had stopped him from doing that.

"Added to that," Piper went on, "you're single and not my legal brother." She paused. "I heard Aunt Rayelle hashing this out with Mama Brenda shortly after she got sick. Mama Brenda told her that she had to take me or that I'd end up back in the system. Aunt Rayelle didn't want to do it, but she was stuck."

Nico had suspected it'd gone down like that, and yes, he'd figured his police record and womanizing were part of Brenda's decision making process.

"Believe me when I tell you that you won't go back into the system," Nico promised her. "If worse came to worst, I could ask Callen and Shelby to foster you." He paused. "In fact, I can do that now if things are bad with Rayelle. You could move here and finish your last two years of high school."

"Things aren't that bad." Piper wiped away her tears with the back of her hand. "Besides, this is going to sound crazy, but I think Aunt Rayelle needs me."

Not crazy, but it was confusing. "What makes you say that?"

Piper lifted her shoulder. "She gets this sad look in her eyes sometimes, and when I see it, I try to cheer her up. It seems to work."

Nico thought about that a moment. "Brenda was her only sister. Rayelle's probably going to grieve for a while." Heck, they all were.

"No. Aunt Rayelle would get that way even before Mama Brenda got sick. I think it has something to do with her secret box."

Color him confused. "What secret box?"

"The one she put in her suitcase and locked up when we were packing to come here."

"You mean like a safe for jewelry and cash?" Nico asked.

Piper shook her head. "It's small and silver with etchings on it. It reminds me of an old cigarette box that I once saw in an antique store. Aunt Rayelle nearly had a fit when I walked in and saw her holding it. She looked very sad then, but when she spotted me, she put it in her suitcase, slammed it shut and locked it."

Nico could picture that, but he didn't know why Rayelle hadn't wanted Piper to see it. Maybe the woman had a secret smoking habit?

"It wasn't the first time I'd seen it," Piper went on. "She had it in her purse once when she was staying over with me when Mama Brenda was in the hospital."

"And you don't have any idea what's in it?" Nico asked.

Piper shook her head and moved back to the horse so she could get on. "But whatever it is, it makes her very sad."

Well, whatever it was, it made Nico very curious.

He hoped it wasn't something dangerous like a gun that she was keeping that close to Piper. Just in case it was though, he made a mental note to have a conversation with Rayelle about it. In fact, he was going to have a conversation with Rayelle about a lot of things.

CHAPTER NINE

Let me know what the doctor says as soon as the appointment's over.

THAT WAS THE MESSAGE that popped up on Eden's phone screen, and she'd known what it was going to say before she even read it. That's because Nico had already told her the same thing in a phone conversation when Eden had "informed" him that she'd be taking Piper in for an exam today.

Piper hadn't fought the appointment, either, but the girl had had some "keeping this quiet" concerns. After all, just three nights earlier, Rayelle had come very close to learning about the pregnancy scare. No way did Piper want her aunt to know about that, and Eden couldn't blame her. Eden had been on the receiving end of too many judgments from her mom so she had some experience with knowing that the judgments only made things worse.

"Thanks for bringing me here," Piper muttered while they waited outside Dr. Meredith Mackenzie's office.

"I was glad to do it," Eden assured her, and she patted the girl's hand.

The doctor wasn't local. No way could they have gone to the Coldwater clinic or the hospital and not have been seen by gossips, and that gossip would have gotten back to Rayelle's ears. Dr. Mackenzie was in San Antonio, and Eden had managed to get a short-notice appointment because of a cancellation on the schedule.

Hopefully, no one in Coldwater other than Nico and she would learn about this checkup. Especially Rayelle, who had seemingly bought the notion that Eden was taking the girl into the city for a shopping trip.

Piper glanced around the waiting room at the dozen or so other patients. "I hadn't really planned on sleeping with Jax," she whispered to Eden. "I was just so down because of Mama Brenda, and I ended up in his arms."

Eden did have some experience with getting swept away. Recent experience with Nico. Unfortunately, the sweeping had only stirred her appetite for more, and more hadn't been possible because of Nico's work and this situation with Piper. A situation that would hopefully be fixed with this doctor's appointment. Piper could get on the pill or some other form of birth control in case she ended up in Jax's arms again.

"You must think I'm stupid or a skank," Piper added, her voice the quietest of whispers. She was no longer glancing around but rather had her gaze focused on the riveting floral pattern of her top.

Eden lifted Piper's chin, turning the girl's face so they'd have eye contact. She wanted Piper to see that what she was saying wasn't just a load of bull. "I don't think either of those things. I was once sixteen, and I remember how things are."

Actually, things were still sort of that way. She was lusting after a hot guy, but this time it wasn't Damien. It was Nico.

"But you never nearly got pregnant," Piper concluded.

Eden shrugged. "No, I never thought I was pregnant, but I did have sex so it could have happened. Even with us using birth control, it still could have happened, but we always took double precautions. Both condoms and the pill."

Piper stayed quiet a moment. "So, you don't want kids?"

Eden hadn't expected the pang she felt in her heart. "I did. I wanted them very much," she admitted. "But Damien didn't."

And it shamed Eden to admit that over the years, she'd let his way of thinking become hers. Before that, she'd let her parents' way of thinking become hers. Eden frowned. Now that she was thinking for herself, she was pissing people off and complicating things.

Not a stellar endorsement for her life decisions.

Still, she preferred to royally screw things up on her own terms rather than go back to the way things had been.

"My parents are old-fashioned," Eden continued when Piper stayed silent. "I knew they wouldn't have understood a divorce, and my mother would have seen it as some failure on her part. She *sees* it as a failure on both our parts," she corrected. "So, I went along with Damien's wishes to hang on to the marriage even if those wishes weren't exactly what I wanted."

"Bad idea, huh," Piper said, and it wasn't a question. It was ironic that a sixteen-year-old girl could see something that Eden hadn't.

"What about Jax? Is he a bad idea or the real deal?" And yes, that was a question.

"The real deal." Piper immediately groaned. "Trust me, I've tried to have feelings for someone who would meet with Aunt Rayelle's approval, but I can't get past what I feel for Jax."

Eden wondered if there was such a guy who would garner the woman's good graces. Maybe, but if so, he likely wouldn't appeal to Piper or any other girl. Hard to get all gushy over a stick-in-the-mud.

It did make Eden wonder how a woman could turn out like Rayelle. Perhaps she'd had her heart crushed and had shut down, vowing never to go through that again. Or maybe she'd taken one risky step too many and something had snapped.

"I swear, when I see Jax, my heart skips a beat," Piper said. "And my chest gets all tight. It's as if I forget how to breathe."

Medically, that probably wasn't a good reaction, but again Eden understood it. "I just go all head-to-toe hot when I see Nico."

Oh God. She'd actually said that aloud, and Eden winced, then groaned.

Piper chuckled softly and patted her hand as Eden had done to her earlier. "It's okay. I see the way you two look at each other, and I'm not clueless. I figure if there's heat, there's fire." She paused. "You're not worried though that his hookups don't last?"

"Yep, I'm worried." Eden figured she shouldn't have continued to jump on the "spill the truth" bandwagon, but what the heck. She'd already admitted that she was in lust with the man. "But I don't want to hold back just because it might not work out. I don't want to look at Nico when I'm seventy and see him as a regret I didn't make. I'd rather see him as one I made."

Eden frowned again, wondering if she was just deluding herself. After all, some folks, including her mom, would argue that a regret was still a regret. But Eden was going to ignore that argument and go for it. Actually, she was going to ignore anything that would stall her from getting Nico naked.

"Nico said he's the only one of his brothers who's never hooked up for something serious," Piper went on. "Callen's with Shelby. Judd's with Cleo. And even Kace used to be married."

True, though Kace's very short marriage had ended in divorce. Coldwater wasn't immune to divorces and such, but because there was little real news in the town, talk of breakups tended to last for a while. Eden figured she was giving folks some gossip fodder that would last for years.

One of the other patients was taken into the examining room, prompting Eden to check the time. The doctor was running a little late. It wasn't a big concern for Eden since she wasn't scheduled to work at the law office today, but she figured every moment they sat there caused Piper's nerves to rattle even more than they already were. The girl's sex life had already been outed to her brother, and now she was going to have to go over it all again with a doctor.

"Will you tell Jax about this appointment?" Eden asked.

Piper nodded and glanced down at the phone she was holding as if she expected to see something from the boy. "He's at work now, but I said I'd text him once I was done. He wants to see me tonight," she added after another pause. "He wants to get back together."

This was tricky territory, especially considering that Eden wasn't family. She suspected that Piper's feelings for Jax truly did run deep. Maybe she was even in love with him. But if Eden encouraged that reunion, and it turned bad, then she would feel as if she'd contributed to the train wreck.

"I guess you have to follow both your hearts and your heads on this one," Eden advised.

Piper made a sound of agreement. Mild agreement anyway, letting Eden know that the girl couldn't follow what was still unclear to her.

"I'm not bad," Piper muttered, barely loud enough for Eden to hear.

There was so much emotion dripping from that handful of words that Eden pulled her into her arms for a hug. A hug that didn't last long though because the nurse called out Piper's name, motioning for the girl to follow her.

"You want me to go with you?" Eden asked Piper.

"No, I'll be fine. Really," she added, and she managed a very thin smile before she went with the nurse.

The moment the door closed, Eden's phone dinged with a text. From Nico, of course. Anything? he messaged.

Eden stepped outside the waiting room and into the corridor just off the front entrance. That way, she could have some privacy and still keep watch through the glass panel to see if Piper came out.

She pressed Nico's number, and he answered on the first ring. "Nothing yet," Eden immediately said. "She just went in, and it might be a while because the nurse told her they'd need to do some lab tests."

Nico grunted an acknowledgment. "I'm just on edge."

"You think?" she teased, but added, "We're all on edge." Then, Eden told him something that wasn't going to help. Still, it was something he should know. "Piper's considering if she should get back together with Jax. Nico, I think that'll happen because she loves him."

Nico somehow managed to groan and curse at the same time. "I want to tear off his dick."

"So noted, but Piper likely wants his dick to stay right where it is. I know that's not something a brother wants to hear," she quickly continued, "but it's the truth. I think you're just going to have to accept that your kid sister is no longer a kid."

"She'll always be a kid," he snapped. Another groan. More cursing. "I'm not sure when I turned into a judgmental tight-ass. God, I don't want to be like Rayelle."

"You're nothing like her," Eden assured him.

He made one of those sounds that could have meant nothing. He was good at those. "Say, did Piper ever mention anything to you about Rayelle having a box?"

Since she seriously doubted that was a euphuism for a lady part, Eden gave him a straight answer. "No. What kind of box?"

"I'm not sure. Piper made it sound like some big secret so it's got me curious. Apparently, Rayelle keeps it under lock and key or carries it in her purse."

Well, now Eden was curious, too, but she couldn't imagine someone like Rayelle having secrets like love letters. Or body parts from a murder she'd committed. Except now that the thoughts of it were in her head, she could indeed imagine it, and she wouldn't be thanking Nico for it anytime soon.

"Two things," he said. "First, I want to thank you again for taking Piper to this appointment. She refused to let me do it."

"Wow, that's a stunner," Eden joked.

She thought she heard him chuckle, but maybe he was just biting back another groan. "Also, I want to see you tonight," he added.

That erased any other thoughts she had. Heck, it erased common sense and modesty. "Please tell me that's a euphuism for more kissing and sex."

"Yes," he confirmed. No hesitation, but in just that one word, she heard the concern in his voice. With reason. This would be an earth-shattering change in their relationship. It could mess up everything.

And Eden still wasn't going to let that stop her.

"Then I'll see you tonight," Eden assured him. She ended the call before he could change his mind. Of course, if he did, he'd just call her back, but Eden thought that maybe Nico was just as far gone as she was. Their hormones had become king and were ruling the rest of them.

Eden was about to go back in the waiting room, but the clinic door opened, and someone very unexpected walked in.

Damien.

She was so surprised at seeing him that Eden gave her head a shake in case it needed clearing. Nope. No clearing needed. Damien was actually there.

As if announcing some kind of bad omen, there was a crack of lightning outside, followed by a low grumble of thunder. The timing seemed perfect, but Eden knew it was a coincidence. Rain was in the forecast. Lots of it. When this first front went through, there'd be another one right behind it.

"Eden," Damien said as if he'd expected to see her standing right where she was. "Good. You're still here. I wasn't sure if the appointment was already over. I'm glad I caught you."

There were so many things wrong with that comment that she didn't know where to start. "How'd you even know I'd be here?"

"You didn't change the password for your online app calendar," he readily admitted.

Good grief. She had all kinds of personal stuff on there, including deadlines for the blog. Even reminders to buy tampons.

And that led her to the next "wrong" thing with this.

"Why are you here?" she demanded, and her tone wasn't nearly as nice as Damien's had been.

He glanced around, and when he spotted the reception desk only a few yards away, he motioned for her to move to the corner of the room. Eden stayed put and repeated her "Why are you here?"

Damien wasn't so quick with the answer that time, but his hands went on his hips and he shook his head. "I'm worried about you."

Oh. She got it then. Well, maybe. He'd seen the doctor's appointment on her calendar—a calendar that would soon get a password change—and he'd thought she was ill or something. Since he now worked in San Antonio, the clinic wouldn't have been too far for him to pop over, but that didn't tamp down the anger that bubbled up inside her over this unwanted interference.

"I'm fine," she said, giving him that much. "Now, you can go." She didn't want him around when Piper came out.

He didn't budge. "I've heard you're having a hard time getting over the divorce," Damien whispered.

"Where'd you hear that?" And Eden didn't whisper. Not by design but because of the surprise and frustration over what he'd just said.

"From just about everyone I run into from Coldwater," he readily answered. "People are saying you're fooling around with Nico, and the only reason you'd do that is to try to get back at me."

"Seriously, the *only* reason?" Eden didn't wait for Damien to try to convince her of that. "Nico is incredibly hot, along with being a good guy." She thought about the way he'd hugged a crying Piper and could add a *very* to her good-guy assessment. "He's also been a supportive friend who's been there whenever I've needed him."

Damien stared at her. *"Friend,"* he said as if relieved by that. "Good. I'm glad you still remember that because it'll keep you from doing something stupid."

She decided to go with the no-filter approach. "You mean like having sex with him the way you are with Mimi?"

"Mimi's different." He groaned and scrubbed his hand over his face. "Look, I know I'm sounding like an ass, but I'm really worried about you."

"Don't be. Like I said, I'm fine." And she realized she was sounding like a disgruntled bitch, but then he had sneaked into her calendar. He deserved some shade aimed at him. "Go on. Get on with your new life and don't have any regrets."

He turned as if he might do that, but her hopes went south when Damien pivoted back around. "Confession time. The sex got stale with us. I don't know why. It just did, and Mimi filled a void for me."

"You're sure it wasn't *her* void you were filling?" She was back to shade and, yes, the snark.

Damien didn't strike back, though. He just shook his head. "I don't expect you to forgive me or understand, but I want to say I'm sorry. I didn't put Mimi up to doing it. It was all her idea, and I didn't find out she'd done it until later."

Eden hadn't had any problems following this conversation until he'd said that. "Huh? What idea?"

Damien fiddled around with answering that before he finally said, "'Hot in the Saddle.'"

Well, that didn't help clear things up. Not until she remembered that was the name of one of the posts someone had sent her for the blog. A post she'd not only answered and published but had also included it in her "Best of Sex" feature.

Since Damien wasn't explaining that, Eden gave it a try. "Did Mimi read 'Hot in the Saddle' and get some ideas about how to fill your void?"

"No," he said, and she could have counted to thirty before he continued. "Mimi wrote it. For fun. She said it was so she could keep spicing up things between her and me, but I think she did it to poke fun at you, too. Sort of a passive-aggressive way of getting back at you." Damien looked her straight in the eyes. "I'm sorry, Eden."

Now he did walk away.

And Eden understood what Damien had fumbled to try to say. "Hot in the Saddle" had been written nearly a year ago. By Mimi. Maybe for some sex spice. Maybe because it would be a thrill for her to get advice from the wife of the man she had in her bed.

CHAPTER TEN

WHEN NICO HEARD the knock on his door, he finished drying off from his shower, dragged on some clothes and hurried to answer it. He hadn't realized he was smiling until he threw open the door and felt that smile disappear. It wasn't Eden as he'd hoped it might be.

It was Hog and Rayelle.

Hog held an umbrella open over Rayelle's dainty head. Apparently, he'd been doing this their entire trek across his yard because Rayelle didn't have a single raindrop on her, and Hog was practically soaked, his shirt plastered to his chest. Nico wasn't sure how this umbrella chivalry had happened because both Hog's truck and Rayelle's car were parked out front.

"I went by your office in town," Rayelle greeted, her voice laced with its usual disapproving bite.

Nico opened the door wider and motioned for them to come in. "Yeah, I left work a little early today so I could check on the livestock before the next wave of rain moved in." Something that had already happened.

And he'd also left early so he would be there when

Eden arrived. Best not to mention that to Rayelle, though.

"Is there a problem?" Nico added, the question meant for both Hog and the woman.

"Miss Devereaux dropped by your office to tell you that the cabin roof is leaking," Hog explained.

"I tried to call you, but it went to voice mail," Rayelle piped in. "Mr. Hannigan became concerned about that and followed me out here."

It took Nico a moment to realize that Miss Devereaux was Rayelle and Hog was Mr. Hannigan. Pretty formal, especially when applied to Hog.

Nico took out his phone and muttered an apology when he saw Rayelle's missed call. "Sorry, I was in the shower." And he would have almost certainly checked his phone once he'd finished if he hadn't heard Hog's and Rayelle's knock at the door.

"I told Miss Devereaux that I'd go over and fix the roof," Hog went on. "But she thought it best if she checked with you."

No, Rayelle hadn't wanted Hog to have any part in this so she'd tried to put him off with that remark, but Hog wouldn't have picked up on a subtext like that.

"We'd better put off the repairs until morning what with the lightning," Nico said. "How bad is it leaking?"

"It's over the sink in the kitchen," Rayelle answered.

Well, if you were going to have a leak, that was the best place for it. Maybe the sink would catch all the water.

Despite Nico's motioning, Rayelle didn't come inside. She stayed put on the porch and cast a very quick glance at Hog. "You can get back to your work now, Mr. Hannigan. Thank you for making sure I got here okay. And thank you again for the use of your umbrella. Mine buckled when I was coming out of your office," she added to Nico.

"I was glad to do it." Hog collapsed the umbrella and handed it to her. "You'll need it when you get back to the cabin. Or do Piper and you plan on staying here tonight with Nico?"

Nico sucked in his breath so fast that he nearly choked, but there was no need for the slam of panic he got because Rayelle quickly shook her head. "No. I'll be going back to the cabin where I'll wait for Piper. Eden and she are baking cookies over at Rosy McCall's. I checked, and Piper's still there, but she's going to call me when they're done."

He didn't doubt that some cookie baking would be going on, but it was sort of a ploy, too. Nico hadn't actually talked to Eden about it, but she'd texted him that Piper didn't want to go straight to the cabin after the doctor's appointment, that she'd wanted some time to "process" everything that'd happened. Eden hadn't sounded particularly enthusiastic about it, but Piper had suggested they take up Rosy on a standing invitation for baking. He was going to owe Eden big-time for helping out with his sister.

"I'll be fine, Mr. Hannigan," Rayelle said to Hog. It wasn't exactly a "don't let the door hit you in the ass," but it was close.

Hog nodded and wiped the rain off his face. "I

was just wondering if I could take you for a cup of coffee or something. You know, while you wait for Piper to call."

Rayelle turned slowly toward him, and her whole mouth tightened. "No, thank you."

And with that, Rayelle finally stepped inside, but Nico figured that was only so she could shut the door in Hog's face. Later, he'd have a chat with Hog and warn him off the woman. Nico was surprised that Hog hadn't already picked up on her dick-freezing vibe.

"Want some coffee?" Nico asked her and added a wink. Some women would have considered that funny charm. Not Rayelle, though. And he wondered if there was anything that made her laugh. Or cry. She seemed to be one-note when it came to emotions.

"Thanks but no." She used the same dismissive voice as she had with Hog. "I'll be leaving in a minute."

Yeah, once Hog had driven off, but since Nico had her here, he might as well bring up something he'd been wanting them to discuss.

"Has Piper said anything to you about her fear of having to go into another foster home?" Nico hadn't sugarcoated it because he wanted to get to the bottom of this.

"No." Rayelle stiffened her shoulders and looked surprised with the question. "I wouldn't do that. I promised Brenda that Piper would stay with me."

And there it was. Nico's concern all spelled out for him.

"I'd hope you wouldn't move her because you want

her with you, not just because of a promise you made to your sister." Again, not a grain of sugarcoating on that.

Rayelle kept her gaze on him, her hand moving to her chest and over her heart. Maybe he had offended her, and if so, he'd apologize. In the meantime, he also kept staring at her, waiting for an answer.

"Piper has been somewhat of a handful," Rayelle finally said. "What with Brenda's death and her breakup with that boy."

"Jax," Nico provided, though it nearly stuck in his throat to coax Rayelle into remembering his name. Still, Eden had said that Piper cared for Jax, and that was enough to make Nico care, too. Of course, his caring came with an asterisk attached. Jax had better not hurt Piper again.

"Jax," Rayelle repeated as if it'd stuck in her throat twice. "Piper's been moody about all of that."

"She's sixteen. Moody is a requirement. I sure was when I was that age."

Since Rayelle didn't jump back into the heart of their conversation, Nico did it for her. "If you don't want to keep Piper with you, then tell me now so I can do something about it," he spelled out.

Her hand pressed harder on her chest. "Like what?"

"Like get Piper in a home with someone who wants her."

"I want her," Rayelle practically snapped, and despite it being a snap, it pleased Nico. That sounded like the sincerest thing he'd ever heard from Rayelle.

He didn't question the woman's motivation for wanting to keep a teen who she'd labeled as moody.

Maybe Rayelle saw this as her only chance to ever have a child. Nico didn't care why.

"I just want my sister to be brought up in a loving home," he added. "She shouldn't be shut away in some box that's locked away."

Okay, that wasn't his best analogy, and it caused something to flare in Rayelle's eyes. Seriously, it was like sparks of gold fireworks, and she turned on her heels so fast that Nico was surprised he didn't feel the breeze coming off the woman.

"I have to go," Rayelle snapped.

She grabbed the umbrella, whipping it up over her head as she sloshed across his yard. Obviously, he'd said the wrong thing.

"I'll be over in the morning to fix that roof," he called out to her. "But I warn you, it'll be noisy with the hammering." Nico was talking to the rain though because Rayelle was already in her car.

Nico didn't shut the door. That's because he spotted a visitor he actually wanted to see. Eden. She drove up almost as fast as Rayelle drove away, and neither of them stopped. Eden pulled up in front of his house, barreled out of her car and into the sheet of rain. Nico fumbled around for an umbrella to go out after her, but Eden made it to the porch before that could happen.

Oh man. She looked good, despite the rain-plastered dress. Or maybe that helped with the good looks. Either way, Nico knew he wanted to kiss her, and he likely would have done that if he hadn't taken a better look at her face.

She'd been crying.

His heart jumped right to his throat. "Is everything okay? Did something go wrong with Piper's appointment?"

Eden walked straight into his arms. "I just found out Damien cheated on me when we were married."

Oh. *That.*

A lot of things went through Nico's mind. How had she found out? And did she know it was more than a onetime thing? Did Eden know that he knew? But he didn't voice any of those questions because hearing the answers wouldn't help her get through this. He just continued to hold her while he maneuvered her inside and shut the door.

"Damien just blurted it out," she went on. "And while he was cheating with Mimi, she was sort of making fun of me. She wrote to my blog asking for sex advice. Advice on how to spice up the sex she was having with my husband."

Hell. Nico figured that had to have felt like a punch to the gut. Damien was an idiot.

"Why did Damien tell you all of this?" he asked.

"I don't know. Maybe to clear his conscience. Maybe because he's a jackass."

It was probably both. Nico had heard his former friend say that Eden wasn't handling the divorce well, but Damien was the one who was doing the mishandling. There was no reason to throw his affair in Eden's face like this.

Eden wasn't crying now, but since she didn't seem so steady on her feet, he led her to the sofa, had her sit and then went to get her a beer. He opened the bottle, but when she didn't take it, he set it on the coffee table in front of her.

"Mimi wrote to my blog a year ago," Eden went on. "So, they were having an affair at least several months before he left me. In fact, she's likely the reason he left. All that time, he lied to me, and she used the advice I gave her to have naughty cowgirl sex with my husband." Her gaze zoomed to his when he sat on the sofa next to her. "And Damien looked at my computer calendar."

In the grand scheme of things, that last part didn't seem to be much of an infraction, but Nico guessed that maybe it'd gotten all rolled into the nasty mix of a cheating ex who couldn't keep his stupid mouth shut.

Nico hooked his arm around her, drew her against him and just held her. It wasn't the start to the evening that he'd planned, but it was what Eden needed. If it helped for them to sit here like this all night, then that's what he would do.

"I don't know why I'm upset," Eden continued several moments later. "I mean, it's not as if I still love him. I don't. But this hurts."

Yeah, because the asshole had betrayed her. Not just with Mimi, either. Nico didn't know exactly how many other women there'd been, but Damien had cheated at least two of the three years he'd been married to Eden. Heck, he'd cheated on her even before that.

And that made Nico feel like shit.

All three of them had been friends, and by keeping the secrets of one friend, he'd hurt another. He'd hurt Eden. And he wasn't sure she would forgive him if she ever learned the truth.

Which, of course, meant he needed to tell her.

No way should he let her go on believing that he was the good guy, someone who'd always been loyal to her. Because if he had been loyal, he would have ratted out her cheating bastard of a husband.

Nico eased her around to face him so that he could add another blow—his confession—to the shitstorm she'd already had dumped on her today. He managed to get his jaw unclenched so that he could speak, but one look at her, and no sound came out of his mouth. Well, except a soft grunt.

Unfortunately, it was the wrong kind of grunt.

Oh man. She looked good. Despite her earlier crying and frazzled expression, he could easily see the woman he'd been lusting after for days. Not good. Eden didn't need his lust-driven moves right now. She needed Nico, her friend. Her *truthful* friend, who didn't keep secrets from her.

Eden was staring at him, too, and she seemed to be holding her breath. Waiting for him to say or do something. Which meant this was the perfect time for him to fess up.

Or not.

She launched herself at him, her mouth landing right on his, and Eden dragged him against her. Of course, she didn't have to put too much effort into the dragging because he seemed to be weak and mindless when it came to kissing her. One taste of her, and he was no longer thinking about Damien, affairs or confessions. He was thinking about getting in Eden's pants.

That confirmed to Nico that this situation had the potential to make him a dick. His friend had come to him with a problem. She'd wanted to vent and verbally bash her cheating ex-husband. She wasn't in any mental shape for sex.

Nico repeated that to himself.

While he continued to kiss her.

That wasn't a good sign, but he did put a mental stopwatch on this lip-lock. He savored, deepened and let the feel of her slide him into some scalding sweet pleasure before he finally caught on to her shoulders. He moved Eden back just a few inches so he could make eye contact with her.

"This is about Damien," he said to jog her back to reality.

The jogging worked, more or less. She looked at him with her heavily lidded, lust-filled amber eyes. "Huh?" she asked.

Considering that she seemed very confused by his comment, Nico wondered if he'd gotten it wrong. Of course, he was wishing he'd gotten it wrong so he could haul her off to the bedroom, but he needed to make sure he wasn't crossing a line here. Damn. It was hard to figure out the rules when you wanted to have sex with a friend.

"I just don't want you to jump into something you might regret," he tried again. "I don't want you using this—*us*—to get back at Damien."

He could see Eden take a second to consider that.

Could also see her dismiss it, and she did the dismissing by going back for another kiss. It didn't just stay a little kiss, either. She fisted her hand in the back of his hair, anchoring his mouth against hers, and climbed onto his lap.

This time, Nico didn't grunt. He groaned, and the sound was a mix of pleasure and pain. Pain because he wasn't going to be able to let this go where Eden wanted it to go. And he had no doubts about the destination she had in mind because she slid her free hand lower to the front of his jeans.

Over the years, he'd used a trick when he found himself running too hot. Like now. He mentally hummed old show tunes. Something too perky to add to the heat and force him to think about anything else instead of getting inside the woman who was on his lap and brushing herself against his erection.

Oh yeah. He had an erection all right. Even "Hello, Dolly" didn't stand a chance against Eden's mouth and squirming body.

After he'd gone through every single word of "Hello, Dolly" that he knew, Nico was still losing ground. Worse, he was doing his own touching now. His hand was also between them, jockeying for position with Eden's so that he could remind himself of just how good her puckered nipples felt between his fingers.

Damn good.

"Eden," he managed to say, and there must have been something in his voice that caused her to pull back. Not to stop touching though—

His eyes crossed when she gave his dick a squeeze.

"I want you," she said.

"Yeah. You made that clear, and that part of me you're squeezing makes it clear that I want you, too." Just in case she'd fried her every brain cell, he gave in to the heat and kissed her again.

Sheez. Why did she have to taste like that? Like everything he'd always wanted but didn't know until he'd tasted her. Nico figured that was going to be a question for the ages and definitely not something he could suss out right now. After all, his hard-on was frying some of his own brain cells.

"Eden," he repeated when he finally forced himself to tear his mouth from hers. "This might not be the right thing for you to do."

Oh, it hurt to say that, and if his hard-on could have managed it, it would have knocked Nico upside the head.

"Why?" she asked, and that one word was filled with her warm breath. A breath that brushed against his mouth like a kiss. *No. More than a kiss.*

He had to clear his throat, and his head, so he could speak. "Because you might be doing this since you're upset with Damien. I get why you're upset," he quickly added. "You have every right to be, but I don't want you to regret something we do here after you've cooled off."

"I won't regret it." Her breathy response rushed out so fast that Nico knew she'd given it exactly zero thought. Under different circumstances, he might have liked that since he'd never thought of sex as a deep thought kind of experience.

But this wasn't normal circumstances.

This was Eden.

"Besides," he went on when he managed to speak, "we need to talk. There's something you should know."

"I don't want to talk. I want to have sex with you," she insisted. "No talking," she added when he tried to speak. "I don't want to hear anything that'll stop what's happening."

Well, hell, that put a lid on his confession. Though it shouldn't have. Nico knew he should push it, that he should make her hear the truth, but Eden put an end to his resolve with just three words.

"I need you," she said in a breathy whisper.

Okay, so that spurred a change in his plans. First, he'd get rid of this lust storm that was bearing down on both of them, and then he could tell her about Damien.

"Just in case you might regret it," he tried again. "We'll do something that might end up causing you fewer regrets. It'll give you some thinking time," he added when she opened her mouth to protest.

Since it was obvious her protest would just continue, he kissed her. No hardship on his part. Eden was just as hot and tasty as she had been a few moments earlier, and Nico could feel his erection testing the zipper of his jeans.

Speaking of jeans, Nico slid his hand into hers. Right past the loose waist and down into her panties. His fingers found her. Wet, of course, which made his stupid dick start to beg him to make this something more than a hand job.

And it was indeed something more.

"You've got a Brazilian," he managed to say once he groaned. Hard to think with discoveries like that. "I didn't expect that."

She nodded. "I had it done a couple of years ago for blog research and decided to keep it. It's good for swimsuit season. You don't like it?"

"I'm a guy. I'll like pretty much anything when it comes to that part of your anatomy. Any part of your anatomy," he added when he ran his gaze down her body. Even though he didn't get that good of a look, he peeked down into her jeans, too.

Yeah, he liked the Brazilian.

His fingers liked it as well because they went to work on her.

Eden gasped, but it was from pleasure, and her eyelids fluttered as her body bowed. "You can't do that," she said. And yep, there was her breathy voice again. Air foreplay. "I won't last."

Nico would thank his lucky stars if that was true because his willpower was waning fast here, and he didn't want to cave in. But then he remembered their sex talk. The one where she'd told him about her quick-draw orgasms.

Her body was still bowing, and her hips still thrusting so that his fingers slid deeper into her. "Alabama," she said, gutting it out.

"What?" Nico managed just as Eden said, "Alaska."

And then she shattered. The orgasm racked through

her, and he could feel her wet slick muscles squeeze his fingers. Tight little spasms that would have felt damn good around his dick. He pushed that aside though and gathered Eden in his arms as she collapsed against him.

Her breath wasn't brushing now. It was gusting, and he could feel her heart thudding against his. Nico gave her a minute, then two before he had to ask.

"Alabama, Alaska?"

She kept her face buried against his shoulder. "It's a trick I use when I run too hot. Which is pretty much all the time when it comes to sex. I recite the states in alphabetical order."

So, it was like his show tune thing, but he liked her trick better and might borrow it. It didn't feel right for a cowboy and rodeo champion to mentally hum "Singing in the Rain."

Eden finally pulled back, looked him in the eyes. "And now you're going to ask how far down the list I've made it before I climax."

No, he wasn't going to ask it, but mercy, he wanted to know.

"That's it," Eden said when he didn't answer. "Never got past Alaska."

For some stupid reason, that made Nico smile, and it made him think something equally stupid.

Eden and he were going to have so much fun trying to make it all the way to Wyoming.

CHAPTER ELEVEN

Dear Naughty Cowgirl,
My sweetie's b'day is coming up soon, and I want to do something extra special for him. Maybe something to do with his hobby since he likes to tinker with fixing up cars. Any ideas?

Raring to Go in Dallas

EDEN FOUND HERSELF smiling when she read the post, and unlike the last couple of months, a lot of suggestions instantly came to mind. Hot, dirty suggestions. So many of them in fact that she took out a notepad from her desk at the law office so she could jot them down. Roy was in with a client, and there was no one else scheduled for an appointment so she figured that she'd have some privacy to whip out some ideas and then narrow down how to respond.

Apparently, Dallas wasn't the only one raring to go.

Her climax the night before with Nico had left her with a nice buzz. Strange, considering that they actually hadn't had sex, but after he'd sated her with that hand job, she had understood his reasoning for what he'd done. He hadn't wanted her to plunge into sex with him until she was positive it wasn't some reaction to hearing that Damien had cheated on her.

And maybe it would have been.

Eden could see that. Now. Maybe she had wanted to prove she was still desirable, and thankfully Nico had answered that question for her. She was. Better yet, she had some strong desires of her own. She couldn't wait to get her hands, and the rest of her, back on Nico.

He'd already told her that he didn't see her climaxing issue as a problem, and she hoped that was true. If not, then it was something she intended to ask him to help her with. Damien had never seemed interested in prolonging sex with her and had in fact become quite a "quick draw" himself. But she wanted better with Nico. She wanted longer.

Heck, she just wanted.

Soon, she would have him, too. Along with repairing the cabin's roof, he'd had business meetings all day and was scheduled to make a quick trip to Austin to deal with some rodeo where he'd be supplying the bulls. But once he was home and she was off from work, they were having a date.

"Raring to Go in Dallas, pretend that you're the car and he's tinkering with you," she jotted down on her notepad.

Go with a head-to-toe inspection where he touches and pleases.

Pleasure yourself while he watches, and

just when you're ready to climax, let him finish things for you in any way that he wants.

Give him a surprise hand job when he's
talking on the phone. While he continues the
phone conversation, stroke away, and it'll be a
hot thrill that only you two will know about.

Eden read through her notes and realized something. She wanted to do all those things with Nico.
In fact, she wanted to give him a sex quiz that she'd
come up with for a blog special about a year ago. Sort
of a sexual show-and-tell.

She went bold and texted him her first idea with
the question:

Can you give me some car repair lingo that will work
with this?

She hadn't expected him to answer right away,
but he did.

Nico texted:

Have her play with his dipstick while he aligns her
chassis.

Oh my. He had really gotten into the spirit of
this and given her a very strong reminder that she
wouldn't mind playing that particular game with
Nico. Maybe it wouldn't hurt for her to take her own
blog advice.

How about this one? She then texted him her idea

about the surprise hand job while the woman's boy-friend was on the phone.

A few moments passed, and she saw the little dots indicating he was typing. Maybe he was smiling, too. And getting as aroused as she was.

Nico's message read:

If she's doing the hand job right, no way would he be able to keep up that phone conversation. Will talk with you more about this later. About to leave Austin. Would be nice if you were at my house when I got there.

She fanned herself and glanced around to cool her-self down. If she were a guy, she'd have an erection right now and be unable to walk. Since she wasn't, she did some walking to the window so she could rein in some heat. If she didn't, she was going to have an orgasm the moment Nico looked at her.

"Alabama, Alaska, Arizona," Eden mumbled as she made her way to the window, and she saw some-thing that did nothing to cool her down.

Nico's brother Callen was in the doorway of his office building, his back against the jamb. His wife, Shelby, was across from him, and they were looking at each other. Not talking. Just looking, gazing into each other's eyes and smiling. Eden was betting there was a nonverbal naughty conversation going on be-tween the two, and a moment later, she got confirma-tion of that. Callen pulled Shelby to him and covered her mouth with his.

Eden turned so as not to watch, but she turned right back and watched anyway. Callen made the kiss something extra by pressing his body to hers. Talk about scorching. And intimate. The kind of intimacy that could only happen between two extremely horny people or a couple in love. In their case, Eden suspected it was both.

God, she wanted that. And wondered if she'd ever had it.

She supposed that years ago, Damien had looked at her and kissed her that way. With so much need that it came off in thick, hot waves. Then again, maybe that's what had been missing from their relationship, from their marriage. Eden had never needed him to gobble her up in the doorway of his office because he'd been taking small bites off her for years. Familiarity had become the thick waves.

Screw familiarity.

She wanted the heat.

Callen and Shelby finally eased away from each other and shared a smile that was somehow just as sizzling as that kiss. After Shelby gave him a quick wave, she turned and made a beeline for the law office. Eden nearly gasped at being caught gawking, though she was certain plenty of other folks on Main Street had seen it, too.

"Yes, I know," Shelby said when she walked in. "I have zero control when it comes to Callen." She was still smiling.

Eden eyed her, then glanced at Callen, who was

making his way back into the building. "You two just had a quickie in your husband's office, didn't you?"

Shelby just kept on smiling. "Maybe. And maybe it wasn't the first time that's happened. In fact, it's possible that I have such fond memories of his desk that I want all our future children to be conceived there."

It was good to see her old friend so happy. Shelby had gone years lusting after Callen, and now they had finally snagged each other.

Shelby glanced at Roy's closed office door before she walked closer to Eden's desk. "I want us to have another girls' night out. It's been way too long since the last one."

It had been a little over six months ago, shortly after Eden's divorce had become final and around the time that Shelby and Callen had become hot-to-trot lovers. Shelby had gathered up a group of friends at her place for some Jell-O shots, jalapeno poppers and a Fifty Shades movie marathon. There'd been plenty of sex talk and a debate over the rating for Christian Grey's ass. The final consensus had been a 9.2.

"This time, it'll be you, me, Cleo, Rosy and Piper," Shelby went on. "I'll send Callen over to play poker with his brothers."

Piper. Eden certainly hadn't forgotten about the girl, but hearing her name was a reminder that she needed to call her and make sure she was okay. She probably hadn't gotten back any results yet from her lab work, but Eden needed to make sure Piper wasn't worrying about it.

Or worrying about Jax.

Eden didn't mind the two teens getting back together, but she didn't want Piper going through another emotional upheaval without feeling that she had someone to talk to about it.

"We'll have this one at the ranch," Shelby explained.

The ranch as in her dad, Buck, and Rosy's place. It was on the edge of town and had been a haven for foster kids over the years. Home for Nico, too, since Buck was the only father he'd ever known since his own dad had run out on the boys when Nico was a kid. Now it was also home for Cleo, Judd and their three foster sons.

"And yes, I'll have to invite Rayelle so she doesn't think we're trying to pull something sneaky and amoral that will scar Piper for life. I'll write down the date and time for you so you won't have the excuse of forgetting," Shelby added, reaching for the notepad, but her eyeballs froze on what was already written there. "A surprise hand job while he's talking on the phone?"

Eden snatched back the notepad, closed down the screen on the computer, too, but clearly she had gotten Shelby's attention. Eden tried to shift that attention back to something else because no way did she want to explain the blog to Shelby.

"You're sure you want to get rid of your guy even for a few hours for a girls' night out?" Eden asked her. "I saw your kiss."

Shelby didn't even blush. "You have to admit, Callen's hot stuff." She tipped her head to the notepad that Eden now had clutched like a lover to her chest. "You've got hot stuff on your mind, too."

"Yes," Eden admitted, because she had no idea what else to say.

"With Nico?" Shelby pressed.

"Yes," Eden answered cautiously. "Are you okay with that?"

"Duh, of course." There was no caution or hesitation in Shelby's response. "Why wouldn't I be?"

"I don't know. It changes the dynamics of things. I mean, you won't be able to joke about the women he's having sex with." Or as Shelby had once called it, bedpost notches. "In fact, I'm the bedpost notch now."

A thought that had Eden frowning. Technically, she wasn't a complete notch since there hadn't been actual sex. So, her clock hadn't started with Nico. But it would start. She had no doubts about that. She wasn't even going to try to resist him, which meant that one day he would be finished with her. Soon, too, if his track record held up.

"Does that bother you, that things might not last long between you two?" Shelby asked.

"It probably should bother me," Eden admitted. "But right now I'm swept away in that hormone tidal wave of lust."

Shelby patted her arm. "That's the best kind of tidal wave. Just enjoy the ride."

Eden figured that enjoyment was the one thing guaranteed in all of this. That and a broken heart, but Eden wouldn't go there yet, either.

"Girls' night, be there." Shelby did another head

tip to the notepad. "I think I'll go across the street and see if my husband's talking on the phone." She added a wink before she headed out.

Of course, Eden would go to girls' night, not only so she could hang out with Cleo and Shelby but also to spend some time with Piper. Being around Rayelle wouldn't be much fun, but maybe she would leave her stick-in-the-mud attitude in the cabin.

Eden went back to her desk to combine her suggestions with Nico's for the blog answer, but she'd barely gotten started when the front door opened again. Not Shelby.

But Mimi.

This time, Eden not only closed down the blog file, she also put her notepad in her bottom drawer. Even though Mimi knew about the blog, Eden didn't want the woman seeing anything connected to *Naughty Cowgirl*.

Actually, she didn't want to see Mimi, either, though it would have been impossible to miss her. The woman was wearing a red above-the-knee dress that clung to her like a sunburn. It was an identical shade to her lipstick and the polish on her fingers and toes.

Very matchy-matchy.

Eden wanted to give her a snarky greeting. Something like "I hope you appreciated all the sex advice I gave you when you were boinking my husband." But Mimi beat her to the punch.

"Are you having sex with my fiancé?" Mimi demanded. Her hands went on her hips, causing those perky breasts to jut out even more than usual.

Eden was certain there was nothing perky about her expression and that she just looked confused. "What?" she managed.

"Sex with Damien," Mimi spelled out. "Are you?"

"Uh, no." Eden stood, but that was mainly so she would be eye level with the woman. "Trouble in paradise?" she asked.

That question caused Mimi's eyes to narrow, and Eden wondered if those baby blues would soon be that same sunburn red as her outfit.

"The only trouble is what you're causing," Mimi insisted. She hadn't exactly whispered that, either. It was loud enough for Roy to open his door and look out at them.

"Everything okay?" Roy slid glances between Mimi and her.

"Apparently not," Eden provided. She figured it was probably low of her to delight in Mimi's unhappiness, but the woman certainly hadn't thought of her or her marriage when she'd started an affair with Damien.

"This is private business," Mimi informed Roy.

"Then, perhaps you should be taking care of it in a private place since this is my law office and I'm with a client," Roy answered without missing a beat. "Eden, would you like for me to show our visitor out?"

"No, thanks. I can do that just fine, and if she stays, she'll just have to use her inside voice. And perhaps tone down her insulting, ludicrous accusations."

Oh, Eden was enjoying this a little too much.

Mimi's face tightened. Her nostrils flared. And Eden was surprised little puffs of smoke didn't spew out of her ears.

"I'll be brief and quiet," Mimi assured Roy.

Roy still didn't budge. He looked at Eden. "My appointment's running longer than planned, but you can leave for the day if you like."

Eden nodded. The timing was perfect. She could hurry home, change, put on some makeup and get to Nico's house so she'd be there when he arrived. She thanked her boss and then gave him a second reassuring nod. Only then did the man give Mimi a reminder glare before he went back into his office and shut the door.

Mimi quickly shifted her attention back to Eden. "I know Damien's been calling you, and he went to see you."

Eden shrugged. "Yes, he did visit, and there were calls and texts."

Annoying calls and texts that she hadn't answered, but Eden decided that fell into the TMI category. She didn't want to get into discussing her feelings for her ex, even when those feelings would have confirmed there was nothing going on between Damien and her. Still, it was a bit of a karma bite on Mimi's perky butt for the woman to think that the man she'd cheated with was now cheating on her.

How original.

"Well?" Mimi added a huff to that demand, but she had stuck to using a much quieter voice. Amazing though how the mean, bitter tone could still manage to be heard even in a near whisper. "Are you having sex with him?" Mimi snarled. "And before you say no, you should know that I've read your recent blog posts, and they're different. Hotter. I can tell that something worked you up, and I think Damien's responsible."

Hotter? If so, Eden could thank Nico for that since she'd been running her suggestions past him. His ideas were a lot better than Damien's ever had been. And as for Damien being responsible for this new tone. *Uh, no. Just no.* It had been a while since Damien had worked her up. Well, unless you counted anger and frustration.

Eden took her purse and her notepad from her drawer. "Look, Mimi, I don't want Damien. In fact, I'm having a hard time remembering why I ever wanted him in the first place."

That was TMI that Mimi clearly wasn't buying because she huffed. "You can't make me believe you no longer have feelings for him, that you wouldn't want to lure him away from me."

Eden looked her straight in the eyes. "Believe it."

It felt so good to say that, but what felt even better was that it was true. Not some fudged truth so people wouldn't know she was still hurting. The genuine truth. Anything she'd ever felt for Damien was gone. She no longer loved, wanted or respected him. But the best part was that she had a whole lot of want for someone else.

Nico.

Eden closed down her computer and hooked her purse over her shoulder. She also locked the desk drawers just in case Mimi took to snooping to find "proof" of her honey's infidelity. The computer would be fine since it was password protected. A password she'd changed after Damien had admitted to seeing her appointment calendar.

And that reminder caused Eden to pause and look at Mimi again.

"The blog," Eden said under her breath.

She steeled herself up in case she saw an aha/gotcha expression on Mimi's face. After all, the woman not only knew about the blog, Mimi could also tell others about it. She could blow Eden's secret life to smithereens. Worse, Mimi was obviously mad enough to do something like that.

So, why hadn't she?

Mimi must have worked herself up into this snit, and during the working up, she could have sent a few texts or dropped a word or two to gossips who would quickly spread it around. If the woman had indeed done that, Eden would have already heard about it so that led her to one puzzling possibility.

"Did Damien tell you to keep quiet about the blog?" Eden came out and asked.

Mimi's mouth tightened—which confirmed that's exactly what had happened. "He said he would be very angry with me if it leaked that you have a smut blog. He thought if that happened, you'd mention that he and I were seeing each other before his divorce was final."

"Seeing each other while Damien was still married to me," Eden automatically corrected.

Mimi gave an indignant wobble of her head. "He didn't want something like that getting back to his folks."

Nope. He wouldn't. So, this was sort of like a standoff. Mimi would keep the blog quiet, and Eden wouldn't rat the bastard out for having an affair. She mentally shrugged. It seemed like a good arrangement for her, especially since Eden had her own new life going on. One that she was betting was better than Damien's, which clearly included dealing with a jealous fiancée.

"Just where are you going?" Mimi demanded when Eden started to walk away from her.

Eden flashed her a smile. It was genuine, too. "I have an appointment for a chassis alignment and a dipstick check."

And Eden headed for the door.

CHAPTER TWELVE

NICO PULLED INTO the driveway in front of his house and groaned when he spotted the boy sitting on his front porch and obviously waiting for him.

Great.

Nico knew he had to talk to the kid. Maybe chew him out for some yet-to-be determined reason, but what he really wanted to do was get inside and grab a shower before Eden arrived.

Would be nice if you were at my house when I got there, he had texted her earlier, and she'd likely be arriving any minute now. He was going to hold on to the hope that he could solve whatever problem Jax had in that short period of time.

Nico wasn't sure it was the smartest idea for him to be with Eden, especially not smart to have sex with her, but he wasn't even going to look for a way to stop it from happening.

"Where's your motorcycle?" Nico asked as he unlocked the door to his house and went in. He hung his cowboy hat on the peg next to the door.

Jax followed along behind him. "In the shop getting fixed. A friend dropped me off. He's going to try to talk Piper into seeing me, and if that doesn't work, he'll be waiting for me at the Gray Mare. He'll come and get me when I call him."

Nico lifted his eyebrow. "You've got a friend old enough to be in a saloon?"

"He's a friend's older brother, and he said he'd only have a beer if he ended up having to wait for me."

"Then make this fast so he doesn't have too much to drink." And so that Jax could get out of there.

Jax nodded. "Something's wrong with Piper."

That was probably one of the few things Jax could have said that would have gotten Nico's mind off Eden. "What?"

"Don't know, but she's real sad when I talk to her. I can usually cheer her up by talking about music or how much I want to kiss her and stuff—" Jax stopped, cleared his throat. "I just can't seem to make her happy no matter what I say, and she won't let me see her no matter how much I ask. I don't think she likes me anymore."

Okay. Nico shifted from his big brother mind-set to one of a guy talking to another guy. "You broke up with her at a bad time in her life. It's my guess she won't be able to get over that. In other words, it's time for you to move on. If Piper wants you back, then she'll let you know."

Jax's forehead bunched up as if considering that. As if also considering what Nico had just told him as some deep philosophical gem that needed to be pondered.

"But what if I still love her?" Jax asked.

Nico sighed, and that sincere puppy dog look on

the boy's face had him biting off something harsh. Like, *you made your own bed*, etc.

"Sometimes, that's the way things are," Nico told him. "But if she doesn't love you, you have to move on. It only works when both of you want it." Since they were still talking about his sister, Nico added, "And it only works when there's deep respect that goes way beyond sex."

At that exact moment, Nico's front door opened. "Ready or not, here I come. I'm so hot right now," Eden announced.

She had been in the process of outstretching her arms, but she dropped them limply to her sides when she caught sight of Jax.

"Uh," Eden managed, and Nico figured it had taken a lot for her just to say that.

All visible parts of her were blushing, and there were plenty of parts for him to see the particular change in color. Wow. She looked ready for him to do a 29-point auto check on her. She was wearing a short loose blue dress with a V-neck and sandals instead of cowboy boots. He could see cleavage and bare legs.

Both very nice. So nice that he wanted to see a whole lot more of them.

"Is everything okay?" Eden asked. "Is something wrong with Piper?"

"Nico and I were just talking about guy stuff," Jax volunteered.

Eden turned to Nico as if confirming that, and he nodded. "Jax is worried that Piper has been a little down."

Eden shrugged. It wasn't exactly a casual/I don't care gesture. More like I'm about to state the obvious here. "Well, you did break up with her at a thoroughly shitty time what with the baby scare and her losing her mom," she told Jax.

Jax admitted that with a nod and heavy sigh. A sigh coupled with a puppy dog look that must have gotten to Eden, because she added, "I'll call Piper later to make sure she's all right."

That put a spark of gratitude in Jax's eyes. "Thanks," he said, then looked at Nico. "I have to be going. I'll call my friend to come and get me."

That sounded like a stellar plan to Nico, and he didn't even consider trying to change the boy's mind. Later, he'd also call his sister and, yes, Jax as well to make sure both were okay, especially since Nico would be swamped with business for the next couple of days. But for now, Jax was out of there. Literally.

Nico shut the door. In the same motion, he whirled back around, hooked his arm around Eden's waist, drawing her to him.

And he kissed her.

Her mouth was like water to quench a very big thirst, and Nico just didn't understand it. He'd known Eden for nearly two decades and had never experienced this kind of need for her, but he was sure experiencing it now.

He ran his tongue over the seam of her lips, sampling and drawing out that taste before he dived in for more. Of course, more was what he'd been fantasizing about all day, and it wouldn't stop with this. Nope. This was just the beginning.

"I don't know how I got away without having a kiss like this all the time," she muttered with her mouth still against his.

He wasn't sure if she was talking about the past twenty-four hours or longer. Best not to question her on that, either, or they'd get into touchy territory of talking about her ex. As a general rule, Nico liked to avoid conversations about exes or past relationships, in part because it would take him too long to get through some of the messed-up ones he'd had. Plus, in this case he didn't want to be pissed off at Damien all over again.

Her mutterings stopped, and she kissed him, pressing her dress and therefore her body against his. She hadn't been holding back anything when she'd blurted out her "I'm so hot right now" greeting.

"What put you in this *mood*?" he asked.

"You," she said, her breathing heavy. "Just you."

Best answer ever. Nico tried to give her the best response ever to go along with it. He backed her against the door, locking it in the process, and Nico did some pressing of his own. Body to body. With his leg between hers. That way he could play with adding some pressure when he put the top of his thigh right against her—

"Oh yes," she groaned out. "That's a good place. A really good place."

He hadn't actually forgotten that she had a quick trigger, but that was a reminder. Too bad he couldn't

Get Up To 4 Free Books!

Dear Reader,

IT'S A FACT: if you answer 4 quick questions, we'll send you 4 FREE REWARDS from each series you try!

Try **Essential Suspense** featuring spine-tingling suspense and psychological thrillers with many written by today's best-selling authors.

Try **Essential Romance** featuring compelling romance stories with many written by today's best-selling authors.

Or **TRY BOTH!**

I'm not kidding you. As a leading publisher of women's fiction, we value your opinions… and your time. That's why we are prepared to reward you handsomely for completing our mini-survey. In fact, we have 4 Free Rewards for you, including 2 free books and 2 free gifts from each series you try!

Thank you for participating in our survey,

Pam Powers

stop himself from giving her another nudge. Nico liked giving a woman pleasure. In fact, it was at the top of his list, and it didn't matter if he didn't have to work too hard to make sure that pleasure happened.

"Do you need another orgasm by hand so you can think straight?" he asked, and he was reasonably sure he'd never asked another woman that particular question.

"That doesn't help me think straight." Eden pulled back, met his gaze, but then she slid her hand over his chest, her fingers dipping lower to the bottom of his T-shirt.

And what she was doing wasn't helping with his clear thoughts, either. Nor was the next kiss he gave her. "Chassis adjustment," he mumbled, doing some touching of his own.

"And a dipstick check," she added.

She ran her hand over the front of his jeans, giving him a rough nudge. Because her mouth was still against his, Nico felt her smile. That's because he was rock hard and she was the reason for it. That smile was the primal seal of approval, her proof that he wanted her, and Nico was sure he'd be smiling, too, once he got his hands in her panties and found her hot and wet.

"I'm counting all of this as foreplay," she whispered. "That way, if I don't make it past Arkansas, you'll still have plenty of memories about what happened."

That had him pausing so he could lean back and

look at her. "You think I'm disappointed about the short time it takes you to get off?"

Eden clamped her teeth over the side of her bottom lip for a moment. "Maybe. Are you?"

He huffed. "Orgasms aren't like twenty-four-hour meds. You can have them often. One right behind the other. Here's the proof of that."

Nico shoved up her dress and went straight to her panties. They were white lace, barely there. The kind of panties that always made him wonder why a woman had bothered to wear anything at all, but then he remembered that he was a sucker for such things. The lingerie industry certainly had his number.

He slid his hand into the elastic at the leg of that strip of lace, enjoying the hitch of her breath and the way Eden threatened him if he stopped. That let him know he was on the right track. But then he did stop when he remembered what was waiting for him beneath the lace.

Or rather what wasn't waiting.

Suddenly, the memory of touching her Brazilian turned him hot, and he made a quick change of plans. *Quick* being the operative word because Eden was pushing herself against him and cursing him for stopping.

Nico caught on to the top of her panties and pushed them down far enough so that his boot could do the rest of the work. He shoved them to her ankles and then went down to his knees. Catching on to the back of her leg, he moved her knee to his shoulder.

"Excuse me a moment," he warned her.

And he kissed her, right there in her wet hot core. Just as he'd kissed her mouth. He used his tongue, his teeth and his lips, and it truly only did take a moment or two. As expected, she flew over the edge when she made it to California. This time, though, he got to feel and taste her climax. If he hadn't already been running crazy hot, that would have done it and pushed him over the edge, too.

He didn't give her long to recover. Nico kissed his way back up her body, bunching up her dress along the way. When he made it back to her mouth, he stripped off the dress over her head and dropped it next to the entry table where she'd already stepped out of her shoes.

Her eyes were still glazed, her breath uneven, and Nico watched her come back to earth. She gave him a dreamy smile. Then, she frowned.

"You still have on all your clothes," Eden complained. "And I only have on my bra."

"Then you've got to do something about that," Nico challenged.

He'd leave his own clothes to her. He hit the front clasp of her bra, slid it off her and with her looped in his arms, he started backing her toward the sofa.

It wasn't exactly relaxing having a naked woman pulling at his clothes. Talk about a way to fire up more heat, and that was the last thing he needed right now. He'd been serious about that frequent orgasm rule, and if he was going to give Eden some "frequency," he needed to throttle back a whole bunch.

He pulled her down onto the sofa, with her straddling his lap. She was so focused on getting his shirt off over his head that it seemed to take her a moment to figure out what was going on.

"Are we acting out the blog?" she asked. She stopped with his shirt still around his neck. "The one where you said she'd get light-headed?"

"No. We're acting out a rewritten version of that." He didn't consider pain from an accident or pulled muscle to be part of this multiple orgasm fest.

Nico helped her finish removing his shirt, but as soon as his mouth was free and clear, he went after her breasts. She wasn't huge or small. She was just right. Tasted just right, too, and he sampled and tugged before he pulled her nipple into his mouth and then sucked hard.

Eden made a strangled sound, a "yes" and an "oh" merged together to make a "yo." Nico took that as a good sign so he did the same to the other one. But he was getting ahead of himself. There was a nice area between her mouth and breasts that he hadn't given much attention.

He took some kisses to the tops of her breasts and started working his way up. Eden gave him some more yo's and wiggled and squirmed to get closer. Specifically, to put her now-naked Brazilian against his jeans-covered dick. It wasn't a very subtle message. Nor was the hand she put between them to unzip him.

Nico was all for unzipping and getting naked, but again, he'd have a problem lasting. He was too primed and ready and wouldn't last past Delaware if he didn't play around and hum a show tune or two.

Eden, however, wasn't humming. She was more in the licking mode, and while her very uncoordinated hands worked his zipper, she leaned in and licked his earlobe. And sonofabitch—she blew in his ear. All hot and breathy as if she was giving him a blowjob there. Hell, she might as well have been doing that because that lick and blow went straight to his erection.

Sonofabitch.

Okay, he could handle this, but since Annie's "Tomorrow" wasn't working worth squat, Nico moved on to the blog reenactment. He caught on to Eden's hips, easing her back so that her upper body and ear-licking tongue were no longer touching him. His coffee table was right there, and he anchored his legs and boots on it so that he could in turn anchor her when he laid her down on her back.

"No fair," she protested. "I can't play this way."

"But I can," he teased. Though he did have to take a few deep breaths at the sight of her. All naked and laid out there in front of him.

Since she was continuing to protest and trying to get up, Nico stopped her with his hand. He pressed the heel of his palm against her mound, against the soft smooth skin. That wouldn't have kept her in place, though, not for long so he found the sensitive knot, gave it plenty of pressure with his thumb and slid his fingers into her.

It was torture.

Not because she protested. Nope. She didn't even

do any more yo's. What she did do was fist her hands in her hair and move her hips so that she was pushing herself into his strokes. Of course, that meant she was also pushing herself against his hard-on, but he made a bargain with that part of himself. The idea was to exhaust all these quickie orgasms so that Eden could experience a nice, slow one.

Nico hoped the wait didn't kill him first.

Maybe she got too involved in what was happening, but Eden didn't start reciting states. Still, Nico figured if she had, they would have made it at least to Colorado before the climax shattered her again.

He'd considered that her quick draw might not make her a good porn star, but at the moment she certainly looked like one. The pleasure was all over her face, in the way her body moved and shuddered. Of course, unlike a porn star, her climax had been the real deal. Nico could feel her tight, wet muscles squeezing his fingers.

As he'd done at the door, he intended to give her a few minutes to recover, but Eden swooped up off his lap and kissed him. It wasn't gentle. Definitely not the kiss of a recently sated woman.

"You've given me two orgasms, and you've had none from me," she pointed out. She didn't sound especially happy about that, either, and she went after his clothes with a vengeance.

He'd never considered that it could be entertaining to have a naked woman tugging at his boots, but it was. It was incredibly entertaining. Her breasts jiggled and swayed. Her butt, too. And that was coupled with her fierce determination and the rosy flush from the orgasm.

She went after his boots, and Nico figured it was the sign of his perv mind, but he was almost hoping they would give her enough trouble that she'd have to clamp the boot between her legs to give it a pull. He was certain that would fuel some lifetime fantasies. Still, he was satisfied when she tugged off his left boot and sock, threw it aside and then did the same to the other.

Eden didn't come diving back at him, but rather she stopped and eyed him. Much the way a starved dieter would eye a display case of desserts. "This time, I'm having you," she said, her voice part purr, part warning.

Nico just outstretched his arms. "Come and get me."

Before Eden could even take a step, however, there was a knock at the door. Obviously, a knock from someone with a death wish. Since Nico didn't want to kill anyone tonight, he just motioned for Eden to keep coming.

She did, but the second knock stopped her again.

"Uh, Nico," the death-wish seeker called out. It was Jax. "Hate to bother you, man, but I got a problem."

"What the hell is it?" Nico snapped.

"Uh, you know that friend who was supposed to pick me up?" Jax didn't wait for him to respond to that. "Well, your brother just arrested him for speeding and having a fake ID. He's in jail and needs us to come and get him out. Oh, and we gotta go because Piper was with him."

THIS WAS *NOT* how Nico had wanted to spend the rest of his evening, and he was betting Eden felt the same way. Yet, here they were, walking into the police station because Piper was somehow involved in a situation involving a fake ID, a traffic violation and an arrest.

The moment Nico, Eden and, yes, Jax—who was right on their heels—stepped into the police station, they saw Piper. No way they could have missed her because she was sitting next to Kace's desk.

And she was crying.

Kace was there, a box of Kleenex in his hand that he had angled at Piper, and he immediately got to his feet.

"She's not under arrest," Kace said. Probably because he saw the fire in Nico's eyes. "She was just in the vehicle with the kid I brought in, and she didn't want me to call Rayelle to come and get her."

That was the only thing about this situation that made sense. Nico cringed at the thought of Rayelle learning about this, though the chances were high that she would. The chances were also high that Nico wouldn't keep it from her whether she heard it or not. Even if Piper had done nothing wrong, Rayelle still needed to hear.

Shit.

That would be about as much fun as being kicked in the balls.

"I'm sorry," Piper said, wiping her eyes and blowing her nose before she stood and stepped into Nico's arms. She continued to sniff back more tears. "All I seem to be doing lately is screwing up."

No, she hadn't, but the pregnancy scare had been a whopper of a situation. She was likely still feeling fragile about that, but Nico wasn't going to let her sink into a pity party. He took hold of her shoulders and looked at her.

"What happened?" Nico demanded.

Piper had to take a moment and clear her throat. "Davy talked me into seeing Jax."

"David Ellison," Kace provided at the same time that Jax said, "He's my friend's big brother."

Piper nodded. "Davy called and said he'd brought Jax to Coldwater, that Jax was all torn up about our breakup—"

"I am," Jax interrupted, earning a glare from Nico.

Nico made sure it was a badass glare, too. One that would hopefully keep him quiet until they got to the bottom of this.

"Anyway," Piper went on. "Davy talked me into meeting Jax. I said I'd give him five minutes, that's all," she quickly added. "So, Davy picked me up near the cabin."

Eden no doubt heard the "near" just as well as Nico had because it caused them both to groan. "You sneaked out and didn't tell your aunt Rayelle that you were meeting with Jax," Nico concluded.

Piper confirmed that with a nod, and her teary gaze shifted to Jax. "I just wanted to tell you…some things."

Things that probably weren't what a brother

wanted to hear, and that might have been why Piper left his arms and went to Eden. Piper hugged her. "Thank you for coming. I'm sorry about all of this."

"It's okay." No glare from Eden. Just a whole boatload of sympathy, and she wiped a fresh tear from Piper's face. "Are you all right?"

This time Piper's nod didn't confirm anything other than she didn't want to worry them more than they already were. Since Eden was giving Piper the TLC that she obviously needed, Nico shifted his attention back to Kace.

"You arrested this Davy guy?" Nico asked.

"Had to. He was speeding through town, and when I pulled him over and ran his license, it was fake. He's nineteen, but according to his license, he's twenty-one."

Jax didn't groan, which meant he knew about the fake ID. Nico would deal with that in a moment.

"Had Davy been drinking?" Nico added to Kace.

Kace shook his head. That was the first piece of good news Nico had heard in this mess, but he still reeled around to Jax. "You sent a guy with a fake ID and a penchant for speeding to pick up Piper. Explain to me why I shouldn't beat the shit out of you for that."

Jax swallowed hard. "Because I didn't know Davy would speed." He didn't say that with much confidence, almost as if it had a question mark at the end of it.

"Don't blame Jax for this," Piper said, easing away from Eden. "I sneaked out, I got in that truck and even though I told Davy to slow down, it was too late. I saw the blue lights from the cruiser."

Unlike Jax, there was no questioning tone in her response. But there was plenty of fatigue and worry. Nico got that. Piper was going to have to face Rayelle.

"Where does Rayelle think you are right now?" Nico asked her.

"Out for a walk. But she's texted me three times already so I know she's worried." And judging from the way Piper was chewing on her bottom lip, she was very concerned as to how Rayelle would deal with that worrying.

"I'll take you back to the cabin," Nico insisted. "Just give me a second."

Nico stepped away from Piper, going to Eden, and since there was no chance they'd have privacy in Kace's office, he took her into the squad room, where at the moment there were no deputies. He was especially glad that the busybody receptionist/dispatcher, Ginger Monroe, had already gone home for the day. However, there would still be prying eyes since Kace's office had a window facing the squad room, and besides, the door was still open.

"I'm sorry, but I'll have to cut this evening short. You should go on home." Nico kept his voice as low as possible.

"I completely understand. You want me to go with you to take Piper back to the cabin?"

Nico considered it, only because an audience might make Rayelle soften the snit she was going to have, but then again, Rayelle seemed to have only one tone when it came to her attitude.

"It's okay. I might be there awhile," he told Eden,

and that brought him to his next point. One that he really hated to make. "I have to leave on a business trip first thing in the morning—"

"I understand," she repeated. "Just go and take care of Piper. My car is here so I can drive home."

Eden had insisted on following Jax and him into town since there wouldn't have been enough room in his truck for Jax, Piper, Nico and her. That had turned out to be a good thing because now he wouldn't have to worry about Eden getting home.

"I'll see you when you get back from your business trip," she said. "Won't I?"

He hated that she even thought she needed to add that last part, but then Eden and he were new at this. "Oh yeah. You'll definitely see me."

Nico wanted to kiss her. Not only to reassure her that he'd keep his promise, but he seriously just wanted his mouth on hers. However, when he glanced over his shoulder, he saw that Piper, Kace and Jax were all staring at them. Instead, Nico settled for a quick brush of his lips over her cheek. It was the kind of kiss he'd given Eden dozens of times over the years.

This one went straight to his groin.

Definitely not a good place for a kiss to go because of that whole audience thing. Plus, he wasn't sure if Eden wanted to keep what was happening between them a secret. She was the one whose reputation would be hurt by this. Gossips would say she was playing around with a guy who played around for sport and that she was probably doing it because she was on the rebound. Nico knew she'd hate the sympathetic looks and the disapproving ones from her folks.

Plus, there was the Rayelle factor. Rayelle didn't want Nico involved with a woman, a*ny woman*, since she'd gotten it in her head that it would be a negative influence on Piper. And Eden could get caught up in Rayelle's attempts to make sure that Nico didn't have a sex life while Piper and she were still in Coldwater.

"I'll see you in three days," Nico added, and because he couldn't stop himself, he gave her another of those cheek kisses before she headed out of the building and Nico went back into Kace's office.

Where everyone was still staring at him.

"Ready to go?" Nico asked Piper.

"Can I talk to her first?" Jax blurted out.

Nico would have nixed that idea, but Piper quickly nodded, along with taking a deep breath. Then, as Eden and he had done, Piper and Jax stepped out into the squad room.

"Shit," Kace immediately grumbled, "you're sleeping with Eden."

"No." Nico could honestly say there'd been no sleeping whatsoever going on. Heck, not any full-blown sex, either, which was probably why he felt ready to explode. Maybe his hard-on would fully soften in an hour or two.

Nico could tell there were things Kace wanted to say. In fact, Nico figured he'd hear a lecture or two in the next couple of minutes so he got some "business" out of the way first.

"What will happen to Davy?" Nico asked.

Kace gave him a look that only a cop could manage. A cop who apparently didn't like putting "business" before a sibling lecture. "Well, you're not going to kick the shit out of him, that's for sure. He's a stupid kid who made a mistake. I've called his parents, and they're on the way here now. They can take Jax back, too, since they're neighbors."

Good. No way did Nico want to have to drive Jax home, but then it wasn't good for the kid to be lingering around, either. Especially since Jax clearly wanted to do that lingering with Piper. At least they weren't kissing or anything, and Piper had her arms folded over her chest, giving lover boy a dose of some very good defensive posture.

"If you're not sleeping with Eden," Kace grumbled, "you're thinking about doing it." He added a disapproving huff to go along with that. "Look—you don't have to nail every available woman in town."

Normally, Nico would have just flashed a cocky smile and joked to his big brother that he did indeed need to do that. But joking about Eden didn't seem right. She was his friend, and no, it didn't matter that he'd had his hand in her panties or had intimate knowledge of her waxing habits. She was, first and foremost, his friend. Heck, maybe that's why the near sex had been so good with her. They hadn't held much back.

"I hope you're at least having second thoughts about screwing around with her," Kace went on.

Nico nodded. Except he had moved on to third and fourth thoughts. And it still hadn't changed his mind.

He wanted to be with her. Despite his bad track record. Despite their friendship. Despite his not being honest with her about Damien's cheating. He still wanted Eden.

"I'll be careful with her," Nico told his brother.

Kace gave him "the" look. The one that mixed together big brother, cop and chief bullshit detector.

"You'd better be. Buck and Rosy think the world of Eden. So do I. If you bang her and discard her, expect grudges to be held." Kace got right in his face to finish up the lecture. "Big-assed grudges. Think before you leap, little brother." Kace's index finger landed against Nico's chest. "For once in your life, *think*."

CHAPTER THIRTEEN

EDEN SIPPED HER wine, listened to the chatter of the women at their girls' night, and she realized one important thing.

She'd had way too much thinking time.

Two days of it with Nico gone on his business trip. She'd believed that the time away from him would give her perspective, that it would make her wonder if she should cool things down a bit and reevaluate what she wanted. But that hadn't happened.

No cooling. No reevaluating. Just the dull throbbing ache in her body. Especially the part contained in her panty region.

Even a refresh of her Brazilian hadn't stopped her from thinking about sex, and while her repeat treatments hadn't been nearly as uncomfortable as her first one, the temporary sting hadn't done a thing to dampen her libido. Man-specific libido, that is. Her hots were all for Nico.

She suspected Nico was dealing with the hots for her, as well.

Of course, Eden had nudged that heat about an hour earlier by texting him a part of a blog letter that she'd be answering soon.

Dear Naughty Cowgirl, help! My latest man isn't packing a lot of heat, if you get my drift. Any suggestions on how to deal with only four inches?

Getting Less than Usual in Laredo

Rosy's hoot and applause drew Eden's attention away from her thoughts of Nico, sex and the blog and back to the kitchen table at the McCall house. That's where Rosy had just put in the last of a 500-piece jigsaw "Puppies Galore" puzzle that Piper, Rayelle and she had been working on.

Shelby was near the puzzlers and was adding more cubes of cheese to the fondue pot on the kitchen counter. Cleo was at the blender, mixing up some virgin margaritas—a follow-up to the virgin daiquiris she'd made earlier.

In the adjoining family room, *Beauty and the Beast* was playing on the DVD though no one was watching it. Just as they hadn't watched *The Little Mermaid* before that, and next up would be *Shrek* if the night lasted that long.

Rayelle was the reason for this G-rated merriment since she'd been the one in charge of movie selection. A much-different atmosphere from rating Christian Grey's ass and using the pause button to see if they could get a glimpse of his junk. That's what they'd done during their last girls' night anyway.

Eden's phone dinged with a message from Nico, and since she still had some semiprivacy in the family room, she looked at his response.

Nico texted:

Dear, Getting Less Than Usual in Laredo, size doesn't matter. Just teach him to hit the right spot, and you won't miss those extra inches at all.

Smiling probably more than she should, Eden texted back:

Usually guys with small equipment say that. You definitely aren't small.

He answered:

You've never seen my equipment. Want me to send you a dirty picture of it?

Oh yes. Suddenly, she wanted that a whole lot even if it worked her up into a heated lather that Nico couldn't cool down. Sure, she said, thankful that a text couldn't detect the way she'd gone all soft and damp.

The moments seemed to crawl by before her phone dinged again. On the screen, there was a cartoon snowman couple, and the female was giving a blowjob to a very short snow penis. The caption was "Sorry, honey, but it keeps melting whenever I put my mouth on it."

Eden laughed before she could stop herself, and it wasn't a soft chuckle, either. It was a good belly laugh, and she quickly put away her phone after she texted Nico a very short reply.

Will have to test this on you, she said, hoping that he was now as needy as she was.

Piper pushed herself away from the table, and as she'd done most of the night, she also checked her phone. Maybe for a message or the time. To her, time had probably stood still. No way could this be fun for a sixteen-year-old.

"The bathroom," Piper muttered, heading in that direction.

Eden watched her as she walked away. Piper had smiled on and off throughout the night, but on a fake scale of one to ten, the smiles were a ten. She was down. Way down. Maybe because of Jax, the recent alarm with her late period or Rayelle's reaction to Davy's arrest. Either way, Eden needed to talk to the girl, and she hoped she could get her alone for a few minutes.

Of course, Nico had filled Eden in on what'd happened after he'd taken Piper from the police station back to the cabin. Piper and he had fessed up to Rayelle, and Nico had thankfully managed to calm Rayelle down by reminding her that at least Piper hadn't been with Jax. Piper had apologized and groveled, swearing never to take a ride with a friend again unless Rayelle knew about it. It had been a Band-Aid fix, and Eden wanted to make sure that Rayelle wasn't still simmering over it enough to make Piper miserable.

"Oh, I nearly forgot," Shelby said, hurrying into the family room with Eden. Shelby hauled out a thick photo album from beneath the coffee table. "Dad was poking around in the attic last week, and he came up with this."

Shelby dropped down on her knees, flipping through the plastic-covered pages that held lots of old photographs, most of them yellowed with age. She stopped when she got to one page and handed off the album to Eden.

"Remember that?" Shelby asked.

Eden set her wine aside, had a look and smiled. It was a group shot of Nico, his brothers, Shelby, Cleo and Eden.

"I think Nico must have been about fourteen when it was taken," Shelby said.

"No, he was thirteen," Cleo corrected as she joined them. So did Rosy and Rayelle. "I know that because Judd and I were both sixteen then. It was, uh, a memorable year for us."

The year they'd no doubt first had sex. Eden wasn't the only one who picked up on that "memorable" though, because Rosy laughed. However, Rayelle got that constipated look on her face, making Eden wonder if the woman had had anything close to "memorable."

"That would have been two years after Nico and his brothers came here," Rosy contributed just as Piper came back into the room. "And about two and a half years before he left Brenda's."

The silence came as it always did when there was any mention of Nico leaving Brenda's. That's because those months in between Brenda's and the ranch had been nothing short of hell. His brothers and he had been beaten and Nico had nearly been killed. Despite that, Nico didn't seem to carry the darkness that his brothers did. But it had taken its toll. Eden knew that. Knew, too, that Nico didn't think of himself as a good man, and she suspected that had its unholy roots in those months of abuse.

"So, you were with Judd even then?" Piper asked Cleo. She pointed to the possessive way that Judd had his arm slung around Cleo's shoulders.

"We were a couple," Cleo confirmed. "But then I moved to another foster home, and we lost touch."

"And were you and Callen also together?" Piper asked Shelby. In the picture, Callen was behind the others, looking both impatient and disinterested. The exact opposite of Shelby, who was grinning at him.

"Definitely not," Shelby assured her. "My dad took in a lot of fosters when I was growing up, and he had one rule. If any of the boys touched me, he would castrate them. You'd be surprised just how effective the threat of castration can be."

That caused Rosy to hoot with laughter, and there were giggles. From everyone except Rayelle, who seemed more the sort to threaten castration rather than to be hindered or amused by it.

"You and Nico weren't together, either," Piper said, looking at the image of Eden as a thirteen-year-old girl. Damien wasn't in the picture because he was the one behind the camera, and in the shot, Nico did indeed have his arm around Eden. But there was no gleam in his eyes like in Judd's and Cleo's.

"No. We were friends," Eden answered. "Best

friends." Looking back though, that's the year things had started to change. Nico had started to notice girls, and they'd started to notice him. "Damien and I were already sort of a couple by then."

"Oh," Piper said, and another long, awkward silence followed.

"It's okay," Eden assured her. Piper had enough baggage without trying to walk on eggshells around her. "Damien and I were together for a long time. I can't exactly do an exorcism or castration to cut him out of my memories."

"Too bad about that, huh?" Shelby said. "Still, I gotta say when I was growing up, I looked at you two and thought—I want that. A guy who's devoted to me. One who sticks." She shrugged. "But I think Damien and you just had all of that too soon and too young. And it fizzled out."

Eden gave her a nod of agreement and sipped more of her wine. Was that it? Was that the reason Damien had cheated on her and then left her for Mimi? Maybe. But if so Eden vowed not to let that muddle her up as Nico's childhood had done to his brothers. It might sound like a corny affirmation session, but she was okay. Nico was okay. And they could be okay together even if it ended up being just an affair. She certainly wasn't going to think about that now because it would stop her from enjoying every second she had as his flavor of the week.

"Damien and I are in a better place now," Eden went on.

Well, she was anyway. She thought about her meeting with Mimi and considered that maybe Damien wasn't in as good of a place as he'd believed he would be.

"Marriage is sacred," Rayelle muttered, and she walked away toward the powder room.

That brought on another silence. A very short one. Probably because pissing off Rayelle was a piece of cake and happened too often to dwell on. Rosy sure didn't.

"I'll bring us some fondue in here while we look at more pictures," Rosy said, standing from the sofa. "Anyone need a refill on wine? Oops. I guess only Eden and Cleo are working their way through that bottle of merlot since Shelby's off the sauce for a while. Sorry that I spilled the beans," she added before she scurried back into the kitchen.

"Yes, I'm knocked up," Shelby admitted, saluting her condition with her virgin margarita.

"I'm so happy for both Callen and you," Eden gushed, and she meant it, but it did occur to her that Shelby hadn't been married that long. "How'd Callen take the news?" she asked.

"He's thrilled and can't wait to tell everyone. But I'm sure everyone will start doing the math and will soon figure out I got pregnant about a month before our wedding."

The words had no sooner left Shelby's mouth when Eden heard a throat clearing. Rayelle was standing there, only a few feet away, and she had an even sourer expression than usual. Clearly, she'd heard what they had said.

"Really?" Rayelle scolded. She even clucked her tongue. "Do you think this is a conversation to have in front of a young girl?" She didn't wait for any of them to attempt to respond to that. She took hold of Piper's hand. "Come on. We're going back to the cabin."

Eden groaned and was about to intercede. She wasn't sure she could talk Rayelle into letting Piper stay, but she was willing to give it a try. But Piper shook her head, and she broke away from Rayelle's hold long enough to hug all four of the other women.

"Thank you for inviting me, Miss Rosy," Piper said.

Piper waved goodbye, and as she headed for the door, she looked back at Eden, their gazes connecting. The girl didn't say another word, but Eden saw plenty in her eyes. Plenty that she recognized as bone-deep sadness.

God, what was wrong?

Nico tossed his truck keys on the entry table at his house, hung up his hat and headed for the shower. One of the last parts of his business trip involved riding Silver Bells, a bull that he had considered buying, and he stank to high heaven. Not to mention that his jeans were covered with dirt and likely some bull shit.

He'd stayed on Silver Bells a couple of seconds longer than he had BYB, but he'd still gotten thrown, which meant he now had fresh bruises on top of where the old ones had only recently healed. Having blue, purple and green splotches on his butt wasn't usually a concern for him, but he'd wanted to be at his best when he saw Eden.

And he would see her.

No amount of self-lecturing had talked him out of doing this. As soon as he'd finished showering off the stench, he'd call her and ask her to come over when she finished at work.

Going to her was out of the question. If he went over to her place and stayed late—which he'd end up doing—someone would see his truck. By morning, the gossip would be all over town about him making a booty call.

If it were just his reputation, he wouldn't mind, but Eden's parents wouldn't want to hear talk of their daughter bedding down with her cad friend. Nico suspected they liked him well enough, but that "like" wouldn't continue if they learned he'd set his sights on Eden.

Rayelle wouldn't care much for it, either, and Nico feared the woman was already on the verge of considering an early return trip to move Piper back to San Antonio.

Nico had heard all about how upset Rayelle had been when she'd heard Eden, Shelby and Cleo talking at the girls' night. Rayelle had stormed out and taken Piper with her after hearing about Shelby getting knocked up before Callen and she had actually said "I do."

That scene had been especially bad since it'd come on the heels of the Davy incident. Thankfully though, a few calls from Nico had calmed things down. Enough so that Rayelle had even agreed to let Piper go back over to Rosy's for the afternoon to ride horses and do more cookie baking.

Of course, Rayelle had a rule or two about the visit. She had insisted there not be any sex talk around Piper. Since it would only be Piper, Buck, Rosy and Cleo's five-year-old foster son, Leo, Nico figured that was one rule that wouldn't be broken. Rosy was more likely to gab on about her latest taxidermy projects than sex anyway.

Nico stripped down, but before he could get in the shower, his phone dinged, and he smiled when he saw the text from Eden.

Dear Naughty Cowgirl,

My guy is a bull rider, and I have to say that seeing him in action gets me hot. All those smooth moves and power between his legs—and yes, I'm talking about when he's on the bull, lol. I want to do something in the bedroom that fires me up the way it does when he's in the arena. Any ideas to buck and ride the night away?

Buckle Bunny in Bandera

Nico wasn't sure if that was a real post or one that Eden had written to make him hard as a hammer. If it was the last one, it had worked well enough that he would have skipped the shower if it hadn't been for the bull stench. That aroma sure wouldn't lead to too much bucking and riding once she got a whiff of it. So he hurried into the shower.

He'd barely had time to lather up though when his phone rang. Obviously, Eden wanted to see him as much as he wanted to see her. He let it go to voice mail, rinsed off and got out of the shower to return what he was sure was Eden's call, but his phone rang again before he could do that. And it wasn't Eden's name on the screen.

It was Rayelle's.

Hell. What now? The only time the woman called him was when she wanted to complain about something. But since that "something" was almost certainly related to Piper, he didn't want to put her off.

Nico took the call, putting it on speaker so he could dry off as he talked. "Rayelle," he greeted, trying not to sound as if he was dreading this, but he was.

"Did you come to the cabin and take something?" Rayelle blurted out.

That wasn't the woman's usual persnickety tone. She sounded, well, panicked.

"No. I just got back from a business trip." Which Rayelle knew since he'd texted her his schedule and an ETA for his return. According to that ETA, he wouldn't be back in Coldwater for another hour or two. "Is something wrong with Piper?"

"Piper's fine. She's with Rosy, and I checked on her not long ago. Did you take something from the cabin?" she pressed.

On a heavy sigh, Nico repeated his "No" and finished drying himself so he could get dressed. "What's the something that someone took from the cabin?"

Silence.

For a long time.

And that silence cut through Nico even more than a shout or tears would have done. "What's wrong?" he pressed.

There was another stretch of quiet before Rayelle said, "Could you please come to the cabin right now?"

Nico felt more of that cut inside him, and while he didn't especially want to spend time with Rayelle— time that he wanted to be with Eden—the woman was clearly upset. That meant this was likely connected to Piper.

"I'll be right there," Nico assured her, and he ended the call so he could send a quick text to Eden.

Got in from my trip but Rayelle needs to see me. Headed to the cabin now and will call as soon as I'm done. Come over and we can work on advice for Buckle Bunny.

He added a winking smile to the text and wished it could be something dirty. Something to keep her mind on sex with him. No time for that, though. The sooner he found out what was bugging Rayelle, the sooner he could see Eden.

Nico threw on some clothes and ran out to his truck, and while he would have liked to have kept his own mind on sex with Eden, it was impossible to think that way when he knew he would have to face

Rayelle's usual look and tone of disapproval. But it wasn't disapproval he saw when he pulled up in front of the cabin and spotted her pacing across the little front porch.

Hell. Had she been crying?

If so, then this wasn't going to be a quick fix. And whatever she had to tell him was almost certainly bad. Maybe she believed Piper had stolen some jewelry from her or something, but no way would Piper do that. His sister wasn't a thief, and if she'd needed money, she would have come to him. After all, he knew the secret about the pregnancy panic that she'd kept from Rayelle.

"Are you sure you didn't take something from the cabin?" Rayelle asked the moment he stepped from his truck.

"Well, unless you count the trash bag and roofing debris I took with me the last time I was here, no."

She actually looked hopeful about that. "Maybe something fell into the trash bag or you picked it up by accident and thought it was trash? Where did you take the bag?"

"To the dump," he answered almost idly. Right now, he wasn't so much interested in giving her that answer as he was in finding out what the heck was going on.

Nico stepped onto the porch with her, and he put his arm around her waist so he could lead her to a chair. She definitely didn't look too steady on her feet, but he expected her to push him away. She didn't.

On a hoarse sob, she went straight into his arms and dropped her head on his shoulder.

Oh shit.

Had she found out about Piper's pregnancy scare?

Nico let the woman cry it out for a couple of moments, and then he got her moving inside the cabin. The AC was on in there, and the sofa would be more comfortable than the wooden chairs on the porch. He had her sit and went into the kitchen to pour her a glass of her preferred unsweetened iced tea from the big pitcher of it that she had in the fridge.

"Thank you," she muttered, taking the tea and gulping some down the way a person would a much-needed shot of booze. Nico nearly asked her if booze would help, but he didn't want her tipsy. Not when she apparently had some big-assed troubling news to tell him.

He didn't say anything or prompt her with questions. That was mainly because he didn't know how much she knew. Best not to blurt out both of Piper's secrets when it might not even be that.

"Something went missing from the cabin," Rayelle finally said. Her voice was shaky and she downed more tea. "Something very personal to me. *Very* personal," she emphasized. Then, she did something he'd never seen her do before. She blushed, the color rising bright pink on her cheeks.

Nico didn't like what first came to mind. Maybe it was a vibrator or dirty pictures. If so, then he might do some blushing himself. Or wincing. He didn't want to think of Rayelle that way.

"It was a silver box," Rayelle added a moment later. "It was small." She indicated the size with her trembling hands, and he estimated it was about the size of a travel package of Kleenex. "It's silver with an etched scroll design on it."

Bingo. That was the box Piper had mentioned. The one that Rayelle locked up in her suitcase or carried in her purse. Nico had forgotten about it, but obviously it was important to the woman and she was upset about losing it. Despite Rayelle's obvious distress, Nico felt some relief. For once, this wasn't about Piper.

Well, hopefully not.

"Have you seen a box like that?" Rayelle was more begging than asking.

Nico shook his head and sat down beside her. "You lost it?" And he hoped she wouldn't say it'd been stolen and then accuse Piper.

She nodded and paused for a long time. "I need to tell you something. I need to tell someone," she added in a hoarse whisper. "And then I hope you'll help me look for the box."

"Of course I'll help you." He would listen, too, but Nico was getting a really bad feeling about this.

"Swear to me that you won't repeat anything I'm about to tell you," Rayelle insisted.

He looked her straight in the eyes. "I swear."

Rayelle nodded, then hesitated again. "Years ago, I made a mistake. I got pregnant."

Nico bit off the "holy shit" that nearly leaped right out of his mouth, and he reined in the sound of stunned surprise that would have followed. If he'd come up with a list of a hundred, no a million, things that Rayelle would tell him, her getting knocked up wouldn't have been on the list. He had always just assumed she was still a virgin.

"My parents were alive then," she went on, "and they were devastated. So disappointed in me." Her voice cracked on those last words, and Nico could hear the hurt that was still there after all this time.

"I'm sorry," he said, and he meant it. He had some experience with other people's disappointment. "What did you do?"

"The only thing I could." She wiped away fresh tears. "Shortly after I found out I was pregnant, I also learned the baby's father was married. I didn't know. I swear I didn't." Rayelle waved that off as if it no longer mattered. "Anyway, when I told him I was pregnant, he said it probably wasn't even his baby and that he never wanted to see me again."

That bad feeling in Nico's gut went up a notch. Hell. Was Rayelle about to tell him there'd been some kind of murder weapon in that box? Maybe a spent bullet casing from where she'd shot the married asshole?

"I was in college then but was working part-time at a private school," she explained. "A church school. And they told me to seek employment elsewhere, that they couldn't have a pregnant unmarried woman working there, that I would be a bad influence on the students."

Of course, Nico found it ironic that Rayelle had put that same judgment on him. And Eden.

"What happened?" Nico asked to break the next round of silence.

Rayelle shook her head, letting him know this wasn't going to be easy for her to say. "I didn't have much money, and Brenda was busy with work and her foster children. I didn't want to burden her so I told her I was going away for a while, taking a long trip. I went to stay with a friend, and after I delivered, I gave the baby up for adoption."

Now Nico needed some silence to process all of that. It was hard to see Rayelle in such a vulnerable position with no emotional support from her family or the baby's father.

"Brenda didn't know?" he asked her because he couldn't imagine Brenda not stepping up to help.

"I told her years later," Rayelle answered in a whisper. "Brenda forgave me for not going to her sooner." She looked at him then. "I need to find that box. It has some things in it from that time in my life."

Crap. That didn't rule out his spent casing's theory. Despite that, Nico repeated his assurance. "I'll help you look for it."

That would mean going through every inch of the cabin, Rayelle's car and the yard. He'd have to cancel his evening with Eden and then come up with something to tell her that didn't violate the vow of secrecy he'd taken with Rayelle. Maybe when he did see Eden, he could just jump right into sex with her and he could pleasure her enough that she would forget any questions he had.

Maybe pigs would fly, too.

Nico stood to send that text, but he stopped when he considered something else. "Do you want me to help you find out anything about the child you gave up for adoption? You know, maybe a computer search or something?"

"No." Rayelle didn't hesitate over that. "She would hate me, I'm sure of it. I gave her up. She'll think I didn't want her." A hoarse sob tore from her mouth, causing Nico to sit back down and pull her into his arms.

Since there was nothing else he could do, he just held her.

"God, I wanted my baby," Rayelle continued, "but my mother wouldn't hear of it. She called me a slut and said I would bear the mark of sin forever. She said I wouldn't be fit to raise a child so I signed the adoption papers."

Nico didn't bother stopping the curse words he muttered. Rayelle and Brenda's folks had passed a few years before Nico had been placed with Brenda so he'd never met them. Good thing, too, because he'd had enough mess in his life without adding a judgmental biddy like their mom. Rayelle had obviously taken on plenty of that judgment, and it explained a lot about how she acted the way she did. She was hurt, broken and still dealing with those shithead remarks.

Rayelle wiped her tears again, eased back from him, and he could see that she was trying to steel herself up. He hoped she wasn't doing that for him. Nico didn't relish the sight of a woman crying, but

he thought it was a good thing that Rayelle was letting out some of this pent-up emotion.

"We need to find that box," she insisted, her voice
a little stronger now.

Nico got up to get the search started. Rayelle did,
too, but her phone dinged with a text. She blinked
hard, trying to read it. Obviously, her eyes still
weren't clear so Nico had a look when she handed
him the phone. Rayelle's heavy sigh, then her groan
let him know that she had seen what was on the screen
after all.

A text from Rosy:

There might be a teeny problem. Jax showed up
when I was upstairs and Piper left with him on his
motorcycle. Hope that's okay.

No. It wasn't okay. Neither was the rest of what
Rosy said in her message.

Piper left her phone here, but Buck saw her leave,
and he said she was upset, crying, so I think you
should check on her as soon as you can.

CHAPTER FOURTEEN

EDEN GRINNED WHEN her phone dinged. *Finally.* Nico had to be texting to tell her to come over, and mercy, was she ready to do just that. Too bad she couldn't just arrive naked and jump him.

Her grin faded, though, when she read the message. It was from Nico all right, but it certainly wasn't an invitation for sex.

Piper went off with Jax. According to Rosy, Piper was upset and doesn't have her phone with her. Please check the diner on Main Street to see if she's there. I'm heading back to my place now in case that's where they went.

Oh God. This couldn't be good, and Eden wanted to kick herself. She'd known something was wrong with Piper and had even called the girl twice. But Piper had assured her that nothing was wrong.

Obviously, it was a lie.

And Eden should have pressed harder. She should have gotten to the bottom of this.

She seriously doubted that Piper would just run off with Jax even if they had reconciled, but heaven knew what kind of emotional turmoil the girl was going through. Maybe Piper had learned something bad from those lab tests that the doctor had run on her. Perhaps Piper had even contracted an STD. Eden prayed that wasn't the case, but something serious had to be wrong.

Eden grabbed her purse and keys to drive to the diner. It was only a short walk from her house, but she wanted her car in case she found the girl and needed to take her back to the cabin.

Where she'd face Rayelle's wrath.

Eden didn't have to know the circumstances that had caused Piper to do something like this, but she seriously doubted that Rayelle was going to accept any excuse. Even a good one.

When she got to the diner, she didn't see Jax's motorcycle, but maybe it was still in the shop. If so, he could have borrowed a vehicle, and there was a blue truck that she didn't recognize. She parked and went to the window so she could take a peek inside.

And there she was.

Jax and Piper were at the far booth in the corner, and they appeared to be having a very intense conversation. Eden felt the relief and the dread. She'd found Piper, and the girl was safe, but there was a bad storm brewing, giving her more concern about that whole possible STD thing.

She took out her phone to text Nico just as she heard someone call out her name. Someone that Eden definitely didn't want to see right now.

Her mother.

She turned to see her folks coming up the sidewalk straight toward her, and she guessed from her mother's creased forehead that she'd noticed Eden on her tiptoes, peeking in the diner window.

"Eden," her mother repeated, her tone very much a scolding.

Eden stepped away, hoping to put a quick end to this meeting, but since she doubted that'd be possible, she went ahead and fired off a text to Nico to tell him that she'd found Piper.

"You look nice," her father said, giving Eden a kiss on the cheek. "See, Louise, she's not with Nico like you thought she'd be."

So, apparently the gossip had gotten back to her mom. Also apparently, her mom didn't approve. Of course she didn't. Nico's profile wouldn't have appeared on Clean Guys R Us dating website.

"You want to have dinner with us?" her dad asked.

Eden shook her head but wasn't sure how much else to say. She definitely didn't want to get into the possible troubles of a teenage girl. "I'm waiting for someone. For Nico," she went ahead and added, since he'd almost certainly be there soon. Since her mom and dad would be eating at the diner, they would see him.

"Nico," her mom said as if he were some form of a persistent rash. "You know I believe he's a bad influence on you."

Eden normally let that sort of thing just roll off her back, but this time, her back went stiff. She was tired of hearing her mom and anyone else bash Nico. "Maybe I'm the bad influence on him."

Her mother huffed. "Don't be ridiculous. Your divorce wasn't your fault so there's no bad influence for you to be. Nico, on the other hand—"

"Is a kind, decent man who loves his family very much," Eden finished for her. "That was what you were going to say, wasn't it?" She kept her firm gaze on her mother, daring her to challenge that.

Her mom stayed quiet, maybe weighing her options about how to proceed. "Nico has had some challenges in life, and maybe that's why he doesn't always make the best decisions. But you're a good woman, Eden, and you deserve better."

Her mother had used the word *woman*, but Eden heard the subtext. She was the good-girl daughter, the one who'd never given them a moment's trouble. Not until the divorce, that is, and apparently they were putting the full blame for that on Damien. Eden didn't mind that—it was Damien's fault—but that "good-girl daughter" label was like a dozen albatrosses around her neck.

"I just don't want to see you end up with the wrong man again," her mom added, and this time her father matched Eden's sigh.

"Maybe we should just tell Eden how much we love her and then go on in and order dinner," her dad suggested. "They might run out of meat loaf if we don't hurry."

Her mom stayed put. "I don't want her good reputation tarnished, and that's what'll happen if she's not careful."

There it was again. That "good" word, which was taking on a "persistent rash" feeling. Along with the hanging albatrosses, that felt pretty icky. Plus, it was as plain as the unnaturally dyed green polyester in her mom's pants suit that the woman was gearing up for more Nico bashing.

"I write a blog giving sex advice," Eden blurted out, and she just kept on blurting. "It's popular and dirty. *Very* dirty at times. Now, that should give you a clearer picture of who I really am."

Her mother's mouth dropped open. So open that Eden was hoping a stray bug or two didn't go flying in there. Her father stared at her a moment, patted her arm.

"Well, okay then," he said, and he caught on to his wife's hand to start her moving. Her mom didn't make that easy for him. Her feet seemed like deadweight as her dad walked her—the way a cop would a cuffed criminal—toward the diner door.

Eden suspected that her mom would soon figure out how to rationalize away what she'd just heard. She would probably dismiss it as some kind of shock statement, meant to get back at her for the unwanted dating advice. That was okay because it might mean her mother would stop bringing up the subject. She might stop bashing Nico, too.

And speaking of Nico, he pulled into the parking lot and was out of his truck right after he braked to a stop.

"Rayelle's not far behind me and will be here soon," he warned Eden. "Where's Piper?"

She tipped her head to the diner. "Jax is with her."

Nico cursed and hurried to the door. "When Rayelle gets here, try to keep her outside. She's running a little emotional right now, and I'd rather not play out family drama in front of an audience. I'll have Piper come out here with us."

Good idea, though they'd still have an audience. Anyone inside the diner, including her folks, would try to get peeks at what was going on, but they'd have to strain their ears to hear the conversation. Well, they would if Rayelle didn't end up shouting. *Running a little emotional right now* definitely didn't seem like a good thing.

Eden didn't want to stand on her toes again to look inside so she just kept watch for any sign of Rayelle. The woman probably wouldn't speed despite this being a crisis. A crisis in Rayelle's mind anyway. It could be just a conversation that the two didn't want the woman to hear.

As expected, Rayelle's car soon appeared, and just as she went to the parking lot, Nico came out of the diner with Piper. Jax was right behind him.

"This isn't Piper's fault," Jax immediately said. "I convinced her to see me."

Eden didn't think it was her imagination that the boy looked a little shell-shocked, but then maybe Nico had threatened him or something.

"Don't be mad at Piper," Jax added when Rayelle came closer. "I just wanted to talk."

Yeah, some definite shell shock, and Piper was clearly feeling some of it, too. Not good. They both looked as if they'd been kicked when they were down, but Eden doubted that Rayelle was just going to let Piper get away with sneaking out again. If that was indeed what she'd done. Since Piper had been staying with Rosy, it was entirely possible that Rosy had given her permission. Maybe even a "that's nice" if Piper had brought up the subject of her seeing Jax.

"Have you finished talking?" Rayelle asked.

Stunned, all four of them turned to the woman. Her voice wasn't uptight, and she didn't look as if she'd just sat on a stick. In fact, her hair was a little mussed, and her eyes were red. Wow, maybe she'd been seriously concerned about Piper and not just pissed because the girl hadn't followed her strict rules.

"We've finished." Piper's voice and body language were uncertain.

"Good. Then, maybe we can go to the cabin?" Rayelle said, and it sounded like a suggestion. Not a demand. "Jax, do you have a way home?"

Obviously dumbfounded now, he nodded and motioned toward the truck in the parking lot.

"Good," Rayelle repeated. "Piper, I'll wait for you in the car to give you a moment to say goodbye to Jax."

Rayelle slunk away, and that's when Eden realized the woman hadn't made eye contact with any of them.

"Did you give her drugs or something?" Piper asked Nico.

Nico frowned. "No." He paused. "Just go easy on her tonight. She was, uh, very worried about you."

"Oh," Piper said, and that seemed to genuinely trouble her. And Jax, who was still volleying glances as if trying to figure out what was going on.

There were folks in the diner, including Eden's mother, who were trying to do the same thing. And Nico noticed.

"It's time to break up this little circus," he grumbled, "so that the monkeys will have to find something else to watch." He turned to Piper, kissed her cheek. "Call me."

Piper nodded. "I will tomorrow. I'm a little wrung out right now." She glanced at Rayelle, who was already seated in her car—and she wasn't peeking. The woman appeared to be riveted to the steering wheel. "You're sure you didn't drug her?"

Nico scrounged up a smile that Eden figured wasn't easy for him, and he kissed his sister again. He also aimed his index finger at Jax. "Don't do anything stupid," Nico snarled.

Jax looked well past the point of doing anything, much less something stupid, and while he was whispering a goodbye to Piper, Nico and Eden strolled in the direction of his truck.

"If I ride with you to your place and leave my car here, it'll give the gossips something to talk about other than Piper and Rayelle," Eden suggested.

This time it didn't seem as if he had to scrounge too hard to manage that smile, and he hooked his arms around her neck, brushing a kiss on her mouth.

Well. That fired up her still-simmering libido, and that would indeed be some fodder for the gossips.

"Are you okay?" she asked him.

Nico met her gaze a moment as they got into his truck. He nodded. "Long night already, and it's barely 6:00 p.m. How about you?"

"Long night already," she agreed. She waited for him to say more, but when he didn't, she added. "I told my parents about the blog."

That snapped him out of the hazy mood. "You what? Why?"

She lifted her shoulder as he started the drive toward his house. "Secrets. They're just so soul-sucking. They're my parents, and I thought I should be honest with them. Of course, it'll still be a secret because you can bet my mom will never tell anyone."

"That's true," Nico said, and even though it was just two little words, she heard the fatigue in his voice. Could also see it in his eyes.

And that meant Eden needed to offer him an out.

"If you want, you can take me back to get my car, and you can go home and get some rest," she said. "Or we could even go over to the cabin so you can talk to Piper."

"Piper's right. Tonight's not a good time for a long conversation. Best to let things settle for Rayelle and her, and I can talk to them both tomorrow."

He seemed adamant about that, though Eden wasn't sure why. Rayelle had seemed docile, which could mean this was the perfect time for a brouhaha. If that's what was going to happen.

"Did you get any sense from Piper as to why it was so important that she see Jax tonight?" Eden asked, and she thought of those darn lab tests.

"She loves him," Nico said without even a pause. "She wants him back."

Well, that was pretty definitive, especially considering that Nico had only had a couple of minutes at most to talk to Piper and Jax, but this could account for Piper's sullen mood. Falling in love was risky business, and there had to be trust issues for her since Jax had broken up with her before. Maybe she was worried about guarding her heart. Since Eden had recently had that debate with herself, she understood.

But in her case, it was a debate Eden had lost.

Yes, she would likely get burned playing with the fire that was Nico, but she was going for it anyway.

"Jax says he loves her, too," Nico went on a moment later. "So, I'm sure I can come up with a big brother lecture of the 'you're both too young, take it slow' variety, but the best thing I might be able to do is just buy them a huge box of condoms."

Eden couldn't come up with an argument for that especially since the teens had already had sex. "How old were you your first time?"

He grinned at her. "Fourteen, and if you tell Piper that, I'll hold you down and tickle you until you pee your pants."

"I'll take it to the grave." She smiled and made a cross over her heart. "Since we're fessing up, I was eighteen."

"I know." He paused, winced a little. "Damien let it slip."

Of course, he had. It had taken Damien years to go all the way with her so he would have gloated about it to his friend.

"And that's all the talk I intend to give your ex tonight," Nico added.

Good. Because she certainly didn't want thoughts of him having any part of this.

With his left hand draped over the steering wheel, he leaned across the seat and kissed her. Not on her mouth. His lips landed on her neck, and he slid his free hand over her thigh. He didn't come out and say, "I want you to stay," but he got his point across, and Eden liked very much the way he'd done it.

Volleying his attention between the road and her, Nico gave her neck a kiss that was actually a borderline lick, and his hand moved higher up her thigh, the movement bunching up her dress so that he was touching bare skin.

She liked the way he got that point across, too. They were going to get naked, and she was finally going to have real, honest to goodness sex with him.

Or not.

Eden became concerned about that when she heard Nico curse, and he moved his hand from her thigh. It took her a moment to get her eyes uncrossed and focused, but she saw the woman on his porch when Nico pulled up in front of his house. Even with the porch light on, it still took her a moment to figure out who it was.

Seeing the protest sign helped.

"What's Miss Liddy Jean doing here?" Eden asked.

That only brought on some more cursing from Nico. "Probably protesting. I haven't been in my office this week so I guess she brought her *cause* to my house."

Nico stopped his truck, and with the weariness back in his expression, he got out. "Miss Liddy Jean, I don't want to do this tonight," he spelled out for her. "Besides, are you even allowed to protest after being arrested?"

The woman made a *hmmp* sound. "That was police oppression."

"You hit my brother with a sign," Nico pointed out.

Liddy Jean gave an indignant shrug. "Purely an accident, and it won't stop me from doing what I feel is right." She turned to Eden. "Imagine how much more interesting Nico's charity rodeo ride would have been if he'd ridden a cow instead of a bull."

Well, he probably wouldn't have had nearly as many bruises. As his potential lover, Eden could see an advantage to that. Still, that argument wasn't going to win anyone but Liddy Jean over.

Nico unlocked his door. "Please go home," he told the woman. "It's getting late, and the mosquitoes are out." As if to prove that, he slapped at one that landed on his arm.

"Mosquitoes don't bother me. Besides, I came out here to do you a favor."

Nico raised an eyebrow and moved back so that

Eden could step inside the house. Liddy Jean reached down into her shirt and pulled out a small silver box.

"I found this in the parking lot at the diner earlier today," Liddy Jean explained. "I think it might have fallen out of that woman's purse. The uppity woman who's here in Coldwater for the summer."

"Rayelle," Nico provided.

"That's the one," Liddy Jean confirmed and added a nod. "I saw her at the diner around lunch time picking up a to-go order. Anyway, I didn't know how to get to the cabin where she's staying so I decided to bring it to you. You'll see that she gets it." The woman handed it to him. "I figure if it's important enough for her to carry around in her purse that she probably wants it back."

"Yes." And that's all Nico said.

Eden was surprised that Nico seemed to know what it was, but he didn't open it. He just stared at it.

"Well, my good deed's done," Liddy Jean announced, picking up her sign again. "I'll be out in front of your office Monday. See you then." She used her sign to wave goodbye and headed to her powder blue VW bug that was parked next to Nico's house.

"What is that box?" Eden finally asked when Nico didn't say anything.

He took his time answering. "Rayelle's secret."

Well, that got Eden's interest. "What kind of secret?"

He shook his head, and when he looked at her, he seemed sorry about something. "I promised her I wouldn't tell anyone, but I need to get this back to her. It's important. Just go in and wait for me. I won't be long."

Before Eden could even get out a "huh?" Nico brushed a quick kiss on her mouth and hurried to his truck.

CHAPTER FIFTEEN

NICO FIGURED THAT Eden was going to have plenty of questions when he finished this errand, but unless he got some kind of signal from Rayelle that it was okay for Eden to know, he wouldn't be spilling the woman's secret. But maybe now that she'd told him, Rayelle could see her way to telling others. It couldn't be good for her to keep her feelings bottled up like that.

And there had to be feelings.

No way would she have kept this box if there hadn't been. And it made him wonder how Rayelle had been before she'd had a baby. Before her parents had labeled her a slut and her life had changed forever—not for the good, either.

Maybe that was part of the resentment Rayelle seemed to have for him. He had essentially gotten away with sleeping around. Yeah, there'd been plenty of judgments from folks, but he'd never had to deal with what she'd gone through.

The moment he pulled his truck in front of the cabin, he saw Rayelle look out the window. He saw her frown, too, and she was probably thinking—what now? But he knew that expression would change when she learned the reason he was there.

He got out, motioning for her to come outside. The cabin was small, and no matter what room Piper happened to be in, she would likely hear anything they said. Would almost certainly want to know the reason for the visit, too, but Nico was going to leave it to Rayelle to explain it any way she saw fit.

"We're fine," Rayelle said in a soft whisper when she came out on the porch. "You didn't need to check on us."

Nico nodded and handed her the box, watching the instant change in her body language. She made a strangled sound of relief, clutching the box in both of her hands. Since she looked as if all the bones in her body had turned to liquid, Nico took hold of her arm to steady her.

"You found it." The relief also washed through Rayelle's voice.

"No. Liddy Jean Carswell did. She found it in the parking lot at the diner and thinks it might have fallen out of your purse."

There went the relief. Any trace of it. And despite the dim light on the porch, Nico managed to see the color drain from Rayelle's face. "Did she look inside it? Does she know?"

Nico had to shake his head to both of those questions. "She didn't say, and I didn't ask." But now he wished he had. "Is there something in the box that could…get you in trouble?"

Rayelle blinked as if confused. "I don't want anyone to know."

All right, that wasn't much of an answer and didn't

help rid him of the notion that Rayelle might have committed some kind of crime with the proof of it being in that box. Since pussyfooting around wasn't getting him anywhere, Nico went with the direct approach.

"Did you do something bad to the father of your baby? Is that what you're hiding in that box?"

No blink this time, but Rayelle's eyes widened. "No." She dragged in a quick breath and repeated her denial. "I haven't seen him since he told me he didn't want anything to do with me. As far as I know he's still married."

Now it was Nico's turn to feel some relief. He gave Rayelle's arm a pat, figuring this would be the end of it, but then Rayelle took the lid off the box and held it out so that he could see what was inside.

Definitely not a bullet.

It was one of those little plastic bracelets that hospitals put on newborns. Nico didn't read what was on it, but he had no doubts that this belonged to the baby Rayelle had given up for adoption. Beneath it was what appeared to be a small piece of folded muslin cloth.

"One of the nurses saved these for me," Rayelle said. She touched the cloth. "This is the knit hat they put on the baby's head."

Nico couldn't imagine how heartbreaking that had been for Rayelle. Hell, it still was, and even though they'd never been close, he still pulled her into his arms for a long hug.

"If there's anything I can do, just ask," he whispered to her. "And if you want me to look at adoption registries or such—"

"No." She pulled away from him, closed the lid on the box and squared her shoulders.

Despite her eyes that were shiny with tears, she was back to the old Rayelle again. Or rather she was trying to be. And Nico wasn't going to fault her for that. Maybe it was that shield that got her through this.

Even though he doubted she would care much for it, he brushed a kiss on her cheek and was about to turn and leave when he saw Piper come into the doorway. Despite it not being late, she was already in her pj's.

Rayelle's back was to the girl so she couldn't have seen the woman's expression, but she must have sensed something was wrong. Of course, she did. After all, Nico was there.

"Is everything okay?" Piper asked.

"Yes," Rayelle jumped to answer. "Nico was just checking to make sure we got home all right."

Nico went with that lie and nodded. He kissed Piper's cheek, too, when she stepped into the doorway. "You're sure?" Piper pressed, and she sounded worried.

"I'm sure," Nico told her. "I'll call you tomorrow. Get some rest."

Though he wondered if rest would even be possible for Rayelle. If he'd thought there was any way he could talk her into counseling, he'd push for it.

For now, he just said his goodbyes and headed for his truck.

On the drive back, he thought of what he should tell Eden about all of this. She might be thinking the worst, that things had bottomed out between Rayelle and Piper. And that box would have definitely piqued her interest. Heck, he should probably just spill everything to her and swear her to secrecy since it was hard to keep anything from her.

Well, most things anyway.

He'd kept her idiot husband's secret of cheating on her, but Nico had only done that to spare Eden's feelings. And now that Damien and she were over, there was no need for her to know about that ultimatum he'd given Damien.

Except it hadn't actually been an ultimatum.

Nico had told him to end the affair with Mimi or else, but he hadn't spelled out the "or else." Nor would there have likely been one since Nico wouldn't have ratted out the man to Eden. Still, it had been enough to spur Damien to action. Instead of ending things with Mimi though, he'd ended his marriage instead.

No. It was best that Eden didn't know all of that.

Nico arrived back at his house, and he dragged in a long breath that he was certain he would need to face Eden and her questions. Of course, she was right there, waiting for him in the entry.

"Are Rayelle and Piper all right?" she immediately asked.

He nodded, tried to find his words, but that became very difficult to do once he looked at her. Yes, she was worried as he had known she would be, but for him to see the worry, he also had to see her face.

And what a face it was.

Despite everything he'd just gone through with Piper and Rayelle, Nico remembered the other thoughts that had stayed with him all day. Thoughts of being with Eden and having her here with him, and just like that, some of the weariness vanished. In its place came an overly healthy dose of lust.

"Want to talk about the box?" Eden added, moving toward him.

Nico shook his head.

She stopped in front of him, waiting, but then she cursed when her phone rang. "My mother," she grumbled. "Again."

When she let the call go to voice mail Nico saw the multiple missed calls, all from her mom. Since they filled up the entire screen, Nico understood Eden's grumble.

"Maybe you should go ahead and call her back," he suggested. "I'll get us some beer."

He could see Eden debating whether or not to do that, and she cursed when her phone rang yet again. She jabbed the answer button as if she'd picked a fight with it.

"Mom, I told you that I didn't want to talk tonight," Eden snapped.

Nico went to the fridge, opened two beers and went back into the living room, where Eden was now pacing.

"Yes, I told you the truth. I do write that blog." She groaned. "You didn't have to look it up or read it."

Obviously, this wasn't going to be a pleasant conversation. Or one that Eden would likely want to prolong. However, at the mention of the blog, Nico did think of something else. That surprise hand job on the phone. He wasn't sure how Eden was going to react to something like that, but it couldn't hurt. This would be like hand-job foreplay.

Nico set the beer bottles aside and went to her. He snagged her by the waist just as she paced in front of him, and he snapped her to him so that her back landed against his chest. She glanced at him, her eyebrow raised, but he decided to soothe away any doubts she might have with a kiss to her neck.

And by lifting her dress and sliding his hand over the front of her panties.

They were white lace and barely there. Perfect for this sort of thing because there was so little fabric between them.

Her breath caught, and even though he could hear her mother chattering on the other end of the line, Eden reached behind her, caught on to his hair and pulled him even closer. She made a not-so-soft moan, but her mother clearly hadn't picked up on her daughter's change in tone because she just kept going with the lecture. Nico caught a word or two and even a sentence.

Naughty. Dirty. For Pete's sake, why'd you do this?

Eden just ignored the question and savored his touch. Nico could tell she was enjoying it not only because of the moans but because Eden was moving her butt against the front of his jeans. Since he was already rock hard, his dick very much appreciated that little maneuver.

It occurred to him that this wasn't ideal circumstances to carry through on a hand job, but he was suddenly starved for Eden. Of course, that appetite for her had been building for days now, and it had gotten to the point where he ached to have her. Nico doubted that was a good thing.

Doubted, too, that he should escalate this, but that's exactly what he did anyway. It helped some with his own clawing need when he ran his hand down into that lace and slipped his fingers into some incredible wet heat.

This time Eden gasped. "Gotta go, Mom. I'll call you tomorrow."

Her words rushed out at lightning speed, and the split second they were out of her mouth, Eden hit End Call and tossed her phone onto the sofa. She whirled around to face him, but she did that without untangling her hand from his hair and while his fingers were still inside her. What with her jockeying for position, and she didn't even get to start reciting the states before her climax started. He felt her tight muscles clamp around his fingers.

"Damn it," she muttered, sounding pleasured and pissed at the same time. "You were supposed to have something other than your fingers in me when that happened."

Yeah, that had been his plan, too, but for now,

Nico just kept his arm around her so that she didn't slide to the floor.

It took her several seconds to recover, to come out of that warm-honey state and regain some focus. And she regained it with a very specific goal in mind.

"Get your clothes off now," Eden said, and she went after his mouth with a hungry kiss.

THERE WAS NO way Eden intended to let this evening end with more hand jobs or oral sex. Not that those things weren't good. They were, especially coming from Nico, but she wanted more.

"The bedroom," she managed to say, despite the French-kissing that was going on. It wasn't just their hands that were battling to get closer and deeper. Their tongues were in on the quest, too.

She didn't mind having sex with him in the living room or anywhere else for that matter, but if they were in bed, the logistics alone would increase the chance that Nico and she might finally have orgasms together. Or rather as close together as her "condition" would allow. To give them a good shot at that actually happening, Eden intended to name as many states as possible, until she reached the brink of insanity.

They started in the direction of his bedroom. Arms and legs tangled. Breaths gusting. But multitasking slowed them down considerably. They were still kissing, and he kept giving her butt a squeeze in between trying to get her dress off. She wasn't faring much better with his T-shirt.

Nico finally paused in the hall that led to his bedroom, reached behind him, grabbing on to the back of his own shirt and dragging it off over his head. He sent it flying. Then, he did the same to her dress, and the walking, tangling, groping and kissing started again.

They still weren't naked, but this was much better. His bare chest was against hers, and she could feel him even through the lace. Bare skin to bare skin. And with her dress out of the way, it made it easier for him to locate the front clasp of her bra. He flicked it open, and her breasts spilled out into his waiting hands.

All in all, that was an amazing place for her breasts to be.

Nico made it even more amazing by flicking his thumbs over her nipples and then lowering his head to tongue each one. That slowed them down on the trek to the bedroom, but it was so worth it, and it caused a whole new fire to flare inside her.

After a few seconds, they picked up the pace, stepping and sidestepping down the hall, and Eden saw stars when her shoulder rammed into the doorjamb. But Nico had a cure for her pain. He mumbled an "I'm sorry," caught on to her hips and ground the front of her panties against the front of his jeans. Specifically, against his erection. And, oh my, that was nice. So nice that it upped the urgency and got them moving again.

Eden pulled Nico's mouth back up to hers so she could kiss him and not bop him in the face when she went after his belt. Of course, this was a rodeo buckle the size of a cabbage so it took her some fumbling to get it open and unzip him.

And finally she gave him some payback.

She slid her hand into his jeans. Into his boxer briefs. Where she clamped her fingers around him.

Oh yeah. His equipment would suit her just fine.

The clamping served another purpose, too. It got Nico moving fast, along with gutting out some grunts of pleasure.

Since Eden was the one who was walking backward, she didn't actually see the bed, but when she felt it against her calves, she dropped back, dragging Nico down with her. Of course, she ended up kissing him again because after all, his mouth was right there, but Eden didn't give up her quest to get him naked. In fact, she quit playing around in his boxers just so she could push his jeans off his hips.

His partial nudity must have reminded Nico that he was after bare-butt nakedness, too, because he got off the bed, and in the same motion, he stripped off first his boots, then his jeans. Then, those black boxer briefs.

If Eden hadn't already been hotter than fire, seeing him like that would have done it for her. He was perfect. Tall, lanky and lean. A cowboy's body with strong arms and a tight stomach. The tat didn't hurt, either, and it was a surprise. A virile-looking bull on his right pec. Like the rest of him, it qualified in the hot-as-all-get-out category, but it was the first time she'd seen it. Then again, it'd been years since she'd seen him without his shirt.

Eden reached out to touch him but immediately got thwarted when Nico did some reaching of his own to rid her of her panties. He was clearly better at doing this than she was, but then she was distracted by all the gawking. Eden just drank him all in while he grabbed a condom from his nightstand, rolled it on and got back on the bed with her.

Except he didn't just get on the bed.

After all, this was Nico, and he had the whole finesse thing going on. Finesse and scalding heat because he kissed her again—right between her legs. And he used his tongue. Lots of times. In just the right spot.

Maybe he thought he had to get her ready for what was about to happen. Perhaps stoking the flames. But she was already stoked, and Eden let him know that by catching on to his hair and pulling him back up to her.

It worked.

Oh my. How it worked. She could feel him all hot and hard between her legs. Could also already feel another orgasm chasing her down.

"Alabama," she said but then lost her breath, possibly her sanity, when he plunged into her.

She couldn't speak, but mercy, she could feel. Every nerve in her body was getting in on this, and she could feel every inch of herself—and every inch of him. So many inches to feel.

"Alaska," she finally managed.

But it was a lost cause. After Nico pushed into her exactly twice, Eden had no idea what planet she was on much less if that planet had states with names. Still, she thought he hurled her to some distant, brilliant star when her climax burst into a giant supernova thing.

She didn't even try to tell him how amazing it felt, the vising of her muscles against the long, hard length of him. Eden just held on and let the pleasure crash through her. She got so caught up in it that it took a moment to realize Nico had quit moving.

Grinning, he was looking down at her. "You're a bonus, you know that?"

"Huh?" she managed, and it was somewhat of a miracle that she could at least say that.

"You're sort of the gift that keeps on giving." Still grinning, he kissed her. "I like that. A lot."

Surprisingly, at the moment, she liked it a lot, too. Except for the blatantly obvious thing that was wrong here. "You didn't take your turn," she pointed out, glancing down between them where they were still joined. Though she hadn't needed to look to know that he was still rock hard.

"I'll get there. I can wait for you if you think you can cum again in the near future. *Very* near future," he added when an aftershock of her climax gave him a squeeze. He made another of those grunts and seemed to be steeling himself.

"I've had two already," she pointed out. "Go for it and let me watch you."

He gave her that smile that was so winning that Eden was surprised it didn't have its own rodeo buckle collection.

"I have a better idea." Nico said, moving his mouth right against her ear. "We'll both go for it and watch each other. I'm sure I make a weird face, and I'd rather you have that image of me somewhat fuzzy because you're making your own weird face."

Eden closed her eyes and smiled when he started nibbling her neck. "Great theory, but I don't think I have another orgasm in me right now."

"Sure you do," he coaxed. "Let's make this one dirty," he whispered in her ear.

Nico moved. That was all it took. One smooth, very effective lunge of his hips. He caught on to her leg, lifting it and then pushing it to the side, opening her up even more. And just like that, Eden realized she was wrong.

There was another orgasm in her.

One that was already getting stoked by the long thrusts that he started making inside her. And as for the "dirty," well, he took care of that, too. He put her fingers in his mouth, wetting them and then moved her hand between them. To her own breasts.

"Touch yourself," he whispered. "I want to watch."

Eden was already so worked up that she would have agreed to shock treatment, and it felt surprisingly good to slide her wet fingers over her nipples. As promised, he watched. And smiled. Before he pulled out and went down on her.

"Keep touching," he insisted.

She did, but he was touching, too. And kissing. And using his breath in a very amazing way.

"Alabama—"

She didn't get further than that before he quit trying to tongue her into ecstasy, and he gave her a different kind of ecstasy instead. He kissed his way up her body, redamping her fingers with his mouth.

"Now, touch here," he instructed, moving her hand between her legs. "Here," he said, sliding her fingers over the most sensitive part of her body. "You stay there because this is my spot." He raked his thumb below her fingers.

Apparently, Eden hadn't been adventurous enough because she'd never done this, and the surprise of what he wanted likely would at least have given her a moment's pause. But Nico didn't give her a chance for that to happen. He pulled her to the edge of the bed, her back slipping and sliding against the comforter, and he thrust right back into her.

All the inches of him at once.

In that spot he'd already claimed.

That eliminated the surprise and the doubt, and Eden found herself touching. Of course, Nico had much better equipment for that than she did. Simply put, his stroke-thing was a lot bigger than hers. Still the two worked in tandem. Her fingers wet from his mouth and his hard erection pumping in and out of her.

"Screw the states," she muttered. "I don't want to say them. I'm ready," she warned him.

But somehow Nico already knew that. Maybe because she was making that weird face. Or maybe because he was just a champion at this, too. Either way, it didn't matter. Eden let go, letting her third orgasm knock the breath right out of her.

And thankfully it was enough.

Because with a dirty grin on his mouth, Nico gave her one last dirty thrust and came right along with her.

CHAPTER SIXTEEN

WHEN SHE TOLD Nico what she'd come to say, he was going to hate her. Rayelle was sure of it. Still, that wasn't going to stop her.

Nico had to know the rest of the truth.

He had to know all the mistakes she'd made. And then he could do something about it. It was possible he would order her to leave Coldwater and never see Piper and him again. It was also possible he wouldn't keep her mistakes and shame private. But if that happened, it would be what she deserved.

Rayelle pulled her car into the parking lot just up from Nico's office and looked around not only at the building but also Main Street. His truck was there, which meant he was inside. Still, she sat there, waiting for nothing more than just to remind herself—again— that she needed to do this. And she had decided she should talk to him here and not risk going to his house.

She didn't like listening to gossip and hearing the ugly things that seemed to excite people who wanted to savor it like bites of well-prepared party food. But it was impossible to miss the fact that many people believed Nico and Eden were having an affair. Rayelle had seen the connection between them. The hungry heat in their eyes. So it was best not to go there to his house and interrupt whatever they were doing.

No need to make this more uncomfortable than it already was.

If Rayelle did see Eden and him together in a post-sex visit, Nico might feel the need to explain why he wasn't a bad influence on Piper. Of course, he might also just tell her that what he did was none of her business, that she had no right to judge him or anyone else after what she'd done.

And he would be correct.

If she'd ever had a right to judge anyone, she had lost that when she'd gotten pregnant and then allowed herself to be pressured into giving up the baby for adoption. However, that weakness was proof that she would have been a lousy parent. A good mother needed backbone. Still did. And that's why she was here.

She couldn't be the one to raise Piper. The facade couldn't continue. She doubted Nico would argue with her about that since it was blatantly obvious that she was doing such a bad job at taking over from Brenda.

It was starting to rain, but Rayelle didn't bother with the umbrella. She hurried out of her car and inside. She remembered Brenda telling her that the building had once been some kind of retail shop, and Nico's brother, Callen, had bought it and converted it to office space.

The conversion had been well-done. The bottom floor featured a reception area as well as Callen's office. His office door was closed, and the reception desk was empty. That was good as far as Rayelle was concerned. She didn't especially want to see anyone other than Nico. Not with her eyes red from crying and with her nerves likely showing.

She made her way up the stairs, and since she'd been there once before, she knew where Nico's office was. Her stomach tightened, though, when she saw that it was empty. She immediately looked across the hall, and her gaze practically collided with his hulking assistant when he stepped into the doorway.

"Ma'am," he greeted.

"Mr. Hannigan," she greeted back, though there was no warmth in her voice, and she didn't look directly at him because she didn't want him to see her red eyes.

"Hog," he automatically corrected. "Or you can call me Wally."

"Wally," she selected, even though she could understand how he'd gotten the nickname. His unfortunate physical features probably had gotten him teased a lot, and considering her mood, that made her feel more sympathetic toward him than she normally would have.

"Nico's across the street," Wally told her. "He had an early meeting with Roy, the lawyer, and then he was going to stop by Eden's, but he should be back soon. You want to wait in his office and I'll get you a cup of coffee or tea?"

"Thank you. Tea would be nice," she said, walking into Nico's office.

"I've got Earl Grey or a nice herbal blend of peaches and mint that I picked up at a shop in San Antonio. Which would you like?"

It was such a surprise to hear him talk of teas that Rayelle looked back at him. He smiled. That was a surprise, too, because it softened his features.

"The herbal," Rayelle told him and she added another, "thank you."

Wally went to a small room next to his office. It had perhaps once been a storage closet, but it was now a small kitchenette area, and he started the tea.

Rayelle was too on edge to sit so she looked at all the pictures that Nico had in his office. Pictures of him and his brothers. Of Brenda.

And Piper.

In the photo, Nico had his arm slung casually around the girl, and they were laughing at something, a moment the person behind the camera had obviously managed to capture. A happy moment—something that Piper hadn't had many of since Rayelle had taken over her care. In fact, Piper had been miserable. Even an idiot could see that, and it cut away at Rayelle.

God, what had she done?

She'd taken this beautiful, amazing girl and made her unhappy and broken. That's why this charade had to stop.

The tears threatened again, and Rayelle was trying to blink them back when Wally came in with her tea. "Here you go," he said, placing the cup in her hands. Hands that she hoped he didn't notice were trembling.

He had his own cup, and while he sipped it, he looked at the photo that she'd been studying.

"That girl can light up the whole Texas night sky," Wally remarked.

It was a kind remark, said with genuine affection, and it caused the tears to fill her eyes again. Because it was true. Piper did have that light, and Rayelle had caused it to dim considerably. If the girl continued to stay with her…

Rayelle couldn't even finish that thought. Nor could she stop the hoarse sob that tore from her mouth.

"Oh God," she muttered. "Oh God."

"There now," Wally consoled. He set his tea on the desk, did the same to Rayelle's and then he gently took hold of her shoulders to turn him toward her.

Since the tears were spilling now, she didn't want him to see that. But she didn't have the energy to move away from him, either, so she did the unthinkable. Rayelle buried her face against his chest.

His arms came around her. A gentle hug. One that she wanted to resist because she didn't deserve it, but she stayed there, letting him hold her and stroke her hair.

"Shhh," he whispered. "It'll be okay."

Despite the tornado of emotions going on in her head and heart, it surprised her to notice just how soft his voice could be. How comforting. Wally definitely didn't look like a man who was capable of holding her as if she were something fragile and precious. But he was wrong about one thing.

It wasn't going to be okay.

She wasn't sure how long they stood there, and Wally certainly didn't rush her. He just kept up those gentle murmurings and the hair strokes.

When she finally eased away from him, Wally immediately produced a pristine white handkerchief from his pocket. She made use of it and didn't miss the fresh scent and the fact that it'd been ironed. The man was certainly a surprise.

But he was also now privy to her breakdown.

She didn't owe him an explanation, she reminded herself. No matter how kind he'd been to her. And despite her knowing that, Rayelle was surprised when she said anything to him. Especially something so personal.

"Have you ever done something that you're deeply ashamed of?" she asked.

"Yes," he answered without hesitation, causing her to look up at him. "When I was a teenager, a punk," he amended, "I was drinking and got behind the wheel of a car with some friends. I wrecked it and one of them was hurt bad enough that he's never fully recovered."

Stunned, Rayelle pulled back her shoulders. She certainly hadn't expected this near stranger to share that. Nor had she wanted to know it. Still, it was hard to ignore that he'd just confessed something very private, very painful, and he'd done that simply because she'd asked.

She wouldn't be sharing that much with him, but she almost wished she could. The burden of her secret was so heavy that it felt as if someone had gripped a meaty fist around her heart and was squeezing the life out of her.

"It took me a long time before I could talk about that to anyone," Wally went on. "An even longer time before I could forgive myself."

"But you did forgive yourself?" she quickly asked.

He nodded and looked at her—not in an examining kind of way as if he'd just put her under a microscope. There was sympathy in his eyes. No, wait. It was empathy. He seemed to believe that he knew what she was going through. Heck, maybe he did, but Rayelle knew she couldn't say her secret aloud.

Not just to Wally but to Nico.

It'd been a mistake coming here. She had to leave and come up with a different way to do this. A better way to tell Nico the truth. Then, once he knew, he would understand something.

That she was the coldhearted bitch people believed she was.

Nico would know about the lie she'd been living. He'd see that there was no way she could continue to pretend to raise Piper. And then Piper would know, too. Because Nico would tell her the very thing that Rayelle had tried to keep hidden all these years.

That she was Piper's biological mother.

EDEN HAD MADE it all the way to Florida before Nico had felt her climax quiver and quake to bring him to his own release. Of course, he'd given her a hand job prior to them landing in her bed so he'd expected it to take her a little while to build back up to the point of finding her second wave. He definitely wasn't seeing her quick draw as a problem. Just the opposite. He could take his time with her and watch her go over and over and over. That added plenty more pleasure for him, too.

"That was amazing," she said, her voice all dreamy and slack.

Actually, the slack and dreamy applied to the rest of her as well since she had collapsed against him after riding him hard—just the way he preferred his rides.

"It's been way too long since I've had a morning quickie," she added. Her face was pressed to the crook of his neck, and he could feel the words as she mumbled them against his skin. It was nice. The calm after the sex storm.

"Then, we'll have to make sure there are a lot more of them," he said.

Because there weren't many of her muscles that weren't touching him in some way, he had no trouble feeling Eden when she went a little stiff. And he immediately knew why. That was not the comment of a guy whose relationships had a shorter shelf life than fresh bread.

Nico considered giving her some kind of assurance that even if the sex ended, their friendship wouldn't, but that was possibly bullshit. Of course, their friendship would be affected. You didn't just forget dirty sex, especially when so many of their conversations dealt with answers to her blog. So, if the sex ended, well… He wasn't ready to go there just yet. That's why Nico made a stupid ploy to distract both himself and Eden.

He located her mouth and kissed her. Long, deep and hopefully hot enough to give her temporary memory loss about what he'd said just moments earlier.

She responded, too. Eden made that purring sound in her throat, and since they were still joined, he felt her internal muscles stir again. Coming to life, and considering how fast she could do that, it meant he needed to take a quick trip to the bathroom to deal with the condom.

He hurried, but then hurried even more when he checked the time. He'd told Hog that he wouldn't be gone long, only about an hour or so, but it had been nearly two hours. First, because the contracts he'd brought to Roy had taken longer to deal with than expected, and then because of getting Eden all the way to Delaware and then a follow-up trip to Florida.

Nico grinned, thinking of that, and wondering if once she made it through all fifty states she could start doing the capitals. Now his grin faded. Best not to mention that because it sounded more long-term than even a string of morning quickies.

He went back into her bedroom and saw her naked, the covers coiled and wrapped around her so that it seemed like some kind of well-placed striptease outfit. His dick reacted, urging him to go for another quickie, but it was going to have to wait. Nico located his boxers and jeans, and he went to her, kissing the frown that was already starting to form on her mouth.

"You have to go?" she asked. Definitely not a purr, more like a protest.

Nico nodded. "And so do you. It's nearly nine, and you'll need to be at work soon. In fact, you're going to be a little late."

Something Eden obviously realized because she scurried off the bed, gathering up her clothes and giving him an incredible view. "Shoot," she grumbled. "Roy has an important client coming in at nine, and he wanted me there to take notes."

Yes, she wouldn't want to rile her boss or the client, but Nico wondered if she knew how hot she was running around naked like that. Probably not. But he put the mental picture of her in his head, something that would ensure he had the makings of a hard-on for the rest of the day.

"I saw you naked once, years ago," he said when he pulled on his boxers.

She'd been in the process of wrangling her very nice breasts into a sensible-looking cotton bra, but she stopped and looked at him. "When you went skinny-dipping with Shelby down at the creek," he added.

Eden's eyes widened, but she continued to dress. "You mean when we were like sixteen?"

"That sounds right. I'd just finished a swim myself when I heard you two."

"And you watched?" she asked.

He shrugged. "Actually, I was doing then what I'm doing now. Putting my clothes back on, but I admit, I peeked a little."

"Perv," she said, but there was no anger or protest.

Just the opposite. As if it'd been a year or two since she'd last had him, she walked closer and skimmed her finger down his still-bare chest. A quick one, since she was obviously still in the hurry mode.

And, oh, it had an effect on him. A bad one. He immediately considered shirking any and all responsibilities so he could get back on that bed with her—and lick her in all the good places.

The sound of the doorbell put that plan on hold, though.

"Crap, that's probably my mother," Eden snarled, reminding Nico that she had that particular issue on her plate. "I really don't have time for this."

Now that her folks knew about the blog, they were probably trying to talk her out of continuing it, and it was a reminder that Nico should ask Eden if she wanted to vent about that to him. There hadn't exactly been a lot of long meaningful talks between them since they'd discovered how nicely their parts fit together.

With the doorbell still ringing, she put on her boots as if she'd declared war on them, and Nico was so concerned with her mood that he was afraid she would end up saying something she'd regret. Not that she shouldn't tell her parents to knock it off, but it was better for Eden to do that with a cooler head.

Nico finished dressing, too, and even though he'd hurried, Eden still made it out of the bedroom ahead of him. He managed one last burst of speed to get to the door ahead of her, and he blocked her from opening it. At their feet, Miss Kitty obviously wasn't happy about any of this because the cat actually bothered to get up from his usual sleeping place by the window and was hissing.

"Take a deep breath," Nico advised Eden. "Recite the states. By the time you get to Minnesota, the timing might be better."

Clearly though, her visitor thought the timing should be faster, because in addition to the constant ringing, there was now a heavy-handed knock. That didn't please Eden, either, so Nico opened the door to see if he could work some magic and calm things down a bit.

He came face-to-face with Damien.

His first thought was that he actually wished it'd been Eden's parents because they might be more clueless about what had just gone on between Eden and him. But Damien took it all in, with a long sweeping glance where he no doubt noticed their disheveled clothes, their messed-up hair. Possibly even the stubble burns on Eden's neck from where Nico had given her some of those tongue kisses she liked.

If the situation hadn't been so damn awkward, it would have been comical to watch as the truth started to dawn on Damien. First, his creased forehead from the confusion. Then, the widening eyes when the confusion wasn't so confusing. And finally, his mouth dropped open.

"What the hell's going on here?" Damien snarled a few moments later. His voice was loud enough to cause Miss Kitty to hiss again, and instead of running to Damien as he usually did, the cat turned tail and went into the bedroom.

"Well?" Damien demanded. "What's happening?"

Eden rolled her eyes and huffed. "None of your beeswax," she snarled right back. "Go home to your fiancée. I don't have time to deal with your pissy mood this morning. I'm late for work."

Without even waiting around to see what Damien's response would be, Eden took her purse from the coffee table, dropped a kiss on Nico's mouth and practically elbowed Damien out of the way and then out of the house and back onto the porch.

Once Nico stepped onto the porch, too, she shut the door, and she headed straight for her car and drove off. Fast.

Just like that, she was gone, leaving Nico and Damien there to stare at each other. Obviously, Eden hadn't thought they'd have a fight, but Nico wasn't ruling that out. Damien looked awfully pissed. That in turn pissed off Nico because, after all, Damien had been the one to leave Eden, and he had no say in what was going on in her life now.

"You fucked her?" Damien demanded.

Oh, that didn't help Nico saddle his anger. "None of your beeswax," Nico repeated. "If Eden wants to tell you anything, she will."

Obviously, that was not an answer that Damien wanted to hear. For a moment, Nico thought Damien might indeed try to punch him. He cursed, and he didn't whisper, either. He was loud enough to be drawing the attention of the neighbors. That meant it wouldn't be long before there was more talk about Eden and him, but now Damien would be added to the tasty gossip mix.

"I'm running late for work, too," Nico informed him. "So, if all you're going to do is stand there and curse, I'm leaving. Once you've calmed down, we can talk." He started down the steps.

"The divorce was a mistake," Damien said.

That stopped Nico. So did Damien's voice. Definitely not the same tone he'd used for all that cursing. Nope. There was a silent groan at the end of that hoarsely spoken comment.

"I want Eden back," Damien added when Nico turned around to face him.

"I'm pretty sure it's a little late for that." Hell, Nico hoped it was anyway. If he'd thought there'd be a mess once Eden and he stopped having sex, it would be a mess times a million if Damien came back into the picture.

A mess that put a hard knot in Nico's gut.

He didn't want to lose Eden, especially not to this dickhead who'd let her go in the first place.

"You're engaged to Mimi," Nico reminded him.

Damien nodded and scrubbed his hand over his face. "But I want to end that and get back together with Eden."

That brought back more than a tad of Nico's anger. "If you really wanted to get back with her, you would have ended things with Mimi first." And he braced himself for Damien to argue that with some bullshit answer.

But Damien only nodded again. "You're right. I'll break things off with her this morning." He paused and stared down at the porch. "I won't be able to get Eden back, will I? I've lost her."

It sure looked that way to Nico, and he was hoping that wasn't all wishful thinking on his part. "Like I said, you'd have to talk to Eden about that." He started to walk away, but like before, Damien stopped him with a question.

"Will you help me get Eden back?" Damien asked.

Nico turned and looked him straight in the eyes. "No way in hell." He didn't even have to think about that, and this time, Nico did leave.

"You'll just break her heart," Damien called out to him.

Yeah, he probably would, and Nico felt the weight of that plow into him like a mean rodeo bull. For a day that had started off darn well, it was sure going downhill fast.

Nico was a good halfway back to his office when his phone rang, and he snatched it from his pocket, figuring it was Eden. It wasn't.

It was Rayelle.

He was so not in the mood to speak to her right now, but considering what she had told him, he had no choice. She could be having another meltdown over the secret she carried in that silver box.

"Rayelle," he greeted when he took the call. "Is everything okay?"

"No," she immediately answered. "It's Piper. She's

crying and locked herself in her room. Nico, you need to come right away. I think she might have found out."

"Found out what?" he asked.

He heard it then. Rayelle was crying. "About what I have in that box. Please come, Nico."

CHAPTER SEVENTEEN

EDEN WAS READY to toss her phone in the trash when it dinged because she figured this had to be from Damien. She had no idea what was so important for him to show up at her house, and she didn't want to know, either. She just wanted him to slink back to his jealous fiancée and stay out of her life.

Her fuming anger vanished though when Eden saw Piper's text on the screen.

Could you please come to the cabin? It's important. I need to see you right away.

Eden got a dose of instant guilt. She'd sensed something was wrong with the girl, and she hadn't pushed hard enough to get to the bottom of it. Well, she was going to push now. Probably push at Rayelle, too, if the woman was adding to anything related to whatever was happening to Piper.

Eden texted back:

I'll be there soon.

Even though she'd just arrived—and late at that—Eden stuck her head in Roy's office. The client wasn't there yet, but Roy was on his computer, no doubt getting ready for him.

"I hate to ask," she said, "but is there any chance you can do the meeting without me? I'm so sorry, but something personal has come up," she added, and hoped that would suffice as an explanation.

Roy studied her a long moment as if he might press for info, but he finally nodded. That was enough to get Eden moving. She hurried to her car and drove off in the direction of the cabin.

Of course, the worst-case scenarios came, and she thought about Piper having an STD. Maybe one that had some medical complications. If that was it, there was no way the girl would want to tell Rayelle. Or Nico. So, it was possible that Piper would need Eden to take her back to the doctor in San Antonio. And she would do that. Even though they didn't have an appointment, they could just go to the doctor's office and wait to be seen.

When Eden pulled into the driveway in front of the cabin, she saw someone she definitely hadn't expected to see. Nico. He was getting out of his truck, and he glanced back at her, a puzzled look on his face.

Puzzled with no visible bruises.

That meant Damien and he hadn't duked it out after she'd left them. Not that she thought that would happen. Things had probably gotten heated between them, but Nico wouldn't have thrown a punch unless he'd gotten to a breaking point that she'd never seen him reach. She, on the other hand, might have lost it and punched Damien right in his cheating, slimeball face, and while that would have felt good, it would have only made things worse.

Damien and she no longer shared a life, but they did occasionally share the same town, and for the sake of their families, she should at least try not to have a public brawl with him. Hopefully, he would stop pestering her. She was tired of his and Mimi's visits and just wanted them to leave her alone.

For now, Eden pushed all that aside so she could try and help Piper with whatever was going on.

"Piper texted me," Eden explained to Nico when she got out of her car. "She texted you, too?"

He shook his head. "Rayelle called."

Oh. So, this was really bad, and Eden was about to ask how they should handle this when her phone dinged again. It was another text from Piper:

Come to my bedroom. Just you. I want to talk to you before I see Nico.

That was more proof of the STD theory. It would be a lot easier to talk about it with another female than with a brother or foster mother.

She showed Nico the message. He growled out some profanity, but he didn't stop her when she went into the cabin. Neither did Rayelle. In fact, the woman was sitting on the sofa and looked as if she'd been crying. Great. Maybe Nico could soothe whatever was wrong with Rayelle while she was with Piper.

Eden tapped on Piper's door, and she immediately heard the snick of the lock. The moment it opened,

Piper took her arm, pulling her inside. Piper closed the door, relocked it and turned to face Eden.

"I'm pregnant," Piper whispered.

She'd said it so softly that at first Eden thought she had misheard her, but judging from the girl's terrified expression, she hadn't. However, Eden did consider that Piper was just wrong about this.

"You got your period," Eden reminded her. But then she skidded to a mental halt. "Did Jax and you have sex again? Is that why you think you're pregnant?"

Piper gave a heavy sigh. "No, we didn't have sex again, and I don't think I'm pregnant. I *know* I am." With another of those sighs, Piper walked across the room and sank down onto the foot of her bed.

Eden joined her there, sitting next to her and putting her arm around the girl. Since she had no idea what to say to her, she just waited for Piper to continue. It took a while, and during those long moments, Piper wiped away tears that slid down her cheeks.

"My period was just some spotting," she explained. "I told the doctor that, and she did a pregnancy test. She called to tell me it was positive. I'm definitely pregnant."

Eden tried not to gasp or make any other sounds of shock. Or dread. Piper definitely didn't need that. But this explained Piper's somber mood for the past couple of days, and again Eden wanted to kick herself for not coming to her sooner. This had to have been hell for Piper.

And it was going to be an even deeper level of hell for Rayelle.

Eden decided not to mention anything about that.

"The doctor said I needed to make an appointment," Piper went on. "That I needed a physical, and we could discuss my options." Piper's voice didn't just crack. It shattered. So did she, and she sagged against Eden when she started to sob. "Oh God. Eden, what am I going to do?"

Oh boy. This was beyond Eden's skill set. Way beyond. So, she took her time, holding Piper and letting her cry it out for several more minutes.

"What do you want to do?" Eden finally asked her. Sadly, that was the best she could come up with.

"I want to dig a big hole and hide in it," Piper answered. "I don't want to face Aunt Rayelle or Nico."

Eden definitely understood that. She might be thirty years old, but she still remembered what it was like to be a teenager.

"Does Jax know?" Eden added, going at this from a different angle.

Piper nodded. "I told him, and do you know what the idiot did?" She didn't wait for Eden to respond. "He asked me to marry him."

Since she'd thought Piper had been about to say that Jax had dumped her again, Eden felt huge relief over that. And she felt some confusion.

"Why did his marriage proposal piss you off?" Eden wanted to know because it was obvious that's what it had done.

"Because we're too young," Piper blurted out.

"We're in high school, and we both need to finish. We don't need to be trying to make a marriage work. The divorce rate is sky-high for teenagers."

That sounded, well, sensible. So, Piper had ruled out saying I do. "How does Jax feel about all of this?" Eden pressed.

Piper dragged in a long breath before she answered. "He was upset when I first told him. He was worried about how his parents would take the news, too. Plus, there's that whole embarrassing thing that now they'll know we've had sex. People will look at us and know."

In the grand scheme of things, that last part didn't seem like such a huge deal, but she knew where Piper was coming from. Eden was dealing with some of that with Nico. The gossips had likely figured out that Nico and she were having sex and were probably hashing out possible details. Still, Nico and she were adults and could handle it. Piper might not be able to do that.

Piper gave her tears another swipe, lifted her head from Eden's shoulder and looked her straight in the eyes. "I have to tell Nico and Aunt Rayelle."

"No way around it," Eden agreed.

No matter what Piper decided to do about this, they had to know. And once they got past the shock, maybe they'd be able to give Piper something she desperately needed right now.

Emotional support.

Then, Eden might be able to talk Nico out of going to see Jax. Nico was way too protective of his kid sis-

ter for him to be having a showdown with the boy
who'd knocked her up.

"Will you go out there with me?" Piper asked.
"Will you tell them?"

"Of course," Eden readily agreed, and even though
she knew she wasn't dreading this as much as Piper
was, there was still plenty of dread.

"Thank you." Piper stayed quiet a moment, but she
did get to her feet. "Once they know, I should be able
to explain everything to them."

One could hope, but Eden might have to muzzle
Rayelle for that to happen. She couldn't see Rayelle
staying quiet about something like this.

Eden grabbed a tissue from the nightstand and had
Piper wipe her eyes and face. Once she'd done that,
Eden put her arm around her again to get her moving to the door. Eden didn't want to delay even a few
seconds to give Piper more time to think about what
she'd be facing out there. Best to get this done fast,
like ripping off a bandage.

It surprised Eden when Piper opened the door and
walked out ahead of her. Both Nico and Rayelle were
there, of course. Waiting. And both looked a little
shell-shocked as if bracing for the worst.

Good.

Because they might see this as *the worst*.

Piper walked closer to them, and she took hold of
Nico's hand. "I'm pregnant," she said.

Well, Piper had definitely done the fast-bandage
move, but she apparently wasn't finished. The girl

glanced at Rayelle before fixing her attention back on Nico.

"And I'm keeping the baby and will raise him or her," Piper added. "Since I'm sure Aunt Rayelle won't approve of that, I want to move in with you, Nico."

NICO FIGURED "OH, SHIT" probably wasn't the most articulate response, but it was all he could manage. Apparently, Rayelle couldn't even manage that because she just stared at Piper. Her eyes were wide, her mouth was slightly open.

Ditto for Eden.

Eden's reaction made him wonder exactly what had gone on in the discussion Piper had had with her in the bedroom because Eden seemed as surprised by this as Rayelle and he were. So, maybe Piper had just done some crying on Eden's shoulder but hadn't spilled this quadruple whammy of bombshells.

Pregnant.

Keeping the baby.

Raising it.

Moving in with him.

"Uh, I thought that was a false alarm," Nico added a moment later, and then he winced because now he'd just confessed to Rayelle that he'd known about Piper's possible pregnancy-related issues.

"I thought so, too," Piper admitted. Even if her hair had been on fire, she couldn't have looked more uncomfortable. "But the doctor ran a test at the clinic and it came back positive. Jax knows," she quickly added.

There were several more revelations in that explanation, not just for him but for Rayelle. Who still hadn't said a word. He didn't think the woman's continued silence was a good thing, either.

"Jax asked me to marry him," Piper continued. "But I said no because we're too young."

Nico nearly pointed out that if she was too young to get married, the same logic applied to her raising a baby, but this didn't seem like the right time to state the obvious. Piper was barely holding it together, and her red eyes told him that her "holding it together" had been a very recent occurrence. This had obviously been tearing her apart for a while now.

But hell almighty, it was doing the same to him.

"And no, I don't want you to beat up Jax," Piper added almost in a whisper. "He didn't force me to have sex. I wanted to be with him like that. And FYI, we did use protection." She paused and tacked on the rest in a barely audible mumble, "I guess something went wrong with the condom."

He had indeed been thinking about having a little *chat* with Jax, one that would have a bite of anger in it. However, her remark cooled Nico down a little.

Yeah, he knew what it was like to be with someone "like that" since it'd been less than a half hour since he'd gotten out of bed with Eden. Of course, the difference was that Eden and he were adults. Still, if you had sex—even protected sex—you ran the risk of making a baby. As Piper and Jax had learned the hard way.

"I'm almost seventeen," Piper went on when no

one else said anything. "I've already checked, and I can take the rest of my classes online so I can graduate. That'll free me up to get a part-time job so I can save some money and eventually get my own place, but in the meantime, I'd need to stay with you."

Nico definitely hadn't missed that part. Hadn't missed immediately thinking how that would change both their lives. Of course, their lives had already changed, but Nico just hadn't been aware of it until a couple of minutes ago.

"Jax already has a part-time job," Piper continued, "but he's going to work more hours so he can pay me child support. I might even be able to live here once Aunt Rayelle goes back to San Antonio."

Wow, she'd thought all of this out. And had likely done all the thinking, planning and, yes, worrying without him even knowing anything was wrong.

"I see," Rayelle finally said.

The woman's voice certainly didn't have the tone of a show of support. That was probably why Eden jumped right in.

"I can help," Eden offered, sliding her arm around Piper. "I'll talk to Roy and see if he can use more help at the law office. I'd wanted to put in fewer hours there anyway to focus on...other things."

Eden meant the blog, and while she had indeed talked about reducing her hours for Roy, she'd never seriously considered it because then she would have had to explain to everyone how she was earning a living.

"I see," Rayelle repeated, and she cleared her throat.

Nico knew this had to be a kick in the teeth to Rayelle, along with reminding her that she'd once been in the same position as Piper. Well, nearly the same position anyway. Rayelle's mother had strong-armed her into giving up the baby, but Piper wanted to keep hers.

Nico wouldn't be doing any strong-arming.

Even though he was still reeling from everything he'd just heard, he went to Piper and pulled her into his arms. He made sure he put as much love in that hug as he could manage. Later, he could gnash his teeth and vent about this situation she was in, but he vowed then and there that Piper wouldn't see any gnashing or venting from him. Well, not about this anyway.

"I'll help you," he promised Piper.

He could actually feel Piper's body relax. Her muscles that had been so hard and stiff went soft, and the breath she blew out was one of relief. No doubt about that.

"Thank you," Piper whispered. "And thank you," she added to Eden. Piper pulled her into the hug, too, making it a group one.

Minus Rayelle.

Nico figured while this might be comforting to Piper, they weren't going to be able to exclude the woman for long, and he was right.

"We need to talk," Rayelle insisted, looking at Piper. "There are some things that need to be spelled out."

Nico made eye contact with her, hoping to give her a silent reminder not to cast any stones here. He wouldn't reveal Rayelle's secret. He'd seen how hard that had been on her. But he wasn't going to let her verbally bash Piper now, either.

"I have custody of Piper," Rayelle reminded them. "I'm legally her foster parent, and she's a minor."

The hug posture stayed in place, but Piper, Eden and he turned and angled so they could see Rayelle. This time, Nico gave the woman a glare because her reminder felt a little like drawing a line in the sand. It must have felt that way to Piper, too, because her muscles stiffened again.

"And?" Nico prompted when Rayelle didn't continue.

"And I believe Piper will be better off with me. In our home in San Antonio," she added. "This is a small town, and there'll be a lot of talk about a pregnant teenager."

"There'll also be talk in a city," Nico pointed out.

Rayelle nodded. "But it won't be something Piper will have to hear every minute of every day. She'll be judged harshly here."

Nico wanted to argue with that, but there was some truth to it. Of course, he could squelch some of the judging. Well, public judging anyway, but he wouldn't be able to stop the gossip. He wouldn't be able to protect Piper from that.

"I think it's best if Piper and I leave and go home. Right away," Rayelle emphasized.

Piper stayed put. "I'm not giving up my baby."

Rayelle nodded again. "Understood. You can have the baby, finish school and continue to live at home. No rent, no expenses. And this way, you'll be able to see Jax more often."

Until she said that last part, Nico could practically feel the argument building inside Piper. But Rayelle's offer might be too tempting for her to pass up.

Piper's silence dragged on. Nico stayed quiet, too, but that's because he was trying to gauge how Rayelle was truly doing. He didn't want this to be the calm before the storm. And he didn't think it was. Maybe it wasn't just wishful thinking on his part and that the woman was truly offering Piper the kind of support that Rayelle herself hadn't gotten.

Was that it?

If so, Nico would have been thankful except for one thing. He didn't want his sister to go.

Hell. When had that happened? Just a few weeks ago, he had thought he couldn't wait for summer to be over so he could get out from beneath Rayelle's scrutinizing eyes. Away from being a bad influence on Piper, too.

But now...

"You can stay here with me if you want," Nico told Piper. "I can try to work out the whole foster thing."

New tears watered Piper's eyes, and he wasn't smart enough to figure out what they meant, but he hoped she was happy. Eden certainly was. She gave him a reassuring smile.

However, there was nothing reassuring about the look Rayelle gave him. "Honestly, I doubt you'll be able to convince Child Protective Services to allow you to foster, and it won't be a speedy process. In the meantime, I'm going to insist that Piper come back to San Antonio with me. Pack your things, Piper," Rayelle added to the girl. "We're leaving now."

CHAPTER EIGHTEEN

EDEN HAD NEVER been a "misery loves company" kind of person, and she wasn't about to start now. But Piper's dilemma helped Eden put her own troubles in perspective.

Yes, her folks were giving her grief about the blog and seeing Nico, but at least she was an adult and could handle the hassles. Piper was just a teenager. A pregnant one, who didn't have control over her own life. Case in point—Piper had gone back to San Antonio with Rayelle.

Eden seriously doubted that Piper wanted to be under Rayelle's roof, but the girl might have wanted to stave off a big battle between Nico and Rayelle. And that might still come since Nico hadn't seemed pleased about Piper caving in. In fact, he was in San Antonio now, not just to make sure Piper was truly okay but also to try to work out the best possible arrangements for the girl.

She figured Rayelle wasn't going to make that easy for him.

But then Eden frowned and rethought that. Rayelle certainly hadn't been judgmental and mean after hearing the pregnancy news that had surely rocked her tidy little world. However, she had been resolute, confident even that Piper's staying with her was for the best.

Whether Piper remained in San Antonio or not, it would be better all around if Nico, Rayelle and Piper could work out a solution that gave them some peace of mind—Jax, too. Because whether or not Nico and Rayelle liked it, the boy had a big part in this and could possibly end up helping Piper raise their baby.

Eden hadn't been anywhere near ready to be a parent at that age. Piper and Jax probably weren't, either, but if Eden had a say in this, she would make sure they got a lot of help. She believed Nico felt the same way, and he'd feel that even stronger once he got past the initial gut-punch of learning that his kid sister was going to be a mom. Nico would do whatever it took for Piper because that's the kind of good guy that he was.

She smiled at that thought and tried to go back to focusing on the blog. It was a losing battle. She'd had her laptop open and in front of her for over an hour now. Had reread the blog post at least a dozen times. And she still had nada. No advice whatsoever to Horny in Houston, who was asking advice about what to include in a home sex tape she wanted to make for her "sweet-cheeks cowboy."

Nico would almost certainly be able to come up with something. Plenty of something, considering how good he was at sex. But she couldn't bother him. No way would he want to think about sex, but Eden was hoping that once he came back from San Antonio that he'd be stopping by her place. Even though she'd had him in her bed that morning, she wanted him again.

And again.

All right. So maybe she could answer the blog after all. She could just think of things—sex games—that she'd like to play with Nico. Actually, there were a lot of things she could think of when it came to Nico, and she frowned again when she admitted that not all of it would involve getting naked with him.

Miss Kitty sprang to life from his sprawl on the window, and when he went trouncing toward the door, Eden suspected she was going to add another hassle to her already hassle-filled day.

And she was right.

When she opened the door, Damien was standing there.

"Don't close the door in my face," he said when she started to do just that. "Please," he added. "Just give me five minutes." He tacked on another *please*, and he scooped up the cat into his arms. Miss Kitty snuggled against him as if he owned every kibble factory in the state.

Eden didn't feel as if she owed Damien one minute, much less five, but she didn't want him going to her parents. Something he'd already done. According to her mom, Damien had called her three times already today, and he'd made it clear that he wanted to get back together. That had caused her mother to hope way too much, and it hadn't completely dashed that hope when Eden had assured her mom that Damien and she weren't getting back together.

"Five minutes," Eden said, "and when you're done, you'll leave me, my family and Nico alone." She hadn't had proof that Damien had actually called

Nico, but when Damien dodged her gaze, she suspected he had done exactly that.

"I ended things with Mimi," Damien blurted out the moment he was inside.

No more gaze dodging. He stared at her as if he expected her to leap for joy. The only leaping Eden would do was if she saw Nico drive up in front of her house.

"I want you back," Damien added, and his tone led her to believe that he actually thought that was something that could happen.

Eden sighed and scrubbed her hand over her face. How had she ever put up with this man? Better yet, how had she ever lived without Nico's kisses? She didn't have answers to either of those, but she did have something to tell Damien.

"No."

She'd thought that by keeping her response simple and direct, that there wouldn't be any confusion. But she wasn't that lucky.

"You can't mean that," Damien insisted.

"But I do," she insisted right back. "I have no intention of getting back together."

"But you love me," he snapped.

"No," she repeated, "and I haven't loved you for a very long time." Since she considered that an end to the conversation, she took the cat and used her free hand to take hold of Damien's arm to "help" him back out the door.

Damien held his ground. "Are you saying this because of Nico?" He toned that question down a little, but there was a big spark of anger in his eyes.

Since she doubted Damien was going to pick up on any subtleties or half answers, she went with the truth. "Yes. I'm falling in love with Nico."

Clearly, that had not been what he'd expected her to say, but Eden realized it was the honest to goodness truth. It would have made her life so much easier if she could just blow it off as good sex, but nope, she couldn't do that. She was falling for her best friend and a first-class womanizer.

Damien just stood there, mouth gaping, and his eyes fixed in a blank stare. It took him several moments of his rapidly passing five minutes to regain the capacity for human speech.

"Falling in love with Nico?" he said, but it didn't actually seem to be a question rather than a questioning of her sanity. He even repeated it—three times—before he finally moved off the broken record observation and went on to something else. "Sheez Louise, Eden, that's a stupid thing to do. You know how he is."

Yes, she did, but she didn't think Damien was talking about how great Nico was in the sack. She seriously doubted that Damien wanted her to give him a laundry list of Nico's other assets so she just stayed quiet, which only seemed to frustrate Damien even more. Of course, maybe her smug smile added to that frustration, too.

"You can't trust him," Damien said as if it were gospel.

"Oh? And why not?" She made her smile even smugger because she doubted Damien could come up with anything.

But Damien didn't seem to have any trouble doing that. "I'll bet Nico hasn't even told you the truth."

No way was she going to drop her smile on just that vague accusation. "The truth about what?" She let go of his arm to tap her mouth in a fake yawn.

The yawn probably wasn't a good idea because it set off a new round of fire sparks in Damien's eyes. Now he got a smug look. "Nico knew I was seeing Mimi when you and I were still married. He knew the whole time, and I'm betting he didn't say a word about it to you."

That caused her smile to vanish, and she shook her head, ready to check and see if Damien's pants were on fire from that lie he'd just told.

But it wasn't a lie.

She could see that past the depths of those eye sparks.

"Think about that before you fall all the way in love with him," Damien went on. "He knew and didn't tell you. He's not perfect, Eden. Nico's a dick just like the rest of us guys."

And with that summary, Damien turned and stormed off.

RAYELLE HEARD THE soft knock at the door and tried to steel herself up. It was probably Nico, returning to try to convince her to bring Piper back to Coldwater. She understood his argument. He loved his sister and wanted to be with her. But Rayelle knew the cruelty of a small town when it came to scandal, and she didn't want Piper to go through what she'd gone through.

It had crushed her.

Besides, she couldn't have Piper leave. She just couldn't. Having Piper there didn't give her the happy family home that Rayelle had once dreamed of, but it was the next-best thing. Her daughter was with her, and even though she couldn't tell Piper the truth, Rayelle didn't want to lose this time with her.

She was surprised when she opened the door and didn't see Nico or Jax standing there. It was Wally. He tipped his cowboy hat before he slipped it off his head and held it almost like a salute over his heart.

"Do you have time to talk?" he asked.

She had plenty of time, especially since Piper wasn't exactly in conversation mode. Rayelle had tried to discuss things with her, but she hadn't gotten anything more than monosyllabic responses on the drive to San Antonio. Once in the house, Piper had gone straight to her room. Rayelle figured she was angry with her for demanding that they leave Coldwater, but maybe Piper would soon see that it was for the best.

It was that "maybe she would soon see" that was troubling Rayelle, and it was likely the reason she stepped back to allow Wally to come inside. Heaven knew she needed to talk to someone, and while Nico's assistant probably wasn't the best candidate for that, he was here. Not only did he know she'd given up a child for adoption, he'd been kind to her. That hadn't especially been a consideration in recent years, but it seemed to be now.

She led him into the small living room that was

still decorated with Brenda's things. What was missing was her sister's casual, haphazard disorder. Books and photos that had once been placed willy-nilly were now aligned. Ditto for the rug that no longer lay at an awkward angle. Rayelle had fixed all of that after she'd moved in with Piper.

"Would you like something to drink?" she asked, remembering her manners.

"No, thanks." He didn't sit until she motioned for him to take a seat on the sofa. "I just wanted to check and see how you were doing. Are you okay?"

She wasn't sure how much Nico had told him, but obviously he knew some portion of what had happened or else he wouldn't be here.

"I'm fine," she said, surprised when her voice cracked. She wasn't sure why she couldn't keep her emotions in check around this funny-looking man.

This nice *man*, Rayelle mentally amended.

"Actually, I'm not fine," she added. "Piper is hardly speaking to me, and Nico is angry. They think I did the wrong thing by insisting Piper come back here." She paused and sat down directly across from him. "But you know what happened to me. I don't want people talking about Piper like that."

He nodded as if he totally understood. Maybe he did. After all, there'd probably been talk and gossip after that accident where his friend had been hurt.

"What does Piper want?" he asked, and there wasn't a hint of judgment or admonishment in his voice.

Rayelle had to swallow hard before she answered.

"She wants to live in Coldwater so she can be near Nico." And darn it, the blasted tears threatened again. "If that happens, I'll lose her. She doesn't like me, and there'll be no reason for her even to want to see me."

Wally calmly lifted one of his bulky shoulders. "I think you could be wrong about that, but even if you're right, there's a fix for this. You could all live in Coldwater. That way, she gets to be near Nico, and you get to be with her."

That sounded so simple. So scary, too, because Rayelle wasn't sure she could keep this secret locked away much longer. It was burning a hole in her, and how much hotter and bigger would that get when she saw her own daughter following in her footsteps?

Pregnant and unmarried.

Of course, Rayelle had been older than Piper. An adult. And yet she'd still caved to pressure. Unlike Piper. As soon as Nico could get custody of her, Piper would leave. She would carry this baby and keep it. She would do everything that Rayelle had failed to do, and if Piper learned the truth, that would make the girl hate her even more.

"Piper's your daughter, isn't she?" Wally said, his voice as soft as a whisper.

Stunned, Rayelle pulled back her shoulders and shook her head. It was on the tip of her tongue to deny it, to lie, but she saw that wouldn't do any good.

"How did you know?" Rayelle asked.

Another lift of his shoulder. "I can see you in her."

Well, other than Rayelle, he was the only one.

Nico certainly hadn't and neither had any of Brenda's friends.

"Did you ask your sister to foster Piper?" he added.

Rayelle nodded. "I'd kept tabs on Piper. *Tabs,*" she repeated with some disgust. "I spied on her, to make sure she was okay. Things were going well until her adoptive parents were killed in a car accident. They didn't have any family willing to take her so she was going into the system. I told Brenda the truth, and since she was already a foster mother at the time, I talked her into taking Piper."

She steeled herself up for him to ask why she hadn't taken the girl herself. Rayelle had been twenty-five then. She'd already finished college and had a decent job. But to take her and to stake a claim on her would have meant coming clean. She hadn't been ready to do that.

She still wasn't.

"Maybe you should consider what Nico and Piper want," he said. "I mean, Piper and you could go back to the cabin for these last few weeks of the summer. That'll give everyone a chance to think things through."

"But the gossip—"

"There's nothing you can do to stop that. People with small minds talk. I figure it's a way of spicing up their own boring lives. But talk will die down, and soon folks will go on to something else. Maybe like Nico and Eden, for instance."

Yes, something was brewing between those two, and Rayelle wasn't sure it was all good. Well, not all good for Eden anyway. She didn't have Nico's history of hopping from one relationship to the other. Even though Eden and she weren't close, Rayelle could feel for her. After all, Rayelle knew what it was to have a man stop wanting you.

Setting his hat beside him, Wally leaned closer, narrowing the already-short distance between them. He reached out and gently took hold of her hands. The gesture surprised her, and she nearly pulled back. Nearly. But then she saw the warm smile in his eyes.

"Just talk to Piper," he suggested. "I think it'll do everybody some good. Even me. Nico can get downright moody when things are unsettled with him. He'll definitely see this as unsettled."

Yes, he would. And it was. Because as much as Rayelle wanted to hang on to Piper, to keep her close, she knew that couldn't happen. Not unless Rayelle changed the course of the path she'd put herself on. Strange that it would take hearing that from Wally to make it sink in.

"Thank you," she told him.

He nodded, smiled and stood. When she stood, too, he brushed a kiss on her cheek. "One day soon I'd like to take you for tea."

She returned the smile because one day soon, she just might let him do that.

Rayelle led Wally to the door, thanking him again and telling him goodbye before she locked up and went back into the living room. She stared at the rug a moment.

"Screw this," she muttered, and she stooped down,

caught on to the rug and gave it a hard yank, turning it at that same awkward angle that it'd been when Brenda had been alive.

With that done, she headed straight to Piper's room. She knocked but didn't wait for an invitation to invite her in since such an invitation might not happen.

Piper was on her bed, using her laptop, but she immediately looked up at Rayelle. Rayelle saw her go on the defensive, preparing herself for a battle.

"So, let's talk," Rayelle said, and she made sure that didn't sound like an order. "Just how are we going to deal with all of this?"

CHAPTER NINETEEN

NICO DIDN'T KICK anything when he walked into his house, but he considered it. Of course, with the way his day had gone, he could just end up breaking a toe or something. Instead, he got himself a beer and dropped down on the sofa to try to figure out if there was a bright light or even a tunnel in this.

Nope.

He couldn't see it.

His pregnant sister was an hour away in San Antonio. Not far, but she was basically being held there—legally—against her will. He had no doubts that he could wrangle custody away from Rayelle, but that wasn't going to happen tonight. Nope, that fun journey would start first thing in the morning in Roy's office, where he'd begin the paperwork that Rayelle would likely fight every step of the way.

He wasn't sure why Rayelle was being so stubborn about this. He got that whole small town gossip thing, but this was where Piper wanted to be. That was saying something considering her baby's father was in San Antonio. Piper would rather be away from Jax than be under Rayelle's roof. Nico couldn't blame her for that, either, but that left him with a massive problem.

How was he going to handle a pregnant teenager living with him?

He'd manage, of course. No way around it. But it would mean a whole lifestyle change. There certainly wouldn't be impromptu rounds of dirty sex at any hour of the night or day. He'd have to limit the sex, dirty or otherwise, to the bedroom and behind closed doors.

Of course, thinking about sex brought Eden to mind. Considering she'd been part of this hellish day, she might not be having romantic thoughts, but he wanted to call her. Not only so he could hear her voice, but also so he could give her an update on Piper.

Which really wasn't an update at all since she was still with Rayelle.

Still, Nico thought it might soothe his raw nerves just to talk to Eden. If he got lucky, she might even need help with a blog post that he could use to distract himself.

He had a long pull on his beer, then took out his phone, but before he could even make that call to her, he heard the vehicle pull up in front of his house. Dreading a visitor, he went to the window and smiled when he saw that it was the only visitor he wanted and the woman that was hot and heavy on his mind.

Eden got out, but his smile went south when he saw her face. *Hell.* Something was wrong, and whatever it was, he could add it to the shit pile of other things that'd gone wrong today.

"I figured you'd be back by now so I drove by your office," Eden said, "but your truck wasn't there so I came here."

That one sentence told him loads. She was looking for him and whatever was wrong, it wasn't something she wanted to get into over the phone. Something that couldn't wait until morning.

Something that had put a very sour look on her face.

He doubted this was something as simple as indigestion. Nope. So, Nico just stepped back to let her in.

"Damien came to see me," she said as she breezed right past him. No kiss. No warm flirty smile.

Nico gave a weary sigh. "Let me guess. He broke up with Mimi, he loves you and he wants you back."

She nodded. Just nodded. And that caused everything inside him to go still. Damn. This could top his shit pile list.

"You're going back to him?" Nico asked.

Some of the sourness left her face, replaced by confusion. Then, what he could only interpret as disgust. "No. He's a cheating sack of dung."

The relief came, damn near an avalanche of it, because he completely agreed. Better yet, because she felt that way about her ex, it meant no reconciliation. But something was obviously still bothering her.

She huffed and glanced around the room a couple of times before her narrowed gaze settled on him.

"Did you know that Damien was cheating with Mimi when he was still married to me?"

Oh. That.

Yeah, this was going to stink and blow up in his face.

Nico nodded. No way would he lie to her, but man, oh man, he was dreading the consequences. "I knew about it," he admitted.

Eden made a sound of outrage and, groaning, she put her hands in her hair and pulled. Hard. Nico moved toward her, but she stopped the hair pulling long enough to motion for him to stay back. Then, she made a circling motion with her finger for him to continue.

He did. But first Nico took another deep breath. "I was at a bar in San Antonio one Saturday night when I saw Damien come in, and Mimi was with him. She was hanging all over him, and he wasn't doing anything to stop it, so I figured things had gone past the innocent flirting stage."

Eden didn't say a word, but he saw the hurt creep into her eyes. Hurt that made him want to hit his head with a rock. Despite the misery this was causing her, she obviously wanted to hear more because she made another of those circling motions with her finger.

"I didn't say anything to Damien about it that night, but I asked him to meet me the following day," he went on. "You were busy with the blog so I think he lied to you and said he was going in to get some work done. I told him it wasn't right what he was doing to you and that I wanted it to stop. I even gave him an *or else*."

He could see from her slightly raised eyebrow that he would need to clarify that. Too bad the clarification might just piss her off more than she already was.

"That's what I said to Damien," he went on. "To stop the affair or else. I didn't spell out the consequences, but I'm sure he believed I would go to you and tell you the truth."

"But you didn't," Eden quickly pointed out.

Nico shook his head. "Damien took the *or else* in a different direction. He went home, told you he wanted a divorce, and he left you."

He waited for Eden to groan or curse him, but she just stood there and stared at him. She didn't need for him to finish spelling this out for her, but Nico did anyway.

"It was my ultimatum that caused Damien to walk out on you," he said. "If I'd just stayed out of it, you two would probably still be together. He'd be living a lie, but you'd be together."

There. It was all out on the table now, and Eden might be angry enough with him to want to hit his head for him.

Eden groaned, took his beer from him and downed the rest of it. Even after she'd finished it, she looked as if she could use another one. Then, she began to pace, occasionally mumbling something that he couldn't catch. Occasionally shooting glances at him, as well. That went on for a couple of minutes before she stopped dead center in front of him.

"Exactly how mad are you at me?" he asked when she didn't say anything.

"That's to be determined. Why didn't you tell me about Damien's cheating either before or afterward?"

That wasn't a hard question to answer. "Because I knew it would hurt you, and I thought he'd come to his senses, stop dicking around and realize you're the best thing he'd ever had in his life."

Apparently, that took some wind out of her sails because her shoulders dropped, and her groan turned to a heavy sigh. "Then, no. I'm not mad at you."

The relief that he felt was fast, strong and so very welcome. Nico reached for her again, and this time Eden let him pull her into his arms. It was like opening the best of the best presents on Christmas Day.

He didn't push things by kissing her. Nico just stood there holding her. Not exactly holding his breath but close enough.

"How many other secrets of Damien's are you keeping?" she asked.

Nico didn't have to think too hard to come up with one. "He kissed that cheerleader, Sarah Beth Daniels, in high school. Frenched her beneath the bleachers, but that's as far as it went. Trust me, Damien would have told me if he'd managed to get in her pants."

Eden pulled back, met him eye to eye. "Anything else?"

"Three other incidents over the past two decades similar to Sarah Beth. I honestly don't know if sex happened, but Damien mentioned making out with them."

Damien had called them his candy on the side. Something Nico had no intention of telling Eden. She had enough details, enough truth without heaping on stuff that would make her want to neuter her ex.

"Okay," she said after a really long pause.

But Nico wasn't sure exactly what she was okaying. She just stood there as if trying to absorb that he'd been a dick of a friend by not telling her the truth about her dick of a husband.

"Okay," Eden repeated. She looked up at him and moved in closer until their bodies were touching. "You so owe me make-up sex. Nothing fancy. It can be fast and still edged with some of this anger and hurt I'm feeling."

Nico smiled. Then, he winced a little. He was probably going to lose his guy card for this, but he had to ask. "Are you sure you want to try sex to fix this?"

"Absolutely. Talking about this won't do anything other than piss me off. Damien screwed around on me, and nothing will go back and undo that. The only thing is for me to move forward."

Now his smile returned. "That's awfully adult of you."

She shrugged, ran her fingers into the small gap between his shirt buttons. "Not really. I don't love him and don't want him so it's easier to be an adult when you haven't lost something important."

Good. Not only because Damien was no longer the big gun in her life but also because she no longer seemed hurt. Or pissed off.

"*'I thought he'd come to his senses, stop dicking*

around and realize you're the best thing he'd ever had in his life,'" Eden said a moment later, and he quickly realized she was quoting him.

Yeah, he had said that all right. "I meant it," Nico confessed. "Damien was an idiot."

"He still is. He came to visit me when you were in San Antonio, and that's when he gave me the useless whine of wanting to get back together with me. How's Piper?" she asked before he could respond to that.

Because she was still playing with his chest, it took him a moment to shift gears. It took him a moment more because he wasn't sure of the answer. "I'm going to keep an eye on her and start the paperwork to foster her. It's possible she can have herself emancipated or something so we can cut through the red tape."

"If there's anything I can do to help, let me know."

Nico knew she meant it, too. She'd given him no dire warnings about him not being suitable or how this would upset his life. Just Eden's blanket offer to help. He wondered if she'd always been this nice and decided that she had been. Well, except for the times they'd gotten into friendly arguments over sushi and some of the women he'd dated.

Eden wasn't just nice. She was special. And because that realization made him tense a little too much, he kissed her. Nico touched his lips to hers and just lingered for a moment there. Sampling and savoring.

"I'm sorry about keeping Damien's secret from you," he told her. Not that he especially wanted to talk about her ex, but he did want to get that apology out in the open. For Nico, it was going to be a hard rule that he'd never break with her again.

"I know you are. Damien said because you'd kept it a secret, that I shouldn't trust you."

"What an asshole," Nico growled out before he could stop himself.

"No argument from me." She did some brushing of her lips against his, too. Then, she brushed her hips in the right area of his groin before she caught on to his chin, angling his eyes to meet hers. "I do trust you, you know."

That sent a nice hit of heat through him. And fear. Because it was true. She did trust him, and he had such a shitty track record when it came to not letting women down. In the past that hadn't mattered too much. Women hadn't expected much more of him than he'd expected of them. But again, this went back to that whole notion of her being special.

"Do you trust me enough to try sushi?" he asked, needing to add some levity to this. Best not to get that hard-on she was working on giving him while there was a tennis volley of thoughts and emotions going on in his head. Hard-ons should come with some focus to carry out the task they were designed to do.

"No," Eden quickly answered. "Do you trust me enough to cheer for the Cowboys?" she countered.

Easy answer. "Nope."

But he was mentally on the right track now, thanks to a follow-up kiss and his running his hand down the side of her leg. He pushed up her dress and slipped his hand into her panties.

"Just checking to make sure you don't need any touch-ups on your Brazilian. All good," he verified after he skimmed his finger over that smooth silky spot.

Since it felt amazing and since Eden's eyes rolled back in her head, Nico kept up the touching.

"What are you doing to me?" she muttered. Not a protest but rather a dreamy, sexy purr. Mercy, she was hot.

"I'm starting the make-up sex I owe you. I believe you said nothing fancy. Fast and edged with…stuff." Because he couldn't remember her exact words.

"Then get on with the fast part," she insisted, and Eden took his mouth with a whole new urgency that hadn't been there just seconds earlier.

That created an urgency for Nico, too. If Eden wanted fast, that worked. For the first hit of the evening anyway. But his hard-on assured him that he'd be up for the job. Of course, that part of him was often a brainless braggart.

The fight to get naked started. As usual, Eden went after his buckle, cursing because it was so hard to get off. Nico knew he should help her, but he first had to deal with his own appointed task. He pulled off her dress, flipped open her bra and sucked her nipple into his mouth.

He was smiling inside when that caused her to melt against him, and her buckle fumbling became a little unfocused and halfhearted. That's because Nico had distracted her, and the distraction kept up until the urgency part kicked in again. The need to squash the sex fire outweighed nipple kissing.

"Get out of this belt," she insisted.

He did. He unhooked it for her, but then went back to his own next task. Panty removal. His favorite. He slid the little swatch of silk down her legs and dipped down to test his mouth on the Brazilian. Eden didn't let him linger there long though, since she had started to pull and yank at the rest of his clothes. He could have staved her off awhile if she hadn't managed to do some of that pulling and yanking on his erection.

It was time for fast, full penetration, make-up sex.

Nico scooped her up and took her to his bedroom, practically dumping her on the mattress. Since time was the enemy now, he snagged a condom out of the nightstand drawer and rolled it on the moment Eden freed him from his boxers. Obviously, she didn't want to wait until he had his jeans off, and since this was her make-up sex, he would play by her rules.

He pushed into her and didn't feel what he'd expected to feel. She was hot, wet and tight—all of which he'd counted on—but she didn't fly into an instant orgasm. However, she was muttering off the states, and her forehead was creased with concentration. It was a nice balance to her carnal moans and her hands digging into his hips to make him go harder, deeper and faster. As hot as he was running, Nico had to launch into a mental show tune, as well.

Man, it was torture. The delicious, sweet kind that drew him right into that deep well of sensations. The intense pleasure mixed with just a trace of primal panic. Panic because his body was begging for release now, now, now but wasn't sure it was going to get it in that *now* moment.

Eden was having her own pleasured panic. He could see it in her eyes. Feel it in the way she was lifting her hips, meeting him thrust for thrust.

And then the panic was sated. Just like that. With one final, very well-timed beat of her body rising to his. Even through the haze, relief and shattering, Nico realized something.

Eden had made it all the way to Pennsylvania before they'd peaked together.

THE MOMENT NICO FINISHED, made a quick pit stop in the bathroom and was back in bed, Eden went straight into his arms for a postsex cuddle. She wasn't surprised that he was as good at that as he was the sex itself. She was benefitting from all the practice he'd had, and she didn't feel the least bit jealous about that.

Okay, a little jealous.

But they both had pasts with many parts of their lives overlapping and intersecting. Heck, Damien had probably even talked to his good buddy Nico about not only their marriage but their sex lives, as well. Eden refused to let that sting or embarrass her. In fact, she refused to feel a lot of things about Damien anymore. She'd already wasted too much time and emotion on him. And besides, she had a hot naked cowboy in bed with her and wanted to concentrate on that.

Eden traced her finger over the bull tat. "What's the story behind this? Was there alcohol involved?"

"Nope, no alcohol. I got it when I started the business two years ago. I think of it like a trademark." He eased a strand of hair from her face, kissed her. "What brought on this argument you had with Damien?"

Considering that she'd just shoved Damien memories aside, she hadn't expected to go back to the subject so quickly. Maybe she should have traced something else on Nico's body to distract him. Because this was touchy territory when it came to pillow talk. Especially since Nico and she hadn't been together-together that long.

"You're frowning," he pointed out.

For a good reason. What had escalated her argument with Damien was what she'd told him. *I'm falling in love with Nico.* That hadn't gone over well at all. Probably wouldn't with Nico, either, which was why she needed to keep it to herself so that he wouldn't feel pressured or trapped.

Except Damien might tell Nico.

In fact, that was something Damien would do to take a jab at her and try to ruin things. Well, heck. Her own confession had put her between a rock and a hard place when all she wanted was to be naked with Nico.

"I told Damien I had feelings for you," she admitted. Not the whole truth but not a lie. Eden steeled herself for Nico to go all rigid and quiet, but he merely kissed her.

"You've been a great friend and stuck with me through some bad times. Thank you for that. Thank you for helping with Piper."

All right, so that wasn't a gushing "I have feelings

for you, too," but it wasn't a boot from the bed, either, which meant maybe he didn't think things were getting too serious between them. Of course, Nico could have had this "great friend/thank you" reaction simply because he had so many other things on his mind. Important things like Piper.

"Do you think it'd do any good if I went to San Antonio and talked to Rayelle woman-to-woman?" she asked. "I'm concerned about how she might be treating Piper."

Nico looked at her a moment, kissed her. Looked at her again. Eden didn't have to guess that something other than the obvious was bothering him.

"Rayelle told me a secret," he said, getting her attention. "She asked me not to tell anyone, but I'm going to tell you. I think if you have the big picture, then you'll see why I'm so troubled."

Now it was Eden's turn to study him. She nodded. "If you're worried that I'll repeat Rayelle's secret—"

"I'm not." He stopped her with a kiss, a very effective way of hushing her. It would have been even more effective at heating her up, but Eden knew this was serious.

"When Rayelle was younger, she got pregnant," he explained. "The baby's father ditched her, and her parents pressured her into giving the baby up for adoption. She hasn't had a relationship since."

Eden stayed quiet while the shock of that settled in, and then she realized the news wasn't all that surprising. She had figured that something had shaken Rayelle right to the core for her to be the way she was

now. After all, Rayelle was young, still in her thirties, but she lived her life more like a prudish spin-
ster. Something had to be at the root of that. But what
Eden couldn't decide was if Rayelle's secret made
her a better choice for dealing with a pregnant teenager. Or if this would be like rubbing salt in a still
very raw wound.

"Jesus," Eden murmured.

"Yeah. Lots of edges and possibilities. I think it
would help if Piper knew, that it would give Rayelle and her a connection. Right now, Piper just sees
Rayelle as Brenda's sister, who was pressured to take
her in."

"I admit that's the way I saw her, too. But Rayelle
is fighting to keep Piper." Or rather the woman was
digging in her heels. That might change though when
the legalities kicked in after Nico started the paperwork for custody. "Do you think Rayelle wants to
keep Piper simply out of loyalty to Brenda?"

Nico lifted his shoulder, and she could see the
slack feeling from sex start to slide away. Yes, this
was weighing on him, and the legal battle would be
just the start. Once he had custody of Piper, he was
going to have to figure out the best way to deal with
her. And fast. Because in about eight months or less,
there'd be a baby, perhaps right here in Nico's bach-
elor pad of a house.

Eden couldn't stop the thought from coming. A
bad thought. Would Nico and she still be lovers then?
If so, that would be a major record for him when it
came to relationship longevity.

And it wasn't likely going to happen.

That was the reason Eden quickly pushed the notion aside. Instead, she kissed him. A much better way to spend their time together. In fact, she could think of something even better than that. A second round of sex. That's why she leaned into the kiss and put some serious heat into it.

Nico responded, adding his own scorching expertise to the lip-lock, but they were soon interrupted by the sound of Eden's phone ringing. She didn't especially want to hear or talk to anyone whose name wasn't Nico, but since this could be Piper, Eden got off the bed and located her phone in the pocket of her dress.

She cursed.

It was her mother's name that popped up on the screen so she let it go to voice mail. Eden had barely managed to push aside the annoyance of the interruption when her phone rang again.

Damien, this time.

Eden hit the decline button for that one. She didn't want to hear what he had to say even in a voice mail and made a mental note to block his number.

She laid her phone back on the nightstand and turned to Nico to resume their kissing, but her blasted phone rang again, and again it was her mother. That call had no sooner gone to voice mail when there was another call, this time from her father. That's when Eden knew something was truly wrong. Her mom had a tendency to nag and pester, but her father didn't. In fact, she couldn't remember him ever calling her before.

"I have to answer this," she told Nico, but he'd already clued into the possibility that this could be a problem. "Dad—" Eden said when she hit the answer button, but that was as far as she got.

"Your mother had me call you," he said, "and don't hang up," he added, probably because that's what she'd been about to do. "It's important. Something happened that you need to hear about. I'm sorry, baby. Real sorry."

Well, crap. It had to be *very* bad for her dad to say that, but Eden didn't even want to speculate. She also didn't want to have to repeat whatever this was to Nico so she put her phone on speaker. It was only a few seconds before she heard some shuffling sounds and then her mother's voice.

"I'm guessing you don't know what's going on?" her mom asked.

"No. What?" Eden managed, and it had better not have anything to do with her having sex with Nico.

"It's Mimi," her mother continued. That burst the anger that had been bubbling up inside Eden. Now, she got a bubble of frustration.

"Damien broke up with her," Eden provided. "Yes, I did hear about that." From the source. A source that probably hadn't treated the breakup with a tender touch. Which led her to another bad thought. "Mimi didn't do something to hurt herself, did she?"

"No." And that was all her mother said for way too long of a time. "She did something to hurt *you*."

Nico automatically sat up, the concern already all over his face. Eden was sure it was on her face, too.

"What did she do?" Eden asked when her mother didn't continue.

"It's about that blog." Her mother's voice pitched high on the last word. "Mimi found out about it somehow. From Damien, I suppose. You didn't say, but I suspect Damien must have known. After all, you two were married when you were writing all those posts—"

"Mom, what did Mimi do?" Eden interrupted, and yeah, there was a flurry of bad thoughts happening now. A hacked site, getting advertisers to pull out. Getting Eden blackballed by some conservative watchdog group.

"Mimi tattled." Her mom had another hitch in her voice when she blurted that out.

Okay, so that wasn't as dire as the other things Eden had imagined. "Who did Mimi tell about the blog?"

"Everyone," her mother said.

That seemed pretty far-reaching for a bookkeeper. "How'd she do that?"

"Eden, she printed out pages of the blog. Pages!" her mother emphasized. "And I'm sure she picked the dirtiest ones she could find."

Again, not as dire as Eden had imagined because there was a big non-dire factor in this. "My name's not on the blog. I use the pseudonym Naughty Cowgirl."

"I know," her mother was quick to agree. "But

Mimi printed out copies of your online calendar, too. I don't know how she got into it, but she did, and she stapled those pages to the blog."

Eden knew. Damien. *Dang it.* She'd changed the password, but Damien could have made copies before she'd done that. So, either Damien had given the info to Mimi or Mimi had scoured through his computer to find it.

"Your calendar does have your name on it," her mother said. "And it's got the deadlines all written out there for everyone to see. *Naughty Cowgirl Talks Sex.*"

Yes, it did indeed have all of that info—because it was supposed to have been a private calendar for her use only.

"Eden, did you really give advice about how to play naked Pin the Tail on the Donkey?" her mom asked.

Nico groaned. That'd actually been his idea, but Eden wasn't going to fault him for it. It'd gotten the site a lot of visitors and comments.

"Mom, put aside the specifics of the blog," Eden advised, "and tell me what Mimi did with all the things she printed out."

"They're everywhere. Everyone knows."

Again, there was that word, *everyone*, which still seemed a little far-reaching for Mimi's skill set. "Did Mimi pass the pages around town?"

"Yes," her mother answered.

So, that was bad. Coupled with her name, everyone in Coldwater now knew the secret Eden had been hiding.

"But Mimi did more than that," her mom went on. "She put the flyers on cars, not just here, but in San Antonio, too. And I don't know how she managed it, but she must have a friend in the newspaper. By tomorrow, it'll be all over the gossip and society news."

CHAPTER TWENTY

EDEN DIDN'T THINK her big girl panties were large
enough to deal with this firestorm, but she didn't have
the luxury of hiding from it. Not any longer anyway.

She'd spent the night with Nico, cuddling in his
very sympathetic and soothing arms. She had ignored
one phone call and text after the other, but Eden was
certain she'd received communications from every
person in Coldwater. There'd likely be repeat attempts
to contact her, including some from out-of-towners,
now that the blog had hit the San Antonio newspaper.
Eden still wasn't sure how Mimi had managed that.
Nor did it matter. There was a metaphorical bag and
the cat was no longer in it.

Speaking of cats, Eden fed Miss Kitty, and said
her usual goodbye to him before she headed out to
work. He didn't hiss or snarl as he usually did, making her wonder if he sensed that she was troubled all
the way to the marrow. Not for herself. No.

There were plenty of others in the mix who could
be hurt.

Her parents, for one. And Roy. She wasn't sure
how he was going to handle this, and he might have
no choice but to fire her if he got enough flak from

their clients. That was okay. She didn't mind losing the job, but Eden had counted on him being an ally if Piper still wanted part-time work when she came to live with Nico.

Of course, Piper could be affected by this, too. Rayelle probably wouldn't encourage the girl to spend time with Eden—and possibly Nico—when she learned about some of the content in Naughty Cowgirl. According to Eden's mom, the naked Pin the Tail on the Donkey had caused quite a stir. So had the saddle sex. That last one was especially ironic, since it was the post that Mimi had sent to Eden.

If she'd been a mean girl, Eden might have let that tidbit leak. Maybe even leak about Damien's cheating. Or that he was a lousy vet whose neutering skills had failed on his own cat. But while spreading that dirt might give her a quick kick of pleasure, it would ultimately just add to the flames that were burning her folks, Roy and Piper.

Maybe Nico, too.

Certainly, by now everyone in town knew they were seeing each other. This stench might affect his business. Or his push to become Piper's foster parent. If so, then Eden might not be able to hold back any meanness that she would aim at Mimi. The woman was a selfish, jealous witch, and the karma bus couldn't run into her soon or fast enough.

Eden didn't drive to the office. She walked even though she knew she would likely run into prying eyes and running mouths along the way. But if she drove, she would just end up delaying the inevitable and she wouldn't be taking the bull by the horns. The eyes would just wait to pry. Mouths would stay on pause to run. Because like her, the townsfolk knew that there was no place for her to hide in Coldwater.

Heck, even moving wasn't an option. Her parents would still be here, and she wouldn't be near Nico. It was worth putting up with all sorts of flak just to be with him.

For however long that would be.

"Eden?" someone called out before she'd walked less than a minute. It was Silla, the queen of mean, and she was waving like a loon and making her way to Eden. She was moving surprisingly fast, too, considering she was wearing strappy hooker heel sandals.

"I'm on my way to work," Eden told her, though she figured that wasn't going to deter Silla.

It didn't. Neither did the fact that Eden kept walking in the direction of Roy's. Silla just switched directions after she caught up with Eden and began to walk next to her.

"OMG, I heard about your blog," Silla said. "I can't believe it. No one can. I mean, you just don't seem the type. But it's true. I know it is because we all saw the proof printed out for us to read."

Eden started to say there'd be no requirement for her to actually read it, but that would delay Silla telling her whatever it was she wanted. Maybe just to try to rub some salt in the wound.

"Your mom's probably ready to murder you or something," Silla went on. "Roy, too. But I'm guessing Nico's having fun with this." With those heels making annoying woodpecker taps on the sidewalk, Silla sidled up even closer to Eden. "Say, do Nico and you ever playact with things you suggest? Because if so, I can see why he's taken a liking to you."

Since Silla finally paused and seemed to expect some sort of response from Eden, she grunted. That guttural sound was enough to spur things right along.

"Say, I read the one about the woman being on the guy's lap while they're on the couch," Silla went on, "and I was wondering if you'd tried that personally. I mean, it looks as if a girl could get hurt doing that."

Yes, Eden had actually tried a modified version of that with Nico, and it had been extremely satisfying.

"You're smiling," Silla pointed out. "So I'm guessing if I ever got adventurous in that kind of way, then that might be one to try."

Eden grunted again, but she didn't drop the smile. Or at least she didn't until she saw Jax hurrying up the sidewalk toward her. Definitely no smile now, and she rethought this whole stupid plan of walking to work and taking the bull by the horns. She no longer wanted to latch on to any proverbial livestock projectile parts.

"Silla, you'll have to excuse me," Eden said as politely as she could manage.

"Oh." The woman looked at her, then at Jax, again as if she expected Eden to provide some kind of explanation.

"A friend of a friend," Eden told her so that Silla wouldn't speculate. "He has a very contagious strain of strep throat and a rare form of jumping body lice, and he wants to talk to me about it to get a recommendation for a doctor. I wouldn't get close to him if I were you. I'll sure be keeping my distance."

Silla repeated her "oh," but this time there was a horrified look in her eyes. She gave a girlie wave and rat-a-tat-tatted her way to the other side of the street. *Far* on the other side, and she nearly broke into a run to put some distance between them.

"Uh, you know I don't have lice or strep, right?" Jax asked her.

"Yes, I know. You're here to talk about either the blog or Piper, but there's nothing I can tell you."

"What blog?" Jax, again.

Since he was probably the only breathing, fully functioning person in town who didn't know, Eden waved that off. "So, you're here to talk about Piper," she concluded, and started walking again. Of course, Jax followed, taking up the position next to her that Silla had just vacated.

"I love Piper," he said. "I love her so much that it makes me feel like an idiot. But it makes me feel good, too. And sometimes bad. It mixes me up. You know?"

Yes, she did know, and that's when Eden realized the falling for Nico had stopped. She was already there. She was in love with him.

Well, shoot. That should add some more complications to the bull-by-the-horns failure of a day.

"Anyway, now that Piper's pregnant for real," Jax went on, "I think she should marry me. That's why I'm here. Can you help me convince her that we should get married?"

Eden stopped, sighed and, because she truly did understand just how crazy love could make you, she patted his arm. "I can't do that. This has to be Piper's decision, and she's probably already getting plenty of input from Rayelle."

The roll of his eyes let her know just what he thought of input like that. "Piper says we're too young, that we can just stay together, and if we're still in love after I finish college, then we can think about marriage."

That sounded like a genius plan to Eden. Of course, Eden was hoping that Piper, too, would go to college or a technical school. She'd need at least some kind of training to be able to support her baby.

Eden started walking again. "For now, I think you should just listen to Piper. Don't hover and insist, either. Give her breathing room." Especially since she doubted Rayelle was doing that. And that was a reminder for Eden to shift the subject a little. "How is Piper doing anyway? Have you spoken to her since she went back to San Antonio?"

He nodded, gave a grunt that didn't sound as disgusting as hers had. It was more of frustration. "I talked to her last night. She said Nico's assistant, Hog, had come over to visit with Rayelle."

Eden forced herself to keep moving, but that put a stutter in her step. "Hog? I didn't even know that he knew Rayelle."

"Guess so. Rayelle and Hog were talking in the

living room while Piper was on the phone with me. She didn't know what they were saying, but she figured Nico had sent him to try to talk some sense into Rayelle."

No. Nico wouldn't have done that. He would have put on his big boy boxers and gone himself. Still, she would ask Nico about that visit later.

Just ahead, Eden saw Cleo waiting outside of Roy's, and she knew she needed to end this visit with Jax. She didn't want him to let anything slip about Piper being pregnant. That was news that should only come from Piper.

"I have to go," Eden told him. "Just remember what I told you about how to handle things with Piper."

"Yeah, I guess." He sounded neither enthusiastic nor hopeful that what she'd said would work. And it might not. But if he went with it, it would give Piper a little thinking time.

Eden left him standing there and went to Cleo, who immediately took hold of her hand and pulled her into the office building. Roy wasn't in reception, but since his office door was closed, he was likely in there with a client. Cleo didn't let Eden go in the direction of her desk but instead took her to the ladies' room.

The moment they were inside, Cleo reached in her pocket and pulled out a shot glass filled with some kind of brown liquid. It had plastic wrap on it, which Cleo removed.

"It's whiskey," Cleo said. "Drink it because you're going to need it."

Without even arguing, Eden tossed back the shot

and grimaced at the awful taste. "It's all true about the blog," Eden told her. "I've been writing it for years, and yes, I've done some of the things I suggested."

Cleo stared at her a moment. "Which ones? Because I was going to use the *pretend I'm a truck* one so that Judd can tinker with me. He's got great tinkering abilities." Cleo winked at her.

Eden appreciated the woman's attempts to cheer her up, but it was going to take more than sex talk and whiskey to do that. "How bad is it?" Eden asked. "Because I figure it's awful for you to come over here like this?"

"It's bad," Cleo confirmed a moment later. "Judd is going to arrest Mimi for littering and placing unauthorized posts on utility poles and private vehicles, but the damage has been done."

Yes, it had been. "How'd you know Mimi was the one to do it?"

"Plenty of people saw her leaving those papers all over town. The bank even has her on the security camera leaving one there."

Mimi was probably too riled to worry if there would be any repercussions for her. But there would be. Once the gossips had picked enough meat off Eden, they'd go after Mimi. Eden didn't know exactly what direction that gossip would take with the woman, but she'd likely get some dirt on her. That was going to have to be enough payback. A tit-for-tat feud wasn't going to help anyone.

"Tell Judd not to arrest Mimi on my account," Eden said to Cleo. "It'll just piss her off even more."

Cleo shrugged. "I'll try, but Judd's pretty pissed. He's the one who gets stuck scraping off that sticky tape."

Good point. So maybe an arrest and Mimi's community service could be tape-scraping. It seemed like a small price to pay, though, for stomping on Eden's life like this. It was a reminder that suddenly gave her a heavy feeling in her chest. She wouldn't cry, but she wasn't going to be a ray of sunshine today, either.

The ladies' room door opened, and Shelby came in. "There you are," Shelby said. She took a small shot glass from her purse. One that she'd balanced in a paper cup. Like Cleo, she'd covered it with plastic wrap, which she removed before she handed it to Eden.

"Figured you could use this," Shelby said. "It's from Callen's prime stash of scotch. Drink it."

Eden did, not because she wanted it but because it might help with the chest tightness and the lump in her throat. She had good friends. Friends who cared enough to bring her booze and check on her. Of course, the jury was still out on whether or not the booze was a good thing. Eden's head was starting to feel a little light.

"So, those notes I saw by your computer were for your blog?" Shelby asked.

Eden nodded. Yes, definitely light-headed.

"And you held out on us all this time?" Shelby grinned and nudged Eden with her elbow. "I know having news like this will make your life shitty but know up front that I plan on tapping you for advice."

"Tap Nico. He helps me with it." The moment the words left her mouth, Eden regretted them. She should have taken her own advice about staying quiet. That was something that should have come from Nico.

"Pay up," Cleo said, extending her hand to Shelby, and on a groan, Shelby fished a twenty out of her purse.

"You two bet on this?" Eden asked.

"Yep," Cleo readily admitted with no shame whatsoever. "I just couldn't see you not using a knowledgeable source like Nico." She leaned in. "Please tell me all that practice has made him really good at making you scream out his name."

Heck, since she'd already spilled too much, Eden just kept spilling. "Oh yes. He deserves a championship title for what he can do."

This, of course, caused Shelby and Cleo to squeal with obligatory delight. Eden would have done the same for them.

"Try the hand job with Judd while he's on the phone," Shelby added to Cleo. "Works great. And I don't think Callen minds that he lost that client when he belted out those curse words."

Shelby winked at Eden, but then her expression got very serious. "Are you okay?" Shelby asked. Cleo moved in closer, watching and waiting for the answer.

Eden was certain she could come up with a marginally convincing lie so they wouldn't worry, but she didn't get a chance to do that.

Damien walked in.

Eden huffed. "What if we'd been peeing in here?" she asked. Not her best effort to confront him, but at least he heard her displeasure. Saw it as well in not only her glare but also Shelby's and Cleo's.

"I'm sorry," Damien said. "I swear I didn't know Mimi was going to do that, or I would have stopped her."

Eden doubted the being able to stop her part, but Damien did look genuinely sorry and rattled. Good. She might not be a mean girl, but she wasn't exactly a good one, either. She didn't mind seeing him suffer.

"What can I do to make this better for you?" Damien asked.

Again, there seemed to be genuine sincerity in his expression and voice, and it was only because of that Eden would cut him a break by not saying something mean or snarky.

"If you truly want to make things better for me, you'll leave. No more visits unless it's to pick up Miss Kitty. No more phone calls. And especially no more asking me to take you back." She looked him straight in the eyes. "Just please stay out of my life and get on with yours."

Clearly, that was not the answer Damien wanted to hear, but she knew in every fiber of her being that he would soon get past the hurt she saw in his eyes. The way he played around, his future ex was out there, and he'd find her.

With his head down, Damien turned to leave, but he couldn't because Roy opened the door. Unlike the others, he didn't come in. However, he stood in the doorway, volleying glances at each of them. Roy, no doubt, could figure out what was going on.

"For you," Roy said, handing her one of the small cone-shaped paper cups that were by the bottled water dispenser. But there wasn't water in the cup. "Brandy," he said. "I figured you'd need it."

Eden sighed and thanked him, but this time she didn't chug it. She took a small sip. Good thing, too, because it had a serious kick and burn.

"How bad is it?" Eden asked her boss.

"Could be worse."

In that moment she wanted to kiss him for his eternal semioptimism.

"You should go on home," he continued. "Take a couple of days off if you like. With pay, of course. I can manage things on my own for a while."

"I can work," she assured him.

Roy shook his head. "I don't have any other appointments this morning. Nico had one, but he's already come and gone. He said he was heading to your place to talk to you, but I guess he didn't know you were here in the bathroom."

No, but that meant he'd be back, and Eden wanted to clear out her "audience" before he returned.

That didn't happen.

Eden heard the clomp of footsteps, and a moment later her mom and dad stepped up behind Roy. As Roy had done, they peered into the tiny room as if trying to figure out what the heck was going on. That wouldn't take them long, especially if Damien started talking, so Eden decided on an attempt to defuse the situation with humor.

"I'm tired of the toilet paper being put on the wrong way," Eden volunteered, setting the rest of the brandy into the sink. Because of the cone bottom, it tipped right over, and she watched with woozy eyes as it swirled down the drain. "This is a little demonstration so that folks get it right. TP placement frustration is a real thing, people."

Okay, she failed at that attempt at humor. Only Cleo and Shelby snickered, but they were on Team Eden and would have supported anything she'd said.

"This is serious," her mother scolded.

"And it's kinda good," her father piped in, making Eden smile. He was on Team Eden, too. "The feed store's been swamped with business. Folks were buying like a storm was coming, but Louise and I knew they were in there just to try to wheedle some news about you. Didn't tell them a thing," he added with a proud lift of his chin.

Her mother's chin definitely wasn't lifted. "I said what you did was some kind of therapy. Sex therapy." She whispered the word *sex*. "But really, it's none of their beeswax, especially since I figure you're giving it up."

Eden was so going to have to disappoint her. Not only did that blog pay her bills, but it allowed her to put money in savings. Eden intended to ride that horse as long as she could. However, she didn't get a chance to say anything else to her mom because she heard Nico call out for her.

"Eden?"

"Back here," she answered. She tried to go to him, but she couldn't work her way through the logjam of people in the tiny bathroom.

Nico managed it, though. He snaked through them, tossing a scowl at Damien before he pulled Eden to him and kissed her. Maybe Nico was just doing that to take a jab at Damien, but it still felt darn good. Of course, Nico probably couldn't give a bad kiss even with an audience.

"You need a drink or something?" Nico asked.

That was the one thing Eden was certain she didn't need. The combination of the booze and the kiss had made her past woozy and on to dizzy.

"I can't see how liquor at this hour would help," her mom answered for her. "I don't think the kiss helps, either."

"Oh, Mom, you're so wrong about that," Eden countered. "That's because I'm in love with Nico."

Suddenly, you could have heard a pin drop in the room. Well, except for the slight gurgle in the toilet. The handle needed jiggling—that was the fleeting thought she had before another thought came.

Holy shit.

She'd said that aloud. To her mother. To Nico. *Holy shit times a thousand. Times a million.*

Quick, she mentally told herself. *Say something to recover. Another lame joke.* But her mind drew a blank. It was hard to think with all that silence, and here were those prying eyes she'd been dreading. Eden wasn't exactly sure though that Nico was doing any prying. That's because she didn't want to look at him.

Soon, there were four other eyes added to the mix. Eden wasn't sure how she managed to see them what with so many people around, but she spotted Rayelle and Piper peering around her parents and Roy.

"Uh, is this a bad time?" Rayelle asked.

No way had the woman meant that as a joke, but Cleo and Shelby burst out laughing. Heck, Eden joined them because a giggle couldn't possibly make this worse than it already was.

Rayelle looked flustered, but her question, and perhaps the maniacal laughter, accomplished something. It got people moving.

"I'll call you later," her mother said.

"Hey, great about you loving Nico," her father contributed, causing Eden to groan. She hadn't figured anyone had misheard her, but hope sprang eternal after two and a quarter shots and blurting out something you hadn't intended to blurt.

"Gotta do something in my office," Roy muttered as he walked away, nudging her parents out with him. Later, she would thank her father and hug both him and her mother. If she hadn't dug a hole and buried herself, that is.

Cleo and Shelby both gave her cheek kisses, squeezed her hand and left, too. Damien didn't budge though until Eden gave him a look that she was certain would have frozen a desert camel's balls.

"You don't deserve her," Damien mumbled, aiming that at Nico. But then he shook his head. "Neither did I." And with that revelation that Eden wasn't going to argue with, Damien finally left.

Even though Eden would have liked to clear the air with Nico, after another look at Rayelle's face, she knew it would have to wait. Something was wrong. Well, wrong with Rayelle anyway. Piper was smiling, and the girl ran to Nico to hug him.

"Aunt Rayelle talked things out, and we're moving back to the cabin," Piper said, and she shifted her hug to Eden. "Thank you for everything."

Eden hadn't thought she'd done that much, especially not with Rayelle, and she wondered what had caused the woman's change of heart.

"Maybe Roy will let you use his office," Eden suggested. That would give them a better place to talk, if indeed that's what Rayelle wanted to do. Of course, any place was better than the ladies' room.

Clearly though, Rayelle didn't feel that way about changing locations because she stepped in and closed the door behind her. She bracketed her back against it as if standing guard and preventing anyone else from entering.

Or leaving.

"I didn't want to tell Piper until we got here," Rayelle said.

That put a fast end to the hugging, and Piper, Nico and Eden turned to face the woman. Rayelle was as white as paper and looked even dizzier than Eden felt.

"I'm just going to blurt this out before I lose my nerve," Rayelle added. She shifted toward Piper, swallowed hard and said, "Piper, I'm your mother."

CHAPTER TWENTY-ONE

ONCE AGAIN, NICO heard himself saying, "Oh shit."

He reeled toward Eden to see if she had a clue about what Rayelle had just said. She didn't. Eden was shaking her head, muttering her own version of "oh shit" and was as dumbfounded as he was.

But their shock was a drop in the bucket compared to Piper's.

His sister wasn't muttering nor shaking her head. She was just standing there, seemingly frozen, her stunned gaze fixed on Rayelle.

Her mother.

Part of Nico wanted to believe this was some kind of joke, a really bad one, but Rayelle wasn't the joking sort. Plus, there were tears in her eyes, and she was pulling that little silver box out of her purse. The one with the secret baby stuff in it. Apparently, the woman had decided that it wasn't going to be a secret any longer.

"Uh, I should be going," Eden muttered.

Nico didn't want her to leave, especially not after what she'd said. *That's because I'm in love with Nico.* Eden had seemed damn adamant about it when she'd blurted that out to her mother, and now Nico needed to find out if it was true. Hell, he hoped it wasn't true.

Didn't he?

But even if it was, he couldn't deal with that now. Not with what Piper and Rayelle were about to face.

"You're lying," Piper said to Rayelle. When Eden started to walk out, Piper caught on to her hand, stopping her. "Aunt Rayelle's lying, right?" Piper then turned to Nico, silently posing the same question to him.

Rayelle was the one who answered it. She walked closer, opening the little silver box she carried, and she showed the contents to Piper.

"I was in college when I got pregnant with you," Rayelle said, her voice thin and watery—a lot like the pallor on her face. "Your father was married. I didn't know that when I was seeing him, but I found out later. After I told him I was pregnant, he abandoned me, and I allowed myself to be pressured into giving you up for adoption."

Piper continued to shake her head, and it got worse with each word that Rayelle said. "But I wasn't adopted. My parents were killed in a car accident. That's why I went to live with Mama Brenda." Unlike Rayelle, there was nothing thin and watery about her. By the time Piper had worked her way to that last sentence, she was practically shouting.

Nico put his arm around her, to try to soothe her. Eden did the same on the other side of the girl. But Nico wasn't even sure Piper felt them. She had her very steely eyes pinned to Rayelle.

"Your parents adopted you," Rayelle insisted, and she lifted the hospital bracelet from the box, extending it out for Piper to take. Piper didn't touch it. "If you look at it, you'll see my name on it and your birth date. Of course, you hadn't been named yet so that's why you're listed as Baby Devereux."

Piper still didn't touch the bracelet, but she did look at it. So did Nico, and yeah—Piper's birth date was indeed there. And on a scale from one to infinity, Nico was infinity sure that Rayelle was telling the truth about all of this. This was a hard moment for both Piper and her, and if there'd been any doubts that Piper was her daughter, Rayelle wouldn't have just made that confession.

Piper made a hoarse sobbing sound, and she sagged against Nico.

"You lied to me," Piper murmured, her attention still fixed on Rayelle. "All this time you lied."

Rayelle nodded, and she didn't even attempt to wipe away the tears that were spilling from her eyes. She just let them fall. "Because I'm a coward. Because I was afraid you'd hate and reject me."

Piper certainly didn't do anything to dispel that notion. She broke loose from Eden and him and, storming past Rayelle, she ran out of the ladies' room. Because Rayelle looked ready to collapse, Nico hesitated a split second, wondering if he should at least make the woman sit on the floor before her feet gave way.

"I'll take care of Rayelle," Eden assured him. "Go after Piper."

With that split-second debate over, Nico didn't even take the time to thank her. He hurried out after his sister.

Nico glanced around the reception area. No Piper. But the front door was still jiggling a little to let him know that she'd gone outside so he raced out, his gaze slashing from one end of Main Street to the other. He spotted her—running in the direction of the diner. He didn't think she would stop there, though. Nope. This wasn't something that a Coke and burger were going to cure.

"Piper?" he called out, well aware that he was drawing attention that would lead to speculation and gossip, but he didn't give a rat's ass about that. Right now, he only cared about getting to his sister and trying to talk her down from this emotional ledge she was on.

It was a pain running in cowboy boots, but Nico pushed himself as hard as he could, and he caught up with her at the end of the street. He expected her to fight him, to try to bolt away again, but the moment he took hold of her, Piper just dissolved into his arms. And, of course, she was crying.

Nico brushed a kiss on the top of her head and glanced around for the nearest place where they could have some privacy. There weren't a lot of options unless he wanted to walk her back to his office. Since that would mean not only crossing the street but also facing anyone who might be there, Nico opted for the back of the alley.

This wasn't ideal, but he led her to the stone retaining wall between Joslin's Feed Store and Patty Cakes Bakery. It was a strange combination of scents what with cattle feed grains and what Nico thought might be freshly baked snickerdoodles.

He sat on the retaining wall with Piper, and he kept his arm around her, but Nico didn't speak. Neither did Piper. She just kept crying.

The lull in conversation gave Nico some time to realize that he didn't have a clue how to handle this. Nor the "I love you" situation with Eden. He was good with most rodeo bulls, but try as he might, he couldn't see how to apply any of that skill set with Piper or Eden. Thankfully, silence brought on by his cluelessness seemed to be the way to go because after about ten minutes, Piper finally lifted her head from his shoulder and looked at him.

"Aunt Rayelle isn't lying about this, is she?" Piper asked.

"No." And he left it at that.

Piper nodded, and she seemed to be trying to steel herself up. At least she wiped her tears, and Nico helped her with that.

"I felt…something," Piper added a moment later, getting his attention. At first, he thought she was talking about the baby she was carrying, but she clarified that a moment later when she added, "I couldn't put my finger on it, but I always felt that Aunt Rayelle looked at me and saw something that no one else did."

Well, that was news to Nico. He'd never felt or noticed anything like that. Only Rayelle's rigid stiffness that he now figured was a facade.

"She always seemed to keep me at a distance," Piper went on, "but there were times when I would catch her looking at me, and I'd see something different in her eyes. Regret, maybe."

That sounded promising if Piper could put that together and understand where Rayelle was coming from. Very adult of his little sister. Of course, since Piper was going to be a mom soon, the adulting was a good sign. Piper didn't need to be fighting battles on two fronts.

"Aunt Rayelle… Rayelle," Piper amended, "would have been what—about twenty when she got pregnant with me?"

Nico nodded, and he thought he knew what Piper was thinking. Rayelle had been an adult. Unlike Piper. And here Piper was planning to keep her baby while Rayelle hadn't.

"You can't compare your life to hers," Nico advised her. "Giving you up might have been the best choice she had. After all, you had great adoptive parents, right?"

"Right," Piper verified. "And life as I knew it was over when they died. Then, I went to live with Mama Brenda and started a new life." She paused. "Why wouldn't Rayelle have stepped up then to take me? Why did she let me go into foster care?"

"Can't answer that for sure, but I believe she thought she wouldn't be good at the mothering thing."

"She's not," Piper quickly said. "She's too uptight."

No argument from him on that. Rayelle was the textbook definition of uptight. But what he'd seen in the ladies' room was a broken woman. One who had her crushed heart on her sleeve. Maybe that would help with her other character flaws.

The minutes crawled by, and new smells hit the air. Jaylene at Patty Cakes now had something chocolate baking.

"Any idea who my biological father is?" Piper asked.

"Not a clue, but you could ask Rayelle. She did say he was married when he got her pregnant and that he abandoned her, so if you find this guy and want to see him, I'll go with you."

Piper didn't hesitate with the sound of agreement she made. Good. Nico didn't want her facing down a potential asshole on her own.

More minutes passed before Piper groaned and scrubbed her hand over her face. "What should I do?"

Oh, this was the sucky part about being a brother. "Can't tell you that." But man, he wished he could fix this and everything else for her. "This is one of those times when the ball is in your court."

He didn't groan out loud, but Nico figured that was the lamest advice in the history of lame advice. He almost expected Piper to tell him that, too, and maybe give him a not so playful punch on the arm, but she got to her feet and nodded.

"Please come with me," she said. "I have to go see Rayelle."

EDEN CLOSED THE silver box and slipped it back into Rayelle's purse. "Come with me," Eden insisted, getting a firm grip on the woman's arm.

She knew there'd be pitfalls on this trek to take Rayelle to her house. It would mean a walk up the street, but since Eden hadn't brought her car to work, walking was her best immediate option.

It didn't make sense for them to stand around in the bathroom, waiting for either Nico or Piper to return. It could be hours before that happened. Or in Piper's case—never. The girl was already on overload what with the pregnancy, and heaven knew what this could do to her emotional state.

It certainly wasn't doing much for Rayelle's.

The woman was no longer crying, but there was a stunned silence about her. Maybe she'd gone into shock. If so, that was even more reason for Eden to take Rayelle to her place so she could get her to lie down and maybe coax her into having something to drink.

Speaking of drink, Eden had to fight off the effects of the alcohol she'd guzzled down so she could try to think straight. Soon, she'd need to know what to say to Rayelle. Even offer some sympathy. And right now, it hard to focus with the booze buzz still playing havoc. Too bad that buzz couldn't blank out that she'd told Nico she was in love with him. It was the truth, but that particular revelation would have been best saved for a day that hadn't also included Rayelle's revelation about being Piper's mother.

As they walked, Eden kept glancing at the woman, trying to pick through her features to see if there was any resemblance between Piper and her. Nope. Well, maybe around the mouth and the shape of their eyes.

"Piper looks like her father's sister," Rayelle volunteered. She'd obviously caught Eden's glimpses and knew what this was about. "I haven't been in touch with him. His name was Ted Draper," she clarified, "and I didn't know anyone in his family, but I saw pictures of his sister. Piper definitely has his DNA."

Eden heard the sadness in Rayelle's voice, and her comment seemed to be some kind of conclusion that because of that DNA, Piper would reject her. Just the way this a-hole Ted had done.

Maybe her quick trigger burst of anger was liquor induced, but Eden suddenly wanted to kick him in the balls. The man hadn't just rejected Rayelle. He'd also rejected his own child. She'd seen firsthand what that sort of thing had done to Nico and his brothers. It had landed them in foster care—some of it really god-awful, too—and it had caused them years of pain and plenty of baggage to go along with it. That could have easily happened to Piper if Brenda hadn't taken her.

Eden mentally stopped on that last thought but kept walking. People were staring at them, and if they stopped, someone might want to chat.

"You convinced Brenda to take Piper?" Eden asked.

Rayelle nodded but continued her blank stare. Which was a good thing since the woman didn't seem to see the behind-the-hand whispers of Silla and her mean girl pack who were walking on the other side of Main Street.

"Brenda was already doing foster care by then,"

Rayelle quietly added. "And she was so good at it. All her foster kids loved her."

Nico and Piper certainly had so maybe that had been the best solution for Rayelle. That way, her daughter would be in a good home, and she could keep an eye on her. Of course, that wasn't a rationale that Piper was likely to accept.

Rayelle and she were still trudging along, one slow step after the other, when Eden had to stop. Not mentally this time, either. That's because she saw a very unexpected sight. Mimi was scraping what appeared to be tape residue off a utility box, and some of the tape bits were stuck to her face and hair. She was a mess. Mimi didn't say a word to her, but she gave Eden a hard glare.

Eden stuck out her tongue at her. Again, maybe the booze had prompted that, but Eden was tired of Mimi's antics even though there could be an advantage in not having to hide her secret blog life. That could be booze thought, too, but Eden was going to choose to see things that way. Especially in light of Rayelle and Piper. Their dilemma was Nico's dilemma, and that in turn affected Eden, as well.

Because she loved him.

God, she loved him.

And she hoped soon that would cause her at least some small shred of joy and not just the dread she felt now at facing him. Dread, too, that he might just end things with her so as to spare her heart. Of course, he would know by now that there'd be no heart-sparing for her.

When her house finally came into view, Eden groaned. There were people milling around. Lots of people. The first one she noticed was Liddy Jean and a trio of other female protestors Eden didn't recognize. They had Equality for Rodeo Heifers signs and were holding them high as they marched in front of her house.

"There were more people here than in front of Nico's office," Liddy Jean promptly explained with an indignant nod. "We take our message to the crowd."

Well, that explained things. Eden hadn't been sure which had come first—the protestors or the people. So, that meant her friends and neighbors were there to get more gossip or to make sure she was okay.

"I'm fine," Eden assured anyone who was there for that facet. "And I'm not going to discuss the blog right now," she added for the others.

At least three-fourths of the crowd grumbled and walked away. One who didn't do any walking was the guy sitting on her porch steps.

Jax.

"I don't have jumping body lice or strep," Jax announced in a loud voice, letting Eden know that maybe he'd gotten some flak about that. Well, Silla was a mean girl so it was possible she'd already started gossip about it. Eden would have to issue a correction on that soon. "No jumping lice," he emphasized, his voice even louder.

Maybe there were some in the crowd who didn't believe him or were just icked out by the possibility of such a thing because that caused a few more folks to scurry off.

Good, the herd was thinning.

"I need to see Piper," Jax went on. "She's not answering her phone and I have to make sure she's okay."

"She's with Nico. I'm sure she'll call you back soon."

Eden wasn't sure of that at all, but she didn't want to get into all of this while they still had an audience. Besides, anything he heard should come from Piper.

"Come on," Eden told Rayelle, getting her onto the porch. She unlocked the door, moved Rayelle inside and turned to Jax to tell him this wasn't a good time for a visit. But, heck, he looked as beaten down as Rayelle did.

"Find something to do in the kitchen," Eden instructed the boy. "Make yourself a snack or something. I need to talk to Rayelle."

Jax nodded and didn't give her a word of flak about that. However, he did hesitate even after Eden closed the front door and sent Rayelle into the living room.

"Uh, is this about Miss Rayelle being Piper's real mom and all?" Jax asked in a whisper.

Eden blinked. "How did you know about that?"

A red blush flooded his cheeks. "I snooped and looked in the little silver box Miss Rayelle always carries. It was in her purse, and I checked it out when she wasn't around. I thought maybe she had a severed finger or some cremated ashes. Or maybe some cigarettes," he added with a shrug. "I wouldn't have smoked one or anything, but I just wondered if she had like a nicotine habit or something."

"A severed finger, ashes?" But Eden waved that off. She didn't want to know how he'd reached those possible conclusions.

"I'll get that snack now," Jax said, and he headed in the direction of her kitchen.

Eden was about to go to Rayelle, but the sound of a text ding stopped her. Until that sound, she hadn't realized just how desperate she was to hear from Nico. But it wasn't Nico. It was Roy.

Just got six calls. All from out-of-towners who are fans of your blog. They want to do business with me and made appointments. Go ahead and take your time off, but when you get back, we'll be mighty busy.

Well, good. That was something at least. She hadn't wanted *Naughty Cowgirl* to hurt Roy, and it apparently hadn't. Thankfully, it had caused business to pick up at the feed store, too, though it might take a year or so for her mother to accept that particular side benefit.

Eden poured Rayelle a shot of whiskey, carefully avoiding the fumes herself since she'd had enough of booze fumes today. She brought the glass to Rayelle and then sat beside her. Miss Kitty put up a token hiss, as if protesting the interruption to his nap before he went back to sleep.

"I've lost her," Rayelle said, taking a dainty sip

of the drink before tossing the rest back in one gulp. "I've lost Piper forever."

Eden opened her mouth to assure her that might not be true, but it turned out that she didn't have to say anything. That's because the front door opened, and Nico and Piper came in. Eden could have sworn her heart did a little jump in her chest, and she forgot how to breathe. She hadn't always had this reaction to him, but she was certainly having it now.

Nico went to her, brushing a kiss on her cheek and giving Eden's arm a hang-in-there squeeze. She returned the gesture and braced herself for whatever was about to happen.

"I don't have lice or strep," Jax said.

Okay, so she hadn't been expecting that. Or the smile of relief that practically washed over Piper. Piper went to him, and despite the fact that Jax was holding an open bag of Cheetos in one hand and a Coke in the other, Piper hugged him. And Jax hugged her back.

"It's okay, baby," he said to her, kissing her cheek.

Piper probably wouldn't care that he'd left an orange smear with his mouth. She just looked, well, relieved that he was there. Their holding and touching wasn't anywhere near the scalding level of the kiss that Eden had witnessed between Callen and Shelby, but there was no mistaking the intimacy. These two cared deeply for each other. Whether it would last was anyone's guess, but it was there for now, and Eden suspected Piper would need that to get her through the next couple of minutes. Along with the next few months.

Rayelle got to her feet, but she didn't say anything. She just stood there and let Piper and Jax hug it out and whisper sweet nothings to each other. Since Eden was well aware that the sweet nothings might rile Nico as only a big brother could be riled, Eden took hold of his hand. A ploy to keep him in place, yes, but Piper wasn't the only one who needed someone to get her through this.

While staying in Jax's arms, Piper finally eased around to face Rayelle. "Don't expect me to just start thinking of you as my mother," Piper said.

Not a lovey-dovey way to begin a conversation, but it was far better than some of the alternatives. No profanity had been involved, and Piper wasn't doling out any stink eye. More of a warning eye.

"No," Rayelle agreed. "Right now, I'd be happy with just a start." She paused as if giving Piper a chance to object to that, but the girl didn't.

"There'll be a lot of or's in what I'm about to say," Rayelle continued a moment later. "But we need to make some decisions. *You* need to make decisions," Rayelle amended. "First thing first. We can stay in the cabin indefinitely or move somewhere else in Coldwater or go back to San Antonio when the summer's over."

"The cabin," Piper said without hesitation.

Rayelle nodded but took her time again before she continued. "Since Jax is clearly important to you and if his parents agree, he can see you whenever possible, or I can arrange for him to get a place to live here."

This time Piper wasn't so quick with her answer. She seemed to give it some thought. "Jax visiting whenever possible for now. I want him to finish school."

Another nod from Rayelle. "I want you to finish, too, and I'm afraid there won't be an *or* with that. You need to finish for yourself. For your baby."

"She's right about that," Nico insisted.

Piper gave him what appeared to be an obligatory little sister eye roll. "All right, agreed."

Along with Rayelle's next nod, she let out a breath so long that it seemed as if the woman had been holding it for hours. "I'll pay for all your expenses, including college, or you can figure out a way to do that yourself. There are no strings attached to what I'm offering."

Piper stayed quiet a moment. "I'll have to think about that one."

Rayelle gave a fourth nod. "And finally I'm so sorry that I gave you up for adoption. I don't have an excuse, not a good one anyway. What I did was on me, and you can choose to forgive me for that—one day—or you can tell me to get out of your life and that you never want to see me again."

There it was. All spelled out for Piper. A bottom line filled with options and or's.

"Even if you don't forgive me," Rayelle said, adding even more to that bottom line, "I'll always love you and my grandchild that you're carrying."

Silence all the way around. Eden certainly wasn't

going to say anything. This was a family deal. If she'd had a bet on who would cave and talk first, Eden would have lost that bet because the winner was Jax.

"Uh, she sounds sincere and sorry and all," he told Piper. "And this baby will be her grandkid since you're her kid. Maybe you could at least give her a chance or something. You know, like maybe just live with her awhile and see how it works out."

Strange that the most inarticulate one in the room could manage to boil everything down to a solution. A very simple solution that didn't involve a gnashing of teeth or detailed plans.

Not for now anyway.

Piper certainly didn't balk at what Jax had said, and after what must have felt like an eternity to Rayelle, the girl nodded. "Okay. We can have a trial run of sorts here at the cabin in Coldwater."

Tears instantly sprang to Rayelle's eyes, but Eden had no doubt that these were of the happy variety. She stood still until Piper started toward her, and Rayelle met her halfway. When Piper hugged her, Rayelle hugged right back.

Tears sprang to Eden's eyes, too. And Piper's. And while Nico didn't cry, there was a sigh of relief as if a heavy weight had been lifted off his chest.

Rayelle pulled back from Piper for only a second to look at the girl. At her daughter. There was lots and lots of love on the woman's face before she went back for seconds on the hug.

Jax beamed and looked longingly at Rayelle and Piper as if he wanted to be included in that love. Rayelle hooked her arm around the boy's neck and pulled him into the embrace. That went on for several long moments and involved a few more tears before Piper finally moved back.

"I've got a bad case of morning sickness." Piper ran her hand over her stomach. "Can we go back to the cabin now so I can lie down?"

"Of course," Rayelle said, running her hand down Piper's hair. "I might have a fix for that. Crackers worked when I was carrying you." Rayelle turned as if heading for the door, but then she stopped. "My car's parked up the street."

"So's my truck," Jax said.

Eden had a fix for that. A small contribution but still one that would help. She took her keys from the entry table and handed them to Jax. "Drive them to the cabin. Stay as long as needed." Though she wasn't sure how Jax would interpret that, Eden had no doubts that Piper or Rayelle would send him on his way when the time was right.

Nico went to Piper and hugged and kissed her. "Call me after your stomach's settled."

Piper nodded. "Thanks…for everything." She looked at Eden and repeated the thanks, and then Nico and she heard other rounds of gratitude. First from Rayelle and then from Jax before the three of them filed out of the house, leaving Nico and Eden standing there in the quiet.

It didn't stay quiet for long.

"Now," Nico said, turning to her, "you and I have to talk."

CHAPTER TWENTY-TWO

NICO DIDN'T MISS the "deer caught in the headlights" look in Eden's eyes, and he knew exactly why it was there. Even with the ordeal they'd just gone through with Piper and Rayelle, that wasn't what had put Eden in the frozen mode. Nope.

It was the: *That's because I'm in love with Nico.*

Nico certainly hadn't forgotten about it, and he was dead certain she hadn't, either. Now he had to figure out the best way to handle this. He started by going to the door, locking it, peering out the sidelight windows to make sure Jax, Piper and Rayelle had managed to get out of there despite the crowd. They had. The only people left were Liddy Jean and her protesting crew, and Nico figured they'd be leaving soon, too, when they realized they no longer had an audience.

He turned back to Eden to further assess the situation. She had her bottom lip clamped between her teeth. It seemed as if she expected him to curse her out or leave. So Nico came up with the best way to approach this. Unlike with Piper, silence and a hug weren't going to do the trick.

"What's your latest blog request?" he asked.

Obviously, Eden hadn't expected that because

she drew her brows together. "Uh," she finally said, "Horny in Houston wants advice about how to make a home sex tape for her sweet-cheeks cowboy."

All right. He'd hoped for something simpler like kitchen sex or role-playing, but he could work with this. It would not only get that nerve-frazzled look off Eden's face, it might also help him think clearer, too. Usually sex or near sex hadn't been a mental palate cleanser, but it had been with Eden.

"Okay, your phone camera or mine?" he asked, and when her blank stare continued, he went with, "Mine then." He took out his phone to get it ready.

Eden's blank stare finally turned into a sigh that had a touch of a huff to it. "Nico, I know you want to talk about what I said."

"Yes, I do," he readily admitted, "but after the ordeal we've just been through, anything we say will be filtered through a crapload of raw emotions. Let's soothe those emotions a little and then the talk will be more straightforward."

She opened her mouth, but she shut it just as quickly. That perhaps had something to do with him clicking the video function on his phone and holding it out for a selfie of them fully dressed.

"Hi, I'm Sweet-Cheeks cowboy," he told the camera, "and this is Horny in Houston here. We're going to make a sex tape."

When he finished his introduction, he looked at Eden and saw that she was fighting a smile. *Good.* That was progress. So was the kiss he gave her because she kissed him right back. In fact, she went right into it, tongue and all.

He held on to the camera, not sure if he had it angled right and not particularly caring since he would have to erase it as soon as they were done. Well, he might watch it if Eden was game. Right now, she seemed pretty game for anything. The kiss had done its job and heated her up. Of course, her kiss had heated him up just as fast.

Nico cleared his throat before he went back to the video portion of this conversation prep. "Every good sex tape requires several things. First, consent from your partner. That's a biggie. Don't be a dick and spring this on a lover after the climaxes are over. The only other things a sex tape needs are getting naked and getting laid, preferably in that order."

To prove his point, he shucked off Eden's dress. Oh yeah. Little bitty panties and a why-bother bra. Then, he reversed the camera so that she could see herself on the screen. Of course, Eden probably didn't see what he did.

That she was a knockout.

And she probably didn't know he wanted her more than the oxygen in the air. So Nico showed her. Kissing her, he dragged her hand to the front of his jeans so she could feel his erection. Not the beginnings of one, either. That sucker was full-blown and ready for action.

This time when she pulled back from the kiss, she was really smiling. "Put your hand in your jeans and adjust yourself."

He'd never understood how that could get her hot, but she probably didn't get the whole itty-bitty under-wear thing. Even though it wasn't going to do any-thing for his heat rate, he unhooked his belt buckle, opened the snap on his jeans and went in.

Just as Eden took his phone from him and recorded what he was doing.

"Horny in Houston will want to watch that again," she said, her voice now filled with smoke and a whole lot of devilment.

Yeah, they'd be watching this again, so Nico wanted to make sure he got better stuff than him giving his hard dick a comfort adjustment.

He reached to take back his phone, but she shook her head. "Strip, sweet-cheeks."

Gladly. Because the sooner he got naked, the sooner he could shimmy off her panties and get on to the sex part of the sex tape.

Nico reached behind him, caught on to the neck of his shirt and pulled it off. Off went his boots and jeans, but he added a warning when he reached for the top of his boxers. "You and I are the only ones who see this. Don't leave a copy around for anyone else."

"Just us," she agreed. "Now, get all the way naked."

He did, but while his boxers were still around his ankles, she was on him. Eden came at him, hugging, kissing and groping all at once despite still holding the phone.

Nico did something about that. He dragged her to the floor, making sure that he took the brunt of the fall. Eden landed on top of him, and Nico used their new position to rid her of the bra and panties.

"Sweet-Cheeks Cowboy will want to watch this again," he said.

He took the phone from her and levered her up a little so he could get a nice body shot. Her choice in genital grooming was now recorded for posterity. Or in their case, a viewing or two which would likely just crank them up again and lead to more sex.

Nico turned the screen toward her, hit a quick rewind for her to give him a thumbs-up or-down. He got a thumbs-sideways when she turned the camera, hit Record again and got a very close-up image of his face. Then, his erection.

He smiled, wondering if she debated the order of which to record first but knew she hadn't. Eden liked the sex, but he was pretty sure she liked his face even more. He certainly liked hers.

While he wouldn't have minded stretching out the sex tape a bit longer, she was starting to wiggle against the second part of him that she'd recorded, and that wasn't good. He didn't want accidental penetration—especially considering how several members of his family were already knocked up.

"Sweet-Cheeks Cowboy here with a reminder to practice safe sex," he said, tossing his phone aside so he could get a condom out of his jeans pocket.

He wasn't sure where the phone landed and didn't care. That's because the moment he had the condom on, Eden took him inside her. Well, it was more like a frantic let's get this done now, but he was used to that. Both he and his recorded dick appreciated it.

She caught on to his hands, pinning him to the floor, and showing some "Horny in Houston" tendencies, she rode him like a racehorse. Nico didn't stop her, not one bit. He just watched, taking her all in, getting lost in the way his erection slid and slid against all that smooth skin. In fact, he got so caught up in it that he didn't realize soon enough that the climax was bearing down on him.

And Eden was still going.

Hell. She was at South Dakota and showed no signs of stopping.

Nico quickly tried to rein in and slow her down, but she would have no part of that. Her eyes were fierce and filled with the power—yeah, power— of what she was doing. Of what she was capable of doing. And what she was capable of was making him explode.

The climax racked through him, on and on, robbing him of his breath and his ability to reach between them and give her a few strokes to help her do some exploding of her own.

But Eden didn't need that anyway.

While his body was racking and surrendering, hers did, too. "Wyoming," she said, and even though it was a murmur, it seemed to be in triumph.

Nico sure as hell wasn't going to dispute that victory, and it was one he'd remember for the rest of his life. Maybe even watch it—if the camera angle was right. For now, though, he just gathered Eden in his arms, kissed her and waited for her to come back down.

She lay there, sprawled out over him for a few moments before she lifted her head. Still smiling, she kissed him. Not some postsex peck. This was the real deal. Hot, deep and it would have gone well past Wyoming if anyone had been naming states. They weren't. They were just putting some icing on this very nice cake they'd just made.

And since they'd had their dessert, Nico figured it was time for that talk before she gathered her wits and her fears about discussing this with him.

"You told your parents you were in love with me," he said.

As expected, she went tense and probably would have moved off him, but that was one of the advantages of him still being deep inside her. His dick became sort of an anchor.

"Was that something you just blurted out to shut them up, or did you mean it?" he pressed.

Oh, the lip nibbling began, and despite the haze of pleasure still glistening on her face, Eden looked ready to teleport to Wyoming or anywhere else that would allow her to avoid this conversation.

So Nico tried a different angle. "I'm in love with you, Eden."

That stopped the lip nibbling, probably because her mouth dropped open. "W-hat?" she managed.

"I'm. In. Love. With. You," he repeated, breaking it down for her. "And that's not Sweet-Cheeks Cowboy talking. That's me, Nico, your best friend and lover."

The stunned silence lasted a few more seconds, quickly followed by a dreamy sigh, smile and some watery eyes—all happening at the same time. He thought those were good signs.

"You love me," she said on a rise of breath. "I thought you were going to break up with me."

Now he frowned. *Good grief.* "I'm not stupid. I know you're the real deal. Plus, you know all my secrets and I know yours. Mix that up with love, sex and blog reenactments, and I think we've got a sweet deal going here."

Well, she sure wasn't frowning now. "I agree." Eden leaned in, her mouth hovering over his. "On a scale of one to infinity, just how sure are you about this?" she asked.

Oh, this was easy. *So* easy. "More than infinity," he assured her, and he dragged her back down for a long, slow kiss.

* * * * *

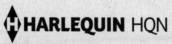

CHAPTER ONE

WATCHING FROM THE window of the police station, Sheriff Kace Laramie wasn't sure if he should deal first with the senior citizen flasher, the traffic violation or the whizzing longhorn.

As a cop in a small ranching town like Coldwater, Texas, Kace didn't usually have to pick between wrongdoings and disturbances, but apparently today they were experiencing a sort of crime wave.

When he saw the flasher, Gopher Tate, reach to unbutton his ratty raincoat, Kace moved him up to the number one spot of which situation should get his attention. There wasn't anyone around Gopher, and the man never flashed a full monty, especially in winter, but Kace didn't want anyone shocked or complaining if they got a glimpse of Gopher's tighty-whities covering his junk.

"Liberty," Kace called out to Deputy Liberty Cassaine as he pulled on his jacket and hat and then headed out the door of the police station. "Go after that idiot who just blew through the red light. Red Porsche, Oklahoma plates."

No need for Kace to specify which light since there was only one, and it was on Main Street, right in front of the police station. It was also next to the clearly marked sign with the posted speed limit of thirty miles per hour. By Kace's estimate, the guy wasn't exactly speeding, but the light had been red.

Liberty leaped up from her desk in the squad room, crammed the rest of a goo-loaded sticky bun into her mouth and hurried out to the cruiser in the parking lot next to the building. Kace went across the street to deal with Gopher.

As Kace walked, he gave the pissing longhorn a glance. Like the rest of Coldwater, it was a familiar sight. It belonged to the librarian, Esther Benton, who affectionately called the bull Petunia.

Petunia had a fondness for breaking fence, wandering onto Main Street and disrupting traffic. Today, though, the bull wasn't in the street but rather had taken to the sidewalk, working its way through the dancing Santas, glittering candy canes and other assorted decorations that the town and business owners had set out for Christmas. Those particular items had been in place for only a couple of hours and had replaced the gobbling turkeys and cardboard cornucopias from Thanksgiving. In a month—specifically December 26—the Christmas decor would be boxed up and the New Year's stuff would be set out.

Coldwater had no shortage of overly done spangles, adornments of questionable taste and downright tacky holiday plastic.

Kace gave Petunia another glance to make sure the longhorn hadn't moved. It hadn't. It was now underneath the awning of the taxidermist's shop, Much Ado about Stuffing, and it had pissed a puddle deep enough to drown an alley cat.

Apparently, hydration wasn't an issue for Petunia.

Once Kace had finished with Gopher, he'd need to get the longhorn moving, call Esther and tell the woman she'd need to pay for another cleanup. Ironically, Gopher often did janitorial services for the town so Kace would be tapping the man for the job if he didn't have to arrest him first.

Gopher still had hold of the sides of his raincoat, but his grip dropped away when he spotted Kace. "You gonna arrest me?" Gopher asked, making it sound as much a challenge as a question.

"Depends. You got a good explanation as to why you're on Main Street, wearing a raincoat when there's not a chance of rain in the forecast?"

Gopher's forehead bunched up as if giving that some thought, and he glanced up at the cloudless blue sky. "I like to be ready in case there's a change in the weather."

Well, it was an explanation all right, but it wasn't an especially good one. "You've got two choices, Gopher. Come with me to the jail or button up that raincoat and clean up after Petunia."

Gopher contemplated that, too. "But I got a different color bow on today, and nobody's had a chance to see it."

Since that bow, whatever color it was, would be tied around Gopher's junk, Kace didn't intend to give the man an audience. "Choose wisely," Kace advised him. "Clean up or lock up."

"Clean up," Gopher finally grumbled, and he continued to grumble while he got busy buttoning the raincoat.

With that task ticked off his to-do list, Kace turned

toward Petunia. He took off his cowboy hat to smack the bull on the butt, but he stopped midwhack when Gopher spoke again.

"Say, ain't that your wife over yonder?" Gopher asked.

That got Kace's complete attention, and he followed Gopher's gaze across the street. Specifically, to the parking lot of the police station, where he spotted the tall blonde getting out of a silver SUV. Not easily getting out, either. She was taking a wriggling, fussing baby from the infant seat in the back, and the kid wasn't cooperating.

But, yeah, it was January Parker all right. *Jana*.

"My ex-wife," Kace corrected.

And because Jana had been his ex for well over a decade, that correction just slid right off his tongue. Of course, Kace had seen her more than a time or two since then whenever she'd visited her mother, Eileen, who still lived in Coldwater. Jana, however, lived about an hour away on a ranch near Blanco.

"Didn't know she had a kid," Gopher remarked.

Kace knew that. Gossip about Jana just seemed to stick in his mind even when he would have preferred that it didn't. Last he'd heard, Jana had had a daughter, and judging from the blond curl haloing the baby's face, this was her child. Kace guessed she was about a year and a half old. Also last he'd heard, Jana was divorced or in the process of divorcing husband number two.

"Jana always did fill out a pair of jeans," Gopher commented. "A little more of her to fill them out these days, but the years have settled just fine on her."

Kace scowled at the man, but there was no way he could deny such an observation even if it had come from Gopher. Jana did indeed have an ass that got noticed, and apparently childbirth hadn't affected that part of her anatomy. Kace could see that firsthand because of the way Jana was leaning into the back seat. The maneuver caused her jeans-clad butt to be aimed in their direction, and the short waist jacket she was wearing did nothing to conceal it.

Jana finally managed to hoist the toddler out of the infant seat and onto her hip. The kid didn't care much for that, either, because she kicked her legs, threw back her head and let out a wail loud enough to start a stampede. Jana ignored that and started walking. She didn't glance across the street at Gopher and Kace but rather kept her attention pinned to the police station.

"It appears Jana's about to pay you a visit," Gopher added.

Gopher was a wellspring of information today. Jana was indeed headed for the police station. Maybe not specifically to see him, though. She could be going inside to file some kind of complaint or report a crime. That didn't help the knot that was already forming in Kace's stomach.

Kace silently cursed. He'd been divorced from Jana long enough not to feel the punch of attraction whenever he looked at her. Thankfully, the lust was tempered with the memories of their god-awful marriage. Of course, plenty would say it was a marriage that should have never happened in the first place. Jana's mom definitely felt that way, and Eileen had made it her mission in life to see that their wedded "bliss" ended as fast as she could manage it.

Fourteen months and three days.

That's how long it'd taken Jana to cave in to Eileen's demands that she divorce her "cowboy husband" and find someone more suitable for their tax bracket and social standing. Eileen might have been a local, but she had always set herself apart from the rest of Coldwater, what with her sprawling house, fancy cars and snobbish ways.

Unlike Eileen, though, Jana wasn't into fancy. Those great-fitting jeans weren't a fashion statement. Neither were the cowboy boots. From everything he'd heard, Jana raised horses and did a lot of the hands-on work herself. Apparently, Eileen hadn't been able to pressure her into giving that up and becoming a socialite.

"I'd best go see what she wants," Kace muttered when Jana finally made it inside the police station, but he shot Gopher one last warning glare. "Keep the raincoat closed and get started on cleaning up after the longhorn." Whether Gopher would actually do that was anyone's guess, so Kace would have to keep an eye on him.

Kace's phone rang just as he started across the street, and he answered it when he saw Liberty's name on the screen.

"Uh, Kace," Liberty said right away. "This guy I pulled over for blowing through the red light says he knows you."

Absently, Kace considered the license plates that'd been on the Porsche. He knew plenty of people from

Oklahoma, but he hadn't recognized the car. Nor had he got a look at the driver.

"That's not going to get him out of a ticket," Kace insisted.

"He's not trying to get out of that," Liberty explained, and then she paused. Paused long enough that Kace had time to get to the police station. "Uh, he says he's your father."

Kace stopped, and his hand froze in midreach for the door. He already had the knot in his stomach from seeing Jana, but now the knot tightened and pulled at his whole body.

"Kace?" Liberty said. "You still there?"

"Yeah," Kace managed, though he wasn't sure where he got the air to speak. His lungs and throat had clamped shut. Too bad there wasn't a lock on the hellish memories from his past.

A past that his so-called father had created.

"According to his driver's license," Liberty went on, "his name is Peter Laramie."

Liberty didn't ask if that was really his father's name. Kace's late mother had called him Petey. Well, she had done that when she hadn't been calling him a son of a bitch and other assorted obscenities.

"He's fifty-four and from Lawton, Oklahoma," Liberty added.

Despite the tornado going on in his head, Kace did the math. His father had been just nineteen when Kace was born. Young. But not so young that he hadn't got married and fathered three more sons. Of course, it hadn't taken more than a signature on a license and some sperm to accomplish those things.

"Kace, you okay?" Liberty asked.

"Fine." And he gathered as much breath as he could manage. "Write him the ticket," Kace instructed, and he hit the end-call button.

If his father was in town to see him and his three younger brothers, then he'd find them soon enough. Anyone in Coldwater knew where to locate Judd, Callen, Nico and him.

Kace put his phone in the pocket of his jeans, dragged in another breath and went inside to face Jana. He didn't have to look for her. Kace just followed the fussy sounds of the baby. Sounds that led him straight to his office.

Apparently, Jana had indeed come to see him. This was going to be his day not only for a small-town crime wave but also for surprises that weren't of the good variety. So far, Jana was running second in the surprise department, though. Nothing was going to beat Peter Laramie cruising into town.

Ginger Monroe, the receptionist/dispatcher, was at her desk, and she had one of her unnaturally red eyebrows raised to a questioning arch while she volleyed glances between Jana and him. Kace was always a little perplexed when Ginger made that expression, or any other one for that matter, because she wore her makeup so thick that it coated her face like a mask. Still, she managed to convey not only some amazement but also intense curiosity.

Kace had some intense curiosity of his own.

"You got a visitor," Ginger said in the same tone she would have informed him of a persistent fungus in the bathroom.

Ginger's reaction was what he'd expected. After the divorce, the town had taken sides, and most folks had sided with Kace. Of course, Ginger did work for him so that might have played into her decision-making process. As for the rest of the town, Kace figured that folks thought he'd been screwed over by Eileen and also by her daughter who hadn't had the gumption to stand up to her mother.

"Jana didn't say what she wanted," Ginger added, using more of that fungal tone.

Well, Kace would soon find out. Pushing aside the rest of his childhood memories and memories of the divorce, he went in to find out why Jana was here. The odds were that their conversation wouldn't be private. Heck, it might not even be heard because of the baby's loud cries, but even if Jana and he managed a whispered chat, the content would soon get around. Kace suspected that Ginger and maybe some of his deputies had taken up lipreading.

Kace took off his cowboy hat and coat and put them on the wall pegs when he went into his office. "Jana," he greeted.

Thankfully, he managed to keep his voice in check. Hard to do, though, now that he was face-to-face with her.

As usual, the front side of her looked as good as the back even though her ponytail was a little mussed, and her expression was frazzled and weary. Kace figured the squirming kid was responsible for most of that, but this visit was likely part of it, as well. Unless it was for a social visit, and this clearly wouldn't be, most people got stressed being in a police station.

The little girl yanked off her pink jingle-bell cap as if it were the thing that'd pissed her off. She let out another loud wail and reached for him. Kace didn't reach back, but that didn't stop the kid from practically lunging out of Jana's grip. The motion unbalanced Jana, and if Kace hadn't caught on to the baby, both of them would have likely landed against him. The baby took advantage of the near mishap and vised her little arms around Kace's neck. She also hushed.

Suddenly, it was quiet enough that even a whisper could have been heard, but it didn't last. The moment Kace tried to hand the little girl back to Jana, the kid started to squeal again. This time, Kace got smacked in the face with that pink hat, and he took some blows from her little kicking feet. For someone whose tiny boots were four inches long, tops, she packed the wallop of an angry mule.

"No! No! No!" she shrieked, and the moment Jana quit trying to tug her from Kace, the kid hushed again. Complete silence that had both Jana and him checking her. Kace could feel her still breathing, but that was the only sound she was making.

Jana gave a weary sigh and pushed some stray strands of her hair from her face. "Marley's teething, and she missed her nap."

Well, that explained the crappy mood, but it didn't address why she'd quieted down in Kace's arms. Or why the kid settled her head against his shoulder as if she belonged there. Of course, none of that hit the number one spot of Kace's questions about this situation.

Why the heck was Jana here?

"Could you please just hold her while we talk?" Jana asked.

She wasn't looking at him. That's because she was fishing around in the huge diaper bag that she'd set on his desk, and she pulled out a bottle of water. Jana guzzled some as if she'd been crawling through the Mojave Desert for days, and then she sank down into one of the chairs.

Kace didn't especially want to hold the kid. He didn't have much experience doing that sort of thing and wasn't sure he was doing it right. Plus, Ginger would no doubt spread some kind of gossip about this that would get back to Belinda Darlington, the woman he sometimes dated. Belinda seemed to live on the eternal hope that Kace would change his mind about marriage and fatherhood and would make those changes with her.

He wouldn't.

Ever.

But if Belinda got wind of his holding Jana's daughter, then that might fuel some jealousy and hope that Kace didn't want Belinda to have. Still, if he handed Marley back to Jana, then the crying might start up again. Jana clearly looked as if she needed a break from that, and having a quiet Marley would help speed things along.

Marley must have been resigned to the current situation, too, because she cuddled the hat against her like a blanket, stuck her thumb in her mouth and started sucking. Kace could practically feel the kid's muscles go slack.

"Thank you," Jana muttered. After drinking more water, she looked up at him with her intense blue eyes.

Eyes that could apparently still do a number on him.

Like her butt, those baby blues gave him a few tugs on the heartstrings. So did her mouth, but it tugged at a different part of him. That mouth had always been a hot spot for him. Kace silently cursed himself for recalling that and shoved that notion aside.

"Marley's always cranky when she gets back from visits with her dad," Jana went on.

Visits, as in a custody thing, and even though he tried to stop his attention from going to her left hand, he looked anyway. No wedding ring. That must mean the divorce was final.

"Since I doubt you brought your daughter in so I could arrest her for extreme crankiness, care to explain why you're here?" he prompted, making sure he sounded and looked like a cop.

Of course, his stern demeanor was somewhat diminished by the fact he was holding a thumb-sucking baby wearing pink overalls and tasseled cowboy boots. Plus, Marley's wispy curls kept landing on his mouth, and he had to blow them away since they were tickling him.

Jana nodded and gave another sigh, but she didn't say anything until she'd stood and met him eye to eye. "Kace, we have to stop this wedding."

He was sure he blinked twice, and Kace searched back through his memory to see if he'd missed something. "Are you talking about my brother?"

Because that was the only wedding Kace knew anything about. His brother Judd, and his fiancée,

Cleo, would be having a small private ceremony once they set an actual date, but there was no reason for Kace or anyone else to stop it. Judd and Cleo had been in love since they were teenagers, so nobody would question why they were taking the "I do" plunge.

Jana pulled back her shoulders, shook her head. "You haven't heard?"

Well, hell. That gave him a new jolt of concern. "Heard what?"

She stared at him. Really stared. And she mouthed some profanity. "I just assumed your father had told you."

Now, that wasn't just a jolt. It was more like an avalanche. "Told me what?" Kace snarled.

Jana's hands went on her hips. "Your father asked my mother to marry him, and she said yes. They're making plans for a wedding, Kace." Her eyes narrowed to fiery slits. "Plans that you and I are going to stop."

Don't miss
A Coldwater Christmas *by Delores Fossen.*
available October 2019 wherever HQN Books and ebooks are sold.

www.HQNBooks.com

I N T R I G U E

*Hank Savage has always believed his old girlfriend
was murdered. Now it's time to prove it.*

*With PI Frankie Brewster's help, can Hank break open
the case…when someone wants it to stay closed?*

Read on for a sneak preview of Iron Will,
*the second book in the Cardwell Ranch:
Montana Legacy series by* New York Times *and*
USA TODAY *bestselling author B.J. Daniels.*

Chapter One

Hank Savage squinted into the sun glaring off the dirty windshield
of his pickup as his family ranch came into view. He slowed the
truck to a stop, resting one sun-browned arm over the top of the
steering wheel as he took in Cardwell Ranch.

The ranch with all its log-and-stone structures didn't appear to
have changed in the least. Nor had the two-story house where he'd
grown up. Memories flooded him of hours spent on the back of a
horse, of building forts in the woods around the creek, of the family
sitting around the large table in the kitchen in the mornings, the sun
pouring in, the sound of laughter. He saw and felt everything he'd
given up, everything he'd run from, everything he'd lost.

"Been a while?" asked the sultry, dark-haired woman in the
passenger seat.

He nodded despite the lump in his throat, shoved back his
Stetson and wondered what the hell he was doing back here. This
was a bad idea, probably his worst ever.

"Having second thoughts?" He'd warned her about his big

family, but she'd said she could handle it. He wasn't all that sure even he could handle it. He prided himself on being fearless about most things. Give him a bull that hadn't been ridden and he wouldn't hesitate to climb right on. Same with his job as a lineman. He'd faced gale winds hanging from a pole to get the power back on, braved getting fried more times than he liked to remember.

But coming back here, facing the past? He'd never been more afraid. He knew it was just a matter of time before he saw Naomi—just as he had in his dreams, in his nightmares. She was here, right where he'd left her, waiting for him as she had been for three long years. Waiting for him to come back and make things right.

He looked over at Frankie. "You sure about this?"

She sat up straighter to gaze at the ranch and him, took a breath and let it out. "I am if you are. After all, this was your idea."

Like she had to remind him. "Then I suggest you slide over here." He patted the seat between them and she moved over, cuddling against him as he put his free arm around her. She felt small and fragile, certainly not ready for what he suspected they would be facing. For a moment, he almost changed his mind. It wasn't too late. He didn't have the right to involve her.

"It's going to be okay," she said and nuzzled his neck where his dark hair curled at his collar. "Trust me."

He pulled her closer and let his foot up off the brake. The pickup began to roll toward the ranch. It wasn't that he didn't trust Frankie. He just knew that it was only a matter of time before Naomi came to him pleading with him to do what he should have done three years ago. He felt a shiver even though the summer day was unseasonably warm.

I'm here.

Don't miss
Iron Will *by B.J. Daniels,*
available August 2019 wherever
Harlequin® books and ebooks are sold.

www.Harlequin.com

The countdown to Christmas begins now!
Keep track of all your Christmas reads.

September 24

- [ ] *A Coldwater Christmas* by Delores Fossen
- [ ] *A Country Christmas* by Debbie Macomber
- [ ] *A Haven Point Christmas* by RaeAnne Thayne
- [ ] *A MacGregor Christmas* by Nora Roberts
- [ ] *A Wedding in December* by Sarah Morgan
- [ ] *An Alaskan Christmas* by Jennifer Snow
- [ ] *Christmas at White Pines* by Sherryl Woods
- [ ] *Christmas from the Heart* by Sheila Roberts
- [ ] *Christmas in Winter Valley* by Jodi Thomas
- [ ] *Cowboy Christmas Redemption* by Maisey Yates
- [ ] *Kisses in the Snow* by Debbie Macomber
- [ ] *Low Country Christmas* by Lee Tobin McClain
- [ ] *Season of Wonder* by RaeAnne Thayne
- [ ] *The Christmas Sisters* by Sarah Morgan
- [ ] *Wyoming Heart* by Diana Palmer

October 22

- [ ] *Season of Love* by Debbie Macomber

October 29

- [ ] *Christmas in Silver Springs* by Brenda Novak
- [ ] *Christmas with You* by Nora Roberts
- [ ] *Stealing Kisses in the Snow* by Jo McNally

November 26

- [ ] *North to Alaska* by Debbie Macomber
- [ ] *Winter's Proposal* by Sherryl Woods

HARLEQUIN
Harlequin.com
XMAS0319BPA